TITLES BY THE SAME AUTHOR
ALL PUBLISHED BY HOUSE OF STRATUS

FICTION:
ANTHONY WILDING
THE BANNER OF THE BULL
BARDELYS THE MAGNIFICENT
BELLARION
THE BLACK SWAN
CAPTAIN BLOOD
THE CAROLINIAN
CHIVALRY
THE CHRONICLES OF CAPTAIN BLOOD
COLUMBUS
FORTUNE'S FOOL
THE FORTUNES OF CAPTAIN BLOOD
THE GAMESTER
THE GATES OF DOOM
THE HOUNDS OF GOD
THE JUSTICE OF THE DUKE
THE LION'S SKIN
THE LOST KING
LOVE-AT-ARMS
THE MARQUIS OF CARABAS
THE MINION
THE NUPTIALS OF CORBAL
THE ROMANTIC PRINCE
SCARAMOUCHE
SCARAMOUCHE THE KING-MAKER
THE SEA HAWK
THE SHAME OF MOTLEY
THE SNARE
ST MARTIN'S SUMMER
THE STALKING-HORSE
THE STROLLING SAINT
THE SWORD OF ISLAM
THE TAVERN KNIGHT
THE TRAMPLING OF THE LILIES
TURBULENT TALES
VENETIAN MASQUE

NON-FICTION:
HEROIC LIVES
THE HISTORICAL NIGHTS'
ENTERTAINMENT
THE LIFE OF CESARE BORGIA
TORQUEMADA AND THE SPANISH
INQUISITION

King in Prussia

Rafael Sabatini

HOUSE OF
STRATUS

This edition published in 2001 by House of Stratus, an imprint of
Stratus Holdings plc, 24c Old Burlington Street, London, W1X 1RL, UK.
Also at: Suite 210, 1270 Avenue of the Americas, New York, NY 10020, USA.

www.houseofstratus.com

Typeset, printed and bound by House of Stratus.

A catalogue record for this book is available from the British Library
and the Library of Congress.

ISBN 1-84232-815-8

Contents

BOOK 2 – THE KING

BOOK ONE

The Prince

Chapter 1

Domestic Scene

Charles Stuart-Dene, Marquess of Alverley, looked at humanity, and wondered why it was.

You conceive the pessimism prompting this spirit of philosophic inquiry. How far it was justified you may gather from the Memoirs of the Margravine of Bayreuth, a lady who was no more curbed by discretion in the glimpses she affords us of her family, and particularly of her abominable sire, than in other matters that are commonly accounted intimate.

Through the bright, prominent eyes that stared out of her young face, which would have been winsome had it not been pockmarked, you may view the scene that is to be regarded as the prelude to all this mischief. It was set in the Porcelain Gallery of the Palace of Monbijou.

Music was being made by the flute of the Crown Prince of Prussia, to an accompaniment by his sister Wilhelmina, the future Margravine, on the lute, and the young Rittmeister von Katte on the clavichord. The three were rendering a sugary composition which the Prince claimed for his own, but which Katte believed would never have been written but for the previous existence of a melody of Scarlatti's.

Monbijou with all its choice contents had been a gift to Queen Sophia Dorothea from her father-in-law, Frederick, the first King in

Prussia; and this spacious Porcelain Gallery, so called because of the immensely tall and valuable Chinese vases that were the most conspicuous objects in its subdued and impeccable appointments, was one of the pleasantest of the palace's chambers. Light and airy, its lofty windows commanded a view of the long gardens that stretched down to the tranquil river.

The audience on this afternoon of spring included the Queen herself; a corpulent, comfortable body in a waistless sacque of yellow brocade that lent her the appearance of a monstrous ninepin, whilst the two flame-coloured patches under her eyes gave her the face of a Nuremberg doll. In attendance upon her were the scarcely less portly Frau von Kamen, whom Wilhelmina elegantly nicknamed the Fat Cow, the equally bovine Frau von Bulow, the majestic and quite foolish Countess of Bollenberg, and, by way of contrast, the fair and delicate Fräulein von Sorensen, who was a miracle of willowy grace. Of the half-score courtiers who completed this intimate little gathering, the most notable were Count Hugo von Katzenstein, a tall, fair man approaching forty, of a serene, distinguished air and an almost French urbanity of manner, and Lieutenant von Ingersleben, a handsome lad in a guardsman's uniform, who was one of the Prince's most constant companions.

Lastly, and in a class apart, with them and yet perceptibly not of them, there was our young Lord Alverley, tall and spare and dark. Under a good brow his narrow countenance was of a melancholy in repose which the too-impressionable Margravine confesses that she found dangerously engaging. In his suit of black – the simulated mourning so commonly adopted from motives of economy by gentlemen of restricted means – he contrasted sombrely with Katte's military blue and silver and the Prince's French splendour of whaleboned, silver-galooned pink satin coat over a lilac waistcoat. His Highness' flamboyance, stressed by the exaggeratedly high red heels of his French shoes and the excessive curls of his pomaded and powdered yellow head, was, thought Alverley, better suited to his mincing airs than the guardsman's uniform in which my lord had hitherto beheld him.

Short of stature and slight of build, the Prince, now in his eighteenth year, was hardly prepossessing of countenance. It was rendered, by the excessively long nose, making a single line with the flat brow, reminiscent of a weasel's. The eyes, however, were unusually arresting: large, pale and prominent, they derived an uncanny brilliance from the fact that the whites were visible all round the iris. Alverley had heard it asserted somewhere at some time that the possessors of such eyes are to be avoided, and so much are we the victims of preconceptions that this may have been at the root of the mistrust and faint dislike with which at the very outset of their acquaintance the Prince had inspired him. Otherwise he might have read in those eyes the wistfulness of one who struggles with frustration, a wistfulness that could arouse in kindly souls a vague commiseration, and, through this, a measure even of devotion.

No resemblance was discernible between the Prince and the sister for whom he had an affection greater than any other woman was ever to command in him. From her small-featured, oval face, which had been comely enough before the smallpox marred it, her lively, darting eyes took a sprightly view of life. Her neat shape was in olive green, the bodice laced to a deep point, the billowing over-skirt caught in folds towards the back and padded into what was called with German delicacy a cul-de-Paris.

She was seated beside von Katte, in order that she might follow the scored pages of music set up on the clavichord. If we are to believe her, it was not a propinquity she ordinarily sought, for she suggests small liking for the Rittmeister – although her father, as we shall see, was to take a very different view of her feelings – and she accepted his society only because of the deep affection borne him by her brother. She describes as baneful the glance of his eyes, of a deep blue under heavy black eyebrows that made a single line. He, too, was pockmarked, deeply so, very sallow, of a remarkable ugliness, but nevertheless a man of irresistible charm. In the middle twenties, he was talented and accomplished, a gay companion, a gifted musician, a painter of some merit and a soldier of great promise.

The sonata faded to a soft conclusion. Applause was led by the perfunctory clapping of the plump hands of Majesty.

"That was entrancing, Fritz. Entrancing." And then, because it was not in her nature to neglect an opportunity for lamentation, she must add: "I could weep when I think how little your father appreciates your great gifts."

The eagerness in which the Prince, ever avid of praise, had turned to receive her commendation, faded a little at this mention of his father. A sigh, a lift of the brows, and a shrug were his only answer, as he turned to Alverley.

His lordship conceived that the Prince invited comment, and politeness, at war with sincerity, prescribed that he supply it generously. He contrived an adroit compromise.

"Your highness aspires to say with Horace: 'Non omnis moriar.'"

"Ah!" The Prince stirred uncomfortably, hesitated, and finally asked: "That means?"

"'I shall not wholly die.' Which is to say that my works will survive as an immortal part of me."

The Prince smiled. "You are not by chance a flatterer, Monsieur le Marquis?" Then the smile twisted into a sneer. "What does not flatter me is that I should need to ask the meaning of your phrase. It shames me. But then the study of Latin has been denied me. My father holds the view that it's for pedants only. Young men of quality, he tells me, are to cultivate valour rather than scholarliness."

"Yet from Caesar's day history abounds in instances of men who have possessed both at once."

"Morbleu! If you can persuade my father of that I'll spare no pains to bring you to audience with him."

The Freiherr von Katzenstein, who had sauntered across to them, ventured, smoothly urbane, into the conversation. "Do not take his Highness seriously, Marquis. He wants to laugh. You would be doing no service either to his Highness or yourself. Indeed you could find no surer way to prejudice his Majesty against you."

They spoke in French, which, indeed, was the common language of the polite world throughout Germany, and commonest in Berlin where, as a result of the revocation of the Edict of Nantes, one-third of the population was actually French. Those Huguenot refugees who had sought shelter in Brandenburg a half-century earlier had brought, in new handicrafts and trades, their civilizing influence into the Electorate.

Prince Frederick's first governess, Madame de Roucoules, had been French, as had been his tutor Duhan, whom Frederick William had driven out with blows of his cane when he caught him teaching his son Latin. The Prince, with his airs and graces and affectations of culture, had come to hold the German language in such contempt, as fit only for soldiers and peasants, grooms and horses, that he was never to learn it thoroughly, never to speak it save with a foreign accent. He used it, as did other members of the family, only in the King's presence, when French was excluded by Frederick William's francophobia, just as in Frederick William's presence music and dancing and the other polite amenities which his Majesty despised were banished. Because of this the members of the royal family eagerly welcomed the King's hunting expeditions to Wusterhausen and other absences that temporarily delivered them from his despotic boorish restraint. To Frederick in particular was it a season of relief, in which without apprehensions he might deliver himself to music and exercise the considerable virtuosity, so savagely execrated by his father.

He was beginning to express it unrestrainedly when the lovely Fräulein von Sorensen came to detach Alverley with word that her Majesty commanded his company.

Ever since Sophia Dorothea's father, the Elector of Hanover, had – as a consequence of the lack of vitality of Queen Anne's long succession of children – been called to the throne of England, she had accounted herself as in some sort English. Considering that she was the daughter of one English king, the sister of another, and still with hopes that Wilhelmina would marry the Prince of Wales, and thus ultimately make her the mother-in-law of a third, it was the least of her extravagances that she should regard an Englishman as all but a compatriot. It was precisely upon this that the alert Katte had counted when first he had taken Alverley to Monbijou. It was his hope to engage her Majesty's interest for him, and he now observed with satisfaction that at last she gave attention to the Englishman.

She received him amiably. "I am pleased with Fritz that he should have brought you to visit me, Milord Alverley." Her fan waved him to a gilded chair beside the little sofa which she occupied, and all but filled. "Be seated, sir. I am curious to learn to what Berlin owes the advantage of your presence."

"Rather should your Majesty ask me to what I owe the advantage of being in Berlin."

"It had not occurred to me that that could be an advantage to anyone." Her plaintive tone suggested the reluctance with which she, herself, abode there. "Certainly not to one who has left the opulent world of London and the elegances of the Court of St James. I cannot figure to myself why you should willingly exchange them for our heavy dullness."

The explanation her Majesty sought was not one that could be offered by a proscribed Jacobite to the sister of King George II, save at the risk of nipping the incipient buds of favour. He sought safety in a half-truth, which is the most formidable, because the most convincing, of all lies.

"I have come to Berlin, Madame, in the hope of studying the military art in its foremost European academy."

"Ah!" She sighed. All things seemed to supply her with matter for melancholy. "That is an answer that will no doubt please his Majesty." The implication was that it did not please her.

Nevertheless, Katte, who had abandoned the clavichord to follow Alverley, took this for his cue. "My cousin hopes to deserve your Majesty's gracious interest with the King, so that his ambition may be gratified."

Overhearing him, the Prince swung towards them, with a short, disdainful laugh. "Ma foi! It's, as my mother says, an ambition that will not fail to find favour with the King. The source of all my misfortunes is that such an ambition is not mine."

"Indeed, Fritz, you were born for nobler things," his sister flattered him.

"I hope so. Indeed, I hope so. Meanwhile I am constrained to meaner ones: to drills that are death to my soul; to a uniform that is a shroud to my body. And these things, Milord Alverley, are your choice, who enjoy the freedom that I envy. I have often thought that God is very unjust."

This scandalized his mother. Her massive bosom quivered. She raised a plump, ring-laden hand. "Hush, Fritz! That is not a thing to say. You should not laugh, Rittmeister."

"Truth is so often indecent," said his Highness, primly sententious. "It goes naked, I believe."

"Fie, Fritz!" She turned again to Alverley. "I shall be happy, if you think it will really profit you, to speak for you to his Majesty when he returns. You'll have been told that at present he is at Wusterhausen. Hunting bears, or boars, or wolves, or something. That is his favourite pursuit when he is not hunting giants, or drilling them." Plaintively she continued: "You'll have seen his regiment of monster grenadiers, brought together from every country in Europe."

"An imposing body of men, Madame."

"Imposing? Say grotesque. An overgrown, knock-kneed lot. I hear of a recent arrival, over eight feet tall; a Hungarian, I believe, acquired at fantastic cost." Again she sighed, almost lachrymose. "Half his Majesty's revenues are squandered on the monsters. We cut down expenditure beyond the limits of dignity so as to waste money on these museum specimens. Oh, and then the trouble it makes with foreign princes, whose subjects they are! That and the reckless Prussian recruiting in foreign lands will end by landing us in a war with someone. But – alas! – it's all of a piece with Prussian ways, as you'll discover, sir. Believe me, it was not worthwhile to leave England for what you may find here." She ceased waving her fan, and peered at him over the top of it.

His smile deepened the gentle sadness of his eyes. They were naturally sad and kindly, from their slightly downward slant, contrasting oddly with the rather bitter set of his lips. A thoughtful contemporary observed of him that whereas he owed the shape of his eyes to nature, it was experience that had modelled the lines of his mouth. In itself that is an indication of his history.

Smiling, he evaded the implied question in her words and glance. "On the contrary, Madame. Your Majesty's graciousness alone makes it worthwhile."

"I should be happy, I assure you, Milord, if I could extend it further. You would, I am sure, be better advised to seek the interest of Baron von Grumbkow. His influence with the King is paramount. Don't you agree, Rittmeister?"

"There is no question, Madame, of Monsieur de Grumbkow's influence with his Majesty; but some question of our influence with Monsieur de Grumbkow."

The Prince flung in a sneer. "There is no question of either. The only question is one of price. There is nothing his Excellency will not do for money. Fortunately you English are rich. Grumbkow's interest may be had by any who can pay for it."

The stricture raised a general laugh among those intimates who were within earshot. Only the Queen offered a half-hearted protest, possibly from dread lest the words be reported to the powerful minister.

"Do not always be so malicious, Fritz."

"There is no malice in truth, mama."

The Princess supported him, as she would in any argument. "And it's a deal less than justice. All the world knows Grumbkow for a crafty, grasping, insinuating rascal."

"The sort of man, in short, to whom my father would naturally give his confidence."

Again the Queen displayed distress, not, however, from any regard for Grumbkow or disagreement with what was said of him. Indeed, she had every cause to detest the Baron, for she believed him to be subsidized by Austria, and hostile, consequently, to her hopes of matrimonial alliances with England. Her heart was set not only upon marrying Wilhelmina to the Prince of Wales, but also upon marrying Frederick to the English Princess Amelia.

"It is not nice, Fritz, to speak so of your father."

"God knows, mama, it is not nice to speak of him at all." Fritz sauntered off to the clavichord again, and took up a sheet of music. "Here is a dance I have composed: in the manner of the Magyar czardas. Will you try it with me, Katte, and you, Wilhelmina?"

Katte laughed. "A change of subject is perhaps prudent."

"And always a pleasure," said filial piety, "when papa is the subject."

"Oh, Fritzchen! Fritzchen!" His mother's lips dutifully condemned what her heart approved.

They fell to their musical task. The piece possessed at least the merit of faithfully reproducing the pulse-quickening Hungarian rhythm, and it was swelling to its climax when the main door of the gallery was suddenly and violently flung open.

Instantly Katte rose from the clavichord and the Princess from her seat beside him, whilst the Prince, with the flute still at his lips, swung round to seek the cause of the interruption in an irritation that at once gave place to dismay. The last note of the flute degenerated into a squeak.

Framed in the doorway stood a man whose girth was equal to his height, and he was by no means short. His blue uniform coat with red facings and copper buttons was tightly strained about his swollen bulk, above which his little head, with its small flat wig, was dwarfed by contrast to a mere knob. His mouth was too small, his nose too short for the breadth of his countenance, now suffused by a purple flush. His little eyes malevolently took in the scene.

"What is doing here?" he trumpeted in German, striking the ground with his cane.

Upon the entire company, now on its feet, a hush had fallen at this sight of a King whom all had supposed safely distant at Wusterhausen. To his question the only answer was a gasp of dismay from the Queen.

11

Frederick William came forward a step or two grasping his cane as it were a sword. His terrible glance raked the courtier group and came at last to settle upon the Prince. Suddenly explosively he addressed him. "Almighty! Why are you not in uniform? Why are you dressed like a French Harlequin? Is this what you do when my back is turned you rascal?" He swung to the quaking Queen the veins swelling on his brow, "And you Madam? Do you abet this fribble in his defiance of me?" He advanced again. "I will not tolerate it. Righteous Lord God! Your son was born to be a king – not a womanish fop, a squeaking flute-player. Don't you realize it?"

The Prince, white and trembling, began a soothing appeal. "Lieber papa…"

"Silence, puppy! You need schooling. You are to be taught that my wishes are to be respected in my absence as in my presence."

The Queen, at the point of tears, dolefully interposed. "But it is such a little thing, such a…"

"A little thing! To be sure. That is all this good-for-nothing will ever do. Little things. Vicious little things. Grosser Gott! He's my son, heir to a throne, and without a single manly trait. I suppose he is my son, Madam. God knows he gives me cause to doubt it."

This precipitated the flow of the Queen's impending tears, with havoc to her raddled cheeks. Wilhelmina and Fräulein von Sorensen drew closer to her as if protectively.

The vertical line between Alverley's brows had deepened. Standing stiffly now at Katte's side beyond the clavichord, he looked in incredulous horror upon this spectacle of unreasoning rage. The remainder of the company was ranged in a motionless, uncomfortable silence.

The King rolled forward on his swollen legs. Violently he snatched the instrument from the limp hands of the cowering Prince. "Have I not told you often enough that I will not have you waste your time piping like a silly shepherd? Let this make you more mindful of my orders." Brutally he struck the youth's unguarded face with the flute. "A flute! My God! I have a flute-player for a son. Prussia has a flute-player for its Crown Prince. Du lieber Gott!" Again he struck the Prince, this time across the head, and then flung the abominated instrument through the open window.

Next he took his son, who had covered his bruised and bleeding face with his hands, by the collar of his fine satin coat. "Who gave you leave to dress yourself in this fashion? Pah! You disgusting, mincing fop! Pink satin! My God! And you stink of civet like a harlot, yet your neck is dirty. You don't even wash. You're an offensive spectacle."

He wrenched at the coat, as if to tear it off, grimacing viciously at the effort. Failing in his purpose, he loosed his hold and raised his cane. But whilst the Prince bounded, shaking, out of reach, his mother and sister, both clamant and in tears, hung each upon one of the royal arms, whilst Katzenstein, serenely calm, moved aside so as to place himself as a screen between father and son. His Majesty was striving in vain to shake himself free of the women, trumpeting the while, when Katte plucked Alverley's sleeve.

Under cover of the royal bellowing he murmured: "The scene becomes a thought too domestic. I fear we intrude."

There was a side door near the clavichord, and by this they slipped quietly from the gallery.

Chapter 2

The Fortunes of Alverley

"It is not given to every man to enjoy the spectacle of a royal family in curlpapers."

Thus Katte irreverently, as the cousins took their way on foot through the park of Monbijou.

"Enjoyment," drawled Alverley, "was not what I experienced. Unbridled rage is rather matter for disgust, inconceivable in a man of birth."

Alverley merely expressed an article of the code by which he lived. He belonged to an amiably artificial age, schooled in restraint, in superficial courtesies and in the masking of emotions, accounting imperturbability the outward sign of breeding. Reared in such an atmosphere, chiefly prevalent in England and in France, Alverley had been fortified in a disposition to which his nature – perhaps by inheritance – was already prone. His complete self-mastery was apparent in his air, his movements, and, above all, in his speech, which never rose above a quiet level however vigorous the expressions he might employ. To Prince Frederick, to whom a demeanour of such urbane calm was as novel as it was attractive, this was amongst the most prepossessing of the attributes he discovered in Lord Alverley.

Saluted by the sentry at the wrought-iron gates of the park, the cousins crossed the bridge over one of the lesser arms of the Spree, and emerged into the town.

The month was June, and the warmth of the weather was rendering the flat capital of Brandenburg, watered by a sluggish river, perhaps the most evil-smelling city in a Europe in which no city could be said to delight the nostrils. The only merit of its ill-paved streets lay in their unusual width, just as the houses, mostly of brick, were unusually low. For the arid land was of such poor value that there was no thought for economy of space, and buildings might sprawl at little cost.

Because the acreage of the city was small for its population, the liveliness of its thoroughfares was considerable, and in the Burgstrasse, at this late hour of the afternoon, there was a steady flow of coaches and sedan-chairs to and from the direction of the Schloss, and a steadier flow of wayfarers of every class afoot. There was a ubiquity of uniforms, from those of glittering officers, sauntering with their ladies under the lime trees that shaded the avenue along the river, to those of gaitered infantrymen moving with the stiff precision of automata. By the bridge that crossed to the island where the best of the city was built, the cousins were obliged to range themselves aside, so as to give passage to a jingling troop of green-coated hussars on its way from the Zeughaus. From somewhere across the river came a bugle-call, and the air was vibrant with a distant roll of drums.

"Berlin, you see," said Katte, "is just a military camp, of which his Majesty is the drill-sergeant, with a drill-sergeant's manners. So if you are to persevere in your intentions here you'll need a less delicate stomach."

"After today, will it serve any purpose to persevere?"

"But why not?"

"We hardly care for those who have seen us at a disadvantage. After what I've witnessed, the King will not be likely to show me favour."

Katte was amused. "You have yet to know his Majesty. He certainly does not suspect that he has been seen at a disadvantage. That was his normal conduct. For the rest, I don't suppose that he will even remember you. Or that he even saw you. Or indeed, that he saw anything but Fritz's coat and Fritz's flute. Poor Fritz! Perhaps you begin to understand my attachment to him."

"Less than ever. I discern in him little to inspire it."

"Surely much, at least, to inspire pity. Abused, distracted, humiliated, thwarted in every aspiration by his outrageous father."

"What are his aspirations, beyond those prompted by his vanity and his malice?"

"There is better than that in him. But it is repressed by his abominable circumstances. He is not the fool he seems; he is hungry for knowledge, and hungry for affection; a starved soul. There you have the source of his appeal to me. Take a kindlier view of him, Charles. I know him disposed to be your friend, and that he would help you if he could, not only for my sake, but for your own. However, for the present I don't think we can reckon upon him. We will take the Queen's advice, and pay our court to Baron von Grumbkow."

"But if this Baron requires to be bought? Or is that merely little Fritz's malice?"

"Oh, no. It's true enough that his Excellency neglects no chance of making money. It is even whispered that he is in the pay of Austria. But for all that he is not incapable of a disinterested action, and he owes some favours to my grandfather and yours, the old Marshal. So we'll try him."

"As you please, my dear Hans. But you'll remember that I am in no case to bribe anyone above the rank of a lackey."

You may account this an odd statement if you remember that the Manor of Dene, of which the Stuart-Denes had been lords for a century before they were raised to the rank of marquesses, is amongst the wealthiest in England. Nevertheless it is a fact that Charles Stuart-Dene was tramping the world with empty pockets.

To find the cause we must go back to the year 1700, when Henry Stuart-Dene, second Marquess of Alverley, was making the grand tour.

His lordship came in the course of his travels to the court of the Elector of Brandenburg, and there met, wooed and married Fräulein Caroline von Katte, daughter of the Marshal of Wartensleben and lady-in-waiting to the Electress. Of this marriage Charles was born at Dene two years later, and there might have lived out his life without adventure had not his father accounted his loyalty due to the dynasty from which his house derived its broad acres (bestowed by James I) and with which it claimed kinship. As a result he had lost his life in the rising of 1715.

The confiscation of his lands and the extinction of his titles were avoided only because Caroline had become persona gratissima with the Princess of Wales, Caroline of Anspach. The full penalty was avoided by payment of a crippling fine, which, if it left the House of Alverley still standing, left it sadly in disrepair. It became necessary for Charles to seek to rebuild its fortunes, and since he chose to regard service to the House of Hanover as an outrage upon his father's memory, it only remained for him to seek that fortune abroad.

Reluctantly yielding to his wishes, his mother exerted such influence as she possessed in her native land, with such good results that at the early age of eighteen Charles left Oxford in order to take service under that great master of war, Prince Eugène, who at the time was Governor of the Netherlands. It was a service destined to last little more than a year; for the fortune which he was seeking to build abroad his mother conceived that she had found ready-built for him at home. So that when in 1724 Prince Eugène gave up the government of the Netherlands to become the Imperial Vicar-General of Italy, Charles, perceiving no prospect of campaigning, in which alone was rapid advancement to be won, yielded to his mother's prayers and returned to Dene.

Caroline's native shrewdness had discovered how to turn a title into a marketable commodity so as to obtain the means to deliver the house of Alverley from its crippling mortgages and restore it to its former splendours. Her diligent quest had ended in the discovery of Edward Gatling, an opulent nabob newly returned from the East Indies, enriched, more or less dishonestly no doubt, and greedy of honours to adorn his millions. Gatling possessed two daughters. Caroline would have preferred that there had been only one. His fortune, however, was adequate to provide each of his girls with a dowry to dazzle any impecunious nobleman, and the girls happened to be comely enough to command devotion on their own account.

Had it been otherwise Caroline's secret scheme would hardly have succeeded quite so easily. As it was, Charles, at the impressionable age of twenty-two, fell in love with Marion Gatling, the nabob's elder daughter. She was two years his senior, and although her affections were already pledged elsewhere, she was sufficiently her opportunist father's daughter to set the advantages of exalted rank above sentimental considerations. Not in her most extravagant day-dreams had she seen herself a marchioness, with the high position at court assured her by the circumstance that her husband's mother was the intimate friend of the future Queen.

Her father's millions disencumbered for the bridal couple the debt-ridden Manors of Dene and Revelstone, and Charles, restored by his marriage to all that his father's politics had lost him, looked forward to a future of ease and dignity and happiness.

It happened, however, that Marion's winsome exterior cloaked a nature fundamentally base. Nobility, after all, is not acquired from one generation to another. It is the result of a more gradual refining process. In her case too, the sentimental attachment which she had so cynically stifled in order to become the Marchioness of Alverley may have played its part in the unhappy sequel.

A misogynist has said – and the adoring Charles was all too soon to realize it in bitterness – that behind the woman you marry there is another who does not disclose herself until the season of rapture has begun to fade. Under provocation, and the nabob's daughter, spoilt darling, was easily provoked, her mincing speech gave place to the strident railings of the shrew. Mistaking for weakness the restraint which Charles' breeding imposed upon him in the face of her liberal contumely, her authoritarian manner towards him became ever more insufferable as time passed, until disillusion was followed in him by distaste, and the love he had brought to the union was turned to loathing for a termagant who embittered all his days.

Meanwhile, as by an irony, the early rapture was bearing fruit. A son was born to them within a year of the wedding. Vain and short-lived was Charles' hope that motherhood would engender gentler moods, to make life possible at least. Instead, matters became worse, and at last she did not even shrink in her tantrums from informing him that the rank and station which he supposed he had bestowed upon her by marriage were hers by right of purchase.

It is possible that this taunt may have been responsible for much that followed. Already the evil conditions of his home were driving him to seek distractions abroad. Loyalty to the beloved memory of his father rendered him sympathetic to the Stuart cause, notwithstanding the consideration which his mother had procured from the House of Hanover. Thus he was fertile soil for the temptations that came his way after the death of George I in 1727, and almost light-heartedly he allowed himself to be swept into one of those plots that were ever simmering for the overthrow of the Hanoverian dynasty.

He may have been foolishly incautious, or it may have been far from his imaginings that in spite of their ill relations his wife could be guilty of betraying him. Nor perhaps would she have done so but for her affright when her ever hostile vigilance discovered his treasonable traffic. She reasoned, I suppose, that if the Alverley estates had all but been escheated when they were his father's, it was certainly not for her to suffer them to be escheated now when she regarded them as her own purchased property and her son's heritage. There was one sure way of avoiding it, and that way she took without warning or compunction. She sought Sir Robert Walpole, and, huckstering daughter of a huckstering sire, she sold him, in return for guarantees that the Manors of Dene and

Revelstone should remain immune from escheatment, the information that should enable him to crush the incipient conspiracy. Whether considerations of that earlier attachment of hers, and a hope not merely of security but of widowhood, played any part in this we do not know. But if they did, she was disappointed of at least this portion of the reward. For it happened that a wise government desired no Stuart martyrs, whose blood might prove a seed of further treasons. Perhaps had it been otherwise, Sir Robert might not so easily have accepted the bargain that she offered. A warning was secretly conveyed to Charles, as to other leading members of the plot, that only by instant flight could he hope to save his head.

Thus it was that he came to tread the cheerless path of exile in which we discover him.

With only exiguous and rapidly shrinking resources, and with nothing but his sword to offer in the world's market, he had first sought employment at the court of the Pretender in whose cause he had ruined himself. But the Pretender's own manifestly straitened circumstances afforded him no hopes, and so in the end he had come to seek opportunity under the aegis of his mother's family in the notorious militarism of the new kingdom of Prussia.

Frederick William was known to be building up an army so ludicrously out of proportion to the two and a half million subjects that inhabited his scattered territories that it might reasonably be said – and was being said – that Prussia existed only to maintain this army. To achieve his ambition the King shrank from no sacrifice and from no measures, licit or illicit. His recruiting officials were sedulously at work in every state of the Empire, and even beyond it, to the constant indignation and frequent protests of neighbouring princes, especially when this recruiting went the lengths of kidnapping, as not infrequently happened.

Frederick William's vain and pretentious father, the Elector of Brandenburg, had looked on with jealous eyes when his neighbour the Elector of Hanover had become King of England and his other neighbour, the Elector of Saxony, had been elected King of Poland.

Accounting himself at least as good as either of them, he knew no rest until he had succeeded in pestering the Emperor into a bargain, whereunder, in exchange for the royal dignity, the Brandenburger relinquished certain vague claims to some lands in Silesia.

To accomplish this, and against the advice of Prince Eugène, who with remarkable vision foresaw trouble for the world from such a stimulation of Hohenzollern ambition, the Emperor raised into a Kingdom the remote, diminutive, barbarous province of East Prussia, formerly under Polish suzerainty, and bestowed the crown of it upon the Elector Frederick. So that whilst still no more than a Margrave in Brandenburg, he now became a King in Prussia. In order to give weight and substance to his new title, he brought his subjects in Brandenburg, and in the other odd scraps of land which he owned here and there between the Rhine and the Vistula, gradually to be described as Prussians. It was much as if the Elector of Hanover upon becoming King of England had insisted that his Hanoverian subjects be described as Englishmen.

Like any other parvenu the new king considered it necessary to impress his neighbours. So he yielded a free rein to ostentation, spent upon his coronation the outrageous sum of six million thalers, and set himself to ape the splendours of the King of France, who continued contemptuously to refer to him still as the Marquis of Brandenburg. He created a swarm of court officials, loaded himself with jewels, ate to a fanfare of trumpets, held levées in the French manner, and went processionally to bed. Having become a king it was necessary to be royal. Thus, in a parody of the Sun King, he wasted the substance grimly wrung from the sweat and labour of his scanty subjects.

It was far otherwise with his coarser successor, Frederick William. Instead of inviting ridicule by an emulation of the prodigality of the French court, he swung to the other extreme, and by a Spartan effacement of all splendours, sought to advertise his contempt for the pomps of Versailles. He sold the jewels on which his father had laid out a fortune, swept away the elaborate retinues and idle, costly offices, and reduced even his table expenditure to a bourgeois level of which he kept strict account. But the parvenu's need for self-assertion remained; and if he abolished the ostentation for which his rude nature had no taste and the refinements of which he had no understanding, he scraped and saved and ground his subjects in order to build up a mighty army. Thus he strove to the pompous end that his ramshackle kingdom, frontierless, and of scattered provinces that had come to the Hohenzollerns gradually by marriage or inheritance, should be reckoned amongst the great powers of Europe.

In such a kingdom it seemed to Alverley that employment might be found for one who, at least, should not lack for sponsors in his mother's high-placed kin. So he had sought his mother's father, the old Marshal von Katte of Wartensleben, and by the House of Katte he had been warmly welcomed. Not only did the ties of blood lend him interest in the eyes of his mother's people, but his title, literally translated, made him Markgraf von Alverley to them; and in Germany a Margrave's was a sovereign rank, the equal of that of their own sovereign in Brandenburg. However straitened might be their kinsman's circumstances, his Brandenburger cousins felt that the family gathered lustre from his presence.

From Wartensleben he had brought letters for King Frederick William, in which the old Marshal recommended his hoch-und-wohlgeboren grandson to his Majesty's favour, and in Berlin, whilst awaiting the return of the King from his bear-hunting at Wusterhausen, Katte had presented his English cousin to the Crown Prince, and had taken him to the Queen at Monbijou, in the hope of enlisting their interest on his behalf as a supplement to the Marshal's letter.

Chapter 3

Dorothea

Baron von Grumbkow was absent from Berlin, and Alverley, attaching importance to a personal presentation to the King, was the more content to await the minister's return, deeming it desirable that any fugitive impression of himself which his Majesty might have gathered in those distressing moments at Monbijou should be given time to fade.

He was lodged with Katte, who occupied a square house facing the Arsenal, small but commodious enough for his bachelor estate. A German housekeeper, a French cook and a French valet made up his modest establishment. The ground floor comprised, in addition to the domestic offices and the servants' quarters, Katte's dining-room, all oak and leather, entirely Germanic of character, and a long bare room which he erroneously called his manège, being really no more than a fencing-room. It was in daily use when Katte was in Berlin; for he was as athletic as he was cultured, and excelled as much in bodily exercises, in horsemanship and swordmanship, as in the pursuit of the arts. On this account Alverley was doubly welcome to him as a guest, for in Alverley he found not merely a swordsman with whom to exercise himself, but one from whose uncommon address there was much to be learned.

It was in this fencing-room, on the occasion of one of Prince Frederick's unceremonious visits to Katte, that Alverley had been presented to his Highness. The Prince had insisted that they should not interrupt the practice at which he found them, and he had sat down to watch them with envy in his eyes. As is common in effeminate adolescents, his Highness was attracted by masculine prowess beyond his own capacity, and his prepossession in Alverley's favour had thus at the outset of their acquaintance been commanded by the long, lithe Englishman's display of speed and strength and science.

Above-stairs, in addition to the bedrooms, there was the spacious chamber that Katte called his study, the main room of the house. It was elegantly equipped in the French taste, with well-furnished bookcases, a clavichord in satinwood, and some good pictures by Katte himself, rather in the fanciful Watteau manner.

Into this room, on the third morning after that domestic scene at Monbijou, the Prince came unannounced, with the familiarity he used towards Katte.

Alverley was with his cousin at the time. Lounging on a couch, he was seeking amusement in the pages of Scarron's Roman Comique, whilst Katte, at his easel, was at work upon a miniature of the Princess Wilhelmina, partly from memory and partly from a little portrait supplied him by Prince Frederick.

His Highness had shed his foppish plumage and his high heels, and he looked the better for it, in his colonel's uniform, though his carriage, with the slight body thrusting forward, remained ludicrously unmilitary. A blue-black contusion under the left eye, where a paternal blow had caught him, lent a sinister, lowering air to his pointed countenance.

"No ceremony!" he growled, as they sprang up to receive him; and he added with a sneer: "God knows I am in no case to command it. Let me sit."

He flung himself into a chair, hitched his sword forward, and dropped his three-cornered hat on to the table. "Enviable to be a prince, is it not? So thinks the world. Yet I doubt if there's a less enviable man to be found in it. Katte, I can bear no more. The limits of endurance have been reached. If there's no other way out I shall kill myself. Something must be done. As my best friend – and I permit myself to count you my best friend – I've come to talk to you about it."

Alverley rose. "You will wish to be private with my cousin, monseigneur."

But the Prince waved him down again. "Tcha! Tcha! Private? Diable! We've been public enough for you already. An edifying spectacle, were we not? Oh, I am used to public canings by now. Used to it. But not inured to it. That is what makes me troublesome. Last night at supper there was yet another disgusting scene, with von Suhm present as well as that damned Austrian, Seckendorf. His Majesty threw a dinner plate at me across the table. A right royal gesture, Pardieu! It passes all endurance. One way or another it must finish."

"It would be an impertinence to commiserate with your Highness," said Alverley's quiet voice.

"It would. It isn't what I seek. My need is advice, assistance. I am so humbled that I'm not above asking for it, and it happens that as an Englishman you may be able to help me. As a gentleman I can depend upon you to respect my confidence."

"That of course, monseigneur; it is more certain, unfortunately, than my ability to serve you."

"Wait, Monsieur le Marquis. Wait. I was hoping to find you here. I should be obliged by your interest for me with your ambassador, Captain Dickens."

"My interest!" Alverley smiled. "Perhaps I have been less than frank with your Highness. I should have mentioned that I am a proscribed Jacobite."

The Prince's eyes goggled at him through a silent moment. "Faith, I begin to understand. Tell it to Grumbkow when you see him. It should commend you to my father, out of his abhorrence of King George. But it's unfortunate for me. Ah well! I shall have to depend upon you alone, Katte, to break the ice for me with Guy Dickens; to take his pulse and find out how he would be disposed."

"At your service, my Prince; but to what end?"

"To the end that I may get out of this. Haven't I said that if I stay I shall kill myself. That's no figure of speech. I am in earnest. I must go."

"Go?" The Rittmeister's rugged, swarthy countenance was blank. "Go? Your Highness isn't thinking of running away?"

"What else is there to think of? Name of God!" He came to his feet; his voice was shrill in plaintive anger. "Do you suppose that flesh and blood can bear this indefinitely? Or that I am without pride? Am I to continue to be humiliated, insulted, caned in public until I put a bullet in my brain? For that will be the certain end of it, Katte, if I stay. As God hears me, it will."

Katte rose, too. "Calm yourself, I beg, monseigneur. How do you conceive that the English ambassador can help you? Surely his very office makes it dangerously impossible."

"I can see no danger to him in informing my uncle of my situation, and asking him if he will afford me shelter in England."

"Is that what you require me to do?"

"Just that. If Dickens is favourably disposed I'll see him myself. But I don't want to see him otherwise. I couldn't endure a rebuff. I've borne too much already." Self-pity made him lachrymose. "If you love me, Katte, you'll do me this little service. My God, I tell you it's to save me from killing myself."

"But, of course, monseigneur. I'll see Captain Dickens without delay."

"Good. And there's another matter on my mind. I have some debts. My father's loathsome meanness has made it inevitable. And anyway they come to no more than some six or seven thousand thalers, a miserable bagatelle for a man in my position. But these debts must be paid before I leave, or my father will come to know of them. I don't suppose you can help me, Katte. But I wonder can your cousin." And he looked so hopefully at Alverley that his lordship was led to suspect the basis of the interest with which the Prince had honoured him.

"My purse, monseigneur, would be at your disposal were it not an empty one."

The Prince's expression was incredulous. "Is it possible? You English nobles are accounted rich."

"Not in exile, monseigneur. My rebellion has forfeited me my possessions. Let me assure your Highness that I never regretted it more than at this moment."

"At least I can thank you for that. If only you were as affluent as you are gracious I should be happier."

"And," added Katte, "your Highness will now fully understand why Charles is here seeking employment."

But his Highness was not at the moment interested in Alverley's concerns. "The more, then, must I look to you, my dear Katte, to see what you can do with Dickens."

"As you may, my Prince. I shall seek his Excellency today."

"Very well. Report to me... Let me see. Report to me at Ritter's tomorrow afternoon at four o'clock. That will be best. And we can make some music there in peace, without fear of violence. Perhaps you will come, too, Monsieur le Marquis, if you care for music."

He was no sooner gone than Alverley was admonishing his cousin.

"I don't like it, Hans. Your light-hearted Prince is little concerned with the risks you may incur."

"Risks?"

"Don't you account it risky to be an accessory to the Prince's proposed escape?"

Katte laughed. "I may be a fool, Charles; but not such a fool as that."

"You relieve me. Or you would if I could trust your head to rule your heart. You're a good fellow, Hans. And the good fellows of this world are for ever being abused by the worthless."

"Why, what is this, Charles? I am to convey a message to the English ambassador. Surely that's no great matter?"

"Enough to compromise you if the object of the message were known."

Katte shrugged. "Who's to know it? Captain Dickens will, at least, be discreet whether he consents to help or not."

"You perceive the need for his discretion. That means that you perceive the risk I am pointing out. Continue to perceive it, and go cautiously."

"Trust me to walk as delicately as Agag."

It was Alverley's turn to laugh. "That's none too happy an image. You know what came of it. Beware his fate."

Katte was justified, at least, of his confidence in the British ambassador's discretion. But for the rest, Captain Guy Dickens – phonetically alluded to in the Margravine's memoirs as Monsieur Gidikins – was a gentleman whose easy manners masked a deal of shrewdness. He looked askance as he listened to the Rittmeister that same evening.

"I could hardly venture," he quietly protested, "to put forward a proposal of that character. And so I had better forget at once that it has been made. You see, my dear Rittmeister. I am by no means sure that if I seriously listened to you I should not be abusing my position. No. No. Definitely, I can have nothing to do with it."

"I understand," said Katte, "and it is not for me to attempt to persuade you."

"You would lose your time."

But as they shook hands, and when Dickens had murmured polite regrets, he added: "You may tell his Highness that if at any time he should wish to write to King George, who I am sure will always be glad to hear from his nephew, I shall be happy to forward the letter by my own courier."

Well pleased, Katte went off to report to the Prince that whilst the sly ambassador would not act as a conscious intermediary, he offered his Highness the use of the ambassadorial post-bag for letters of whose contents his Excellency would decline to be aware. To make this report he took his way, on the following afternoon, as concerted, to the house of Pastor Ritter in the Nikolaistrasse, and Alverley went with him.

It was actually in this house that the friendship between Katte and the Prince had taken its beginnings. The scholarly old churchman had once been Katte's tutor, and had never loved a pupil more since he had never possessed one who profited more flatteringly by his teaching. Their friendly relations had persisted long after Katte had exchanged his school books for the sword, and for this the pastor's only child Dorothea was partly responsible. The link between the girl and the Rittmeister was the considerable musical talent of each, and in the exercise of it Katte would often spend an evening at the pastor's house.

On one such evening, a year or so earlier, the Prince was idly wandering the streets with his devoted friend, Lieutenant von Ingersleben, when in the Nikolaistrasse his attention was arrested by the sound of a flute played with such mastery as to possess almost the qualities of a human voice. From across the street the Prince was able to look into the room whence the sound came. The window stood wide, and the curtains were undrawn although candles had already been lighted within. Thus he was afforded a clear view of the tall performer in a guardsman's uniform, and of the young girl at a clavichord who accompanied him. Ingersleben, looking with him, was able to supply the information his Highness craved.

"It is von Katte of the Guards."

"A soldier! And he plays like that! You know the fellow, then? You shall present him to me."

The presentation was made on the morrow, and there the friendship had its beginning. It was not only that the Prince found the young guardsman attractive in himself, but Katte's intimacy with the pastor and the pastor's daughter rendered him convenient to one of the Prince's needs. The King's hostility to musical pursuits compelled his Highness to indulge them in secret, just as the King's hostility to scholarship had led his Highness to make secret arrangements for the library which had been assembled for him by Duhan – that sometime tutor whom Frederick William had driven out with blows when he caught him teaching his son to decline *mensa*.

Thus Prince Frederick had been brought to Pastor Ritter's house in the Nikolaistrasse, and thereafter became a regular visitor there. At first whilst both the pastor and his daughter had been a little overawed by this royal condescension, Ritter had regarded it with certain misgivings. He judged that the Prince, being manifestly vain and shallow, might also be vicious, and whilst he had every confidence in his child's virtue and wisdom, yet it remained that she was very young and very innocent and might, therefore, not be proof against the flattery of attentions from one in the exalted station of the Prince. So the pastor at first used vigilance, and affected a taste for music which he was far from possessing in order to be present whenever his Highness came to exercise the flute. Soon, however, he wearied of this, and was content to impose a tactful watchfulness upon his housekeeper Theresa when his own duties as a teacher or his labours on a monumental translation of Apollonius of Tyana engaged him elsewhere. Fortunately for Theresa's embarrassments, it was rarely that his Highness came alone to the Nikolaistrasse. Usually he was attended either by Katte or by the blond and light-hearted Lieutenant von Ingersleben or by some other of his young associates. For with characteristic, if in this instance not unamiable arrogance, the Prince had come to treat the pastor's house very much as his own. Thus he had not hesitated not only to give Katte the appointment there, but to invite Alverley also to be of the party.

"You are expected," Katte told his cousin. "It is a command. Fritz, it is clear, desires your better acquaintance."

"A flattering mystery."

"He's probably impressed by your ability to quote Horace. He would like to quote Horace, himself. Or it may be your English phlegm. Or your taste for music which enables you to appreciate his virtuosity. Not all the fathers in Brandenburg would keep him from playing the flute, and he'll never find a better accompanist than Dorothea Ritter, who is as nearly an angel as any woman that I've ever seen."

"And the pastor?"

"He'll not unduly trouble us. He does not live in the world, but in an egoist's paradise: a scholar with few interests outside his library. His wife, perceiving that she was not necessary, had the good taste to die some years ago, and I almost think that his daughter might do the same without seriously disturbing him. Such men possess, I suppose, the true secret of happiness."

Flourishes from a flute greeted their arrival at the pastor's modest house, and in a room of simple daintiness, of green panelling and floral chintzes, they found his Highness awaiting them.

From the clavichord rose a slim, straight shape in grey, gravely to smile a welcome to Katte, gravely to consider his tall companion. Her unpowdered hair, of which a heavy ringlet lay on her white neck, was of a rich chestnut in which there were gleams of gold. Her skin, scorning the aggressive make-up that was the mode, was of a texture so exquisitely and impressively delicate that it seemed to give you the very note of her nature.

The Rittmeister presented Alverley, and her softly rounded arm, emerging from a froth of lace at the elbow, was extended towards him across the instrument. He bowed formally over it, brushing the fingers with his lips. Then, coming erect again, he met the steady glance of clear grey eyes that were gentle as a hind's, and for a moment each of them remained as if seeking to look beneath the surface of the other. In the ineffable purity of her air she might, he thought, have served as the model for a Madonna.

He was recalled by a giggle from the Prince. "Parbleu, Dorothea, now you will know what an Englishman looks like."

Her glance faltered and fell, and there was a faint stir of colour in her cheeks. She resumed her seat at the clavichord, having spoken no word.

His Highness babbled on. "She is my very good friend, Monsieur le Marquis, and my valued collaborator in these days when I am driven to make music in secret." Abruptly he addressed the Rittmeister. "Well, Katte? What news?"

Katte made his report, with regrets that he should have done no better.

"But it is well enough," said the Prince, with a laugh. "The foxy fellow points out the proper course. Thus a letter will travel safely and secretly. I'll write it today, and you shall take it to him, Katte." He turned to the girl. "Pardon, Dorothea. It's a matter concerning this latest decoration with which his Majesty has favoured me." He set a finger to his bruised cheek. "The order of the Royal Flautist." His mockery was bitter. It was as if he employed this mixture of self-scorn and self-pity as a cloak for his shame.

"That is not a good jest, Monseigneur," said Dorothea quietly.

"Oh, agreed. But characteristic of my father. His humour is peculiar. Very German."

Again she used a tone of gentle protest. "But are we not all Germans, my Prince?"

"Peste! I suppose we are. But that is no reason to glory like my father and his cronies in German intellectual squalor. They even use this barbarian tongue."

"We have poets who reveal beauties in it," she insisted. "Your Highness should become acquainted with them."

"Le diable m'en garde! That is the last of my intentions."

"Yet you might find it profitable."

He stared at her in sudden displeasure. "On my soul, you do not flatter me."

She parried his annoyance with frank laughter. "Your Highness comes here for music, not for compliments."

"And now you do not flatter yourself." He leaned towards her, his elbows on the clavichord, and as he looked into her eyes his glance became something of a leer. "Have I ever said that music is all I come for; the only favour in your bestowing? Why, then, must you assume it?"

"Your Highness would be less welcome if I did not."

"Here's cruelty to match my father's. Worse, for his is merely physical. He forbids me to play the flute. You forbid me to do anything else. You are tyrants both."

Katte interposed, to take up a sheet of music. "Shall we seek shelter in harmony, before discord becomes acute? You have something new here, my Prince."

"That is Dorothea's. She seeks to put me to shame as a composer. Another of her cruelties."

"It is but a little song I have made," she told the Rittmeister.

"You shall sing it for us."

"That, no." The Prince was definite. "Not until I've turned it into French." Over Katte's shoulder he read the opening line: " 'Solange sich mein blut noch rühret.' Is that a noise that can be made to music? Are those words you could suffer to hear sung?"

"If Mademoiselle sang then," ventured Alverley, "since she has written them."

"But I have not," she disclaimed. "They are Anton Fechter's, a great poet."

"One of those," the Prince scoffed, "who reveal the beauties of the German tongue. Bah! Germany will never produce a Corneille or a Racine. The language makes it impossible. But you shall judge the sweetness of the melody. You shall hear it on my flute. The words, as I've said, must wait until I've translated them. Come."

Good-humouredly she accepted his peremptoriness. "Since you are royal, sir, you must not be denied."

"Adorable sentiment. Bear it always in mind, and we'll agree famously. Pray begin."

From the armchair into which Katte had thrust him, Alverley was content to listen to a melody which neither her mastery of the clavichord nor the Prince's virtuosity on the flute could redeem from ingenuousness. But if pleasure was denied his ears, amends were made to his eyes. Observing her so rapt, absorbed in her playing, seated in a shaft of sunlight that set a glinting aureole about her head, he conceived that thus might St Cecilia have appeared.

The long room seemed to Alverley imbued with something peculiarly of herself, as rooms are when tenanted by a definite personality. From the cluster of roses in a piece of Delft ware, set on a console of inlaid woods with copper mouldings, to the needlework tapestry on the walnut chairs, all seemed to reflect her graciousness. Against the panelling facing Alverley hung a smiling portrait of her, of some merit, in which he recognized the work of his cousin. Another picture, of less merit, in an oval frame, hung above the overmantel. It was a portrait of her father, painted by herself. Her talent in painting, as in music, was being guided by the

accomplished and generous Katte, and she was responding
particularly as a miniaturist.

As the last chords of the melody faded Alverley rose to utter
civilities of whose insincerity he was unconscious.

She deprecated the praise. "Oh, I am not deceived. It is his
Highness who deserves your compliments. His playing makes much
of my poor little song."

"I have no doubt that is true," the Prince agreed. "But it's none the
less amiable of you to confess it, Dorothea."

Alverley was conscious of irritation. It drove him to hypocrisy. But
his voice was smooth. "The amiability of true talent which ever
depreciates itself."

The Prince looked up sharply. Then he loosed his loud laugh.
"Touché, pardi! But I forgive the hit since gallantry dictated it. That
is, if gallantry did dictate it, and not lack of discernment."

"Monsieur le Marquis seeks to be kind," said she.

"Faith, he succeeds, I think. He follows the true French spirit."

"I hope, Monseigneur," Alverley protested, "that I follow only my
own nature."

"Then are you the more to be felicitated. Oh, and envied a luxury
that I wish were mine. You see what happens when I openly follow
my own nature." Again he pointed ruefully to the contusion under
his eye. Alverley was finding him tedious in this insistence on his
sufferings. "Hence these sly recourses to my friends. But there! Katte,
since you've nothing to say, take my flute, and discourse to us on
that."

With the bright smile that redeemed the ugliness of his pockmarked face, Katte was swift to obey. "I have not his Highness' skill,
Charles. But I'll do what I can with Mademoiselle's assistance."

"What? Do you mock me? Or do you, too, grow modest?" His
Highness sneered. "Faith, Marquis, yours, I fear, is an influence
destructive of self-esteem. You are not, yourself, a musician by
chance?"

"Alas, no. A music-lover only. Let me envy your Highness in my
turn."

The Prince's smile was almost affectionate. "I should like to believe that you have occasion. But to it, Katte. Let our music-lover judge for himself. Play him 'Armida's Lament.'"

Chapter 4

The Champion

The Prince's letter to King George having been delivered by Katte to Captain Guy Dickens, his Highness sat down to wait with such patience as he could command and in the repeatedly avowed determination to shoot himself if his uncle failed him. All his life suicide was to be a declared consideration of his. This, however, did not prevent him from ultimately dying of old age.

In the meantime the all-powerful minister, the Freiherr von Grumbkow, came back to Berlin, and his interest for Alverley was sought by Katte and also by the Crown Prince, who was showing the Englishman an ever-increasing favour.

On acquaintance von Grumbkow displayed none of the odious characteristics imputed to him by the Prince and his sister. A man approaching fifty, inclining to portliness, yet of handsome presence and suave, insinuating ways, he received the Marquess of Alverley with a cordiality that left nothing to be desired. It would be an honour to present his lordship to the King, little weight though his presentation would add to Lord Alverley's letter from a nobleman of such consequence as the Marshal of Wartensleben. Of seeking profit for himself there was no sign, although it may well be, as Katte laughingly suggested, that the Baron, from a sense of decency, postponed this until later.

So Alverley was taken to the Schloss, that vast quadrangular castle between the two branches of the Spree, half-Dutch on one side with its copper-roofed bell turrets, half-classical on the other, with its columned façade, it was characteristic of Frederick William that he should have converted the ground floor of his royal residence into a swarming hive of crown offices, in order that those employed in them should be immediately under his hand and eye. For his personal abode he reserved no more than a matter of five rooms on the first floor, such as would have supplied a lodging for the simplest gentleman. Their rich adornments, frescoed ceilings, tapestried walls, loaded cornices, gildings and the rest, were a legacy from his prodigal father, which he accepted, but in which he took no satisfaction.

Alverley and his sponsor were received in the spacious audience chamber; which upon occasion served the frugal monarch also as a dining-room. His Majesty was at work there with a couple of secretaries, and from the antechamber, whilst awaiting admission, they could hear him roaring and bellowing at those unfortunates. These emerged at last with scared faces and perspiring brows, to inform the Baron that he was awaited.

The King sat at his work-table, rummaging fiercely in the litter of papers that cumbered it. The little blue eyes embedded in that fleshly red face flashed a keen glance upon his visitors.

"Ah, Baron, it is my fate to be served by fools. Devil take them!" He thrust the mass of papers from him, smacked it viciously with his little podgy hand, and flung himself back in his chair. His blue military coat and yellow chamois waistcoat were unbuttoned, for the day was warm, and he suffered from the heat. For the same reason he had loosed the plain white neckcloth about his pendulous dewlap.

"Whom have we here?" The stare of his blue eyes upon Alverley was hard and searching.

The Baron was formal. "I have the honour to present to your Majesty the high and well-born Markgraf von Alverley, an

37

Englishman, who brings you a letter from his uncle, the Marshal von Katte of Wartensleben."

"Wartensleben has a margrave, an English margrave, for a nephew?" Majesty grunted, and added: "That is news to me."

The tone suggested that it was news – subtly magnified by the translation of Alverley's title – that impressed his Majesty, as well it might, since the rank was equal here in Brandenburg to the King's own.

"The Marshal," he continued, "is my very good friend. I give you welcome, sir."

Alverley made his bow. "Your Majesty is gracious."

Relieved not to have been recognized for one of the Prince's companions in the Porcelain Gallery, Alverley presented his letter, and stood silent whilst the King perused it, his thick lips moving as he read.

"So!" Again the little eyes were scrutinizing the stranger. "The Marshal tells me that you seek service with me." He made it plain that he asked the reason.

"Prussia," Alverley explained, "is the most eminent of all schools for a man of military ambitions. The fame of your Majesty's army makes it natural that I should regard it as the highest academy of the military art, the elements of which I had the good fortune to study under Prince Eugène in the Netherlands."

The magic of that name modified the King's expression, softened its odd blend of haughtiness and vulgarity.

"That is the opinion even in England, eh? Sit down, sit down. Baron, a chair for the Margrave."

For a silent moment the keen, hard eyes continued to ponder the applicant's tall, graceful figure in its unostentatious black, the strong, proud lines of his patrician face, and the air of quiet dignity that mantled him. "And so out of all Europe you choose Prussia as your school of soldiering. What active service have you seen?"

"Alas, Majesty, none."

"None!"

This was not so gratifying, and Alverley made haste to explain, as the crafty Grumbkow had prompted him. "My political convictions were against my taking service at home. They are now responsible for my having left England."

Majesty's glance brightened again. "Oho! You are out of favour, then, with that brother-in-law of mine, the Red Cabbage?"

"I am exiled, sire. I am a Jacobite, like my father, who gave his life for King James."

"Gerechter Herrgott! Had there been more like you in England that coxcomb of Herrenhausen would still be Elector of Hanover." It was an explosion of the resentment he nursed of his proud, poverty-stricken brother-elector's elevation to a throne of such antiquity, wealth, power and dignity as that of England, in contrast with which Frederick William was but too conscious of the paltry, upstart quality of his own kingship. It was a kingship so recent that he, himself, had not even been born royal; for his father had been made King in Prussia some time after Frederick William's birth.

At the moment he was smarting, moreover, under a sense that in his marriage projects for Wilhelmina with the Prince of Wales he was being defeated by the deeper guile of King George. He took the view that his brother-in-law had but made a pretence of favouring the marriage in order to dispose of his own daughter Amelia by marrying her to Prince Frederick. There had been on the subject a violent and unseemly scene with Sir Charles Hotham, who, at the request of Queen Sophia Dorothea, had come to Berlin as Ambassador Extraordinary. King George, through this envoy, had declined as a beginning to go beyond the question of the marriage of Amelia, whilst Frederick William, on his side, was equally determined to treat only of the marriage of Wilhelmina. It was intolerable to Frederick William, aiming solely at the disposal of a daughter, to find himself frustrated by an identical aim on the part of King George. It resulted in rendering his brother-in-law more detestable to him than before. Here, then, was enough to predispose him in favour of Alverley, for if a common friend makes a bond between men, a common enemy makes a vastly stronger one.

The King stroked his massive chin. "Loyalty to his rightful sovereign," he dogmatized, "is a gentleman's highest virtue, and honour is magnified by sacrifice in loyalty's cause."

"In our case, Majesty, my father's and mine, it was also loyalty to our care, to our kin. Stuart is among the names I bear."

"So!" The King looked at him with a deeper interest, imagined, as he was later to tell Grumbkow, that he now held the explanation of that quiet dignity, that calm urbanity. In his veins flowed – the words are Frederick William's – the blood of an ancient royal race; no wonder that he had a royal look. What he said at the moment, however, was: "But how excellently you speak German, my Lord Margrave."

Alverley explained that he owed it to his mother, who was of the House of Katte.

"To be sure. So says the Marshal. Yet I felicitate you that you speak it with such fluency in this generation of silly fops who affect to disdain it with their morbleus and sapristis."

He went on to question Alverley on his estates, their extent and character, his pursuits, his education, and the like. He made his lordship talk at some length upon hunting as pursued in England; and at great length, himself an ardent hunter, he dilated upon the sport at Wusterhausen. "You shall come and hunt the wolf there one of these days. You'll find it manlier sport than chasing little foxes."

Upon that he gave him a friendly dismissal. "I'll send for you again when I have considered. Decidedly we shall find you something to occupy you here in Prussia. Meanwhile, Baron, you must bring him to our next Tabagie. You'll enjoy yourself. And now let me return to work. It's no light thing being King of Prussia."

Alverley bowed himself out well pleased.

We know that Grumbkow held the view that to the instant and unusual favour which his lordship found in the eyes of Frederick William the circumstance of his being a proscribed Jacobite, and consequently an enemy of King George's, contributed more than a little. Grumbkow, who had his vanities, may have leaned to this opinion because it flattered his judgment in having urged Alverley, as an ingratiatory measure, to avow himself a Jacobite. It is certain that the result justified him, although it is too much to suppose that it was the only factor in what followed.

Reassured by his interview, Alverley resigned himself without impatience to await the King's pleasure. Meanwhile, as best he could, he took his own. With Katte he made excursions into the surrounding country, flat and uninteresting in every direction save that of Potsdam. There he found refreshment of spirit in the pleasantly wooded banks of the Havel. There, too, he witnessed more than one of those parades at which Frederick William played the drill-sergeant, and in which the troops displayed that miraculous precision into which they had been schooled by that ageing warrior Prince Leopold of Anhalt-Dessau, a precision which no other troops in the world could pretend to match. The automatic movements of these regiments were like the movements of a clock, as if each man, always in place, were but a piece of the machinery. It would have rejoiced the heart of Prince Eugène, thought his lordship, to have beheld action so smooth, easy and unfaltering, and yet so vigorous. If this swift precision could be maintained in the field, and under fire, such an army should be formidable indeed.

Alverley wondered for what purpose so mighty a weapon should be forged, and at so extravagant a cost, by a King who in all else was of a wretched parsimony. It was a question that all Europe was asking, the more puzzled because, however despotic and bullying at home, Frederick William displayed no aggressiveness whatever abroad, but, rather, a marked pusillanimity in his dealings with other powers. The truth was that in the matter of troops he was merely a collector, with all a collector's avarice. He assembled them from pride of possession, as ornaments to his kingship, for the consciousness of strength which they gave him and in just the same miserly spirit as the gold which he hoarded in the cellars of the Schloss. He was careful to keep the peace because he could not contemplate the dissipation of one or the other of these well-nurtured sinews of war. Covetous he might be of land and glory, but he would risk no actual possessions in order to increase them.

41

Having no means to fathom the mystery of all this, my Lord Alverley looked upon the incessant drilling, training and manoeuvring as the whetting of a sword with which soon to be carving destinies. And because in the career which he had chosen, as the natural career for a necessitous gentleman, it was only by campaigning that advancement was to be won, he was content that circumstances should have guided his steps to Brandenburg.

He saw the Crown Prince frequently in those weeks of idle waiting, sometimes at Katte's house, and sometimes at Pastor Ritter's. It was the Prince who sought these meetings, out of a manifest eagerness to learn in detail what he could of life in England, where he hoped soon to find himself. Had time been available it is even possible he might have sought lessons in English from Alverley. Without that, however, a certain intimacy crept into their relations, and it might have become closer still had not Alverley's mistrust of the Prince's bonhomie dictated a wary restraint. It happened also that he was secretly deprecating the too-easy familiarity with which his Highness at times perceptibly embarrassed Dorothea Ritter. She was too fine and pure, he thought, to be exposed to the liberties of speech and manner which the Prince occasionally permitted himself Alverley never saw her without recalling Seele's lines on the Lady Elizabeth Hastings: "Though her mien carries much more invitation than command, to behold her is an immediate check to loose behaviour."

Because of this he came gradually to disapprove in his heart of these musical gatherings at Ritter's. Inevitably, it seemed to him, they must result in scandal and damage to the repute of a girl too unworldly and innocent to be aware of the risk she ran, whilst her father, accustomed by now to these visits of the Prince and his associates, and having found their conduct sober, had conquered his earlier misgivings, and tranquilly pursued his classical labours. That Alverley was right was very soon and very terribly to be proved.

The first hint of it came one evening when, with Katte, Ingersleben and three other officers of the Berlin garrison, he sat in the pleasant tavern known as the Weintraube. They were joined by a lieutenant of dragoons named von Stein, who sauntered uninvited across to their table, a big, fair, coarsely jovial fellow with whom Alverley was already acquainted.

Seeing so many of the Prince's cronies together, he must hail them with a: "Where's his Highness?" to which he added with a suggestive laugh: "Practising the flute in the Nikolaistrasse, I suppose. Lord God! What chances we miss who are not flute-players. I'm told the Pastor's girl is as sweet a piece of flesh as may be seen in Brandenburg. The talk is all that his Highness is growing up."

There was no echo from the table to his coarse guffaw. Katte looked at the man with cold dislike. Young Ingersleben sat stiff and frowning. But Alverley was stung to answer in his quiet drawl: "The foul must talk foully."

The big red face grew redder. "Potzteufel! How am I to take that, sir?"

"For what it is. A truth too manifest to be contradicted."

"I'll need a plainer answer, if you please. To whom do you allude?"

Alverley answered without heat. "To the foul, who talk as you tell us. You'll hardly deny their foulness."

"Of course he won't," Katte cut in with intent to avert an ugly situation.

Stein uttered a sneering laugh. "Et tu, Brute! My faith! what a hornet's nest of little puritans. I give you joy of one another." And on that, conceiving that he went off with the honours, the lieutenant swaggered away.

Alverley half-rose to follow him, when Katte gripped his arm.

"Quiet! Take thought. A quarrel would wreck your chances in Berlin. And it would do Dorothea the very harm from which you seek to protect her. Let the drunken oaf go."

"I suppose you are right," Alverley yielded with a sigh. "But the clown would be the better for a lesson."

It was Ingersleben's fault that the matter did not end there, as Alverley was to discover a couple of days later. The Prince and Katte were to meet him at Pastor Ritter's, but arriving before either of them

Alverley found himself alone with Dorothea, who at once took him to task.

"I don't know whether to thank you or scold you."

"Do neither, then."

"I must do both. Yet I am so touched by your defending me, that I hesitate to scold your indiscretion."

"So that is it? But, faith, if I blame myself at all it is for being too discreet. And I am sorry, anyway, Mademoiselle, that you should have been troubled with this trifle."

"It is not a trifle." Her clear grey eyes met his with steady candour. "But I am too insignificant a person to deserve a champion. Nor, I hope, do I need one."

"It rather seems you do. For there's a lesson in all this. It is that the breath of a prince's favour is blighting to a maid's repute."

She frowned as she looked at him. "More so than a margrave's?"

He became serious. "I perceive that I offend."

"Oh, no, I want you to realize how idle are your assumptions."

"It was with assumptions that I quarrelled. And they were not mine, you'll remember, if the matter was correctly reported to you."

"That man!" She was scornful. "What do his assumptions matter? There could be no better answer than you gave him."

"What you should remember is that he did not claim to be original. He merely made himself the echo of what is being said. It might suggest to your friends that the Prince's visits are more frequent than is good for your repute."

There was a little movement of impatience. "You know why the Prince comes."

"Of course I do. But that is nothing to the matter. If he came to pray with you it would still be the same. Indeed, I permit myself to wonder that your father, who can hardly share your own sweet innocence, should have made no protest."

"My father is a good man. A saint. He thinks no evil, and he has confidence in my good sense. For the rest…" She smiled affectionately. "Poor father! He scarcely lives in this world."

"That seems to be a family trait. But perhaps I become impertinent."

She set a conciliatory hand upon his arm. "You are not to suppose that there is any resentment in me. How could there be? How could I not be touched by your desire to protect me? It may not have been discreet, but it was the action of a true friend."

Although at the time it seemed to him that he had failed, he was soon to realize that, on the contrary, seed had been cast on fertile soil. Quite how she contrived it he did not know at the time, but he rightly supposed that she had made use of the Stein incident so as to impose upon his Highness the condition that he must never come to the Nikolaistrasse unaccompanied. It went near to putting an end to his visits altogether, for he received the condition petulantly.

"I rarely do. But, mon Dieu, my girl, what is this nonsense?"

She answered him in Alverley's phrase about the blighting quality of a prince's breath. That set him crowing with shrill laughter.

"Blighting, do you say? Dieu me damne! Have you never heard of Melusina von der Schulenberg, who was more than queen in England in my grandfather's time? The royal breath made her a duchess. An enviable blight. And that's to mention only one of thousands who have been magnified by royal attention."

"I do not aspire to be so magnified."

"A pity. For it would rest with me to make you as great in Prussia."

"Your Highness is mistaken. It does not rest with you."

Grinning, he thrust his weasel face within a foot of hers. "Is that a challenge, petite vierge?"

"It's a reminder, monseigneur, of the respect I have the right to claim."

This annoyed him. "But you forget the respect you owe me in claiming it." He swung aside, and strutted about the room. "You would be well served if I did not come here again. You cast your good name at me. How has my notice hurt your name? Before my visits you were just Pastor Ritter's girl. Now if any speaks of you, it is as the Fräulein who is the friend of the Crown Prince. Is that nothing to you?"

"So much that I think it will be better if you do not come again."

He checked in his pacing, and stared amazed. "Name of God! I talk in vain, then. You don't listen; or else you don't understand."

"But I understand perfectly, Highness."

Before her quiet firmness he changed his tactics, subduing his irritation and his arrogance, and turned to appeal. "Dorothea, my dear little friend, this is unkind. I have told you so much about myself. Consider how little there is, prince though I be, to cheer my life. Will you deny me one of its purest joys?" He had come to stand beside her as he spoke. "Dorothea!" He set an arm about her slim waist, and drew her against him. Because she passively suffered it he was emboldened. "Come, now. Confess that you are only rallying me. Am I to be denied the happiness of these hours with you merely because of the chatter of some jackanapes? You couldn't be so cruel, knowing me so devoted. Surely you love me a little, Dorothea. You…"

"No!" She disengaged herself abruptly from that slyly tightening clasp. Standing taller than he, she looked down upon him, her breathing quickened. "This is not right. I am not to listen to it." She was severe.

"Oh, very well." He was petulant again. "But coyness can be pushed too far. It becomes tiresome, and I can find elsewhere all the tiresomeness I can endure. I had better go."

"I agree, monseigneur, that it will be better."

"And not come again?"

"Not alone. Please spare me by understanding that."

He glared. "Is that a thing to say to your Prince?"

"With all respect, Highness."

"Oh, go to the devil." He clapped his hat on his head, and stalked out, leaving her with mixed emotions of anger, amusement and relief.

But he was back again on the morrow in penitent mood, bringing Katte with him. He abased himself in excuses, whined about his unhappiness, which he urged in exculpation, and vowed that hers was the only house that offered him facilities and security to devote himself to his passion for music. Thus he wrought upon the generosity of her nature, which, after all, was not entirely emancipated from a sense of deference to his rank.

Their peace was made, and it was preserved thereafter by the Prince's scrupulous observation of the condition she had made, always coming accompanied by at least one and usually more of his young associates. Alverley, himself, continued frequently to be of these little gatherings, and sometimes, too, he ventured to come alone. He had made friends with her father, and ostensibly it was the pastor he came to visit. It is possible that he believed it, although it is beyond doubt that Dorothea was the true lodestone, her society affording him an imperceptibly increasing pleasure and solace. Friendship between them, as is no matter for wonder, had ripened into intimacy with their almost incipient quarrel over the Stein affair.

One day when he lingered with her in the green-panelled room after she had been playing for him, she expressed the irony that was at the root of their present relations.

"Are you never conscious that in coming here as you do, you encourage in me the freedom of conduct you have condemned?"

"Condemned is too harsh a word. Besides, I come to see your father. That I see you as well is but a natural accident." He laughed. "And anyway I am not a prince."

"I think I suggested to you before that what is wrong in a prince cannot be right in a marquis. And since I've taken your lesson to heart, and practised it with his Highness, as you'll have noticed, am I to ignore it with you?"

"You may be right," he conceded, "to require that I practise as I preach. If you insist I shall reluctantly obey you."

"There was no reluctance in my obedience to you."

"Not ultimately. But at first you were not merely reluctant, but resentful. And you were in the right; for I was guilty of presumption."

"I do not call it that."

"Whatever you call it, will you not answer the question you have raised?"

She was smiling. "Perhaps, after all, there is a difference between a prince and a marquis. Certainly a great difference when the prince is the Crown Prince of Prussia."

This was a conclusion that made vain their argument, since it banished the very question she had raised. Thereafter the chivalrous, courtly deference he used, blent with an affectionate comradeship, set her completely at her ease with him, whilst, on his side, the contrast he drew between her nature, so frank and artless, and that of the calculating woman who had bought and sold him, served dangerously to deepen his regard.

Chapter 5

The Tabagie

Whilst nothing in those days afforded him greater pleasure and refreshment than his visits to the house in the Nikolaistrasse, be it alone, be it in the company of the Prince and his associates, Alverley was not so utterly engrossed in Dorothea Ritter that he could not give time and thought to his real aims in Berlin. Nor was his patience unduly taxed. It would be some ten days after his interview with the King when Grumbkow sought him with a command to attend a Tabagie, or Tabaks Collegium, that singular mixture of carousal and informal parliament so dear to Frederick William, who had invented it. How unkingly was the invention Alverley could never have realized without the evidence of his senses. He was no more squeamish than any other healthy young man of his years and times; but he had been reared in certain traditions of conduct for men of breeding, which, however superficial, made him look askance upon the gross character of the assembly to which Grumbkow introduced him.

There were gathered together in the main hall of the King's apartments in the Schloss some two dozen men of Frederick William's Court, and there were a few others besides. There was Count Seckendorf, the Austrian representative, a burly, stolid man of fifty with the airs of a prosperous farmer. It was whispered, as we know, that he was Grumbkow's paymaster, bribing the minister to direct the royal policy in the Austrian interest. Nevertheless, or, indeed, perhaps as a result, he enjoyed Frederick William's highest esteem. There was Baron von Suhm, the Saxon envoy, a slight, delicate man of a frigid elegance, also highly esteemed by his Majesty, though perhaps less highly than usual at the moment. For there had lately been a breeze between the King and himself on the subject of some shameless crimping by Frederick William's recruiting officers in the territory of the Elector of Saxony, who was also King of Poland. The great cordiality that existed between the two monarchs had momentarily stood in peril, and von Suhm had been instructed to ask for his passports unless the kidnapped subjects of his master were instantly set at liberty and enabled to return home. Frederick William had yielded, but had been left resentful; and this, in fact, was von Suhm's first appearance at a Tabagie since the dispute.

The Crown Prince, too, was present, with his two governors, Colonel von Rochow and Rittmeister von Keyserlingk. He came forward with a friendly greeting for Alverley, and remained to point out to him some of those present. It was from the Prince, who treated the matter with malicious humour, that Alverley learnt of the Saxon affair, knowledge this which was to remain in his memory, and to be turned by him later to opportune account.

That famous old warrior, Prince Leopold of Anhalt-Dessau, was perhaps the most important person in the assembly, for, invaluable to Frederick William, he was the real organizer of the Prussian army. Short and sturdy, he was disfigured by a clipped, snuff-laden grey moustache, grotesquely incongruous with his powdered wig. His eyes were smiling and friendly, despite his ferocious reputation. Then there was Gundling, the President of the Academy of Sciences, a portly, untidy fellow in rusty black, with a loose, humorous mouth in a big red face that was marbled by drink and gluttony. And there was the tall, blond, handsome Freiherr von Katzenstein, lately appointed aide-de-camp to Frederick William, and highly esteemed by the Prince.

They stood about in groups, talking noisily, until the double doors were thrown open by a chamber hussar. Then the chatter died down, and, with a deferential bending of backs, the company turned to face the entering King.

Frederick William rolled forward, planting his feet heavily and leaning upon his cane. He paused, to wave it like a sword.

"To table, sirs."

He made his way to the head of it, to occupy a seat that was neither chair nor stool, but a hybrid of the two, equipped with arm-rests but no back.

Beside each plate on both sides of the long table there was a clay pipe, a jug of beer and a glass, whilst in the middle of the board there were baskets containing coarse tobacco. But, as soon as the company was seated, the chamber hussars, whom Frederick William dressed in the French fashion, in order to mark his contemptuous opinion that such modes were fit only for lackeys, came to place on the table long silver trenchers of sliced ham, sliced veal, and slabs of cheese, together with platters of bread and butter.

The Prince had found himself a seat as far from his father as the length of the board permitted, with Katzenstein beside him and Colonel Rochow opposite. Alverley, also on the opposite side of the board, midway down, between Grumbkow and von Suhm, observed the expression with which his Highness advertised his distaste for the gathering. There was a curl to his lip as if an evil smell were offending his long-pointed nose, and there was only contempt in the dull glance with which he raked the table. His queer, sensitive nature, and his affectations of delicacy and culture, may well have found here little that was to his taste; but only his natural insolence could prompt him to parade his feelings under the eye of his father. Nor was his father's eye slow to observe it, or his father's spirit slow to take up the challenge.

A Hungarian wine was being offered to Seckendorf and von Suhm out of deference to their ambassadorial rank and foreign taste. Seckendorf refused it, perhaps sycophantically, knowing that he would deserve the King's approval by preferring beer. As the cellarer was withdrawing, wine-jug in hand, the Prince beckoned him and

pointed to his glass. The servant, advancing to pour, was checked by
a sudden bellow from the King.

"Take that away. His Highness will drink beer, like the rest of us."

Scared, the Prince achieved a sickly pacificatory smile. "Ach, gern,
lieber papa."

But Majesty, being roused, was not so easily pacified. "Willingly,
eh? Willingly under compulsion, you mean. That's the only way you
are ever willing. Am I always to be ashamed of you, you milksop?"
The Prince's superciliousness had supplied a spark to dangerously
combustible material. "I saw you riding this morning on the road to
Charlottenburg with the English Margrave. A pity you don't copy his
deportment in the saddle, instead of sitting a horse like a monkey on
a dog. Keyserlingk, why the devil don't you teach the Prince to ride?"

With a grunt of contempt, he took up a pipe and reached for a
tobacco basket. The assembly, which his manner had momentarily
frozen in discomfort, thawed again, and a murmur of conversation
arose.

The Prince, cowed and sullen, but resolved to provoke no further
humiliations before a company most of which he permitted himself
to despise, lighted himself a pipe, and, at the risk of being made sick
by a practice which he abhorred, began to smoke.

Katzenstein, under cover of the general conversation, murmured
a word of sympathy, which almost brought the young man to tears.
Otherwise, however, out of a kindly desire to spare him, little notice
was taken of him. Whilst some were eating, others smoking, and all
drinking, the conversation, directed by the King, took the course
that was common to it at these gatherings.

It began as usual with politics, which, if not the actual motive,
supplied at least the justification for the tabagie. The King, either
indulging his natural antipathies, or with the aim of goading his
Francophile son, dealt with the condition of things in France as a
preliminary to sneering at all things French, at old Cardinal Fleury,
at the legacy of licentiousness left by the Regent, at the nation's
narrow bigotry which had expressed itself in the persecution of the
Huguenots. Next his Majesty passed to speak of England, and, just

as contemptuous on the subject of his brother-in-law the Hanoverian sovereign, ended by inviting Alverley's judgment on the situation of the throne in Britain.

There was universal attention, to hear the opinion of one who was taken to speak with authority.

Alverley delivered himself quietly. "My own loyalties compel me to hope that the Hanoverian dynasty is transitory. Hope, as Aristotle tells us, is no more than the dream of a waking man. It can vitiate judgment, by encouraging beliefs that may be unfounded. Yet, hope apart, I have cause to know that Jacobite feeling is strong in England, and stronger still in Scotland, where the country is solidly in favour of the legitimate king. Jacobite failures hitherto have resulted from ill-prepared and premature action. But I think the lesson has been learnt and will be applied when the time serves."

The quiet tone, the assured manner of one at home in any assembly, lent impressiveness to his words among men addicted to vehemence.

The King beamed malicious satisfaction. "If the stewing of the Red Cabbage is as likely as that, my judgment was not at fault in the marriage negotiations." His loose fleshiness shook with mirth. Being in these gatherings without reticences of even the most intimate matters, he went on: "He could have had my daughter for the Prince of Wales, but not at the price of marrying his daughter to the Crown Prince of Prussia. Oh, he was cunning over that; but not cunning enough for me. As if it could matter to me that Wilhelmina should become Queen of England. Lord God! The House of Hohenzollern is illustrious enough not to need further royal titles. And from what you tell me, Margrave, it is unlikely that she would ever have come to that estate, in which case I should have committed myself for the sake of a few apples and pears."

He roared laughter at his own wit, and some of the company laughed with him. The Prince was not of these. He sat sullenly biting his lip. He had always favoured the English match, and, abetted by his intriguing mother, he had, behind his father's back, gone so far as to urge King George to content himself at the moment with the marriage of the Prince of Wales to Wilhelmina against Prince Frederick's solemn pledge to marry the Princess Amelia afterwards. King George, however, had proved as little willing as King Frederick William to engage his son without making sure of disposing of a daughter.

Finding his father's malevolent eye upon him, and fearful of provoking further insults, the Prince addressed himself with sudden vigour to his detested pipe, and his equally detested beer-mug.

The talk flowed on to other topics. Seckendorf was relating hunting experiences in the Tyrol, and presently the King was capping these with boasts of his own exploits at Wusterhausen.

Tobacco smoke hung above the company in a cloud, and from copious drinking voices grew louder, laughter less restrained. From sport with game the talk shifted as by a natural transition to sport with women, and Gundling, more than half drunk by now, drew howls of mirth with a lewd story unctuously related. After that, the degeneracy was complete, and as some became more and more drunk, all pretence of decency was abandoned.

Alverley was in prey to an amazed and only mildly amused disgust which both prudence and good manners compelled him to dissemble. He was helped by the fact that if Grumbkow on his right was somnolently fuddled, the delicate von Suhm on his left, who drank very sparingly, like himself remained sober, and was soberly entertaining him upon Polish politics.

The Prince, on the other hand, similarly moved to disgust, though it was rooted in quite different sentiments, made no effort now to disguise it, having drunk enough to discard caution. He confided in Katzenstein. "I shall be ill tomorrow, if indeed, I am not ill tonight. I have no head for this hoggishness, and, God knows, no taste for it."

Katzenstein raised his tankard to make himself a screen. He spoke under cover of it. "Careful, Highness. The King is watching you."

"Much may it profit him," sneered the Prince. "I'm a fool to let myself be bullied into drinking beer; doubly a fool to submit to this slavery."

But the pot-valiance went out of him when the King's voice boomed above the general din. "What is he saying, Katzenstein?"

"The Prince is drunk," was the evasive answer, and one that Katzenstein supposed should mollify the King.

"Drunk!" The King crowed in amazement. "Bah! Don't be fooled, Baron. He's shamming. He's not man enough to get drunk. But what does he say?"

The Prince groaned and shrank at that insistence. Katzenstein lied boldly to save him. "Actually, sire, he was telling me how much he loves his father, that to please him he drinks beer although it makes him ill."

"He said that? Gerechter Herrgott! Then he must, indeed, be drunk." And he turned to talk of other things with the old Dessauer.

That evening when Alverley reached home – the Tabagie had been held, as usual, in the afternoon – he expressed himself frankly to Katte, who had just come off duty.

"It's been a liberal education in boorishness, Hans."

"I hope you didn't tell them so."

"Be easy. The luxury of such frankness is beyond my means. It's my misfortune that the need to live almost confines me to Brandenburg."

Katte was thoughtful. "We are certainly not nice at the Court of Prussia. But that makes it the easier for a man of your parts to succeed, to achieve distinction here. Let that console you."

"It may when it comes to pass." Alverley spoke without conviction.

"In the meantime, Charles, the experience should teach you patience with the weaknesses of our unhappy Prince, dwarfed and repressed by the King's dislike of him and violence towards him."

"You are charitable, Hans."

"I count myself his friend, and loyalty is a friend's first duty. To judge charitably comes naturally to loyalty. But not on that account is my judgment warped. I know the kindliness and affection of which the Prince is capable. These are the qualities that make me his devoted servant."

Alverley's smile was a little quizzical. "Even if you should be mistaken, the mistake is one that does you credit," he said.

Chapter 6

Forebodings

Utterances that flatter our hopes commonly make for our esteem of the utterer. It may well be, therefore, that Alverley's urbanely expressed opinion upon English politics at the Tabagie, being added to the good impression his personality, military bearing, and manifest culture had made upon the King, materially advanced his cause. The determining factor, however, Alverley probably owed to the kindly shrewdness of the old Marshal of Wartensleben, taught by experience how to play upon the weakness of Frederick William. Somewhere in Pomerania an agent of the Marshal's had discovered a young giant between seven and eight feet tall, and had bribed him with a matter of a thousand thalers or so to enter Prussian service. This son of Anak had been dispatched by the Marshal to Potsdam. With him had gone a letter to his Majesty informing him that this addition to his Majesty's giant grenadiers was offered as a token of respect and admiration by the Marquess of Alverley.

Persuaded by this that his high opinion of the Englishman had been an underestimate, his delighted Majesty at once reciprocated, not only by giving Alverley a company in the horse guards, but by appointing him his extra aide-de-camp, whereby he was Prussianized to the extent of being designated henceforth as Rittmeister der Markgraf von Alverley.

Perceiving here a stepping-stone to greater things, Alverley devoted himself to the assiduous study of his new duties, and gave every attention and thought to the drills and parades at Potsdam when he went there in attendance upon the King. And now, whether at Potsdam or Berlin, he had his quarters in the royal residence, with a kammer-hussar of his own to attend him, a matter, this, in which he took little satisfaction since it removed him from his pleasant lodging with Katte.

His appointment proved no sinecure. A King who must be giving his personal attention to everything, from kitchen arrangements to foreign diplomacy, provided abundant and even excessive employment for those immediately about his person, and from the outset Alverley discovered that his office of aide-de-camp included the duties of a military secretary and some others. Nevertheless a little time remained him for his own devices, and some of this he still spent with Katte, some at Pastor Ritter's, where Dorothea's satisfaction in his advancement, and in the blue coat with red facings that so well became him, was of an ingenuous candour.

Although all the noble houses in Berlin were now open to him, the only one that he frequented at all freely was that of the Freiherr von Katzenstein, known for its splendour as the Katzensteinerhof. Friendship had grown rapidly between Alverley and this man of a kindly, endearing urbanity. He was a widower with one only child, Stéphanie, a long-legged, lively, golden-haired girl of nine or ten, who tyrannically ruled her indulgent father. The Freiherr's friendship for Alverley may have ripened the more quickly because of the attraction which from the outset the Englishman had exercised upon the child, and the delight which she took in his company. Such firm friends did they become that Stéphanie out of a consequent reluctance to use him with ceremony, yet hesitant to call him Charles, as did the Count, had compromised by giving him the name of Quixote. It resulted from hearing her father one day, when Alverley had been touching upon his Jacobite adventures, use the phrase: "It seems to me, my friend, that you chose to tilt at windmills."

"At windmills?" quoth Stéphanie. "Tilting at windmills? How does one do that?"

"One doesn't," laughed Alverley. "It is only your father's way of saying that he accounts me mad." And he went on to tell her of the frenzy of Cervantes' hero, couching his lance and riding at a windmill in the insane belief that it was a giant with waving arms, and of how, caught up by one of the gyrating sails, he had been dashed violently to earth.

"That is what your father thinks I did in another sense."

This was but to whet the child's appetite for more knowledge of the gentleman of La Mancha. To satisfy it Alverley told her of Don Quixote leaving home to go up and down the world like a knight-errant of old, to do his endeavour.

"Like you?" she asked, to Katzenstein's amusement.

"Just like him," the Count laughed. "You see, Charles, that I am not alone in discerning a likeness between you and the Knight of the Rueful Countenance."

"No, no." Alverley disclaimed the comparison. "His end was a different one. A nobler one. He was on a quest for the Lady Dulcinea del Toboso, and ready at all times to break a lance in her honour with any who denied that she was the loveliest lady in the world."

The child's eyes shone. "That was brave. Why don't you do the same?"

"Alas! I have no Dulcinea."

"But if you had, you would. Wouldn't you? I know you would."

"It is possible."

She was standing beside his chair, and now she leaned affectionately against him.

"Then let me be your... What was her name?"

"Dulcinea. With all my heart." He laughed, and kissed her cheek, an arm about her shoulders. "With whom shall I break a lance for you, Dulcinea?"

"Why, Quixote, with any who says that I am not the loveliest lady in the world."

"But none will ever say so."

"Lord, Charles," interposed her father. "Will you turn her head completely with your make-believe?"

The make-believe, however, in which he was Quixote and she Dulcinea, was to persist. It built itself into an enduring game between them, which came to assume something of reality in the affection of the man for the child and the devotion of the child to the man, which grew out of it.

It followed naturally that from this should result a closer bond between Alverley and her father, so that the Englishman was an ever-welcome guest at the Katzensteinerhof.

Most of Alverley's leisure, however, was still spent with Katte, and it was at Katte's that one Sunday afternoon of early July, when he had been dining with his cousin, the Prince descended upon them without warning whilst they were still at table. He was in a state of manifest excitement, only partially repressed to offer Alverley his congratulations upon the still-recent attainment of his desires.

"Though, as you know, I don't regard it as enviable," he added. "For myself, I'd sooner be a foot-boy in Paris than a field-marshal in Berlin. However, de gustibus non est disputandus."

"Disputandum, monseigneur," Alverley corrected upon an impulse of which he was instantly ashamed.

"Eh? Oh! Disputandum, is it?" There was a flash of annoyance from the Prince's eyes. "Much obliged. A pity I have no learning, for which I thank my father." He flung himself into a chair, and turned to Katte. "Bear with me, my friend. I abuse your friendship, and make free with your house."

"Both are very much at your service, my Prince."

"I know. I am grateful, and some day I'll repay you, Katte." He took a breath before continuing. "I have a message from Captain Dickens asking me to see him in private audience. It will be that he has heard from King George. I have made bold to request him to be here at two o'clock. Hence this intrusion. You forgive the liberty, Katte?"

"I am proud to be used, monseigneur."

"You're a good fellow. Dickens should not keep us waiting."

Alverley, who had remained standing, offered to withdraw; but the Prince would not hear of it. "What the devil? I don't want to incommode either of you more than I must. There's not the need. So stay, I beg, and add your prayers to mine that King George is consenting to receive me in England." Again there was that threat of suicide, which Alverley was finding tiresome. "If he refuses I swear I'll kill myself. Sometimes I think it is what my father wishes."

Katte was still protesting that he should not harbour such thoughts, still enjoining patience, when Captain Dickens arrived, plump, benign, and fastidiously appointed. His low-lidded eyes keenly surveyed Alverley, when presented.

"Honoured," he murmured. "I have heard of Lord Alverley."

"With disapproval, no doubt."

"Officially. But unofficially, I am your lordship's humble servant."

The Prince was losing breath and growing fretful from impatience. "A chair, Captain. You'll have news for me. I have no wish to delay you."

"Nor would it be prudent." The envoy disregarded the proffered chair. "His Majesty King George desires me to assure you in the strongest terms of his profound sympathy."

"Ah!"

"But…"

"Oh!"

"…in terms equally strong he begs you to do nothing for the moment. The step your Highness has been considering could not be taken without the gravest political consequences. If King George were in any way a party to your flight international complications might ensue. Your Highness will perceive that his Majesty cannot contemplate such a risk."

His Highness sat down as if suddenly boneless. His face, which had lost colour, looked more pointed than ever. Tears trembled in his faltering voice. "But…but if it were not known?"

"How could that be if your Highness made England your destination?"

"In short, then, my uncle refuses to receive me." His disappointment was shot now with a sudden viperishness.

"So anxious is his Majesty to ease your Highness' lot that what he can do he certainly will do, and he is quite prepared to pay the debts of which your Highness spoke in your letter. If your Highness will oblige me with a note of the amount, I am empowered and shall be happy to place the money at your disposal."

"Tiens! I ask for a meal, and I am offered a cup of water."

The ungraciousness left Captain Dickens unruffled. He smiled. "Let us at least say of wine, Highness."

The Prince shrugged ill-humouredly. "God knows I am in no case to refuse anything. As for my debts now..." He broke off, considering; and the lean, pointed face went blank, as if a mask fell over it. "Fifteen thousand thalers will cover them." He glanced at Dickens with an anxiety that Alverley thought he understood, for, from what the Prince himself had formerly said, it was clear that he now more than doubled the amount.

Captain Dickens bowed slightly, in cool acquiescence. "The money will be at your Highness' disposal tomorrow. How shall I convey it to you?"

"If you will be so good as to have it delivered here to Rittmeister von Katte, he will take charge of it for me."

"It shall be done." The envoy looked at Katte. "At noon tomorrow, then, shall we say? Excellent. Then I will take my leave, Monseigneur." But he paused, as if waiting, and added, after a moment: "If your Highness should wish to write to his Majesty in acknowledgment..."

"Better not since his Majesty is so apprehensive of being compromised." There was more than a suspicion of a sneer in his tone. "It will no doubt suffice that you convey to his Majesty my thanks for this little loan."

The envoy's lips tightened. "Very well, sir," he said, and on a short and frosty leave-taking he departed.

The Prince sat gloomily thoughtful for some moments; then a sly smile came slowly to lighten his countenance. "If the damned skinflint won't receive me, at least I've squeezed out of him the means for my escape. Seven thousand thalers, or so, will cover my debts. So that there will be plenty left for our travelling expenses, Katte." He got up. "So far, so good, then. It remains only to determine where we shall go."

Alverley was shocked at this abrupt inclusion of Katte in the Prince's plans. "Your Highness does not consider that King George's warning of political consequences should be heeded?"

"That? Bah! The man spoke out of selfish concern for himself. Little he cares about political complications so long as he is not, himself, embroiled."

"But should not your Highness care?"

"I? Why? Suppose that they arise. How can they hurt me? I have to think of myself. It's a selfish world, Monsieur le Marquis, and who forgets it, suffers."

It was an aphorism Alverley was to repeat when the Prince had gone.

"A selfish world, and who forgets it, suffers. Lay the lesson to heart, Hans, while it's time. He takes it for granted that you'll accompany him in his escape. You heard him say 'our' travelling expenses."

Katte, however, was not yet disposed to take the Prince seriously. "There will be no escape. I know Fritz too well. He won't go unless a safe asylum is offered to him, and that he is denied. This is mere play-acting on his part, like his talk of suicide. He sees himself as a nobly pathetic hero out of Racine or Corneille."

Alverley dubiously shook his head. "As for suicide, I agree with you. He would never hang himself unless he could be sure of someone to cut the halter. But for the rest, these histrionic temperaments are often mastered by the parts for which they cast themselves. Your Fritz is vainglorious and weak. The part of a prince in flight from parental tyranny may seem to him of irresistible appeal to the world. He looks to become a figure of romance."

"Maybe, maybe. But I hope you haven't perceived any such weakness in me. And I flatter myself I have some influence with him.

Enough, I think, to restrain him in this madness before he takes any irrevocable step."

"Then why not make the attempt at once?"

"Because if I did he would turn to others, who to win the favour of the future king might accept the risk of helping him in this folly."

"That would not be your blame. Meanwhile, by acting as his agent with Captain Dickens you are already compromising yourself."

"Oh, that!" Katte dismissed it with a laugh. "Faith, I've done worse. I've lent him money; some two thousand thalers; and I've sold some diamonds out of his decorations for him. But certainly not in order that he may run away. Set your mind at rest, Charles. I am not the man to commit so crude a folly."

But Alverley was not reassured. Out of his affection and esteem for Katte he was troubled by forebodings.

Chapter 7

The Plot

For the latter half of that month of July the King had planned a royal progress through the scattered Hohenzollern possessions as far as Wesel, and the preparations for it were afoot.

The Crown Prince was commanded to accompany his Majesty, and for once the Crown Prince acceded very readily to his father's wishes, for in this progress he perceived his opportunity. Somewhere in the course of it the chance should be afforded him of slipping across a frontier, and so making good his escape.

The high spirits resulting from this prospect, and the unusual affluence in which he found himself as a result of King George's contribution, made him generous. Whether at the same time some less noble emotion actuated him we do not know. What we do know is that he paid a visit to Stefan Kahn, the court jeweller, and laid out the heavy sum of a thousand thalers on a diamond bracelet of some magnificence. After that, and accompanied by Ingersleben, he took his way to the Nikolaistrasse.

There he played the flute to Dorothea's accompaniment, with Ingersleben ever in attendance in order to conform with the condition from which Dorothea would now tolerate no departure. The evening was warm, and the windows stood wide. Even so, after a while, Ingersleben, who no doubt had his instructions, complained of the heat, and sauntered out into the pastor's garden, leaving them alone together. Dorothea, engrossed in her playing, did not notice his absence until the piece had come to an end. Then she casually wondered what had become of him.

"He went out into the garden. A soulless audience. No matter. I'll call him in a moment." He had set down his flute, and he stood, with his hands behind him, at her side. Her left hand still rested on the keys, and his eyes were on her softly rounded arm, displayed by a sleeve that ended at the elbow. "You will often have been told how lovely is your arm, Dorothea."

She looked up without smiling. "This is foolishness," was her forbidding comment.

"Oh, no. The fact. And here's something to adorn it."

Before she knew it, the shimmering, flashing hoop of jewels was clasped about her wrist, and the Prince was kissing her hand. "With my love, Dorothea."

"What is this?" Slowly she withdrew her hand, and gazed frowning at the bracelet. "You should not... You know that I cannot accept this." She was making shift to detach it again, but he stayed her almost by force.

"You must. I have received so much from you here that I must give something in return."

"But I do not want anything." There was annoyance in her voice. "Please let me unclasp it. You must take it back."

"Do you want to offend me, Dorothea?"

"I do not want you to offend me. That is all. Such presents are not for me, and certainly not from your Highness. My father would not like it. Please release my hand, Monseigneur."

But he did not obey. "How cruel! How cruel and how cold! As cruel and cold, as you are sweet and desirable."

This brought her to her feet in a flush of indignation. "Highness!"

"Wait, wait. You don't understand yet. I am not making love to you, Dorothea – unfortunately for me; for you don't imagine that music was the only power that drew me here. But you have chosen to be just marble to me; and, anyway, it's too late to talk of it now. This trifle, Dorothea, is a parting gift. I am going away. You won't see me any more." Having surprised her by that assertion, he paused before adding the question: "Now can you accept it? Even your father could take no exception to this acknowledgment of all the happy hours I've spent here, of all the help and cheer I've had from you."

"You are going away?" she echoed soberly. "Where is your Highness going?"

"I scarcely know, myself, just yet. But when I leave on this progress with my father next week, Berlin will see me no more." His air was tragic. "I shall not be coming here again before I set out. That is why I take this occasion to make my parting gift. Keep it in memory of me, Dorothea. In memory of a faithful, devoted heart."

This made a difference, of course. The bracelet was no longer to be regarded as an illicit offering, a bribe designed to corrupt. She put aside her indignation.

"But a gift of such price, Highness!" she protested.

"In return for gifts that have been priceless," said he, and released her hands. "Hush! Here is Ingersleben."

The Lieutenant, as opportune in his coming as in his going, sauntered in, and saving some further words of thanks from her at parting there was no more mention of the matter. But her gratitude remained laden with misgivings and with self-reproaches for having even in these circumstances accepted a gift which it was not fitting for a maid in her station to receive from a prince. For this reason she could not bring herself to wear the bracelet, or to speak of it to anyone. But not on that account did the jewel fail of fate's purpose with it, which was to change the whole of her life, shaping it to a pattern very different, indeed, from what it must otherwise have been.

Of that farewell visit of his to Ritter's house the Prince was to hear on the morrow in unpleasant circumstances.

On this, the very eve of setting out, the King held a last Tabagie, this time at Potsdam, and his Highness was required to attend it. It supplied a setting for yet another of those disgusting scenes between father and son, provoked this time by that drunken clown Gundling,

67

the President of the Academy, who possibly in sincerity but probably in malice commended the Prince's musical talents.

"Musical talents!" barked the King. "If he wants music let him sing to the organ, as becomes a Christian gentleman, and not pipe on a flute like a silly Arcadian goatherd."

"Ah!" rejoined Gundling in his lisping, unctuous voice. "But his Highness possesses what the Italians call maestria. To hear him once is always to recognize his playing. It is sui generis. Why, but yesterday evening as I was walking down the Nikolaistrasse, I heard the notes of a flute, and I knew at once it must be his Highness; for never Pan piped more seductively."

"In the Nikolaistrasse?" quoth the King, glaring a question through the haze of tobacco smoke.

The Prince shook his head, and snarled at Gundling: "One flute is like another, you fool."

Gundling leered, and set a finger to his nose. "A fool, am I? He, he! I was no fool when I recognized that flute for your Highness'; for I looked, and saw your Royal Highness through the open window. I saw more." He hiccoughed, and his leer broadened. "I saw the nymph to whom your Royal Highness piped."

The Prince shrugged contemptuously, and with the King's brooding eyes upon him took refuge in his tankard. Seckendorf came to his rescue, claiming the King's attention, and so the matter was for the moment dropped.

But a half-hour later, when the company had broken up, as the Prince was slipping from the room, his father called him back.

"Fritz! A moment, if you please."

Besides Alverley, who was in attendance, there now remained present only von Rochow, the Prince's governor, and General Buddenbrock, who was waiting to accompany the King on an inspection.

"What house do you frequent in the Nikolaistrasse?"

"None," was the sullen answer. "Gundling was drunk, as usual."

"Drunk or sober, he saw you. You heard him say so. You and the baggage with whom you amuse yourself. Why do you lie to me? Have you no shame at all?"

His Highness was stung to insolence. "Sometimes I think that I have nothing else; that shame is my portion in life."

"Righteous God! Will you be pert with me?" He raised his cane. But the Prince shrank away out of reach, and the King did not attempt to follow. "Get out of here," he shouted. "Let me see you on parade. March!"

The Prince departed with insolent leisureliness, and the unhappy witnesses of the scene, thankful that it had gone no further, disposed themselves to follow with the King. None was more relieved than Alverley that the matter should be at an end and that his Majesty should not have pressed further for the name of the Prince's friends in the Nikolaistrasse.

It was not yet the end, however, though it might well have been but for the Prince's misplaced vindictiveness. For lack of hired bullies to do his will, he stirred the sympathy of Ingersleben and another of his young intimates, Lieutenant von Spaen, and begged them, as they loved him, to teach the President of the Academy a lesson in reticence.

As a result, when, on the following evening, Gundling left his house by the Halle Gate in order to take the air, he was followed by two young men in plain civilian clothes. As in the course of his walk the President followed the deserted avenue along the left bank of the Spree, he was hailed by one of them.

"Herr Praesident! We have something for you. Something to remind you that it is not wise to talk too much in drunken malice."

Gundling observed, to his sudden disquiet, that their round hats were pulled down over their brows, overshadowing faces already dim in the fading daylight, and that they carried whips. He was to make other discoveries even more painful.

On the following morning he limped from a carriage that brought him to the palace at Potsdam, seeking audience of the King.

He told a terrible tale of violence suffered at the hands of two unknown ruffians, from whose words it was clear that they had been hired to this infamy, a violence that left him in his present crippled condition. But for the intervention of some passing strangers it was probable, he wailed, that he would not have escaped with his life. For having beaten him the ruffians had flung him into the river. He ended his complaint with a demand for justice. There was scarcely the need. The King who, with his two aides-de-camp, was on his way to a review of his regiment of giants, had swelled with wrath as he listened. The words Gundling's assailants had used left his Majesty in no doubt of the instigator of this outrage. His hard inflexible little mouth tightened.

"Very good, Sir President. I think I know where to find the culprit. Leave this to me."

Gundling departed. The King stood brooding for a while. Then, abruptly: "Come, sirs," he barked, and marched out, striking the pavement with his cane at every step.

They came to the main hall, where a group of officers waited. The Prince was amongst them, laughing gaily with Spaen and Ingersleben over the sorry spectacle Gundling had afforded when limping out of the palace.

"Fritz!" The King's voice cracked like a pistol-shot.

Startled, the Prince hastened to him. "Papa."

Whilst you might count ten the King just scowled at him, his great red face growing marbled with white streaks. Then, without warning, he swung his heavy malacca, and struck.

The Prince recoiled, a hand to his bruised shoulder. "Papa!" he squealed.

"You scoundrel!" screamed his father. "You'll send your bullies to assault my servants, my friends, will you?" And he struck again, recklessly, viciously, with no regard for the half-score witnesses of this royal degradation.

"I didn't. I didn't. This is not true, lieber papa."

"Not true, puppy! That lie won't serve. Your bullies betrayed themselves. You coward! You're not even man enough to vent your

70

spite with your own hands. So you must hire ruffians to do your work." Down thrashed the cane again. In too hasty a movement to dodge the blow, the Prince tripped and fell, to be struck again and yet again where he lay.

"Get up. Get up." The King seized him by his hair, so as to hasten his rising. "Spitzbube! I'll school you. I'll teach you to maltreat my servants." He paused to glare at him, standing dusty, dishevelled and almost in tears. Illogically he added: "Almighty! If my father had so treated me I'd have killed myself. But you are shameless. You would submit to anything, you flute-playing popinjay." Then, abruptly: "Follow me," he ordered, and stamped across the hall, past the officers who stood ranged, uncomfortable witnesses of this detestable violence. "Come along, gentlemen."

The Prince, scarcely able to stifle his whimpering, perfunctorily dusted his blue coat, and followed, his eyes on the ground. Near the door Colonel Rochow drew alongside, as if to give him support. This led him in his emotional condition to express himself with a freedom he would not otherwise have dared to use with his governor.

"This must not occur again, Colonel." He was sobbing. "It is not to be suffered. I will not submit to any more of these humiliations. It is the end. I know what to do."

"Calm, Highness. Calm," Rochow sought to soothe him.

"You heard him: if his father had so treated him, he would have killed himself. It's what I must do if I did not know how to do better."

They were crossing the courtyard to their horses. "Whatever you do, Highness, let me pray you to do nothing in anger."

"It will not be in anger. Oh, no; nor suddenly."

The tone made Rochow so uneasy that he thought it well to mention the matter to the King that evening. "I account it my duty to warn your Majesty that I have cause to suspect that the Prince is contemplating some rashness since…ah, since the…little misunderstanding this morning."

"That's not all your duty," growled the King. "It is your part to see that he doesn't commit it."

"Your Majesty may depend upon me to do my best."

Yet his vigilance though keen was not keen enough to prevent or even discover the secret meeting which the Prince held that night with Katte among the bushes of the park at Potsdam. To summon Katte his Highness had employed young Keith, a lieutenant in the foot guards who was devoted to him, and who was a kinsman of the exiled Jacobite Scottish Earl Marischal, also in Prussian service. Katte had ridden out from Berlin at once, and Keith brought word to the Prince that he was waiting.

"You've heard what happened this morning, Katte, and in public?"

"I am more shocked and grieved than I can say, my Prince."

"Say nothing." The Prince's manner was portentous. "The time for words is past. We must act."

"What does your Highness command?"

Although he had protested that the time for words was past, his Highness used a good many. He was to be dragged at the King's tail on this progress, so that the King could keep his heel on his neck, so that he might continue to subject him to these vile humiliations, so that he might be made to feel a slave. This and much more of the same kind before reaching the appeal which had caused him to send for the Rittmeister.

"My mind was already made up. This has but hardened it. In the name of God, Katte, don't forsake me now."

"You know that I should never do that, my Prince. But how exactly can I serve you?"

"You must come with me, Katte. I cannot go alone. You'll see that as I see it now; now that I am face to face with the fact of escape. And there is none upon whose wits and strength I can depend as upon yours, none whom I could trust as I trust you."

Katte turned cold. Sympathy and duty were here in conflict. Slowly he answered: "I am an officer in the King's service, bound to it by oath. Your Highness is asking me to desert."

"I am asking a deal, I know. But my need is desperate, and there is no one else to whom I can turn. One day I shall be king, Katte; and for what you do for me now…"

Katte ventured to interrupt him. He conceived that he had found an argument that might deter the Prince from this mad course, of which until now he had refused to believe that the Prince's contemplation was really serious.

"Can your Highness be sure of that? Of being king one day if you should carry out this plan? I implore you to reflect upon the consequences, which may be terrible."

"Could anything be more terrible than to remain at the mercy of this tyrant, to suffer these daily humiliations? Diable, Katte! Use some understanding."

"It is what I am endeavouring to do, my Prince. I am remembering that like myself you are an officer in the King's service, and bound in the same manner. The King... Your Highness has described him as a tyrant. You have said that you fear for your very life with him. If that fear is well-grounded, consider how you would place yourself at his mercy by this flight. If he posted you as a deserter..."

"I should be out of his reach by then."

"Never, Monseigneur. His wrath would always find a way. You have often said that he pampers your brother Prince William as assiduously as he persecutes your Highness. Is it not possible that he might even exclude you from the succession?"

"The succession? Name of God!" He was momentarily startled. But momentarily only.

"Oh, but the Emperor, then? The Emperor would never assent to that. Never. And without his assent the succession cannot be altered."

"Not without good cause, Highness, I agree. But the Emperor might be importuned into regarding desertion as cause enough."

There was a pause. The Prince stood beating fist into palm, and his impatience of these objections, hitherto repressed, flashed out.

"Say at once that these are pretexts to cover your reluctance; confess yourself a lukewarm friend, your service mere lip-service, and have done."

"Does your Highness really believe that?" Katte's tone was heavy with reproach. Possibly the Prince was moved by it; probably, intent upon winning Katte's assistance, he accounted it prudent to retract.

"No, no, Katte. I don't know what I am saying. I am distracted. I know your loyalty. I count upon it. Whatever the risks, I must take them. Death, I tell you, is the only alternative; therefore I may as well be shot as a deserter, as shoot myself, or go and drown myself in the lake down there. And that," he added with a sudden ferocity, "is what I swear I shall do this very night if you abandon me."

"For God's sake, Highness!" cried Katte, himself reduced to despair. "There has never been any question of my abandoning you. I only point out the risks you must face." On an impulse of generosity he added: "But if you still decide to face them, vogue la galère, I'll face them with you."

In both his hands that were hot and moist the Prince caught one of Katte's, and gripped it hard. "My friend! My best of friends! I'll never forget this. If I live you shall come to bless this night."

The Prince passed on to details, showing in what minuteness all had been considered by him. Since Katte was not to be of the King's following in his progress, he must get leave of absence from his colonel; for to go off without this would almost certainly mean his being caught and brought back before he was over the frontiers of Brandenburg. Having obtained it, he would join the Prince at Wesel, whence they could slip across the border into Holland. Of the moneys received from the King of England, a thousand pistoles or so remained in Katte's possession together with some of those jewels from the Prince's decorations, which his Highness had entrusted to him for sale. These resources he was to retain since he would act as purse-bearer in the flight.

"Besides," added his Highness. "Watched as I am, the money might be found in my possession, and I might be asked to explain the presence of so great a sum. So all is settled."

"Unless when you have slept on it," said Katte, who already may have been repenting his too-generous impulse, "your Highness should change your mind, which, as your friend, is what I must still hope."

"As my friend, dismiss the thought. The decision is irrevocable."

They gripped hands again in the dark, and Katte swung himself into the saddle to ride home, committed out of good-natured weakness to a course the folly of which he fully recognized. With every mile of the road to Berlin his misgivings grew blacker.

Chapter 8

The Discovery

Two days later, on the 15th July, the King, having kissed his Fifi – as he fondly called the Queen in rare moments of uxoriousness – set out with a train of a score of carriages, in one of which went the Prince with his governors, Rochow and Keserlingk.

Retarded by foul weather and almost impassable roads, five days were consumed in a sluggish journey to Anspach, whose Margrave was married to Frederick William's second daughter Frederica.

At the Margrave's court, in its attractive park by the Rezet, there followed days of feasting and hunting which rejoiced the heart of the King, but in which the Prince took no interest, nervously engrossed as he was in the contemplation of his approaching adventure. As day followed day without any word from Katte, the Prince became so fretted that in the end he wrote to the Rittmeister, reproaching him with his silence, and reminding him that he was expected, come what might, at Wesel. He enclosed for his sister, the Princess Wilhelmina, an affectionate note of farewell, informing her of his intentions.

That letter, however, crossed with one from Katte, prudently addressed to Alverley. In this Katte informed his cousin, to his cousin's profound relief, that he found it impossible to obtain leave of absence, as he was announcing to the Prince in the note which he enclosed and begged Alverley to deliver. Alverley received this communication just as he was on the point of setting out on a day's excursion with the King. His Majesty being already in the saddle, and Alverley not daring to keep him waiting whilst he sought the Prince, entrusted the delivery of the note to Keith, whom he knew to be fully in the Prince's confidence.

Keith found the Prince in his room with his valet Gummersbach and a tailor, trying on a gaudy red coat of French design. It commended itself to the Prince as a suitable disguise; and it had been necessary to procure it here in Anspach because he travelled with none but military garments.

Keith, who was scatterbrained, used no secrecy. "This has come for your Highness from Berlin."

Eagerly, in manifest excitement, the Prince snatched the note, and tore it open with trembling fingers. Then, as he read, the life seemed to go out of him. He dropped into a chair like a man exhausted, and sat, his elbow on his knee and his chin on the fist that held the crumpled sheet, staring at nothing. After a while, "That will do, Keith," he said. "You may go."

After he had similarly dismissed the tailor, he sat on, alone with the discreet and patiently waiting Gummersbach. When at length he roused himself it was to order the valet to light a candle. With no word said, he went to thrust the paper into the flame, and dropped it, burning, on to the empty hearth.

Anger was now his emotion, with Katte for its object. What need for the fool to ask for leave, with the risk of its being denied him, when by urging an indisposition, which, for a few days at least, would explain his disappearance, he might have slipped quietly away. If Katte could not use his wits to better purpose, they could hardly be of the resourcefulness with which the Prince had credited them. And what the devil did he mean by this simple announcement that he could not get away? How the devil did he think the Prince was to contrive without the moneys that were in Katte's keeping? Altogether it seemed to the Prince that Katte was behaving with a reprehensible casualness, as if he did not understand the gravity of the occasion, or else as if he did not care.

With the cooling of his indignation and the return of reason, he realized that his intentions were not necessarily frustrated. What Katte had lacked the wit to do on his own initiative in the first instance, he must do now at the Prince's suggestion. So he sat down, and wrote a letter to the Rittmeister, instructing him how to get away without being immediately missed, and to go not now to Wesel but straight to the Hague, where his Highness would meet him at the British Embassy. He added, by way of a reproach to Katte for his thoughtlessness on the question of money, that fortunately he had a bare sufficiency for the first stage of his journey.

A royal courier would be leaving on the morrow for Berlin, and the letter was placed by the Prince, himself, in the courier's letter-bag.

After that his Highness' next step was to find Ingersleben, and send him into Nuremberg to cash a letter of credit for a thousand thalers. Then he sat down to consider the reshaping of his plans now that Katte was no longer to join him at Wesel. Mannheim, when they reached it, would offer him, he determined, the best opportunity to get away. Thence, once across the Rhine, he could snap his fingers at pursuit, and the way to the Hague would be clear.

The royal party left Anspach on Thursday, the 27th, and was at Augsburg on the following Monday. From there it went on to Ludwigsburg, to pay a visit to the Duke of Württemberg, and after that took the road to Mannheim, making the last stage of the journey thither at Steinsfurt. There on the night of Friday the 4th of August they were more or less encamped in barns, owing to the scant accommodation the place offered. For the King and the Prince, however, and for their immediate attendants, room was made in the inn.

The Prince's plans were complete. He was to leave next morning, and he had now prevailed upon Keith to go with him, congratulating himself upon this, since in England, when he ultimately reached it, Keith would be an even more appropriate companion than Katte. The point of departure was to have been Mannheim, where he had counted upon sleeping that night, and Mannheim was still some ten miles distant. Not on this account, however, did a postponement seem necessary; therefore he instructed Keith to meet him at half past two o'clock on that Saturday morning at the Steinsfurt horse-market, bringing the horses which he was entrusted to procure.

Accordingly, soon after two o'clock, the Prince quietly rose, dressed himself, putting on the red coat which had been made for him at Anspach, stole out of his room and groped his way on tiptoe to the stairs. Reaching them sooner than he reckoned, in the dark, he stumbled and thudded on the topmost step, saving himself from falling by a sudden clutch at the rail.

Gummersbach, who slept on a mat on the landing, was instantly awake and sitting up. "Wer da?" he challenged.

"Sh! It is I, Gummersbach."

The valet was on his feet. "Does your Royal Highness require anything?"

"Nothing. Do not disturb yourself. I am going down to speak to his Majesty."

"A moment, Highness. Let me find you a light."

"No, no." It was the last thing the Prince desired; for a light would reveal his French coat. "It is not necessary. I can find my way." He was halfway down the stairs as he spoke.

Now, whilst it was true enough that the King slept below, yet it seemed to Gummersbach an odd thing that the Prince should go stealing down to him, like a thief in the night, at such an hour as this. Besides, he had received precise instructions from Colonel Rochow to be vigilant. So whilst his Highness crept down the stairs, the valet was scratching at the Colonel's door, across the landing.

Rochow was instantly afoot and arousing General Buddenbrock, who shared the room with him. Within a very few minutes, and still buttoning themselves into their clothes, they were below stairs. The inn door stood open, which deepened Rochow's alarm. Old Buddenbrock, disgruntled at having been dragged from his bed, and with memories of his own disorderly young days, scorned the Colonel's alarms at what was probably no more than a wenching adventure on the Prince's part.

"My God, Rochow, were you never young?" he grumbled. "You won't be thanked for this."

But grumble as he would, assume what he would, Rochow dragged him out into the chilly air of approaching dawn, and through the silent and deserted streets. It did not take long to scour the whole of Steinsfurt, and their search came to an end beside the horse-market. There a carriage stood without horses, and beside the carriage, a slight figure was pacing to and fro. At once Rochow recognized his charge, and breathed more freely. But instead of advancing upon him, he drew back, and restrained his companion. He desired to discover what the Prince might be about.

They had to wait some time, as had the Prince, and even Buddenbrock's impatience was as nothing to his Highness'. He fumed as he waited, cursing Keith who might yet ruin all by his dilatoriness. Day was breaking, and the growing light began to be revealing. What it revealed to Rochow was that the Prince was not in uniform. That sufficed. Out of the shadows, with Buddenbrock beside him, the Colonel strode across the open space, to the carriage and the young man beside it.

The Prince swung round at their approach.

Rochow was sardonic. "You are an early riser, my Prince."

"So are you, Colonel," snapped the Prince in a simmer of rage.

"I? Oh, but then it's my duty to be watchful."

"You make it plain," snarled his Highness. Then he deemed it wise to add: "I could not sleep in that foul-smelling hovel. I needed air."

"Of course. What else could I suppose? But these airs of dawn are treacherous, Highness. You should not expose yourself."

The silence of the streets was broken by an approaching clop-clop of hoofs.

"The town begins to stir," Rochow continued. "We had better be returning to the inn, Highness."

"It does not yet suit my convenience to return, Colonel," answered the quivering Prince. "But do not let me detain you. I do not require anything."

"By your leave, Highness, you require a change of clothes. And urgently. His Majesty will be stirring. For God's sake don't let him see you in that coat."

And then Keith arrived, riding a horse, and leading another. He pulled up out of countenance at the sight of the two officers.

Rochow advanced a pace or two. "Good morning, Keith. What are these horses."

Taken aback, and without time for thought, Keith lied clumsily. "They...they are for his Majesty's pages, my Colonel."

"I see. So you've been promoted. You are now horse-boy to the King's pages, are you?" Then, abandoning sarcasm, he let wrath flame forth. "Go to the devil with your horses. Take them back where you got them from and report to me later. I shall have something to say to you, I promise you. Be off with you." He turned away, growling. "Impudent young dog." Then, courteous but firm, he addressed the Prince. "Come, Highness. You have no time to lose if his Majesty is not to catch you out of uniform."

Sullenly, raging inwardly, but realizing his helplessness, the baffled Prince, without another word at the moment, allowed himself to be led away between his governor and General Buddenbrock. Before they reached the inn, however, he had recovered some of his wits.

"There's no need to make an affair of this, Colonel. It's only that Keith and I had planned a frolic. The fool came too late."

"That," said the Colonel, committing himself to no opinion of his own, "is just what General Buddenbrock was supposing."

"And there's no need to tell my father. He wouldn't understand."

"Very likely not," was the vague answer, which nevertheless sufficed to reassure his Highness.

It did not, however, soothe his rage at the missed opportunity and the need by which he was now confronted to make fresh arrangements, attempting escape a second time in the face, perhaps, of increased obstacles.

Not until evening, by when the King and his train were housed in the vast red sandstone Castle of Mannheim, was Keith able to approach the Prince with his explanation of the delay that had wrecked the morning's plans. The fault was with the stableman who supplied the horses. Instead of having them ready at two o'clock, as had been arranged, the fellow had been in bed and asleep when Keith arrived. In rousing him, and in waiting after that whilst he went to get the horses, the valuable time had been lost.

The Prince was not mollified. "Why the devil must you wait until the last moment before going to the stables? I am not pleased with you, Keith. If you had been really concerned and trustworthy you would have gone in good time, and this would not have happened. I can't forgive your carelessness."

The lad flushed under the rebuke. "My orders to that sluggardly lout were precise. I could not suppose that he would fail me."

"In my interests you ought to have supposed it. Then you would have run no risks. That lout, as you call him, was not the only sluggard. In God's name, see that you do better tomorrow night."

Resentment of the injustice was blent with dismay at this announcement that the attempt was to be renewed. "Tomorrow night, Highness?"

"That's what I said," snapped the Prince. "Tomorrow night. Or, rather, Monday morning. At the same hour. Arrange for the horses; saddle-horses this time; we shall have to do without the carriage. I am at the loss of that. However, we'll say no more about it. Meet me at the bridge at half past two, and see that this time you are punctual."

"But is it safe now? I am sure that Colonel von Rochow is suspicious."

"Ha!" The Prince looked at him sharply. "What had Colonel von Rochow to say to you?"

"I haven't seen him since this morning."

"It follows, then, that he attaches no importance to the matter. If he questions you, tell him you don't know what I had in mind. That I had spoken only of a frolic. As for his suspicions, let him suspect what he pleases. If you are punctual, we shall be away and across the Rhine before he can interfere."

"But he'll be watchful, Highness," Keith protested, and he added beseechingly: "I am sure it is too dangerous at the moment, my Prince. Let us leave it for another time. Let us wait a few days at least."

"Fool! Don't you see that if we are really suspected, there is all the more reason to make haste away. For you are committed now, Keith. You had better remember that. You are in it with me, and it wouldn't be safe for you to remain. So make the arrangements. And, above all, see that you keep to them this time."

Perceiving that he was, indeed, compromised, and that even if he now refused to accompany the Prince and the Prince were to go off alone, there would be ugly consequences for him, Keith very reluctantly yielded.

On that they parted, and the Prince re-entered the castle, leaving Keith to pace the ramparts where their interview had taken place. The young man's thoughts were gloomy with self-reproach for having ever lent himself to this silly plot, and his gloom was deepened by the selfishness the Prince displayed. If they were caught, as most probably they would be, his Highness, safeguarded by his royal blood, would escape with a reprimand, or at worst a caning from his father, but Keith, himself, would certainly be broken for his part in the attempt.

A night's sleep brought no easing of the Lieutenant's fears. Indeed, when he awakened on that Sunday morning they darkened his outlook like a thundercloud. He thought of taking counsel with Ingersleben and Spaen, the other two accomplices; but they were not immediately to be found, and he was still seeking them when the time came for him to accompany the King to church. When he returned, and was supposing himself at liberty, he was suddenly confronted by the tall figure of von Rochow in the entrance hall of the castle.

The Colonel cleared his throat noisily, an operation that he was perpetually performing, as if troubled with some obstruction in his breathing.

"Ha, Lieutenant Keith. You were to have reported to me yesterday. You didn't. Perhaps you hoped I should forget."

"I am sorry, Colonel. It…it quite went out of my mind."

"Oh, you have a mind, have you? Oblige me by unburdening it. What was the purpose of those horses yesterday morning?"

Keith obeyed the Prince's instructions faithfully. "They were for his Highness, of course." He attempted to speak casually. "What he wanted with them I don't quite know. He spoke of a frolic."

"A frolic at half past two in the morning, when his Majesty intended to set out for Mannheim at daybreak. That didn't leave much time for a frolic, did it?"

"Not very much time. No."

"What are you hiding, Keith? Why are you lying?"

"My Colonel!" Keith drew himself up in outraged dignity.

"Bah! Man of honour, aren't you? Not to be given the lie. Well, I give it you, and I'll have none of your airs and graces. Come along, my lad. Come and tell the King all about it. He's asking for you."

The Colonel took him by the arm before he could recover from the shock of this announcement, and hurried him off in panic to the room where dread Majesty waited.

The King stood squarely before him, his hands on his corpulent hips, an intimidating scowl on his swollen face to deepen Keith's dark forebodings.

"What is this that Colonel von Rochow tells me of horses for the Prince yesterday morning at Steinsfurt?"

"They… I…" The stammering young man cast a look of anguish at the big, impassive Rochow.

"Come, come," croaked the King. "You told Colonel von Rochow that they were for the pages."

"He now tells me, sire," Rochow interposed, "that they were for the Prince, for a frolic that he had in mind."

"A frolic? What kind of a frolic?"

"His Highness did not tell me."

"Yet you were ready to go with him, and at that hour?"

Again Rochow interposed, mercilessly. "I have pointed out to Lieutenant Keith the unlikelihood of setting out for a frolic within an hour of the time appointed for your Majesty's departure for Mannheim."

"And what does he say to that?"

"Nothing so far, sire."

"Invention fails him, eh? Come, sir. Better let me have the truth."

You will have perceived, even as Frederick William perceived, that Lieutenant Keith's was not an inventive mind. But even had it been, invention here would have been sorely taxed. In helplessness and fear before that gross, terrifying figure, the lad's courage broke.

"I had better tell your Majesty the truth."

"Much better," was the grim agreement. "Out with it. What did the Prince want with the horses at that hour. He meant to desert, did he not?"

Keith gulped. "To escape, Majesty. Yes."

The King showed no satisfaction at the accuracy of his guess. Stolidly he put the next question, "Where was he going?"

"Over the Rhine, to France, and then to Holland."

"And ultimately to England, eh?"

"I... I believe so, Majesty."

"And you were to accompany him, of course."

"That was the intention. I humbly beg your Majesty..."

"Get out of my sight." The terrible voice suddenly raised, the inflamed countenance, the cane quivering in the royal grasp, all heralded violence. Keith fell back some paces. "Go. Go to your quarters, sir, and count yourself under arrest. You shall hear from me."

Too scared to utter another word, Keith went out with alacrity, backwards. He sought his quarters as bidden, but by no means to stay there as bidden. Since he was as good as broken, there was nothing for which to stay. The savagery of Frederick William might call for other sacrifices even more unpleasant if he lingered. Between the wrath of the father, and the wrath that must await him from the son, whom he dared not even stay to warn, Lieutenant Keith conceived that his Prussian days were over. So that if he lacked invention, he certainly does not appear to have lacked foresight. Swiftly he pocketed what money he possessed, assembled what else he most required, and then made his way at top speed to the stables. Within less than half an hour of quitting the royal presence, he was riding across the bridge of boats over the Rhine, and so out of this narrative in which his part was played.

It might have been grimly otherwise had not the raging King wasted a full hour in the indulgence of his passion, stamping up and down the little room. The tempest of his fury rolled about the Colonel's stolid head when he had listened to further particulars supplied by von Rochow. These included Gummersbach's report of the Prince's suspicious intimacy with Lieutenants Ingersleben and Spaen.

"Why did you not tell me all this before? Why did you not tell me yesterday morning?"

"I did not wish to distress your Majesty without good reason."

"Righteous Lord God! Had you known your duty you would have come to me at once. And you are so cursedly careless that but for an accident Fritz would have got away. A deserter. A deserter, do you understand? You know what that means. You're a soldier, aren't you?"

The pause on the question gave the Colonel at last the chance to speak. "Majesty, he could not have escaped. I had taken all precautions."

"Precautions? Beloved God! Did you suspect the intention, then? And you never told me!" Again the cane quivered in his grasp.

Rochow remained unperturbed. "Was I to trouble your Majesty with suspicions?"

"What were your precautions?"

"Gummersbach slept outside the Prince's room, and Gummersbach, as I've shown your Majesty, is entirely reliable. He and my other agents are now keeping his Highness under observation. I repeat, sire, he could not have escaped, and he cannot escape now."

"You'll answer for it with your head, Rochow, if he does. With your head." His Majesty stamped about the room again, panting with rage. "And then these accomplices of his: this rat Keith; and Spaen and Ingersleben. How many more of them are there?"

"I know of no more, sire."

"Then you're a fool. What of this letter that Gummersbach reports him to have received from Berlin? A secret letter that he was careful to burn immediately after reading it. Almighty! What sort of a conspiracy is threatening me? How many are engaged in it? To what lengths does that mincing rascal mean to go? Is the earthworm turning into a viper? Is my life aimed at?" He stood appalled before the spectre suddenly raised by his own suspicions, and this fabrication of his mind grew, as such things will, by pondering them. "From whom was that Berlin letter? That is the first thing to ascertain. It must be ascertained, Rochow."

"It was Keith who was the bearer of it to the Prince. He should be able to tell us whence it came."

"Keith? Why did you not say so before? Go and get him, man; and have Spaen and Ingersleben arrested at the same time. Put the three of them under lock and key. About it. March!" Rochow was already turning to obey when he was checked. "No. Wait." The King's little eyes had grown cunning. "Let them be for the present, but keep them under strictest surveillance. See where they go and with whom they consort. That should lead us to discover the others." He caught sight of the clock on the overmantel. "Almighty! It is past the dinner-hour. I can't stay now. You know what's to do, Rochow. Meanwhile not a word to anybody." He rolled to the door, which the Colonel hastened to hold for him. "And don't forget, Rochow: if the Prince should escape I'll have your head."

He stamped out, an incarnation of gross rage. When he came to table, however, his appetite did not seem impaired. He ate and drank with his normal gluttonous zest.

Chapter 9

The Arrest

News of the flight of Keith, when served up to his Majesty after dinner, did not prove a good digestive. It flung him into a fresh passion, and, what was worse, it went to increase his black suspicions that he was dealing with a conspiracy whose scope was murderous. It is possible that in his secret heart he knew what he deserved. Nothing by now was too alien to confirm those fears. So extravagantly was this the case that when, in the late afternoon of that Sunday, the Governor and officers of Spandau arrived unexpectedly from France, he conceived that the homage which they came to pay him might be but a cloak under which to assist his son. That the visit supplied no evidence of this did not allay his mistrust. Unreasoning suspicion, once afoot, especially if based on jealousy or fear, is not readily checked. The more groundless its origins, the more recklessly will it discover grounds.

Fritz, his Majesty had by now fully persuaded himself, was impatient for the succession. Such things had happened before in the history of princes. His object in flight was to create a scandal that would shake the foundations of Frederick William's throne in preparation for its overthrow. And no doubt the Prince would find no lack of scoundrels to support him. More than ever did the King realize the necessity of observing secrecy until more facts had been discovered. But the very malice of his nature defeated him in this.

For when the Prince came to join him at supper that evening, he raised his brows and assumed a false joviality, yet with a hint of the savagery behind it.

"What! Is it you, Fritz? Still here? I imagined you by now in Paris."

The Prince stood still, his frail figure momentarily drooping under this fresh wrench of nerves already ragged. He had been troubled all day by the lack of word from Keith, and had vainly sought him, only to learn that he was not in the castle, though none could tell him where or when the Lieutenant had gone. His quest of Ingersleben, and then of Spaen, had been equally fruitless. They had been sent ahead to Frankfurt with other officers, as harbingers of the King to the city of imperial elections. It gave the Prince an unhappy feeling of being isolated and defenceless against the evils now definitely heralded by his father's sarcasm. Nevertheless, as he took his place at the table, he contrived an air of pertness.

"In Paris? Faith, I should be there if I had wanted to go. But why should you suppose it, dear papa?"

"A passing thought," said dear papa, with a wicked twinkle in his little eyes, and he fell upon his food with noisy relish.

No more was said; but the Prince observed from that moment, with increasing misgivings, that he was never alone. Either Rochow or some other officer was always at his elbow, and meanwhile there was still no sign of Keith; so that, to his bitter chagrin, the notion of escaping that night must again be postponed. And when next, he asked himself in vexation, would there be such a chance as Mannheim afforded?

The royal progress moved on by way of Darmstadt to Frankfurt, which was reached early on Tuesday, the dignitaries of the wealthy imperial city waiting in the Römer to receive his Majesty.

It had been decided that at Frankfurt the royal party should leave the carriages for the waiting barges, so as to complete by water the journey to Wesel.

It was a pleasant enough mode of travelling in the summer weather, by Mainz and Bonn to Cologne; but not for the frustrated

Prince, whose plans had all gone awry. Spaen and Ingersleben had rejoined the party. Of Keith, however, there was still no sign, and nothing could have been more disquieting to the Prince and his two remaining friends than this mysterious disappearance. His Highness had enlisted Alverley's assistance to solve the mystery, and Alverley had made discreet inquiries; but since none but the King and Rochow were aware of the truth, he was unable to discover anything.

"If only Katte were here," the Prince sighed, and for a week thereafter, until that leisurely progress reached Cologne, he continued tormented by suspense. Here it was abruptly and terrifyingly ended for him.

The Archbishop-Elector of Cologne had prepared a reception to do honour to the King of Prussia and the Crown Prince, and for this they landed there. On the quay the King turned to Rochow and Keyserlingk, who came after him, with the Prince between them.

"Understand me," he shouted, in a voice that carried far and startled his following. "You are not to leave his Highness for a moment, and you will deliver him on board again alive or dead. Alive or dead. So, forward."

Shrinking under the astonished gaze of the electoral officers ranged along the quay, and with rage and fear and shame blending in his soul, the Prince moved on in silence, his eyes upon the ground, between his governors whom already he must regard as his gaolers. But his torment of suspense was to continue for another three days, until Wesel was reached, and they stood once more on Prussian ground. He had not seen his father since the reception at Cologne, and was not to see him until the morning after their arrival at Wesel. Then, without any warning of what was intended, he was conducted by Rochow to a room in the castle where the King, at a writing-table, sat awaiting him.

Behind the King stood his Majesty's aides-de-camp, Katzenstein and Alverley, and Rochow went to join them, leaving his Highness face to face with his father. The Prince dissembled his desperate uneasiness. He strove to put amiability into the smile that was like a spasm on his painted, foxy face. "Good morning, dear papa."

The King took a long look at him, without returning the greeting. Then he began quietly. "You are a soldier, Fritz. At least that is what I have sought to make of you. It's true that you have profited little by my endeavours, but at least, I suppose, you will have learnt the meaning of desertion and its consequences."

"Desertion?" echoed the Prince, blankly.

"How else would you describe what you were attempting at Steinsfurt?"

The Prince stared in dumb helplessness at his father.

"Answer me," he was bidden. "And don't trouble to lie. You will waste your breath. I am too well informed already."

"You said 'desertion', papa. I had no thought of that. I mean, I had not considered it as that. It is true, I had arranged to escape."

"So! Will you tell me why?"

"Why?" The Prince gaped a moment, undecided. Then his wrongs supplied the answer, and it poured from him in a torrent. "Because I am hated by you. Because every day you give me proof of your hatred. You ill-treat me and shame and humiliate me in public and in private beyond all endurance. It was the despair to which you have reduced me that prompted flight."

"I see," said the King, and his calm, so unusual, was portentous. "Tell me now! What accomplices had you besides that wretched fellow Keith?"

"No other accomplices."

"So. Then perhaps you can tell me for what purpose Lieutenant Spaen purchased the carriage that was ready for you at Steinsfurt. Was it on your instructions?"

"No. Certainly not."

"No? No matter. He shall tell us, himself. For I have just ordered his arrest. And there are others. At Mannheim you had a letter from Berlin. What was that letter? Who wrote it?"

Alverley felt himself stiffening with apprehension. Was Katte after all to be compromised in this miserable business? Only Keith could say that the letter had come through the good offices of Alverley, and Keith was far away. But would Fritz betray the writer?

On the Prince's part there was a moment's hesitation. In that moment his glance sought Alverley, standing straight and stern behind the King, and the stern force of will in Alverley's steady eyes may well have governed him.

"That…that was nothing. It was from a tradesman. Holzapfel, the bookseller, about some books I had ordered from him. That is the truth, papa."

"So you say. But your word is evidence of nothing. It shall be tested at once, and it will be the worse for you if, as I suppose, you have lied. And now, another detail. It has come to my knowledge that you have something over a thousand thalers in your possession. That is a large sum to carry about with you."

Thus the Prince was brought to realize how well he had been spied upon by Gummersbach.

"It was natural," he said, "that I should provide myself with money."

"Of course. Of course. But how did you provide yourself? How did you come by this sum, and what other moneys do you possess?"

His Highness was by now beginning to recover his self-control, and with it some of the insolence natural to him. This was reinforced by vanity, which urged him before these witnesses to meet this browbeating in kind.

He drew himself up, a ridiculously stripling figure, and looked his father between the eyes. "A thousand thalers is no great sum in the purse of the Crown Prince of Prussia. Your father would not have thought so."

"No. But in your spendthrift case it is."

"Spendthrift!" The Prince almost crowed. "Could I possibly be that on the stingy allowance I receive from you?"

The King's restraint began to slip from him. The colour began to darken in his bloated face. His hands closed and tightened into fists. His neck swelled. But still his voice remained level. "You have from me what your needs demand. Neither more nor less. And it certainly should leave you no balance for conspiring. That is why I am asking you whence this money comes." And on the heels of that he fired another question: "What has become of the jewels in your decorations?"

This time the Prince answered promptly. "I have sold them."

"You make that admission without shame?"

"The shame is for the tight-fistedness that drove me to it."

The King's fingers drummed ominously on the table. But still he held himself in leash. "How much did you realize by the sale?"

"About a thousand thalers."

"Which, of course, you brought with you from Berlin?"

"Of course."

"Ah! And the letter of credit Ingersleben cashed for you in Nuremberg? What was the source of that?"

For a moment the Prince was out of countenance again. He felt that he was treading on ground as treacherous as a quicksand. Then, recovering, he flung out in reckless effrontery, "I had some money from my uncle, the King of England."

His Majesty leaned forward, his brows drawn down until his eyes had almost vanished. "The King of England!" he echoed. And again: "The King of England!" as if this were something quite beyond belief.

Having committed himself, the Prince went on. Malice in him was very closely allied with insolence. *Schadenfreude*, the malign joy in the pain of others for which only the German language has a word, attracted him irresistibly. The clear perception of where he might strike to hurt drove him to strike without thought for the consequences.

"I wrote to him. I told him how I was placed; how treated; how kept without even the means to support the dignity of my station."

The fist of Majesty crashed down upon the table. His voice soared in a scream of rage. "You did that, you scoundrel! You dared to do that!"

Perceiving that he had, indeed, struck home, the Prince began immediately to wish that he had not. His father appeared to be breathing with difficulty, and his fingers were plucking fiercely at his neckcloth. Darker grew those suspicions of his that what he perceived was but the surface of some vile plot in which this unnatural son might be aiming at his very life.

"You have dared to do that!" he repeated. "Righteous Lord God! You hold me up to shame in the eyes of foreign princes. Rascal! You seek by your lies to make me an object of contempt to the world. God save all honest folk from the ways of unnatural children." He thrust himself violently back from the table, and heaved himself up. "God is my witness that I have tried everything with you: kindness, severity, warnings, punishments. All has been vain." He shambled round the table. "But this time I'll make an end."

To the horror of the three witnesses he lugged out his sword to strike at his son, who recoiled in terror before the maniacal fury he had provoked.

It was Katzenstein who, greatly daring, and at the risk of being charged by this madman with lèse majesté, sprang forward to seize and hold the royal arm as it was drawn back to thrust. "Majesty!" he remonstrated. "Majesty!"

Glaring, Majesty strove to wrench his arm free, whilst the Prince, in abject fear, all insolence blown out of him now, was on his knees, wailing: "Mercy, papa! Have mercy!"

"What mercy had you for me, you gutterling?" Then voicing yet another newborn suspicion: "Was your mother in this?" he asked. "Did that intriguing woman advise you to write to her brother?"

"I take God to witness that she did not."

"Who's to believe you? You are without religion; without fear of God. I know you, you jackanapes. You'd never scruple to forswear yourself. Here." Suddenly, the murderous frenzy spent, he thrust his sword upon Katzenstein. "Take it before I save the hangman his job. But let him get out of my sight. At once. No. Wait. Rochow! You will take Colonel Frederick's sword. You'll convey him a prisoner to the fortress of Cüstrin, and you'll deliver him there alive or dead. Understand me: alive or dead. If there should be any attempt at a rescue, you will see to it that there is only a corpse for the rescuers. Go."

Gravely Rochow inclined his head in acknowledgment of the order, and approached the Prince. He spoke gently. "Your Highness hears."

"Here is no highness," the King shouted. "There is only Colonel Frederick; and there may not long be even that. Away with him."

Chapter 10

The Chaplain of Cüstrin

That journey to Cüstrin was to Prince Frederick a veritable journey through the Valley of the Shadow. The fear of death, which had entered his soul the moment when his father, with his own hand, would have killed him had not Katzenstein forcibly intervened, was not to be dismissed.

The travelling arrangements were strictly as his father, with that passion for petty detail in all matters, had prescribed. Colonel von Rochow and two other senior officers occupied a carriage with his Highness. A major and three captains rode in a following carriage, as a further guard upon his person, and a troop of dragoons acted as escort. They carried a supply of food and wine for the journey, and never for a single moment in the whole course of it was the Prince to be permitted out of the sight of his custodians.

Of arrogance there was now no sign in him. Never yet had he been so utterly cowed. His large, prominent eyes, in a pallid face that seemed to have grown narrower, were wistful as a beaten dog's. When he did not sit huddled in brooding silence, he was uttering laments, and protesting that he had intended no such evil as the King supposed; that he had merely sought to escape the hatred of a father whom he loved; and finally – after the fashion of weaklings, who must ever be blaming others for the troubles they have brought upon themselves – that he had been led astray by evil counsellors.

Rochow accounted it in the Prince's own interests, as well as in the King's, to play upon these fears. "If you can persuade his Majesty of this," he said, "you might then be hopeful of an appeal to his mercy. I dare not say that a frank avowal of your full intentions, with the disclosure of all your accomplices, will save you; but I dare say that nothing else will."

When at last they came to Cüstrin and its grim fortress set in the bleak marshes of the Oder the signs were still more ominous. The Governor of the fortress, forewarned by a courier who had ridden ahead, received his exalted prisoner in accordance with the stern instructions he had been given. It was a reception that scarcely differed from that of a common felon. His Highness was bestowed in a cell that was little more than a dozen feet square, with a small barred window overlooking the ramparts. A table, a chair and a truckle bed, all of the rudest, made up its furniture.

On the threshold of this den the three senior officers who had brought him from Wesel took their leave of him. A gaoler closed the door and shot the bolts, and he was left alone with his wretchedness. His immediate impulse was to write to his dear papa, to protest his innocence of any evil intentions towards him, and to implore his mercy whilst yet it was time. But he could not yield to this, because writing materials were denied him, as were all books, saving the Bible conspicuously, displayed upon the table.

Morning found him blear-eyed from lack of sleep, following upon a night of physical and mental anguish, throughout which he had tossed continuously, half-dressed, upon his miserable pallet.

At eight o'clock, the bolts were drawn, and two officers entered. They were followed by two orderlies, one bearing a basin of water for the Prince's toilet, the other a breakfast tray. One of the officers informed him that he was accorded seven minutes in which to perform his toilet and eat the unpalatable food. The meat had been cut for him, and only a spoon was supplied with it.

When he attempted to engage the officers in talk, he was curtly told that conversation was interdicted.

He ate a little, and then thrust the platter from him in disgust. The tray was removed; the orderlies departed, followed by the officers; the door was closed again; and he was left in a condition of increased despair.

There was no alleviation of this when, towards noon, the door opened once more, to admit a gaunt man in the black cassock and bands of a clergyman. Lugubriously the stranger announced himself as the prison chaplain, sent to offer the prisoner such spiritual help as by God's grace he might command.

To the Prince this man was a terrifying apparition, his advent the prelude of the end; for in his dread condition he could not but regard the chaplain as the forerunner of the hangman. He broke into a cold sweat.

"My God!" he cried. "Am I to be put to death without so much as a trial?"

"No, no." The chaplain tried to soothe him. "There is no question of death. At least, not yet."

"Not yet!"

"Perhaps not at all, if by a true penitence you deserve the clemency of his Majesty."

His Highness, who had risen, flung himself down again upon the bed. "But I am penitent. Truly penitent. How could I not be? Let me have pen and paper, so that I may write to my dear father."

"Penitence is not to be established by words, but by proofs, my son. There is not true contrition without the purpose of amendment."

"I have that purpose," was the whimpered answer. "I was mad. I was led astray. I listened to wicked advice."

"From whom?" The question was instant and sharp.

"What does that matter? If the King will forgive me, I swear that he shall never have cause to complain again. He shall find me submissive in all things. I desire nothing in the world so much as his love, and I shall spare no effort to deserve it."

"God be praised that I find you in so chastened a spirit." The chaplain was unctuous. "It will rejoice his Majesty to be informed of this. He will readily believe that you have been led away by wicked counsellors. He requires only that you name them to him. That would persuade him of the sincerity of your penitence."

The Prince sat hunched, his elbows on his knees, and groaned.

The chaplain came to set a large bony hand upon his shoulder. "Come, my son," he coaxed. "Unburden your soul. Be open and frank, as you hope for mercy from God and man. His Majesty regards the starting-point of all this mischief to be a letter that you received at Anspach from Berlin, a letter you took some pains to burn immediately. That was no letter from a bookseller, as you pretended. This has been ascertained. From whom was it? You must shield no guilty person from the King's justice if you would have your repentance accepted."

Conscious of the guile that was being used, the Prince looked with revulsion into that long-nosed, swarthy face, its cheeks blue-black from the razor.

"This is odious," he protested. "To ask me to betray my friends..."

"You have said that you were led astray by evil counsellors."

"I was. I was."

"Then you can really call them friends who brought you into this terrible position?"

"Two are already in prison and a third in flight for their association with me. Do you suppose that they are not on my conscience? How can I add to that burden?"

"But isn't the one who remains undiscovered – your correspondent in Berlin – perhaps the chief culprit?"

"No. Why must it be assumed that he had anything to do with my escape? He had not."

"All the better, then. There can be no reason not to disclose his name, and so enable his Majesty to dismiss his suspicions."

Feeling himself akin to a cornered rat, the Prince displayed exasperation. "But the matter is a private one. It concerns someone else. I will not have it raked through, and scrutinized. It is monstrous to ask it of me, on a mere suspicion."

The dark-faced chaplain pondered him with sorrowful eyes.

"Your Highness forgets how much cause you have given for these suspicions, which are not otherwise to be laid to rest. To refuse this disclosure is to rush upon your ruin. I'll leave you to consider it, praying that the Almighty may lead you to a wise decision. I will come again tomorrow – hoping that the night will have brought you better counsel."

But neither the night nor the fears that haunted its wakeful hours could help the unhappy Prince. He writhed on his pallet as on a rack, and the morning found him with exhausted, shattered nerves. The dumb service under the guard of the two officers was an added irritation. The chaplain when he came found him pitiable to behold: pallid, unshaven, unkempt, dirty, his clothes crumpled and in disorder. His mood, however, was now violently rebellious.

"You try to frighten me," he accused the priest. "But you waste your time. The King would never dare to go to extremes. For above the King there is the Emperor, and the Emperor would never condone my death. My father knows that." His high-pitched voice was shrill with the emphasis whereby he sought to convince not only his listener, but his own self. "I am not so mean a thing that I can be lightly put away and no questions asked. I am the Crown Prince of Prussia."

The chaplain sighed. "Alas, my son, do not be deceived. The least of your dangers is that you may cease to be Crown Prince of Prussia. You may be deprived of your heritage in favour of your brother."

Here was a new and unexpected threat, almost as dismaying to Prince Frederick as that of death itself. It was only too convincing. His father's affection for Prince William, which did not make Frederick love his brother, might urge the King to grasp at this chance to alter the succession in his favour. He was aghast.

"God in Heaven! Is...is that actually in my father's mind?"

The chaplain's eyelids drooped. "I believe it to be under consideration should you prove intractable; should you withhold the full disclosures his Majesty requires."

"But I have disclosed all that matters. The King knows everything."

"And the letter from Berlin?"

The Prince paced in silence to the wall and back. He flung himself petulantly down upon his bed, and with elbows on his knees and brow in his hands, he sat brooding. Over him stood the gaunt black figure of the chaplain. At last when the Prince spoke he did not trouble to maintain the pretence that the Berlin letter was not concerned with his escape.

"If I refuse to speak," he complained, "I face death, or, what is worse, the loss of my birthright. But rather that than betray a faithful friend."

"I tell you again that he is no faithful friend who counselled or helped you in this rebellion. A true friend's part was to advise against it, or, at least, to refuse to assist in it."

"I will not dispute with you on that. It may be as you say. But if I betray him, if I deliver him up to my father's vengeance..."

"To your father's justice," the chaplain interrupted to amend.

"Oh, what does a word matter? If I do that I shall disgrace myself in the eyes of all the world."

"A vain consideration. Fiat justitia, pereat mundus."

The Prince continued huddled in thought, and in those moments of desperate search for an outlet from this trap the inherent slyness of his nature was at work. At last he looked up. There was a stir of colour in his cheeks. "May I regard you as a friend, reverend sir?"

"In all things lawful, my son."

"I stand parlously in need of help. Will you help me?"

"To the full extent of my power – in all lawful things."

Again the Prince was silent for a moment, selecting his words. Then he spoke with a sudden feverishness. "There is perhaps a middle course. If I tell you the name of this friend, the best of all my friends, the only one of those who helped me whose name has not yet been discovered, will you go first to him and warn him, so that he may make himself safe, before you disclose his name to my father? Will you promise to do that?"

"What deceit are you asking me to practise?"

"No deceit. Surely there is no deceit in this. I ask you to go to him, and explain to him my wretched case. Tell him how I come to be faced with death if I do not divulge his name, and that I beg him to escape before the knowledge reaches the King. Tell him that it was only after I had your promise to do this that I consented to disclose his part in my attempted flight. Tell him that, without that promise, I would go to my death rather than betray him. For that is what I shall do unless you consent. Thus, at least, you will have saved me from the dishonour the King would force upon me. Well, sir?" He rose, and gripped the chaplain's arm. "Will you be my friend, and do as I require?"

The chaplain stood with bent shoulders, his head bowed. He was obviously troubled, and the lean, crafty face, overcast now with thought, was hardly a face to trust. At last he spoke.

"This is not…straightforward. It…it almost amounts to trickery."

"Have I a choice? Are not the dice cogged against me? Then I, too, must cog my dice. And what a little thing I am asking after all! What a little price I ask you to pay for serving me. Sir, do not be hard. Do not drive me to extremes. You call it trickery. But can you say that I am not the victim of trickery? Can you say that you were not sent here to practise upon me? Surely it is lawful to meet trickery with trickery."

The chaplain tightened his lips. "You take that view, do you? So be it. Tell me the name of your correspondent, and what he wrote."

"You will do as I have asked?"

"You can trust me."

"Very well. That letter was from Rittmeister Hans Hermann von Katte. He was to have accompanied me in my flight; but he wrote to say that he could not join me as arranged because he could not obtain leave of absence from his colonel. That is all, and it amounts to very little, as you see. When you have carried my message to Rittmeister von Katte, you may tell the King."

The chaplain bowed his head. "I pray, Highness, that his Majesty's heart may be softened by this disclosure! that he may see in it a proof of your penitence. I will leave you now. God keep your Highness."

He was gone, so suddenly as to leave the Prince with some misgivings.

Chapter 11

Anxieties

It is manifest in the sequel that the Chaplain of Cüstrin did not keep faith. It is matter for speculation whether he ever intended to keep it. Similarly it is matter for speculation how far the Prince was really concerned that he should keep it. There is no reason to doubt that the Prince would have preferred, and may strongly have hoped, that he should do so; but should he fail, the condition his Highness had made would still set a gloze of loyalty upon the disloyal thing he did. Thus far the appearances would be saved.

As for the chaplain, we may suppose that he would reconcile his conscience with the breach on the ground that his first duty was to the King, and that subterfuges for the perfection of that duty were justifiable, if not laudable. A casuistical mind can persuade itself of anything.

But to the facts.

The leisurely homing Frederick William was met at Halberstadt by the chaplain, who had taken pains to be with his Majesty at the earliest moment. There were no witnesses of the interview. But we may assume that the pastor, adopting the role of Prince Frederick's advocate, would urge his Highness' penitence, his plea that he had been seduced by evil counsellors, and that the first of these was the Rittmeister von Katte, writer of the mysterious Berlin letter, whose contents were now disclosed.

The King kept his own counsel; but that something had happened was apparent to everyone in the sudden end of his leisureliness. He completed the journey to Potsdam as swiftly as the vile roads permitted, arrived there late one night, slept there, and in the morning was off again, to Berlin.

My Lord Alverley, anxious to see Katte and to inform him of what had taken place at Wesel, had obtained twenty-four hours' leave of absence, and was in Berlin before the King, not indeed suspecting that his Majesty intended to visit his capital that day. Because of this ignorance he was not perturbed when he found Katte absent from his quarters in the Zeughaus Platz. The Rittmeister's housekeeper, Frau Körner, believed that von Katte was at the Palace of Monbijou. He was expected home for supper.

Alverley left word that he would return to sup with his cousin, and went his ways. The delay was of no moment, since he would still be seeing Katte in good time to warn him so to order matters that he left no traces of his participation in the Prince's plans of escape. The arrest of Spaen and Ingersleben, who were to be court-martialled, was a sufficient indication of what must happen to any other discovered associate of the Prince's. This had left Alverley far from happy. Affection for his warm-hearted cousin sharpened his own distaste for the environment that imperilled him. He was discovering in these Prussians little to admire and much to contemn. The evil smells of Berlin, which the August heat was again rendering almost insupportable, seemed to him symbolical.

"It stinks like their own natures," he told himself.

The spaciousness of the streets, which once he had admired, moved him now to scorn. "Where land is worthless, streets may well be wide."

Some antidote to this disgruntled mood was supplied at Pastor Ritter's house, to which he took his way. He found Dorothea in the garden. She had set up her easel there, and, using a clump of laurel as a model for her background, she was attempting – faithful to her master – a pastoral piece, of the kind that Katte loved to paint. Alverley was given a glad welcome by the girl, and presently a civil one by her absent-minded father, who was insistent that he should stay to dine with them.

Before the Pastor made his appearance, however, Alverley sat beside Dorothea in the grateful shade of the limes that fringed her garden, watching her brushwork.

After a little while, she set aside her palette. "That will do for today," she announced, and turned to consider him. "You have been absent so long," she complained.

"I rejoice that it should so have seemed. A sweet flattery, to make me vain."

"If I perceived that danger I should choose my words more carefully." She laughed lightly, and rose, tall and virginally slim above the billows of her panniered petticoats. "I do not judge you easily made vain."

He had risen with her, and sauntered now beside her down the garden path.

"You would never be hard in any of your judgments," he said. "That is for little souls. But are we not, all of us, made by what we feed on?" They were beside a bed of roses of spindle growth, with ill-formed, anaemic blooms on drooping stems. "Consider these poor starvelings. I know the rose for the proudest, hardiest flower in all the garden, exuberant of petals, dazzling of colour, intoxicating of fragrance. Such is the rose as we in England know it. But here, in this arid Prussian soil, it struggles pitifully for a bare existence, its noble nature lost in weakness."

She put up her eyebrows as she looked at him. "This is a parable, I think."

He smiled. "Of course, Mademoiselle."

"There was a betraying bitterness in your voice. It is not only the soil that you find arid in Prussia."

"I confess it."

"Then why do you remain?" Her tone robbed the words of reproof.

"I am poor. My needs constrain me."

"Then – forgive me – should not gratitude constrain you, too?"

"Perhaps I deserve the rebuke. Perhaps I don't. Perhaps loyalty to the few friends I possess here justifies my feelings. You shall judge."

Moving slowly beside her, where the laurels made a shade, he told her of the happenings at Wesel, the arrest of the Prince, the persecution of his Highness' friends, and his anxieties concerning Katte. She heard him in growing dismay, for, apart from the Prince, those he named — Ingersleben and Spaen and Keith — were well known to her, almost friends, having been with his Highness frequently her visitors, whilst Katte, known intimately for years, from the days when her father had been his tutor, was the object of feelings almost sisterly.

The plight of the Prince distressed her deeply, until she assured herself that his rank must shield him from any dangerous consequences of his rashness. Alverley's anxieties on the score of Katte, however, she refused to share.

"What, after all, has he done?" she asked.

"As much or as little as those others who are to go before a court martial. The King is all vindictiveness. As I read him, he has been badly scared, and that is something he can't forgive."

"But only his Highness knows of Katte's part in all this, and his Highness will never fail in loyalty. He loves and admires Katte too much for that."

"I hope you may be right. But it's in my mind that he loves and admires himself still more."

"Are you not unjust to him?"

"I hope so. Devoutly I hope so. Yet even if I regarded his loyalty as a rock, I must still be anxious. Daily with the King since this has occurred, I have watched the malign growth of his rancour. It embraces all who were ever the Prince's friends."

She turned towards him, a new gravity, almost a fear, in her clear eyes. "But that would include you!"

"Me?" He laughed easily. "Hardly. And, anyway, I have seen no sign of loss of favour."

"Still, you are Katte's cousin and close friend. If he were implicated, what then would be your position? Might it not be assumed that you were in his counsels?"

In sudden concern her hand closed impulsively upon his arm. The little gesture moved him oddly. A warmth of tenderness responded in him and his smile, as he shook his head, was gentler than she had ever known it. It swept the last vestige of sternness from his face.

"It would be mere assumption, after all," he said.

"But has not all been done upon assumption?"

"Certainly a deal. But in each case the assumption is based upon some fact of conduct. There is no single such fact in my case."

She seemed to breathe more freely, and she would have withdrawn her hand, but that his left closed over it and made it prisoner. "Your thought for me is the sweetest thing I remember since... Faith, I don't know since when. It must have been very long ago, Dorothea. If ever."

It was the first time that he used her name. That and his tone may have darkened the colour in her face and made her glance falter.

"Monsieur!" she gently protested, and withdrew the hand which he now made no effort to retain.

He sighed as he let it go. "I speak the simple truth," he asserted. "Ah! Here comes your father."

"It will be to bid us to dinner. Better not speak of these things to him. In his heart I do not think he likes Prince Frederick."

Alverley was to form the opinion that it would have mattered little to the pastor, for all the attention he would have paid to it, if the Prince's misfortune had been discussed. This tall, lean, ascetic man, almost humpbacked from a lifetime spent over books, displayed after all only a secondary interest in the world about him. He may not, as Dorothea said, have liked the Prince, but there was no vigour of dislike in him for any man.

At the moment he had graver concerns than a daughter's conduct, and at dinner he confided them to Alverley, in whom he had discovered a certain scholarliness that buttressed his esteem. He was still labouring upon his deeply annotated German rendering of Apollonius of Tyana. But the more deeply he penetrated into the work, the graver became his doubts whether this was indeed a fitting task for a Christian divine, and whether the book was one that it would be prudent to make known to Christians, whether it might not lead them to disquieting parallels. Yet to abandon the task after so much and such loving labour would entail a self-denial and sacrifice that daunted him. Humbly he sought the advice of his guest.

Alverley congratulated himself upon his utter ignorance of Apollonius, since this he imagined would effectively dispose of a subject that went none too well with roast goose and a hock of fragrance and dignity that might have come from the famous cellar of the Bremen Rathaus. But all the difference his confession of ignorance made was that, instead of a discussion, there was a protracted lecture from the pastor, calculated to improve his guest's knowledge.

Chapter 12

Katte's Desk

Lord Alverley would have taken his ease less nonchalantly at Pastor Ritter's house had he known what was happening at about the same time at the Palace of Monbijou.

They had been gay there during these weeks, profiting as usual by Frederick William's absence from Berlin. As we have seen, Queen Sophia Dorothea seldom failed to make the most of these little lulls in a stormy existence, and to lead the court into those gaieties upon which his puritanical Majesty frowned disapproval. She held drawing-rooms and gave balls and banquets, to which were bidden all who in Berlin were accounted noble. In addition there were more intimate gatherings for a chosen few, at which they made music, danced, gamed, performed comedies, and were generally merry. And in this merrymaking none was more active or contributed to it more richly than Katte. He was at hand to play the clavichord or the flute as occasion required, to take the leading part in a comedy, or tread a measure with incomparable precision and grace.

He had never been gayer than in this month of August, possibly in reaction from the preoccupations with which his mind had been burdened touching the Prince. The fact that leave had been denied him by his commanding officer supplied a sufficient reason why he should not join his Highness, whilst the fact that he held the Prince's money was a sufficient assurance that the Prince could meanwhile perpetrate no such rashness as he had contemplated. Easy in mind, therefore, both on his own and the Prince's account, he abandoned himself wholeheartedly to the festivities to which he was urgently bidden by the Princess Wilhelmina.

On her side, too, it was similarly a happy season of reaction from anxieties on behalf of a brother between whom and herself the bonds of affection were peculiarly close. Her suspicions that he was planning an escape, and her dread of the consequences to him at the hands of her violent father, had been confirmed when Katte secretly delivered to her his Highness' valedictory letter from Anspach. But even as these fresh fears were aroused, so were they partly allayed by Katte's intimation of his inability to join the Prince.

"So be at peace, Madam. His Highness will not now make the attempt."

Despite the gravity of the matter, there was mockery in the pale eyes that considered his dark, rugged face; for she was not without her streak of the malice that marked her brother.

"You are telling me that your consequence to him is such that he will not go without you?"

"Just that, Highness."

She sighed, and fingered her little pointed chin. "I wish my opinion of you were as exalted as your own."

Katte took no offence. He laughed. "It's an opinion that brings me reassurance. For your Highness, however, since you do not share it, there is something more. I carry the purse. Prince Frederick's treasury is in my keeping: a matter of some four thousand thalers. If you disbelieve that he would go without me, believe, at least, that he could not go without money."

"Why didn't you tell me this before?" There was no mockery now; but only relief. "Bless you for the assurance." She became expansive, almost coquettish. "I'll confess, my dear Katte, that I have suspected you of being more than a partner in this plan of which he had given me a hint; I thought that you might actually have advised it. I am glad to find that I have done you an injustice."

"Indeed, my advice has always opposed it, and, confession for confession, since I now know that it will deserve me your regard, I have actually conspired against it. I requested leave of Marshal von Natzmer in such a manner as to make sure that it would be refused."

She set a hand upon his arm. "So that being without the money, Fritz would be unable to travel."

"Without the money and me," said Katte, smiling.

Her laughter, made possible by relief, trilled again in derision of him.

The incomparable Fräulein von Sorensen came up to them, as lightly as if she were thistledown. "You are merry," she said, and looked from the Princess to the Rittmeister.

"With von Katte that is inevitable."

"It is my fate to be mocked, Mademoiselle," he protested.

He was to protest this again, and less gaily, to himself, some four days later, when he received the Prince's second letter from Anspach, summoning him to the Hague, to the house of Lord Chesterfield there, where he would find his Highness under the name of Count Amberville.

This letter, revealing a rashness in the Prince with which Katte had been far from counting, reduced him to distraction. To desert – as he must if he were to obey the summons – would be not only to ruin his career as a soldier, but to bring grief and shame upon his family. To ignore the summons would be to leave the Prince suspended at the Hague. For since Katte held the purse, his Highness would lack the necessary resources to go forward, whilst his father's violence would make it impossible for him to return. It was as intolerable to leave the Prince in this predicament as that Katte should ruin himself in order to deliver him. Such was the dilemma into which, as he perceived, his amiable weakness had landed him; and he blamed himself now for having lacked the firmness advocated by Alverley to dissociate himself frankly at the outset from the Prince's crack-brained plan.

When he had slept on the matter, however, some of the difficulties vanished. The Prince's predicament need not be as desperate as he supposed. After all, seeing him committed to the adventure, Lord Chesterfield, no doubt, would advance him the funds necessary to complete his journey to England. If Katte did not find in this conviction quite the peace of mind that he desired, at least he perceived in it a sufficient justification for disregarding the summons.

That letter had reached him a week ago, since when he had not dared to show himself again at Monbijou, out of a reluctance to distress the Princess Wilhelmina with the news of this unexpected turn in the events. But on this Monday of Alverley's return to Berlin he had received a note from her Highness bidding him to dine at the palace. She shared her brother's pretensions to originality and creative effort, and like him she was for ever dabbling at musical composition. She had written, she announced, a new piece for her lute, for which she desired Katte's opinion and accompaniment.

In the Porcelain Gallery, to which he was conducted on arrival, he found no more than an intimate family gathering. The Queen was there with two of her ladies-in-waiting, her daughters, the Princesses Amelia, Charlotte and Sophia, Mademoiselle von Sorensen, and Prince William, the rather dull, blond lad who was his father's favourite.

Her Majesty greeted Katte with a vague, goggling stare, and offered him her hand to kiss. Prince William, who had little affection for Fritz, and therefore none for his friends, was supercilious. The Princesses, however, with all of whom Katte was a favourite, were at pains to make amends for this.

After a family dinner, neither as frugal nor as coarse as those which the King approved, they were all peremptorily conducted to the music-room by Wilhelmina. Her Majesty settled down to a game of backgammon with Frau von Kamken, having Frau von Bülow as a spectator. Prince William, having overeaten, disposed himself torpidly on a settle, whilst his sisters, with Mademoiselle von Sorensen, came to group themselves about the clavichord, to which Wilhelmina had commanded Katte. He was invited to improvise an accompaniment to the piece for the lute, of which a manuscript sheet was set before him.

His fingers wandered through tentative arpeggi, which did less than justice to his talent, for his mind was divided. Now that he was in Wilhelmina's company, his silence on the score of her brother, his pretended preoccupation with her music, left him with the sense of practising a deceit. Yet it was impossible to broach the matter in the presence of those others, equally impossible to draw the Princess aside in order to be private with her.

He was still fumbling over a keyboard on which he was usually so much at his ease, and a puzzled frown at this was beginning to knit Wilhelmina's brows, when suddenly the door of the chamber was thrown open with a violence unpardonable in such a place.

Their startled indignation was instantly quelled upon beholding the King whom, as once before, they had imagined many a league away, standing in wrath before them, like a gross incarnation of Nemesis.

At first Katte wanted to laugh. The interruption ludicrously reminded him of the domestic scene enacted there on that June day when the King had belaboured the Prince with his flute. This inclination to mirth, however, did not long endure.

Alverley had by no means overstated the matter to Dorothea when he asserted that the King's malign vindictiveness embraced all those who were known to be the Prince's intimates, and who, therefore, might be in the plot, whose ultimate aim he was now persuaded was to destroy him.

Among the first who must be brought to account were the Queen and the Princess Wilhelmina, and it was with this object that the King had repaired that day to Monbijou.

On the palace steps he was met by Marshal von Natzmer, whom an hour ago he had dispatched to Katte's house, charged with the Rittmeister's arrest. The Marshal was followed by an orderly, carrying a portable writing-desk.

"Why the devil are you here?" shouted the King. "Have you got that rascal?"

"I am informed at his lodging that von Katte is here at the palace."

"Here? Lord God!"

"I am on my way to arrest him, sire. Meanwhile I have taken possession of his papers. I have them with me. This is his desk."

"Ha! Come with me."

He led the way to a small chamber on the ground floor, normally used as a guardroom, but now empty. He addressed the orderly, pointing to a table. "Set the desk down. Break the lock."

The desk was a mahogany box some two feet long by eighteen inches wide and a foot deep at the front of its sloping lid. This lid the King threw back. Then he curtly dismissed the orderly, bade Natzmer set a chair for him, sat down, and rummaged fiercely through the contents. After some bundles of papers he pulled out a stout and very heavy linen bag which proved to contain a little over a thousand pistoles in gold, a small leather bag in which there were some precious stones, and two miniatures in ivory, framed on gold, both portraits, one of Prince Frederick and the other of the Princess Wilhelmina.

The first of these pictures he tossed contemptuously aside. Over the second he goggled a moment, to explode: "Lord God! Does that scoundrel presume to… And that baggage Wilhelmina… Lord God!"

He dropped the miniature, and thrust savagely among the papers. They were letters, and for the moment a glance sufficed for the majority. But there were three in the handwriting of the Prince. One of these revealed that the money and the jewels belonged to his Highness and that Katte was acting as his treasurer; the other two were the letters from Anspach, one of them enclosing a note to be delivered to Wilhelmina, the other acknowledging Katte's letter and ordering him to join the Prince at the Hague, at the house of Lord Chesterfield.

Growling incoherently, he thrust these letters into his pocket, stuffed the remaining papers and other objects back into the desk, for later closer examination, and left Natzmer to consign it into the orderly's keeping. Then, having informed himself of where the

Queen was to be found, he stormed forward, sweeping obsequious lackeys aside with his slashing cane.

On a flood tide of fury, with Marshal von Natzmer at his heels, he surged into the music-room, and stood a moment on the threshold, the menace of his gaze petrifying its tenants.

Lute and clavichord tinkled into silence. Wilhelmina and Katte rose with the others. The backgammon board was knocked over by the Queen in her clumsy, nervous haste, and clattered to the ground, scattering draughts and dice.

The King's baleful glance came to settle upon Katte, and quenched the Rittmeister's incipient amusement. "You!" he roared, and pointed with his cane. "You have the effrontery to be here, you scoundrel! Natzmer! Take his sword."

Katte stood at attention, straight and stiff, his head high, his glance steady, betraying no sign of his sudden dismay, whilst the Marshal, his own commanding officer, approached him with a troubled countenance. Katte guessed at once that he was somehow compromised in connection with the Prince. This, however, was neither the time nor the place for argument. So without question or comment he unbuckled his sword-belt and surrendered the weapon.

"Take him out. March!"

Natzmer's wave of the hand was half-command, half-invitation, and Katte responded without demur or hesitation. That self-possession and the pride and grace of the Rittmeister's bearing were as fuel to the fires of the royal passion. As the officer was passing him to reach the door, the King exploded.

"Rascal! Traitor! You carry your head high; but I'll lower it for you." He struck at him savagely with his cane.

Natzmer gasped audibly in shocked reproach, whilst Katte checked; his heels came together, he stood very straight, his face white with anger.

"This is brave," he said.

"What's that?" The King's little eyes, buried in his congested countenance, glittered like a boar's when about to charge. He spoke in a strangled voice, delivering another blow. "Impudent buffoon!"

Katte bowed stiffly and resumed his march to the door. He was followed by a scream of rage. "Take him out, Natzmer. Take him out before I kill him."

Then Majesty swung to face the shivering women. He stormed at the Queen. "There goes a fit companion for your disgraceful son. But you are not likely to see either of them again. Your son is dead, Madam."

"Dead!" she gasped, uncomprehending.

"As good as dead. He's a deserter, a traitor, and I'll deal with him as a deserter should be dealt with. That is the fruit of all your plotting and intriguing; the result of the godlessness in which you've reared that nincompoop."

Livid, speechless, wobbling, she had sunk down again into her chair, her hands to her massive bosom as if to repress its heaving. He marched upon her, and suddenly found Wilhelmina trembling before him in an attitude of intercession.

"Out of my way, you slut!" he roared, and she has left it on record that he grew black in the face and foamed at the mouth. "Have you the impudence to stand before me? Out of my way! Go and join your dissolute brother. Go!" He struck her in the face as he spoke, and followed the blow by a second one, so violent that it knocked her down. She tells us that she would have split her head against the wainscot if Fräulein von Sorensen had not caught her in time and eased her fall. And she goes on to tell us that, seeing her fallen, the King, no longer master of himself, would have trampled on her, but that her mother, her sisters and her brother, stirred at last to action, placed themselves in his way whilst Fräulein von Sorensen and Frau von Kamken supported her to a window-seat. He strove like an infuriated bull to toss aside those who hindered him. But at the risk of blows his four children withstood him, the youngest of the princesses embracing his knees and appealing to him for mercy.

Thus balked, he continued to hurl invective at Wilhelmina. What he actually called her it is impossible to determine, for she writes in French, and translates, perhaps too mildly, the offensive word as "canaille". He was remembering the miniature found in Katte's desk and interpreting its presence there in his own fashion.

"You shameless baggage! You are an accomplice of your brother in his treason. You are no better than he is. But I'll have you schooled. I'll deal with you, you slut, just as I'll deal with your lover Katte."

Fräulein von Sorensen stirred. His Majesty was now implying something that reflected upon her office as governess. "That, at least, is not true," she asserted with a firmness and courage that left him open-mouthed. He seemed to fight for breath in his amazement that any living creature should dare to stand before him and give him the lie.

Slender and lovely and regally proud she confronted him. "Recollect yourself, sire. God hears you. May He forgive you for impugning the honour of a princess as circumspect as I know her Highness to be."

He glowered at her in silence. He was by his lights a devout, Godfearing man, and her invocation of the Deity sent a spasm of awe to ruffle his arrogance.

"You are very bold to address me in such language," he stormed at last. "I may have a word to say to you on this again, Fräulein." His glance swung past her to the afflicted Queen. "As I shall to you, Madam," he added, and on that he turned abruptly and stamped out.

He left desolation behind him. The Queen's ladies fluttered helpless about her Majesty, who sat rocking herself, and moaning, "My son! My son!"

The Princess Wilhelmina reclined pale and faint on the window-seat, with Fräulein von Sorensen murmuring vain words of comfort. Her three sisters were all in tears, whilst the stolid Prince William looked on in youthful misogyny at these feminine displays of futile emotion.

Chapter 13

Peril

Lord Alverley came back to Katte's house that afternoon, an hour or so after Natzmer's visit, to find confusion there, with Frau Körner fluttering and cackling like a distracted hen. She sobbed out a dismal report to his lordship. Marshal von Natzmer had come to arrest the Rittmeister, and had gone on to Monbijou for that purpose, carrying off Katte's writing-desk.

Alverley was aghast. He realized the vanity of his hopes that Katte's prudence had left nothing to connect him with the Prince's plans. He asked himself now what link had been discovered and by whom. Someone clearly must have betrayed the Rittmeister. It was possible that Ingersleben or Spaen might have gathered from some indiscretion of the Prince's how much he was depending upon Katte, and under rigorous examination, perhaps even under threat of torture – for he rightly conjectured that in his panic the vindictive King would stop at nothing – had disclosed the fact.

Further reflection, however, diminished some of his misgivings. He came to realize that, when all was said, and as must transpire in examination, Katte's only offence had been that he had not informed against the Prince. Even so, considering the vile humour of the King, it was likely that the military career by which Katte set such store might well be broken. Out of his love and deep concern for his cousin sprang a natural eagerness to discover some way of assisting him. There was, after all, some testimony that he could supply in Katte's favour, and the moment to supply it presented itself when he returned to duty at Potsdam on the following morning.

He had gone to report himself to the King and to inform him that his regiment of giant grenadiers was drawn up on the parade ground. He found his Majesty closeted with the debonair Grumbkow, with the little plump Judge-Advocate-General Mylius, and the black-a-vised Attorney-General Gerbeft. With them were two officers, General Schulz and Colonel Mazen. These five were ranged in line before the writing-table at which the King was seated. The Freiherr von Katzenstein was at the royal elbow.

"Your grenadiers await your Majesty's inspection," Alverley announced.

"Eh?" Majesty looked up, startled. "So! Devil take it, this damned business puts everything else out of my head. I ask myself how I have sinned that God should punish me in such a fashion. Well, well, sirs, you are sufficiently instructed, I think, for the examination of this scoundrel Katte. About it! See it done, Grumbkow, and warn the fellow that if he doesn't choose to make a full and frank confession, I'll find a way to break his obstinacy. Go."

He waved them all away. Grumbkow led them out, and the King got to his feet. He scowled at Alverley.

"What do you know of this cousin of yours, Margrave?"

"Nothing to his disadvantage, sire."

"Wirklich! Indeed! But nothing to his advantage either, I can swear."

"Something, I think, in this unhappy matter of the Crown Prince. Something which should be known to those who are to examine him."

"Ah? And what may that be?" The tone was sullenly mistrustful.

"It happens, sire, that I had the Rittmeister's confidence, and it is in my knowledge that far from favouring the Prince's purpose, as may appear, he did his utmost to dissuade his Highness."

"You mean that this is what the fellow told you. A man who is a traitor and a deserter will not boggle at a lie or two."

"Neither, with submission, sire, will he make unnecessary confidences."

"Yet, by what you tell me, that is just what he did. And what were you doing that you received these confidences and did not divulge the plot? Was not that in your duty?"

Alverley became aware of the need to go cautiously if he were not, himself, to be swept up into the net of the King's vengeance, in which case there would be an end to any hope of serving Katte.

"I naturally shrank from needlessly distressing your Majesty whilst convinced that the plan would never be carried out, and that Katte, himself, would prevent its being carried out."

"Prevent? How, pray?"

"By withholding the moneys his Highness had entrusted to him. Without these it would be impossible for the Prince to travel."

"You believe that?"

"I have Katte's own word for it."

The King shrugged in ill-humoured contempt. "You make it plain, Margrave, that you are not as intelligent as I supposed. It is clear that you have no information to give my commissioners. I am lawyer enough to know that what the prisoner may have told you proves nothing. And the regiment is waiting." It was an abrupt change of subject. "Let us go. Come, Katzenstein."

Yet when that evening Frederick William received the report of his commissioners and Katte's written statement, which Grumbkow brought him, a man less blinded by prejudice must have seen something in the prisoner's favour in the absolute agreement of his admissions with what Alverley had stated.

Katte had borne his examination well. Calm and dignified before his examiners, he had answered their questions with an unhesitating candour that had strongly prepossessed them in his favour. He had derided as ludicrous the King's suspicion of any design against the State or the person of his Majesty, and defied the production of any scrap of evidence to support it. There had never, he swore, been any question of more than the Prince's escape from his father's persistent anger.

Here Mylius, the President, had interrupted him. "Never more than that, you say. Pray, is not that enough? Or are we to understand that you regard it lightly, that perhaps you even sympathize with the intention?"

"As to that, I will not deny that I was sympathetic. But if sympathy with the Prince is to be counted a punishable offence, I am afraid, sirs, you are likely to be busy. For his Highness does not lack for sympathizers among the many who have witnessed his treatment at the King's hands."

"Sir!" thundered Gerbett. "You are singularly presumptuous, singularly bold to criticize his Majesty, to intervene between your King and the successor of your King."

" 'Intervene' is too strong a word, Excellencies. I am guilty of no intervention."

"Was it not an intervention to give the support of your sympathy, as you admit?"

"That is a very liberal interpretation of sympathy," he answered, and he went on to protest that far from abetting the Prince he had constantly sought to turn him from his project, and that by keeping control of the Prince's money he had confidently believed that he was placing an insuperable obstacle in the way of the Prince's escape.

"There is," said Mylius, whose voice was as harsh and rasping as his appearance was benign, "a letter that you wrote to Colonel Frederick whilst he was on his travels with his Majesty."

"To whom do you say that I wrote?" asked Katte, bewildered.

"To Colonel Frederick. It is thus that his Majesty at present designates the Crown Prince." Beyond a lift of the brows, Katte made no comment. "You do not mention that letter."

"Because it can hardly do other than support what I have said. The letter announced that I could not obtain leave of absence, and would, therefore, be unable to join his Highness."

This was confirmation of what the Prince, himself, had stated the letter to contain. But Gerbett did not consider that the matter could be left there.

"If," he asked, "you had obtained leave, would you have joined Colonel Frederick?"

Katte permitted himself a smile. "That question hardly arises. For if I had really desired leave, I could have urged such reasons that my Colonel would not have refused me."

"So that you actually deceived Colonel Frederick?"

"In his own interests. It might be so construed. I did not wish to hurt his Highness by a blunt refusal. I took the line of least resistance in order to keep within what I accounted my duty."

There was a pause. Then Mylius resumed the interrogation.

"Among your papers we find a letter from Colonel Frederick urging you bluntly to desert and join him at the Hague. That hardly seems the proposal to make to an officer who had – as you represent yourself – always opposed the plan."

"I agree. But it was made."

"Naturally you can't deny it since we hold the letter."

Katte's answer was sharp. "Your holding the letter has nothing to do with my admission. Do me the justice to bear in mind that I am a man of honour."

"That is by no means res judicata. It is precisely what we are here to test. Now, the fact that you did not depart on receipt of Colonel Frederick's letter proves nothing, since, naturally, you would first wait to hear that Colonel Frederick had got away. But answer me this, as a man of honour: if word had reached you that Colonel Frederick had succeeded in escaping should you have gone to join him as he bids you?"

Katte considered for a moment before replying. He smiled quietly and shook his head. "That, sir, is not a juridical, but a hypothetical question."

"So! You are to teach me law? View the question as you please, but let me warn you that it is one to which his Majesty will require an answer. If you do not supply one, it will be assumed from your silence."

"But only until you, sirs, as jurists, instruct his Majesty that assumptions are not admissible in judgment."

Mylius was annoyed. He smiled unpleasantly. "The complete lawyer, eh, Rittmeister?"

"I hope it may avail him," sneered Gerbett. "But I think he would be better advised to remember that he is a soldier, and to consider the obligations of that station, against which he is charged with having offended."

"Charged, but not proved, Excellency."

Gerbett shook his big head. "Proved, at least, that you failed in your duty by not disclosing the plot. However, it is for his Majesty to judge."

Katte went back under guard to the room in the castle assigned to him as a prison, there to prepare his written statement. He did not fail to perceive that his career as an officer was in jeopardy; yet he was sustained by the hope that when the King came calmly to consider his case, his Majesty would understand that the offence was, after all, no more than technical, and so would not be unduly harsh in his sentence. To the frank and reasoned statement which he drew up he added a prayer for pardon for any indiscretion of which he might be considered guilty.

The King, however, when he came to consider Katte's case, together with the cases of Spaen and Ingersleben, who had also been examined, was nowise moved by this prayer. Frederick William's vindictiveness remained fiercest against Katte for no better reason than that he was the closest of the Prince's friends.

"Almighty!" he cried. "Am I to be hoodwinked by these half-truths? This fellow must be brought to talk more freely, even if we have to stretch him on the rack."

Grumbkow, who had brought him the reports of the commissioners, shook his head. "Is so much necessary, sire? Your Majesty may think it well to remember that von Katte's statement agrees in the main with what you were told by Milord Alverley. It will be further tested by the admissions of his Highness when he comes to be examined. If there is anything more, a court martial will, no doubt, bring it to light."

The King yielded. "Very well. I will, myself, appoint the court."

Chapter 14

Emotions of Dorothea

It was mid-September before the court martial assembled. In the meantime, without awaiting its findings, which he promised himself should be as he decreed, Frederick William was striking with maniacal rage wherever his son might be wounded. He had deprived him of his regiment, and bestowed the command of it upon Prince William. He had sold the Prince's horses, and dismissed his servants. When his agents discovered the library which Duhan, the sometime tutor, had assembled for his Highness, he ordered the books to be seized, packed and dispatched to Hamburg to be sold. As for Duhan, across whose back he once had laid his ever-ready cane, when he caught him teaching Latin to the Prince, he was packed off to exile in Memel for the offence – equally odious in the eyes of Majesty – of having provided this library. When Frederick William's ferreting agents discovered that the Prince had purchased a bracelet from Kahn the jeweller for a thousand thalers, he ordered them to discover the strumpet for whom it had been bought, swearing that if they failed he would wring the information from the Prince himself, on the rack. He brutally derided the Queen's anguish on her son's behalf, and taunted her with being a contributor to the scoundrel's present misfortunes. Finally, he kept the Princess Wilhelmina in close confinement and threatened her with worse.

Walking again with Dorothea Ritter in her garden, whither he came frequently in those September days when the King was in Berlin, Alverley spoke unhappily of these things, but not of the hunt that was afoot for her, of which he knew nothing. The rehearsal ended by renewing an earlier alarm.

"Do you never fear that you, too, may become a victim of this senseless persecution? You are Katte's cousin and friend, and you have even ventured to defend him, The Prince, too, counted you among his intimates, and you were often at Monbijou, and in favour with the Princess. Have you thought of all this?"

He smiled upon her gravity, warmed by the friendship it displayed.

"Yes," he confessed. "And there is, no doubt, a change in the King's manner towards me. He no longer uses me with the former geniality."

"And you are not apprehensive?" There was a catch in her breath.

"No. For, at least, he spares me the boorishness with which he treats most others."

"To be sure you are a margrave," she remembered, and provoked his laughter by the implication.

"A likelier reason is that I am an Englishman. Although in exile, it doesn't follow that the exile is eternal. Nothing enrages the King more than the fear of the opinion that may be held of him by the Queen's family. It was from England that Prince Frederick received the money he needed, and it was to England that he would have fled. I have heard the King say that he would have invaded Hanover and laid the country in ashes if Fritz had succeeded in reaching England. He goes in angry dread of the tale of his brutality that Keith may have spread there. It may be that he will not put me to flight, too, lest I should make my way to England, despite the ban, to confirm Keith's tale."

"Do you believe that?"

"Did I say that I believed it? Oh, no. It is not a belief. It is a surmise."

"And you will leave yourself in jeopardy upon no better grounds?"

"I see no signs of jeopardy. But even if I did, I must still remain. One reason is that I could not think of going whilst there is any chance to be of service to Katte. Another is that I have nowhere to go."

"The world is open to you."

"It is. And I may starve in it."

"A man of your rank? Of your attainments?"

"My attainments are no more than those of any gentleman. My rank is not a marketable commodity."

"It is a powerful recommendation. It commands consideration for you. It opens doors that are close-barred against meaner folk."

"All this it does when it is accompanied by the means to maintain it. But an impecunious marquis, seeking employment, is as much a nuisance as any other down-at-heel. No, there is no market for my rank – save one, and that one is no longer open to me. There is many a wealthy burgess who will handsomely fee a nobleman to marry his daughter."

"That is something that you would never do."

"Would I not? Whence the flattering conviction?"

"From my intuitions, if you will. From my knowledge of you."

"It does not go deep enough. I did it once, you see."

"I do not believe it."

"Yet it happened."

"What happened? You may have married a woman of wealth. But you would not marry her because she was wealthy. Of that I am sure."

"I thank you for the conviction," he answered slowly, sadly. "Nevertheless my present troubles are the result of my marriage. But I am not to complain, My wife bought me, and, therefore, had the right to sell me again, I suppose."

"That woman was vile," she said, surprising him by a sudden fierceness, and then she set an impulsive hand upon his arm. "Forgive me if I talk too freely. And forgive me if I have blunderingly stirred sad memories."

"They are sad only as concerning my child. For I have a son, Dorothea. He will be just seven. The loss of him is naturally a grief to me; like the thought of the influences surrounding and forming his young life. For the rest I have no regrets; only the bitterness of disillusion. What else could there be, remembering the avowal implicit in Lady Alverley's action? She would have sent me to the headsman had I not escaped to beg my bread abroad. Alien bread!" he mused, and quoted Dante: " 'How stale it is, and, how it tastes of salt!' Yet I must accept it where I find it. Here in Prussia I may make myself a career as a soldier. My friends have set me on the road to it. Elsewhere there is no such influence to help my beginnings. So I stay, and hope for the best."

"As I do for you." She spoke quietly, thoughtfully. "I should be sorry if you went. You have become..." She broke off.

"I have become...?" he asked.

She laughed without embarrassment. "It is not easy to express. You have become something in the nature of a habit, and a habit is not easily lost. It leaves a want." She laughed again, less freely this time. "This is not elegant. You must take my word for it that there is more grace in the thought than in my expression of it."

"I have no fault to find with the expression. I had begun to fear that I trespassed by coming much too often. I am glad to know myself a habit that leaves a want when broken. I could not desire more."

They had come to a standstill, facing each other, and, for the first time in their acquaintance, her clear eyes were troubled as they met his wistful glance. She lowered them almost at once, and there was a stir of colour in her cheeks.

"I am glad," she said, "that you are so easily content." But the tone of banter did not quite succeed. "Let us go and find my father. He is always glad to see you. He, too, I think, begins to form the habit of you."

Chapter 15

Colonel Frederick

The court martial appointed by the King to consider the evidence which the commissioners had gathered from their examination of the prisoners consisted of three major-generals, three colonels, three lieutenant-colonels, three majors, and three captains, under the presidency of Lieutenant-General von Schulenberg. In addition to the case of the Crown Prince, himself, they were required to sit in judgment upon the officers described as his accomplices: Rittmeister von Katte, Lieutenants Ingersleben and Spaen, and Lieutenant Keith, contumaciously absent,

They came first of all to consider the commissioners' report of the examination of the Crown Prince, an examination which had been conducted along the lines laid down by the King. His Majesty had dictated some two hundred questions that were to be put to the prisoner.

The Prince's spirit had been all but broken during those weeks at Cüstrin, in a confinement so strict that he continued to see no one but the two captains who supervised in silence the brief service of his exiguous meals, and he was allowed no books save the Bible and a volume of psalms, neither of which could be said to conform with his taste in literature. He was reduced to such dejection that for days in succession he did not even trouble to put on his clothes, but remained in bed, dishevelled and unwashed. This last may not have troubled him unduly, for he was never cleanly in his habits.

Nevertheless, when he received the summons to appear before the commissioners, he braced himself at the urgings of his vanity. He reminded himself that he was the Crown Prince of Prussia. He conceived that his rank imposed upon him a definitely prescribed role in this tragi-comedy, and that role, come what might, he would play becomingly.

So he washed himself, combed his yellow hair, and tied it up as best he could, deploring the lack of means to adorn it with those curls which were so offensive to his father. He dressed himself in his crumpled uniform, pulled on his boots, and allowed the two silent captains to conduct him. Their dumbness so enraged him that he promised himself that when he was king he would render them permanently dumb by having their tongues cut out. Under their escort he marched into the chill, bare hall where he was awaited by the four commissioners who had examined Katte. He set a supercilious mask upon the haggardness of his pointed face, and strutted on his toes, his hands clasped behind his back, his body thrusting forward.

Whilst under orders to address him as Colonel Frederick, the commissioners could not forget that he was the Crown Prince, wherefore they stood up to receive him, bowed low, indicated the stool provided for him, and waited for him to take his seat.

For all his inward misgivings he was quick to perceive an advantage in this deferential attitude and he adopted a greater haughtiness of manner. Deliberately he kept them standing, whilst his arrogant glance took time in pondering them: the portly, genial Grumbkow; the red greasy, countenance of the peering, short-sighted Mylius; the lean, dark-faced Gerbett, conspicuous in a red cloak; and the two officers, General Schulz and Major Maxen, stiff, correct products of Frederick William's drill-yard.

At last he sat down, and in a moment Mylius was opening the proceedings, informing the Prince that he was brought there to be examined in the matter of his recent attempt at desertion, and that he was invited in his own interest to deal frankly with the commission and place it in possession of all the facts. Before Mylius had finished his exordium the Prince was interrupting him.

"I am the Crown Prince of Prussia, successor to the crown of which you are the subjects. As such you have no jurisdiction over me, and this is no more than an illegal mummery. I have nothing to say to you."

Grumbkow gently interposed in his soft, melodious voice. "We are here, sir, in loco regis, the representatives of the King's Majesty, empowered and instructed by him to conduct the inquiry along lines which he has himself prescribed. That should dispose of your objection, Colonel Frederick."

"Colonel Frederick!" The Prince looked up sharply, startled. "What does that mean?"

"By his Majesty's orders you are so to be addressed, and in no other way. It is a reduction in rank which we fervently hope may be no more than temporary. But it may serve to show you that for the moment the succession to the crown, which you have urged as your aegis, is in abeyance."

There was in this a dark menace that turned the Prince cold. His prominent eyes dilated, his lips twitched. It was a moment before anger sufficiently revived his courage to enable him to answer.

"That cannot be. I am not only the future King of Prussia, but the future Elector of Brandenburg, and Brandenburg is a fief of the Empire. I cannot be deposed without sentence from the Emperor following upon trial by the Imperial Court. If my father wishes to invoke that, we shall see some pretty things; some very pretty things."

"You do not help your case, sir, by such words," Mylius warned him.

"Let us forget them," said Grumbkow, smoothly tolerant, "and pass on."

"I do not wish you to forget them. They supply reason why I will not admit your right to sit in judgment upon me."

"We are not sitting in judgment," said Mylius. "Judgment is for the King and the court martial which he may appoint to assist him. We are only to examine you, and prepare the evidence."

"Then I do not admit your right to examine me. You waste your time. I will not answer your questions."

Grumbkow intervened again, and the smoothness had now left his voice. "Come, come! This is idle, sir. I have told you – unnecessarily, I think – upon what authority we act."

"And I have told you, also unnecessarily, that I am your Prince. You are not to forget it."

"Our orders are to remember only that you are the accused. Accused of desertion."

"A senseless accusation, as you should know."

"What we know, from the facts in our possession," said Mylius patiently, "is that you intended to desert, and that if desertion did not follow that was only because it was prevented. We do not lack witnesses, and their depositions have been taken: your governor, Colonel von Rochow, the valet Gummersbach, and your accomplices Spaen, Ingersleben and Katte."

"Katte!" the Prince echoed, with a flash of temper. "Has he testified against me?"

Grumbkow had been drumming with his fingers impatiently upon the table. "That is a frivolous question. Rittmeister von Katte was implicated by yourself and examined as a result of that implication, an implication that was in itself an admission of your guilt. In denouncing him as your accomplice, you denounced yourself as the principal. That should be plain to you, Colonel."

It was plain, indeed; plain that his meanness here recoiled upon him; plain that in seeking to profit by accusing Katte, he had merely denounced one who under subsequent inevitable examination must perforce, and despite of loyalty, be a witness against him. Yet, notwithstanding this clear vision, it was not against himself that he raged, but against Katte, and his rage made him venomous.

"I see that you are confusing principal with accomplice." His voice was shrill. "What did Katte testify? Did he admit that it was he who persuaded me to take this step?"

"Ah!" Mylius sucked in his breath. "That is something. Set it down," he bade the notary. "It is a beginning. Now, if you will tell us…"

"I will tell you nothing. I will answer no more of your questions."

"Let me beg you…"

"Beg nothing. Go to the devil."

"So!" Mylius leaned back in his high chair.

Gerbett broke out. "This is most deplorable, most unseemly."

The two officers, stern and wooden-faced, grunted agreement. Mylius' raised hand checked any further expression from them. His eyes were peering at Grumbkow. As if in response to the glance, the minister cleared his throat, and leaned forward. His voice was smooth again, but of a smoothness deliberately overdone.

"It is due to you, Colonel Frederick, to warn you that our explicit orders from his Majesty are to stop at no measures to compel your answers to certain questions he has, himself, dictated. We are not – I say it with deep regret – we are not to hesitate to employ the rack at need."

"The rack! For me?" The Prince bounded to his feet. Beads of sweat gleamed on his pale brow. "You scoundrel, Grumbkow! Only a hangman such as you would dare to threaten me with the tools of his trade."

Grumbkow flushed under the insult; but his voice remained cold. "Again I beg your Highness to discriminate. It is not we who dare. It is his Majesty. Those are his orders, and we, who are but his servants, dare not disobey them. We perform this task with infinite regret and distaste, and we pray, and pray fervently, that you will not constrain us to the lengths I have been compelled to name. I speak for all of us when I say that nothing in the world could pain us more deeply."

White-faced, the arrogance bludgeoned out of him, his frail figure shaken by sudden sobs, he stood and glared at them. "This," he panted, in menace, "is something that I shall never forget. Never.

Never." He sank to his stool again, and sat with his head in his hands, weeping quietly.

Considerately they waited, giving him time to regain command of himself. Then, very quietly, Mylius began again where he had first been interrupted. He recited a reconstruction of the events, and ended by asking the Prince if he agreed with it.

"Yes," the Prince answered shortly, miserably, without looking up.

Mylius passed on to the particular questions dictated by the King. Did he admit that he had written to the King of England, to complain that he was badly treated by his Majesty? He did. Did he not, by begging foreign powers for money, lead them to suppose that his father had none?

"No. Only that my father withheld it from me."

That the answer had been provided for was shown by the next question: "Did not his Majesty tell you once that he would pay your debts, provided you behaved differently and with honest intentions?"

"My intentions have never been other than honest."

"Was it honest to spread abroad this tale of ill-treatment by the King?"

By now the Prince was reassembling the wits that had been scattered by panic. He perceived the trend of the questions, and began to suspect that their aim was not so much to incriminate him as to clear his father's conscience of the sense of his own guilt, of the brutality which had driven his son to plan the escape.

He took courage again from this perception. "Since it was true, as, to my shame, is almost common knowledge, where is the dishonesty?"

Grumbkow intervened. "You say to your shame. Would not your shame have been infinitely increased by a flight that must have filled Europe with a resounding scandal?"

"It is possible. But at least it would have put an end to my intolerable humiliations."

"Is that all that you can urge in your defence?"

The question cowed him again. "That I have done wrong, I must admit. But there has been nothing criminal in my intentions, nor has it been part of my aim to harm the King in any way." He was growing tired physically as well as spiritually. His head ached. He craved rest above all else, and so he sought to make an end. "For what I have done I ask my father to forgive me."

But they had not yet dealt with all the questions his Majesty had set down. There were still some which they well knew should have no place in proceedings of any legality, and which certainly would have had no place in these but for the King's insistence.

"What," asked Mylius, "do you consider that you deserve, and what punishment do you expect?"

"I have said that I cast myself upon the mercy of the King."

"That does not answer the question. What does a man deserve who stains his honour and plots a desertion?"

"I do not consider that I have stained my honour."

"Is not desertion dishonourable? In view of it can you consider that you still deserve to spend your days with men of honour?"

Wearily he answered: "I have expressed deep regret for my offence; I can add nothing to that, and I cannot view it as you insist."

Mylius paused, then sternly fired the next of those questions that had been set down for him: "In view of what has occurred do you still deserve to be King?"

This was to drive the fear deeper into his soul. Yet, striving against it, he contrived to answer with some show of dignity.

"It can hardly be asked of me that I be my own judge."

Relentlessly Mylius continued: "Do you wish your life to be spared? Yes or no?"

"I have already said that I cast myself upon the mercy of the King."

Mylius, however, could not leave it there. He had his orders. "The breach of honour you have committed, whatever your own view, renders you incapable of succeeding to the throne. If, therefore, you wish to save your life, are you prepared to abdicate from the succession in such a manner that your abdication will be confirmed by the whole Empire?"

This was suddenly to shatter the conviction upon which such courage as he possessed was founded. The necessity for confirmation by the Imperial Diet of his abdication had been foreseen, and now, at the price of his life, he was asked to make this abdication in terms that would leave no room for Imperial intervention. Could such terms be found? He must suppose they could.

Livid and shaken, he faced his tormentors abjectly for a long, speechless moment. At length he rallied, reminding himself that at all costs he must play out his part en prince. "I am not," he said "so much in love with life as that." Then, conquered again by fear, he added: "But his Majesty, my father, whose pardon I beg, whose mercy I beseech, cannot wish to treat me with such severity."

On that the examination closed, and he was conducted back to his prison, to resume there the living entombment, the agonizing suspense, until his fate should be decided by the court martial which the King had appointed.

This court martial, having acquainted itself with the evidence elicited by the examining commissioners, as set forth in the protocol of each of the five accused, and having deliberated, passed to sentence.

The case of Keith was clear. He had made it so by his desertion, for which death was the penalty. The court ordered that he be summoned by a roll of drums, and upon failing to appear that he be degraded, his sword broken, and himself hanged in effigy.

Of the parts played by the other two lieutenants, the court took a lenient view in the case of Ingersleben, who was sentenced to six months' imprisonment, but were not so lenient in the case of Spaen, who by procuring the carriage for the Prince's flight had been more directly engaged. He was to be cashiered and suffer two years' imprisonment.

Lenient, too, was the judgment of Katte. Whilst the court found much in his conduct that was reprehensible and merited punishment, yet in extenuation it could be urged that, as was established, he had frequently sought to dissuade the Prince. A term of imprisonment should purge his offence.

On a misty October morning his Majesty sat in his cabinet considering these findings. Grumbkow was in attendance as well as the two aides-de-camp. Over what related to the first three officers Frederick William merely grunted, wasting no words, however savage he might feel towards Keith, who not only had escaped him but might now be defaming him in England.

When, however, he came to the findings relating to Katte and the prince, his temper exploded.

"What's this? Gerechter Herrgott! What have we here? I thought," he raged, "that I had chosen men of honour, who would be mindful of their duty to me, and not forget it in worship of the rising sun; men who would respect only their consciences and the honour of their King. Instead... Look at this, Grumbkow. In spite of my orders that my rascally son should be to them only Colonel Frederick, a deserter, they treat him as the Crown Prince. They decline, as vassals, to pass judgment upon him. They refer the matter back to me. And what have they made of it? His desertion is translated into 'absentierung'; his conduct described as a youthful levity, an escapade. Righteous God! Did I appoint a court martial to sit in judgment upon a youthful escapade? This is gross defiance of my orders.

"And there is more defiance in the case of this Rittmeister von Katte, this other flute-playing rascal. They extenuate – they have the effrontery to extenuate – his offence. Haven't they got it in my son's own depositions that it was Katte who persuaded him to this rascally step? Don't they know that Katte dared to plead in his own defence that I treated my son badly? Doesn't Schulenberg realize that it is nothing less than lèse-majesté for a subject to dare to intervene, with a criticism of his king, between the King and the successor of the King? Yet in spite of this the dolts go on to find in Katte's favour. They stress the fact that although he had promised to assist in this wicked plan, he had fixed neither time nor place, and they pretend that in such a case they must distinguish between the intention and the act.

My God! Was Schulenberg drunk when he came to that conclusion? Send these papers back to him, Baron." He gathered them up, and flung them fiercely across the table. "Order the court martial to sit again, and deliver a proper judgment. A judgment such as I require. Tell Schulenberg that I know law enough and Latin enough to be guided by the motto 'Fiat justitia et pereat mundus'. Let him be guided by it also, or it will be the worse for him."

Alverley had listened to the tirade with an impassivity that betrayed nothing of his inward torment even when enlightenment had been supplied him of the one point that hitherto had been obscure. It had been a shock to learn that the Crown Prince, himself, was Katte's betrayer, aggravating the betrayal by the infamous lie that Katte had persuaded him to attempt the escape. It was something that Alverley could not have believed had he heard it less categorically stated by the King.

A cold rage against the contemptible Prince swept through him, to be mastered, however, for the moment, by his apprehensions for Katte. He perceived that his cousin had irretrievably ruined himself by having dared to urge in his defence that his sympathy with the Prince sprang from the King's ill-treatment of his Highness. Alverley knew enough of human nature to realize that to such a man as Frederick William there could be no such festering wound as that of unflattering truth. What punishment the King would account condign he could not judge, since he had not even the advantage of knowing what was the sentence proposed by the court martial. But that it would be severe he could not doubt.

His heart was heavy in those days, with loathing for the abominable man he served and contempt for himself that he continued in this service, discharging it with mechanical courtesy and always in the hope that his position might yet enable him to be of some avail to his unfortunate cousin.

And then, abruptly, that befell which changed everything for him.

Chapter 16

Flight

Frederick William's was not the only vindictiveness that disturbed the Prussian atmosphere in those days. Gundling, the flabby, drunken President of the Academy, still smarted in the soul of him from his beating and his immersion in the cloacal waters of the Spree, and he would continue to smart until his wounds were salved by the balsam of revenge.

Whilst it would have delighted him to see the ruffians hanged who had committed this outrage upon his bloated, soft-fleshed person, yet he well knew that they were no more than agents. They had been hired to their ghastly office by either the Prince or the lady who entertained him, or perhaps by both. And whether the lady were guilty or not, he would certainly be striking at the Prince – who undoubtedly was guilty – if he struck at her. You perceive here a similarity between the mental operations of those worthy associates, Gundling and Frederick William.

The President's difficulty lay in finding the lady; for he had not been able again to identify the house. Had his wits been less addled by the Hungarian wines in which they were constantly steeped, he must earlier have made those inquiries which were ultimately prompted almost by chance.

There was in the Nikolai Platz a bookseller named Böhme, with whom Gundling had occasional dealings. It was in this shop one day that it belatedly occurred to the President to inquire if knew what ladies in the neighbouring Nikolaistrasse were given to music, and were performers on the clavichord.

Böhme thrust up his wig, the better to scratch his head, and considered. "There is Frau Schatz, at the corner of the Square, who gives music lessons to young ladies of the nobility. And there's Frau Müller, who plays the organ at St Nicholas; she's next door to Armstadt, the glover. And then there's the young Fräulein Ritter, Pastor Ritter's girl. But we mustn't talk about her, gnädiger Herr Praesident." Böhme sniggered. "She's a friend of Prince Frederick's. He's often at her house, they say. Goes there to play the flute – he, he! – and God knows what else."

Böhme's leer was lewdly eloquent. But it went unheeded by Gundling. The President was trembling with excitement. "Potzteufel! What do you tell me? Often at her house! And playing the flute! Du lieber Gott!"

Gundling's quest was at an end, and he was furiously blaming himself for not having earlier thought of seeking information in this quarter.

Betimes next morning he was at the Schloss, backing his prayer for audience by the announcement that he brought information of the first importance.

The King had had a bad night, following upon yesterday's Tabagie, in the course of which he had drunk too much. He was being tormented in body by an attack of the gout and in soul by the wailings and plaints of the Queen and by what he accounted the mutinous conduct of Schulenberg and his court martial. So Gundling found his Majesty in savage mood.

He was still dealing with the day's correspondence. Two secretaries stood receiving his petulant instructions. Alverley lounged in a window embrasure, awaiting the end of the business, and marvelling that a man should dissipate so much energy in unnecessary ill-humour.

"Be brief," he sourly admonished Gundling. "I have to go to Potsdam."

The President smirked, lisped and washed his hands in the air. There was a flush on his flabby face, a glitter in his red-rimmed, watery eyes.

"May it please your Majesty, I have discovered the siren whose music decoyed his Highness."

It was a moment before Majesty's mind absorbed the fellow's meaning. Then there was a wicked eagerness in the long, interrogative intake of breath. "Ah–h?"

"The strumpet's name, Majesty, is Dorothea Ritter. The daughter of Pastor Ritter."

Alverley, who from one of the windows, was watching the changing of the guard in the courtyard, span round on his heel with an involuntary start, his face set. But Gundling was too intent to observe the movement, and the King's back was turned upon his aide-de-camp.

"So! Pastor Ritter has a daughter, has he?"

"Who lured the Crown Prince regularly to her house…to make music. I leave your Majesty to surmise what else they did." He giggled as he spoke, and Alverley, eyeing him in disgust, accounted him the very incarnation of Silenus.

"Grosser Gott!" Majesty's fist crashed down on the table. "You are sure – quite sure?"

"Should I venture otherwise to trouble your Majesty? Oh, there is no possibility of error." And he advanced in evidence the information gleaned from Böhme the bookseller.

"So! So! Now we know why he bought diamond bracelets. And I suppose that all Berlin knows of this." Majesty groaned. "Is there no shame that this dissolute, godless son of mine will spare me?"

His gross bulk sagged over the writing-table, on which he had set an elbow, resting his head on his hand. Thus he remained, in silent brooding, his eyes narrowed, his lips tight, until Katzenstein arrived with word that his Majesty's carriage waited with the escort.

He nodded gloomily. "In a moment. In a moment. You can go, Gundling. You'll find the Staatsrat Klinte waiting in the ante-room.

Send him in to me. By God! I'll make an example of this wench. I'll send her somewhere where sirens won't feel disposed to sing."

Then he dismissed the secretaries. "Here, take these papers. They'll have to wait. I'm too bedevilled now. Almighty! To be so plagued and vexed."

They withdrew as Klinte, the State Councillor, came in, a stocky, keen-faced man in a yellow wig. He bowed low to the King, and nodded pleasantly to Katzenstein and Alverley.

"Pay attention, Klinte," snapped the King. "You'll send me a sergeant's guard to Pastor Ritter's house in the Nikolaistrasse at once with a warrant to arrest his trull of a daughter. You'll have her lodged in the town gaol until I send you further orders."

He set his hands on the table to heave himself up. Then with a gasp sat down again. "Ai! Curse this gout. As if I had not enough to plague me! As if the Lord God did not punish me enough in giving me a son without religion, morals, or even decency. By God, Katzenstein, the worst disservice you ever did me was when you prevented me from running a sword through him. A vile seducer who has been whoring with this daughter of that doddering old fool Ritter."

Out of his deep devotion to the Prince, Katzenstein was surprised into an exclamation of protest. "Sire!"

"Well? What? Do you doubt it?" roared the King.

"I cannot judge, sire. I do not know the evidence."

Then Alverley spoke, uttering his indignation. His face was grey. "There is none yet. At present it is no more than the tale of a drunkard."

Majesty slewed round in his chair to stare at him in furious amazement. "Is that the way to speak of the Worshipful President of the Academy?"

"With submission, sire, the President's way was not the way to speak of the Crown Prince of Prussia, of an intercourse that may well be innocent and of a lady who may well be virtuous."

"Virtuous!" The King's face was empurpling. "Do virtuous women in her station entertain crown princes? Do they receive diamond bracelets from crown princes?"

"It is not impossible, sire."

Majesty vented angry scorn in laughter. "Not impossible! Righteous God! Where have you lived, Margrave? In a cloister? Not impossible? Perhaps not. But highly improbable. And, anyway, we'll make certain. It shall never be said that I want for justice; that I act rashly upon assumption. That is not at all my way. Attend to me, Klinte. When you've lodged this girl of Ritter's in gaol, you'll send a surgeon and a midwife to examine her, and then report to me. You shall have my final orders for her disposal after that. And meanwhile, chaste or not, the girl shall be taught not to practise her blandishments on the Prince of Prussia. Have her publicly whipped tomorrow morning. If Madam finds the weather chill for stripping, the whips will warm her. Let her be whipped first before the Town Hall, then before her father's house, before the Cathedral and before the Zeughaus. That should suffice as a beginning. Afterwards I shall probably have her shut up for life at Spandau. Such women must be sent where they can do no harm. You can go."

The Councillor's face betrayed something of his distaste for the loathsome task imposed upon him. Not for him, however, to argue with Majesty. He bowed himself out.

Behind the King's back Alverley and Katzenstein exchanged a look of sheer horror.

Then his Majesty stirred again, and Katzenstein stepped forward to assist him to rise. Leaning on the Baron's arm, and further supporting himself on his cane, he limped and grunted his way to the door.

Alverley followed, walking like an automaton. His dominant thought was that, cost what it might, these bestialities must not be perpetrated upon Dorothea. Merely to think of that pure, delicate body subjected to treatment that would be brutal if administered to a harlot's was to be taken with physical nausea. This, as it happened, was to help Alverley to his ends whilst still his wits were beating themselves frenziedly against the problems of how to avail her. That rescue her he must if it cost him his life was a thought as natural as the drawing of breath.

His Majesty had entered his carriage, and the aides-de-camp were turning to the horses which two troopers held for them, when Katzenstein, chancing to look at his companion, was startled by the haggard greyness of his face.

"Charles!" he ejaculated. "Are you ill?"

"Do I look ill?"

"Worse than that." With a hand on Alverley's shoulder, the older man's tone was one of affectionate concern. "Are you fit to ride? Shall I say a word to his Majesty?"

"No, no." Alverley needed time to think. He must do nothing upon impulse.

Already the forward half of the escort, in blue and silver, was trotting out of the gates, two leading trumpeters blaring a flourish to clear the way for the royal coach-and-six.

"It is nothing," said Alverley. "A weakness I must conquer." With a smile that made his white face ghastlier, he turned to take the reins, mounted, and wheeled his horse into place at Katzenstein's side behind the coach.

With the remainder of the escort following, they went jingling out of the courtyard, across the bridge, and wheeled into the Zeughaus Platz at the head of the avenue leading to the Potsdam Gate.

By the time they reached the Arsenal, Alverley's resolve had shaped itself. Taking advantage of Katzenstein's supposed discovery of indisposition in him, he spoke to his companion.

"I fear you are right, Katze. I am not in case to go on. I'll fall out and rest a moment here at the Brandenburger Hof."

"That is wise," the Count approved. "And no need to hurry. If you do not overtake us before Potsdam I'll explain to his Majesty. I hope all will be well with you."

"Oh, I think so." He touched his hat in salute and swung aside, letting the escort trot past him. Then he walked his horse into the courtyard of the great posting-house.

An ostler came forward with the alacrity due to an officer of the royal party.

"I require," said Alverley, "a post chaise and pair as soon as may be."

"Zu befehl, gnädiger Herr. Dare I ask where it is going?"

"To Potsdam. On the King's business. You are required to make haste."

Fifteen minutes seemed to him an hour; but at last the chaise rolled out of the coach-house, the post-boy buttoning his jacket as he rode.

Alverley, who had waited without dismounting, led the way at a sharp trot over the bridges spanning first the narrow and then the wider arm of the sluggish Spree, swung right along a narrow street, driving the wayfarers against the walls, crossed the Nikolai Platz with the carriage trundling after him, and brought up at Pastor Ritter's house.

In an instant he was out of the saddle, tossing the reins to the post-boy and hammering on the door. It was opened at once by the broad bosomed Theresa, her jolly countenance disfigured, her apple cheeks besmeared with tears.

"Your mistress?" cried Alverley.

"Gott sei uns gnädig! The Fräulein has been taken...arrested... the soldiers came..."

Alverley turned cold. He cursed Klinte's diligence. And then, espying the tall, bowed figure of the pastor in the gloom of the passage, he strode past Theresa, and went in.

"What is this?" the afflicted cleric hailed him. "In God's name, what is this? What does it mean? I always feared that no good would come of receiving the Prince's visits. But this... Just Heaven! This passes everything. This is wicked. Monstrous. To be publicly whipped like a common harlot! My Dorothea! A tender, innocent child of eighteen!" He clutched his head in anguish.

"So! Klinte has not only been prompt; he has been communicative." Alverley bowed his head. "Let me think, sir. Let me think. I came to save her. I have brought a carriage, so that you might take her away at once, beyond their reach. But Councillor Klinte in his zeal has been too quick for me. What now?" he demanded. "What now? What is there we can do?"

"Why, what I intended. I am going to Potsdam at once: to the King. They tell me he has gone there. He shall give me reason. He must. They have told me what else he intends out of his foul suspicions. But it shall not be. God will not permit that a pure and innocent virgin be so abused."

"The calendar of saints is full of virgin martyrs, sir."

"In other times, sir." The pastor was impatient. "These are enlightened days."

"Not at the Court of Prussia, by what I have seen."

"I shall know how to plead. I am a father, and I have ever been a faithful servant of the Gospel. The Almighty will prompt me. The King shall hear reason from me."

"That madman!" Alverley scoffed. "He doesn't know the language. Sir, you don't understand the King's unspeakable mind. He cares nothing for your daughter. It is the Prince whom he desires to mortify and shame. Himself and his own brutality that he seeks to justify. To that end he uses Dorothea as he is using others: Katte, Keith, Spaen, Ingersleben, Duhan, even the Princess Wilhelmina. How can you hope, then, to prevail with such a maniac acting from policy?"

The deepening pain in the pastor's eyes showed the yielding of his mind. "What then, my God? What then?"

"What I came to enjoin. You must take your daughter beyond the King's reach."

"But she is in prison already." The voice rose in exasperation.

"I must get her out. Leave me to try. Pray that I accomplish it. Whilst I am about it, prepare for the journey. Get together your valuables, your money and what else is of immediate need to yourself and Dorothea. Make haste. Let Theresa pack such things as Dorothea will need so that you are ready to set out as soon as I return."

Already he was turning away when the old man seized his arm. "Set out, do you say? But where am I to go?"

"Anywhere out of the dominions of the King of Prussia."

"But my work here!" the pastor plaintively protested. "How am I to live away from Berlin? It is unimaginable."

Alverley was stern. "What is unimaginable is that your child should be martyred. For the rest, you are a churchman. At least have faith in what you preach that the Lord will provide. I cannot stay to argue, sir."

He was gone, followed by quavering supplications which it is fortunate that he did not stay to heed, for he had not overstated Klinte's swift zeal.

He came briskly into Klinte's office on the ground floor of the Schloss, and demanded to see the Staatsrat at once, announcing himself as from the King. In a moment he was ushered into the Councillor's presence.

Klinte rose to receive him. "At your orders, Monsieur le Marquis."

Alverley was stiffly formal. "In the matter of the girl Ritter, it will not now be necessary for you to take action. His Majesty has considered further and has decided himself to examine her in the first instance. My orders are to conduct her to Potsdam. That is all, sir."

The Councillor of State looked perplexed. "But action has already been taken. Not only is the girl already in prison, but Hochbauer, the surgeon, and a midwife have this moment left me, to carry out his Majesty's instructions." His solemnity was overspread by a complacent smile. "I do not dare to permit myself delays in the execution of the King's wishes."

"Neither do I. Therefore, my dear Councillor, you will oblige me with an order on the prison. I will then do my part."

"At once." Klinte sat down, and took up a pen. "I trust that his Majesty's questioning of the girl may remove the need for the further measures he had in mind."

"The hope does you credit, sir. I permit myself to share it; for it must give pain to Prince Frederick to have this lady subjected to such indignities."

"Indeed I understand." The Councillor sighed, dusted his writing with pounce, rose and handed the sheet to the aide-de-camp.

Within ten minutes Alverley was drawing rein before the gloomy portal of the penitentiary, the carriage ever at his heels.

The head gaoler put on his spectacles to read the order.

"The Fräulein Ritter again! She keeps us busy. The Herr Doktor Hochbauer is with her now. He has just gone to her."

Alverley repressed a shiver of disgust.

"Then we will hasten so as to save him trouble. His offices are no longer necessary." His voice was firm and hard, and for all that his pulses raced, his countenance was that of the emotionless officer on duty.

He hurried the too-leisurely gaoler along a vaulted gallery, wherein presently he caught the echo of voices: first a woman's whose words were inaudible; then a man's, loud, clear, stern: "Idle to protest, Fräulein. We are in our duty, by the King's orders. Resistance will only increase your distress."

The gaoler had reached a door, and he paused there to grin over his shoulder at the officer. "The Fräulein is being coy, and..."

"Open, you dog."

"Almighty!" The gaoler was taken aback by the sudden fierceness. He made haste to fling wide the door.

Within the bare, narrow cell a small man and a large woman turned sharply as Alverley crossed the threshold. Beyond them, her shoulders touching the wall, in an attitude of fierce defiance, her face deathly, her eyes wild, a hand to her heaving breast, stood Dorothea. She wore a simple, high-necked gown of sapphire blue; she was without hat, but a shawl of purple silk draped her shoulders, its ends entwined about either arm.

At sight of Alverley her eyes seemed to dilate still further, the heave of her breast increased, her breath came in dry, hard sobs.

He made haste to end her horrible suspense. He spoke sharply, rapidly. "You will be Doctor Hochbauer. I have to tell you that your services are no longer required here. His Majesty has changed his mind." He stood aside, and motioned them out.

"My instructions are from the Herr Staatsrat Klinte," the surgeon objected.

"This cancels them." Alverley thrust his order under the man's nose.

Hochbauer scanned the order, and bowed. "Perfectly. The Fräulein will be relieved. My duty to you, Herr Rittmeister." He bowed again. "Come, Frau Schacht." He led his female companion out.

There was a gasping sob from Dorothea. Her arms sank inertly to her sides, and she swayed a little in that sudden release from unutterable tension.

Under the eyes of the gaoler, Alverley maintained a stiff, military formality. "Be good enough to accompany me, Fräulein."

She inclined her head, and kept it lowered after that, looking neither to right nor to left, faltering a little at first in her stride as she paced beside him along the stone gallery and out to the waiting carriage.

Leaving the order of release with the gaoler, Alverley handed her into the chaise, closed the door, and mounted. "Follow me," he bade the postilion, and again led the way to the Nikolaistrasse.

In the chaise Dorothea sat quietly weeping, in reaction from the abominable horror that had confronted her. Thus Alverley found her when he opened the door of the chaise.

"Poor child," he murmured. "But come now. It is finished. Your father is waiting to take you to safety, beyond the reach of these savages. Come."

In the open doorway Theresa stood waiting to receive her, and enfolded her to her generous bosom. Alverley thrust both these weeping women into the house, and followed.

"The pastor? Where is he? There is no time to lose."

Theresa showed him a countenance pale with misgiving. "He is gone, sir. Gone to Potsdam."

"Gone to Potsdam!" Alverley stood frozen. "Gone to Potsdam!" he repeated. "God help us! The madman!"

"It's what I feared," wailed Theresa, her misgivings changed to certainty. "I begged him not to go; I begged him to wait, at least, until your worship returned. But he would not listen. He swore that righteousness, must prevail; that he could not become a wanderer among strangers at his age. The King must do him right. A righteous God would not permit an iniquity. That is how he talked. He was gone five minutes after your worship left."

Alverley clenched teeth and fists in desperation. The pastor's crazy rashness wrecked all his plans and left him nonplussed. "Fool! Fool! What could he hope for at the hands of such a man as the King? As likely as not he'll find himself gaoled for his pains. And meanwhile what are we to do? What is to become of Fräulein Dorothea? Every moment wasted here increases her danger."

Dorothea, more and more mystified, was, nevertheless, by now bravely mistress of herself. "I don't understand," she said. "If my release was ordered…"

"It was not ordered," Alverley interrupted, harsh in his impatience. "It was procured by a trick, a lie. I told the Staatsrat that I was commanded by the King to conduct you to Potsdam. That's how I obtained the order for your release and delivery to me." To answer her wide-eyed amazement he added fiercely: "There was no other way."

"There was," she answered quietly. "You could have left me to my fate."

"Could I?" he glared at her. "Could I leave you to be stripped and whipped in public to satisfy a madman's beastliness? Could I? What am I, then?"

To his wonder a wistful little smile broke through the fear and sorrow of her white face. "Do I need to tell you?" Then the smile vanished. "And for this you have ruined yourself?"

"That's no matter." Anger was still his dominant emotion. "What matters is that this should not have been done in vain. In spite of your father's crazy action."

"My father must have thought only of saving you from this sacrifice. He owed you that."

But Alverley in his anger would admit no excuses for the pastor's folly. "He did not even know of it. He did not know what I intended. He lacks even that justification. But we waste thought and time. What remains is to make sure that you are not rearrested. Since your father has gone off on this senseless quest, you'll have to travel without him."

"Travel? Travel whither?"

"No matter whither, so long as it is out of Prussian territory."

"Go abroad? Without my father? That is impossible."

"What is impossible is that you should stay here."

"But if I go, I go only from one evil to another."

"But at least to a lesser one; for nothing could be as horrible as what awaits you here. You do not yet know the extent of it."

"I think I do. They did not spare my feelings."

He shook his head. "They could not tell you all, for they don't know it. These indignities and cruelties are no more than a beginning. That horrible man Frederick William spoke of shutting you up in Spandau for life, and God alone knows what else he may have in mind. He stops at nothing to vent the foul spite that fills him. You must go."

"Alone? How can I? It is impossible." She sank to a short bench that was set against the wall. "Oh, God help me! God help me!"

Alverley had found a solution. "Listen to me. You cannot wait here for your father; but he can follow you. It must be so. Whilst you get your things together – no more than enough for immediate needs – I will write a line to await his return, telling him to rejoin you over the border, in Saxony; that because it's the nearest frontier. And not too close to it. Let us say at …Wittenberg. That's it. Come, Dorothea, make haste. Take her, Theresa, and help her to make ready. We must be well away before my trick is discovered."

She checked in the act of departing. "We?" she echoed. "You say 'we'?"

"Of course. As far as Wittenberg you shall have my escort."

She looked at him from moist eyes. "Oh, my friend, I could not permit it. You have done too much for me already, God knows."

Impatience blazed from him. No trace remained of his habitual imperturbability. "Were you supposing I could remain in Brandenburg after this?"

That reminder of where he stood, which was meant to conquer her hesitation, only served to deepen her distress. "Dear God! I was forgetting. Oh, why, why have you done this? I have no claim upon you that you should put yourself in peril for me. How can I possibly accept it?"

"It is not a gift that you are asked to accept, but a situation. I am committed. The thing is done, and cannot now be undone. Are we to stand here talking until we are caught? Pray think of me. The chaise is waiting. I must be on my travels for my own sake. And whilst I'm about it I'll carry you to Wittenberg, whither your father can follow us. Here, Theresa, take her before she ruins us both. Make haste."

This was the tone to take, and Theresa's response at least was prompt. "Come, schätzli, come. The Lord Margrave is right. You must not delay." She set a powerful arm about the girl's slender body and, whilst Dorothea still hung balanced between the horrors in store for her if she remained and the dread of a leap into the unknown, carried her off to make ready, leaving Alverley to write his note to her father. In this he bade the pastor follow at once to Wittenberg, and seek them there at the Einsiedler Inn where they would await him. It was a hostelry on the outskirts which Alverley remembered from his passage through the town in the course of the recent royal progress.

Theresa's concern and energy made short work of the preparations. She brought Dorothea back to him, cloaked and hooded, almost as soon as the note was written. He sealed it and left it with Theresa for delivery to the pastor immediately on his return.

Then he took up the small portmantle she had packed for her mistress, and, stifling Dorothea's last misgivings, swept her out and into the chaise.

It rolled away, with Alverley riding ahead, leaving the afflicted Theresa staring after it from the doorway, her great bosom shaken by sobs that had been bravely restrained until their shedding would trouble none but herself.

Chapter 17

The Fugitives

Next to the fact that Alverley did not know where to go or how to live once out of Prussian service, his only regret in quitting Brandenburg was concerned with Katte. He had nourished the hope that sooner or later his attendance upon the King would supply an opportunity to be of assistance to his cousin. To depart now, whilst Katte's fate hung in the balance, savoured to him of desertion. Against this feeling all that he could set was the probability that his hope was a vain one, that his absence would make no difference, and that, after all, however unreasonably vindictive the King might be, Katte's case was in the hands of a court martial of honourable men who would never permit themselves to be driven quite beyond the bounds of equity. Upon some such reasoning he gave himself up entirely to his more immediate concern for Dorothea.

From Berlin he boldly took the road to Potsdam, which was perhaps less bold than appears. The hunt would hardly be up just yet, and if he did chance to be seen in the streets of Potsdam by any who knew him, his presence there would be too natural to excite notice. As a starting-point for the real flight, none could be better, since it was the last place in which pursuers would seek to pick up a trail. His true reason, however, for going that way lay in the hope of meeting the returning Pastor Ritter, and delivering his daughter at once into his care.

But when in the dusk of that October evening, deepened by the mists that were rising from the Havel, they came to the gates of Potsdam, there had been no such meeting. From this he supposed that the pastor must still be at the palace.

He led the way straight to Potsdam's posting-house, the Adler, demanded a room in which his sister could be private for an hour or so, and there bade Dorothea lie close until he returned.

Next he sought the postmaster. He and his sister, he explained, were in haste to reach Rathenow, where another sister lay ill. With night descending and twenty miles to go, the journey was to be made only on horseback. Could the postmaster provide him with a horse and a lady's saddle? The postmaster possessed the very thing, a tall grey, strong as a charger and gentle as a gazelle; but it was for sale, not for hire. He conducted the worshipful Rittmeister to the stables, and at twenty thalers a bargain was struck, with an additional three thalers for the saddle.

Alverley left the Adler, to go afoot to the palace. This course was attended by some slight risk, but must be faced. All that he possessed, a matter of between two and three hundred thalers, was in his quarters there. On the staircase by which he approached them he came face to face with Katzenstein descending.

"Ah, Charles! Here already! You are better, then?"

"Thank you, Katze. It was nothing. I am quite recovered. Have I been missed?"

"Only when we arrived. I explained, but faith, I need scarcely have troubled. The King was in such torment from the gout by then that he had little thought for anything else. He has been screaming like a baby and as savage as a tiger, dealing curses and blows to everyone within reach. Pastor Ritter was here this afternoon, clamouring for audience. It was not a happy moment. The King sent him packing with a threat to teach him to bring up his daughter as a harlot. Oh, we've been merry. But at least you need not show yourself tonight. His physician is all the company he craves."

Alverley murmured civilities and passed on. At least he was relieved by this assurance that the way lay open for his easy departure. If only the pastor had been less cursedly obstinate matters would be easier still. As it was, Alverley must keep to his plan of conducting Dorothea to Wittenberg, and trust that nothing would occur to delay her father in following.

He reached his quarters, dismissed the orderly whom he found in charge there, and went briskly about the business that brought him: he packed his money into a broad, hollow belt, fashioned for the purpose, changed from his guardsman's blue and red into a plain brown riding-coat, and covered this with a blue military cloak. His boots and leather breeches were not very different from those that any traveller might wear.

Back at the Adler he found the tall grey already saddled; but whilst eager to be away from Potsdam, yet the haste was not so desperate that they could not think of their physical comforts. So before seeking Dorothea, he ordered meat and wine to be served in the room where she waited.

She sprang up to greet him. "At last! How long you have been. I was growing afraid for you."

He smiled reassurance. "It has seemed long. But all is well. Your father has returned to Berlin. He was sent empty away, as I knew he would be. But at least we know him free to follow us, and that is all that matters. I have a horse for you, and as soon as we have eaten we'll set out."

She protested that she could not eat; that anxiety was choking her. But Alverley was persuasive. "There's neither strength nor courage in an empty stomach, and you'll need both. We have twenty miles to ride before we sleep. I would spare you the saddle if I dared. But to travel post is to leave a trail, and there may be pursuit."

"Must you be excusing yourself?" she wondered.

"Naturally, since I put you to discomfort."

"And I have been so swaddled that I cannot bear any. You have a brave opinion of me."

"The bravest, or I should not ask you to ride through the night."

"Is it for your benefit or mine that we ride?"

"For mine as well as yours. Don't forget that I am a deserter now."

"Which I have made you. Am I likely, do you think, to forget it? Or do you suppose that I could have accepted your sacrifice if I had known of it before you were committed by your actions?"

He laughed. "I take leave to be glad that you could not help yourself."

"But why? Why? Why should you do this for me?"

He looked at her, and the bitter lines of his mouth disappeared in a smile of infinite gentleness. "Say that I was weary of Berlin and its smells, and wearier still of the boorish King of Prussia, glad of any good reason to be gone."

Her lip trembled. "And I am a good reason?"

"I should look in vain for a better. But here is supper."

A waiter had come to set down a laden tray, and Alverley fell to work upon a rich Westphalian ham. He set some slices on a plate for her; poured wine from a black flagon; and whilst he played the host with insistent grace, she forced herself to eat and drink, and so won his approval.

When they were in the saddle, he was at pains to let postmaster, grooms and ostler know that they were riding to Rathenow.

"It's a plausible destination," he explained to her as they ambled gently down the street. "If it is reported to the King he will assume that we are making for Hanover."

As if they were, indeed, taking the road to Rathenow, they rode past the Old Market, and then followed awhile the left bank of the Havel, which flowed like a river of silver under the rising moon. A breeze had swept away the mists of sunset, and the night air struck chilly.

Not until Potsdam lay some three miles behind them did Alverley judge it safe to change their course. They crossed the river by a stone bridge and headed south, with Treuenbrietzen, on the borders of Saxony, for their destination. At first, being on a by-road winding through wooded country, with here and there a gleam of water, they progressed slowly, as if groping their way. But once they had debouched on to the highway they rode at a brisk round pace that devoured the miles. Through village and hamlet they clattered, following a road that Alverley remembered from the recent royal progress in which he had ridden it.

So well did they make up for lost time that by ten o'clock, three hours after leaving Potsdam, their hoofs rattled over the cobbles of Treuenbrietzen and came to a halt in the yard of the town's best inn, the Preussische Krone. They represented themselves as French, Monsieur and Mademoiselle Corbeau, on their way to Leipzig.

Betimes on the following morning, with none to stay them, they peacefully resumed their journey, and crossed the border into Saxony, shaking, as Alverley lightly commented, the dust of Prussia from their hooves.

Dorothea's humour, however, was not light. For her this flight remained, as she had said, the lesser of the evil choices that had been forced upon her. She rode into the unknown in a mood of dark foreboding, from which Alverley exerted himself to deliver her.

"What need you fear?" he asked her. "Saxony is a land on which the muses smile, and Dresden is the Athens of the north. A scholar of your father's worth will thrive there as he never would have thriven in Berlin. He will not want for pupils or for honour, and he will come to bless the evil that drove him out of Prussia."

Gradually such arguments, the optimism of youth, the comforting knowledge that they were beyond pursuit, and the pleasant, fertile, autumn-tinted lands, gay in the October sunshine, so wrought upon her that when towards the hour of dinner they were in sight of the spires of Wittenberg, her gloom was conquered.

They rode into that Mecca of Lutheranism by the Elster Thor, beyond which, some two hundred years before, the great reformer had burnt the Papal Bull, and they found the dusty, ill-paved streets busy with country folk, for this was Thursday, a market-day in Wittenberg. The Market Place, which they had to cross, was thronged with lanky-haired men in round hats and short jackets or smocks and apple-cheeked women in voluminous petticoats. Many were there to buy; others had brought their produce to the town, their cheese and hams and cereals. There were stalls and carts piled with vegetables and with fruits newly harvested and kegs of cider newly brewed. Through that press and clamour and clatter of wooden-soled shoes Alverley and Dorothea walked their horses, respectfully greeted by these rustics, who recognized their quality.

The Einsiedler Inn, to which they made their way, lay to the south, near the bridge, just outside the massive fortified walls of the city, with a pleasant garden running down to the waters of the Elbe.

Monsieur and Mademoiselle Corbeau announced themselves as Huguenots on a pilgrimage to this city of Luther, where they might remain for a few days. The announcement earned them a reception of cordial solicitude from the host of that comfortable, unpretentious house.

Although late in the year the weather was so fine that after they had rid themselves of the dust of travel, they sat down to dine in the open, by the river, under a pergola of vine which had yielded up its fruit and whose leaves were already reddening. There were fat trout from the Elster, a roast of the famous veal of Wittenberg, newly-baked rye bread, which they found palatable, an apple cake, and a sharp cheese of the district that quickened the flavour of the new cider, sweet and cool, of that autumn's brewing. At the end, in a mood of content, Alverley called for a pipe, sat back, and gazed dreamily at the broad river.

"Can the world offer anything better than this?" he wondered, and made philosophy. "Man rages through life, vexing his soul in quest of a happiness that lies easily within reach in sweet and simple things."

She mocked him. "You express no more than satisfied appetite. It's a mood that will pass with digestion. Then you'll discover that there are finer things in life than veal and cheese."

"Is that all you perceive here? Fie, Dorothea. There is this garden with its late roses, the sunshine, the flowing stream, and, best of all, this sweet companionship. Are these things of no account?"

She avoided his gaze. Scarcely perceptible was the deepening of colour in her cheeks. "Certainly of more account since dining than before." And with a little laugh she changed the subject. "Is it possible, do you think, for my father to arrive tonight?"

"Possible. But not likely. And why be impatient?"

"Do you ask?"

He sighed. "There's not the need. Impatience is natural in you, I suppose; just as it is natural for me not to share it."

"How?" Her brows were knit.

"Consider. When your father arrives my task is done. I go my ways, and it is unlikely that our paths will ever cross again. Can I be eager to hail the end of as dear a friendship as I have known?"

Her glance softened. Her lip was tremulous as she answered. "I am glad to hear you call it that."

"Did you doubt it?"

"I should not after what you have done. There could be no greater proof of it. Yet I must doubt my own deserts. I am of no account: the simple daughter of a simple churchman; whilst you belong to the beau monde, walking as an equal with princes."

He was frankly amused. "And whither has this walking led me? Into penniless exile. A fine commendation."

"It does not diminish your quality."

"Nor is yours diminished by being, as you say, the daughter of a simple churchman. You are fine lady enough for any man." More lightly he added: "And your case is much like mine. It is as a result of walking with princes that you, too, are now in flight."

"Alas! How right was my father in his early misgivings."

"I shared them, you'll remember. A prince's breath, as I offended by telling you, can bear a withering blight. Yet but for Monsieur Fritz I should never have known you."

"Which would certainly have been to your advantage."

"Never say that, Dorothea."

"Not even when faced with these consequences?"

"I could conceive none happier. Which is why I am without impatience of your father's arrival."

"This...this is but transient," she reminded him. "A peaceful interlude. I look beyond it, and I am afraid."

"I have told you that all will be well."

"For me. Perhaps. But what of you? You may pay too dearly for your chivalry."

"Dismiss the fear. I could have left the service of King Frederick William in no better cause. If there is a debt between us, it is from me to you, for having set a glamour about a course of action that would otherwise have been merely self-interested."

"It's a point of view, of course," she mocked. "But I am not likely to adopt it. To me you will always remain the most generous friend I have known."

"It will be something to be so remembered since in your life I am doomed to be a memory only."

This produced a silence of some gloom, at the end of which she asked him: "What are your plans? Where shall you go from here?"

"I've scarcely given it thought. No doubt I could still find friends in Rome, at the court of the Pretender – that is the Stuart King of England. But I was there before, and left it because already there were too many courtiers there with empty pockets. I have vaguely thought of France, where Jacobites are well regarded. But there is so little that I can take to market. Having been born a marquis I was brought up a gentleman, which is to say that I have all the useless accomplishments. I am not even a musician, like Katte, or a Greek scholar and teacher of philosophy like your father. But somehow I'll contrive."

He laughed at the gravity with which she was regarding him, set down his pipe, and rose. "We are pilgrims, remember. We should be seeing the sights of this home of theology, visiting the Augusteum and Melancthon's house and what other shrines there be. Will you walk, Dorothea?"

"Willingly."

So forth they went to wander in the town, to view the Augustine monastery where Luther had turned rebel against Rome, the Rathaus with its relics of the great reformer, the Schloss Kirche on whose doors he had nailed his denunciation of Papal indulgences, and much else that this busy university town could show its visitors. And in the course of their wandering, Dorothea recovered her normal bright spirits, and the assurance that there would be a happy issue to this queer adventure.

Chapter 18

Wittenberg

Tomorrow slowly crawled by, each successive hour of it bringing Dorothea an increasing anxiety. She could not be induced to leave the inn lest her father should arrive in her absence, and she started up at every hoof-beat that betokened an arrival. Thus the day wore itself out in vain waiting, and supper-time arrived.

"It will be for tomorrow," Alverley reassured her when they sat down to their evening meal in the dark-panelled room above-stairs, and in pretended light-heartedness he set himself again to do the honours of the table.

She sighed and smiled in one, and out of consideration for him made a gallant show of responding to his optimism. Thus until a growing clatter of hoofs once more brought her, breathless, to her feet. "This may be he."

Alverley shook his head. "Too numerous a company, I think."

Nevertheless he rose and stepped to the window, to look out into the twilight. After a moment, she caught the sound of his quickly indrawn breath, and when he turned again the alteration in his face filled her with dread.

"What is it?" she asked.

He took time to answer, and in the pause his eyes seemed to grow larger as they stared at her. "An outrage," he answered grimly. "Prussian dragoons here in the Electorate of Saxony. Frederick

William seems to have as little respect for frontiers as for the decencies."

"Are you...are you sure?" she asked, a hand on her breast.

"Sure. There are six troopers and an officer. I saw his face in the light from the inn door, and recognized him. A drunken, swaggering bully named Stein."

"Do you suppose?..." She broke off. "But of course. What else is to suppose? They have come after us." Fearfully her eyes questioned him.

"The last thing upon which I could have reckoned." He spoke with quiet bitterness. "I was sure we had left no trail; so sure that being out of Prussian territory we could not be followed. But now..." He broke off. His composure left him, and he grew fiercely vehement. "They do not take you back to Berlin. They shall not."

The perception of what this would mean, the recollection of the insult and horror from which she so narrowly escaped, wrung from her the cry: "I would sooner die."

"As I certainly will before it happens," Alverley assured her.

A servant entered with candles. One branch he set upon the dining table, the other upon a console that was ranged against the wall. He was turning to depart again, when Alverley sharply stayed. him. "Wait, Franz!"

A memory had stirred in him, bringing inspiration in its train. There were writing materials on the console. He stepped to it quickly, found a sheet, and took up a pen. He wrote briskly, standing, whilst Franz, drawn by the clatter and jingle below, moved to the window to look out.

"Almighty!" he muttered. "Here be company. Troopers they be. They'll be needing me."

"A moment," Alverley detained him. He had folded, and was superscribing the note.

The house rang with a sound of heavy steps, a jingle of spurs, and lastly a loud, jovial voice. "Monsieur Corbeau, to be sure. That's the gentleman I seek. I'll go up."

The heavy tread was already on the stairs, and they could hear the clank of a scabbard against the rail.

Alverley addressed the servant with swift, impressive urgency. "Take this, Franz. See it delivered at once. At once. And not a word to anyone." He fished a thaler from his pocket, and pressed it with the note into the gaping fellow's hand. "Two more thalers for you when you bring the answer. Run."

With a ready promise to use all speed, the servant turned to go. Alverley's hand was on Dorothea's shoulder, pressing her down. "Sit," he bade her. "Compose yourself and take no heed of whatever I may say or do."

He had time for no more. The door was flung open, and on the threshold stood the burly form of Lieutenant von Stein: that same Stein with whom Alverley had all but embroiled himself some months ago. There was a grin on his wide, flat face, a fresh-coloured face, with a short nose and nostrils almost as large as his mean little eyes. A moment he stood surveying them. Then he advanced, leaving the way clear for the servant, who passed swiftly out. He bowed in mockery, making it plain that he meant to amuse himself. He addressed Alverley in guttural French.

"Ah, my dear Monsieur Corbeau – or is it Crapaud? No matter which. Either will serve; for, in effect, you are the man I seek. And the lady! Fie, Monsieur, fie! To run off with our Prince's little doxy!"

"You intrude, Lieutenant von Stein – or is it Schwein? Either will serve. This room is private. You had not realized it, perhaps?"

Stein, who had momentarily stiffened at the deliberate insult, smirked again. "It is you who are slow to realize. Perhaps it will help you if I trouble you for your sword." He held out his hand for it. "In the King's name."

"The King? What King?"

"What King? Comedian! What King but the King of Prussia. I am here to arrest you. You and the pastor's pretty daughter."

"And since when, pray, has the King of Prussia's warrant run in the Electorate of Saxony?"

"Don't let that vex you," laughed Stein. "It runs wherever he is in strength to enforce it."

"And you can enforce it here?"

"As you'll discover if you give me trouble. That would be very foolish. I have two troopers at the foot of the stairs. Shall I whistle them up to make you fast, or will you be sensible, and yield?"

Alverley spoke coldly. "This is an outrage, a violation of international rights, for which the Elector of Saxony will demand a stern account."

"It's possible. But you'll be safe in Prussia by the time that happens. Ah, bah! You waste your breath. King Frederick William will know how to answer the Elector. You should know that they are cronies."

"Even so, the Elector is not likely to condone a kidnapping in his territory."

"Who cares whether he condones it or not? You are wanted for desertion, my friend. The Elector will not view that with such favour that he can blame us for being a little...high-handed."

"You admit it, then?"

"Oh, all you please, if it will end this silly argument. Your sword now, and we'll go peacefully, like good friends."

Alverley stood a moment frowning, as if in thought. Then with a sudden air of yielding, he shrugged and began to unbuckle his sword-belt. "Ah, well! I hope I am a good loser. It was never my way to waste my strength in battling with the inevitable."

Stein received his sword. "That's the wise spirit." He turned to Dorothea, and bowed again with an urbanity so exaggerated as to be an insult. "If you will make ready, Mademoiselle, we'll..."

Alverley intervened sharply. "What have you to do with Mademoiselle? She, at least, cannot be charged with desertion."

"Not with desertion. No." He leered. "Her crime is of a more amiable nature. But she is included in my orders."

Alverley did not pursue the point. It was an oddly weak surrender. "I see. How soon must we set out?"

"At once, of course. We'll lie at Treuenbrietzen for tonight. You'll understand my wish to cross the border before we sleep."

"I understand it perfectly," was the dry answer. "But at least you'll allow us to finish supper before we ride. We were just sitting down to it. Perhaps you'll drink a glass with us. This is a pleasant Rhenish."

Stein's little eyes searched his face in silence. Then he looked at the well-spread table, and hesitated. Possibly he found this sudden amiability suspicious. If so he must have accounted himself unassailable. And, as Alverley supposed and calculated, he had not eaten for some hours.

"I am not inhuman," he laughed at last. "The partridges are plump. The ham looks moist. Faith," he mocked, "I'll not be so churlish as to refuse your hospitality. I'll be the better for a lining." He pulled up a chair. "By your leave, Madam." He sat down, and began to pile himself a plate. "It's a pleasure to have you for a prisoner, Monsieur le Marquis."

"You do me too much honour." Alverley fetched another glass from the side-table, and poured wine for the guest. Then he sat down facing him across the board.

Thus Dorothea, at the table's end, had one of the men on either hand. She sat very stiff and white.

"I suspect you of mockery," said Stein. "But that's no matter." He raised his glass. "I pledge your bright eyes, Mademoiselle," he said, and waited. She did not shift her glance, but continued to stare straight before her. "You lack courtesy," he growled. Then he guffawed. "You are rancorous perhaps. A pity. In other circumstances we might have been good friends. If I am a marplot, faith, I cannot help myself. I am under orders. The slave of duty. So I drink to you just the same." And he drained the measure. "That was good," he commended the draught, smacked his lips, and set down the empty glass.

With the solicitude of a courteous host, Alverley filled it for him again. Stein watched him warily, and whilst he fell to eating with noisy relish, the darting glances of his little eyes followed the Englishman's every movement.

Suddenly Dorothea spoke, urged by the need to resolve a doubt as tormenting as her present situation. "You appear to have found us very easily, sir."

Stein spoke from a full mouth. "Lord! The lady has a tongue, after all. Found you easily? To be sure we did. You see, I knew where to look. There was a fool letter in the Pastor Ritter's pocket when we took him yesterday." He wagged his head derisively at Alverley. "That was not prudent, that letter."

"You took my father yesterday?" she echoed in dismay.

"When we found you had flitted," he explained. "His Majesty ordered the pastor's arrest. But don't be alarmed, Mademoiselle. He'll come to no great harm. There's nothing against him save that he's your father, which – if you'll permit me to say so – is highly to his credit. It takes a churchman to get as lovely a child. Who can blame his Highness if he lost his heart to you? Not I, faith. I envy him his fortune." He winked and leered, and raised his glass again. "To the brightest eyes and fairest skin in Brandenburg. Small blame to the Prince, I say again. For I vow there's never a princess in the empire fit to compare with you."

"This flattery will make her vain, Lieutenant," said Alverley.

"Eh?" Stein glowered at him. "Given to irony, are you? I shouldn't be too free in exercising it."

Alverley smiled. "Is that a threat?"

"It might be."

"You are duller even than I suspected, Lieutenant, if you don't perceive that a man in my position is beyond the reach of threats. What can happen to me worse than is happening?"

"In your place I shouldn't defy discovery of it," was the surly answer.

Alverley's amiability remained unruffled. "Of course anything is possible to a guardsman turned mouchard – a catchpoll."

The Lieutenant, in the act of pouring wine for himself, checked, glared, then took up the half-filled glass and cast the contents in Alverley's face. Dorothea flung herself back in her chair with a cry of horror.

"That's to answer you," said Stein, and refilled his glass.

"Certainly forceful. But not very witty." Calmly Alverley wiped his face and his drenched lapels with a napkin. "How am I to take it, Lieutenant von Stein? As a gentleman's challenging provocation, or as a gaoler's cowardly brutality to a helpless prisoner?"

Stein laughed offensively. He drank before replying. "You are as full of pert tricks as Harlequin in the Comedy, my friend. But I am not fooled." He became peremptory. "Finish your supper. It's time we were moving."

"I see." Alverley sighed. "The brutal gaoler. No use to complain, then, though I don't care to have wine thrown in my face. It's not only offensive; it's a waste of good liquor."

"My apologies to the wine," Stein scoffed.

With a smile grown sorrowful, Alverley reached for the bottle, and slowly filled his glass. "That is something, of course." He set the bottle down. In the very act of doing so, he shifted his hand upon the neck, so as to grasp it like a club, and then, so swiftly as to leave no time for parrying, he had launched himself across the table from his seated position and crashed the heavy bottle against the Lieutenant's brow.

The blow took Stein across the right temple with fulminating effect. He sank sprawling athwart the table, with arms flung forward among the dishes, his wig rakishly awry. A trickle of blood from his forehead went to mingle with a trickle of wine from his overturned glass that was dripping to the floor.

Dorothea, startled into rising, stood wide-eyed, with heaving breast, shocked and dismayed by this culmination of a conduct in Alverley which throughout had bewildered her by its oddness. "What have you done? How will this help us?"

Deliberately Alverley set the bottle down and coolly smiled upon his work. "As I told the gallant von Schwein, I don't care to have my face washed in wine. Besides, as long as he was content to sit and guzzle and chop wit I could be patient. But he began to talk of going, and that doesn't suit me just yet. Now he'll remain quietly. And he won't talk for a while, which is just as well; in fact, important."

"But his men?" she reminded him. "He said that two of them are posted at the foot of the stairs. They will never suffer us to go."

"Oh, I hope so. I think so. Sh! Listen."

From the street a sound that had been audible to his attentive ears before he struck the Lieutenant was now rapidly swelling. It was the tramp of men marching at the double.

"Soldiers! More soldiers!" she cried.

He nodded. "The Elector's men, I believe. Coming to deliver us, I hope."

"How can you know that?"

"Because I sent for them. So be easy. That note I gave Franz was for the Burgomaster. Did you really think that I invited Lieutenant von Stein to supper for the pleasure of his company and the delight of his conversation?"

A command rang out below, and swift upon it sounds of tumult surged into the inn: stamping of heavily shod feet, shouts of anger, a sound of blows, a pistol shot, and, drawing nearer above the hubbub, a clattering of steps upon the stairs. The door was flung open to the cry of: "Where is this Prussian crimp?"

A compact, red-faced man in a black coat strode in on gaitered legs. He carried a stout cane. His air was one of authority, and from his scowl his mood might be judged angry. Behind him pressed Franz, who had conducted him, and behind Franz others could be seen dimly on the landing.

Alverley received him with a bow. "Herr Bürgermeister, you can never have been more welcome."

The man's glance raked the room, paused an instant on Dorothea whilst he removed his hat, then swept on to the silent Stein, prone across the table among the dishes.

"So! Is this your crimping scoundrel? What ails him?"

"The drunken dog had the impudence to make himself free of our table. When I protested he flung my wine in my face." Alverley displayed his empurpled neckcloth. "To square the account I did the same by him, with the bottle. So that now he's at your orders."

"That is good. It saves trouble. It was a happy thought to send for me. I thank you, sir. These impudent Prussians are crossing the border as they please, to carry off men for the armies of their King. It's not to be suffered." He called over his shoulder. "Here, my lads!"

Franz was thrust aside, and four Saxon gendarmes entered the little room.

"There's your man. Away with him." A sergeant entered. "Ah, Hobner. Have you got them all?"

"All six of them, sir; snugly tied up, and no harm taken."

"They may thank God for that. If any man of mine had been hurt I'd have hanged the offender out of hand. March them off, and take this drunken officer of theirs with them."

As Stein was being carried out, Alverley motioned Dorothea to a chair. She sank to it, with a pale smile for him, and he turned to the Burgomaster. "I am your debtor, sir, for more than I care to imagine."

"Potzteufel!" answered him that rasping voice. "It is I who am obliged. I am glad to have caught these insolent dogs red-handed. The Elector is too lenient with this damned recruiting. He sends mild protests of which these Brandenburgers take no notice. The kidnapping goes on just the same. But I'll teach these dogs a lesson. I'll kennel them awhile in the town gaol. I'll leave the King of Prussia to ask for them before I even report their presence in Wittenberg." And then on a change of tone he asked: "What brings you here, sir?"

"We are French Huguenots on our travels. We came to Wittenberg attracted by the fame of your university and on a pilgrimage to the shrine of your great Luther. Perhaps the fact that I am a stranger encouraged the Brandenburger to suppose that…"

He got no further.

"Righteous God!" The Burgomaster interrupted. "That makes the matter worse. We were shamed, indeed, if it were known that a pious stranger may not visit Wittenberg in safety. Apologies are due to you and to the gracious lady. I fear she has been scandalously distressed. But I promise you the Elector shall hear of it. It makes a strong case for action on his part."

"You are very good, sir. His Highness is well served in Wittenberg. He should reward your zeal."

"I am fortunate in the occasion to display it. I take my leave, gracious sir. My duty, Madam."

With his hat over his heart, he bowed to each in turn, and marched stiffly out. A moment still they heard his rasping voice marshalling what men of his remained. Then the tramp of marching feet receded, and peace fell once more upon the Einsiedler Inn.

Alverley and Dorothea stood looking at each other. She laughed with tears in her eyes. "But it is a miracle," she said.

"Say, an inspiration. A happy thought, the Burgomaster said, to send him that note. The happy thought was an opportune recollection of the Saxon Ambassador von Suhm's recent indignant protests to Frederick William against Prussian crimping in Saxony. It made me send two lines of hopeful appeal to the Burgomaster against this fresh attempt. And then I knocked the swinish Lieutenant over the head so as to make sure that he shouldn't contradict me. As he reminded me, the Burgomaster might not as readily have extended his protection to a deserter."

"I see," she said slowly, to add more quickly: "But when he comes to hear the Lieutenant's tale…"

"We shall be far away, I trust. From what he said the Burgomaster will be in no hurry to interrogate Monsieur Stein. He'll hardly trouble him before morning. Still, in order not to tempt Providence, we'll be off tonight."

The landlord came in, accompanied by his wife. They were excited and voluble in indignation and regrets, cursing all Prussians, and thanking Heaven for a Burgomaster in Wittenberg who would suffer no nonsense from them. The hostess had a special vehemence for the sufferings of the gracious lady. She hoped that strong action would be taken in punishing that brutal officer and his men.

All this was very civilly accepted, and finally met, to their hosts' increased dismay, by a request for their bill and their horses. They would be quitting Wittenberg at once. There were protests, loud and pained. The night was no time for a delicate lady to be travelling; it would be to the shame of Wittenberg that they should depart thus.

Alverley remained courteously firm. His sister's was a timid nature. After what she had endured, impossible for her to know peace so near the Prussian border. Of course, there was no danger of another crimping expedition, but the hostess, as a woman, would understand that after such a shock it was not easy for his sister to recover peace of mind, particularly on the actual scene of the outrage.

So the hosts, distressed at the loss of guests so esteemed, left them to make ready for departure.

Only then did the deepening helplessness of her position become fully apparent to Dorothea. "Whither now?" she asked him fearfully.

"For tonight we'll make for Prietsch. It's a matter of only twenty miles. Tomorrow we'll consider further."

"What remains to consider? My father is a prisoner. You heard. We can no longer hope that he will join us. What am I to do?"

He set a hand upon her shoulder, seeking to quiet her distress.

"We'll consider, as I've said. But this is not the moment. Nor is this the place. Something will be found. Be sure of that. Meanwhile, courage and patience. Go and make ready."

She looked at him in piteous perplexity. Then by an effort she contrived a smile that but deepened the pain in her eyes. "Very well. I'll obey. I owe you that at least."

Chapter 19

Prietsch

In a dismal room of an indifferent inn – the Weintraube – at Prietsch, where they had lain the night, they applied their minds on the following morning to the formidable problem of Dorothea's future.

They were facing each other across a table and the remains of breakfast when she raised the question to which a sleepless night had provided no answer. "And whither now, Monsieur le Marquis?"

"My notion is to set out in an hour for Leipzig. We should be quite safe there, and there we can consider further at our leisure."

"Would it not be better to consider now? There can be no purpose in going farther if in the end I am to return to Berlin."

"To Berlin?" He was aghast. "That is out of all question."

"Is it? And the alternative?"

"Any alternative you please. You should realize that the fate that awaits you there is made the more certain now by your flight. Oh, I am not thinking only of the public whipping; but of your final disposal. Frederick William announced the intention of shutting you up for life in Spandau."

"Perhaps I should not live long," said she.

"That, of course, would be your best hope. But I haven't brought you out of Prussia to no better purpose."

"Aren't you forgetting that things have changed since I fled? Had I foreseen that my father would be prevented from joining us I think I must have remained. What else could I choose to do?"

"Would that help your father? Would you deny him in his prison the one consolation of knowing that you are safe?"

"Safe? What is this safety? Where am I to go? What is there for me?" Then through her distress surged fierce anger. "Oh, it is vile, infamous, to visit this horror upon the helpless. If I were a criminal I could not be more cruelly punished. And I have done nothing. Nothing. It is monstrous that any man should have the power to do this. God punish that monster as he deserves! May he be brought to such despair as now is mine."

"He'll rot in hell for his iniquities, no doubt. But that is not important, and it won't help you."

"Nothing will."

"Do not persuade yourself of that. Come. Let us count your assets."

"My assets? Some odd thalers and my few jewels, of which the best is a bracelet which you thought his Highness should not have given me."

"I seem to have been right, for it is answerable for a good deal of your trouble. However, I was thinking of your more enduring riches. You are well instructed, a good musician, a fine needlewoman, and you paint well enough to teach the elements of the art to the young. In France or England you could find employment for these qualities."

She looked at him in wide-eyed amazement. "You have been thinking for me!" She was breathless. Then she controlled herself and added: "But even if it were as you say, we are not in France or England."

"Not yet. No. But you didn't suppose I was thinking of setting up house in Leipzig? That is only a stage on the way to the Rhine, to Frankfurt, and thence to France."

"And you think I could launch myself on such an adventure? It is a compliment, I suppose. But you overrate my enterprise. Let us face what is."

"No, no. Let us face what might be, and face it with the courage that commands it. We ride to France."

"We?" she echoed, and stared at him. "Were you thinking that we should go together?"

"Were you thinking that I meant you to go alone?"

"But how could I allow you to go with me? Haven't you already done enough, risked enough, lost enough through me?"

He smiled. "I thought we had disposed of all that."

"It will never be disposed of. Argue as you will, you have ruined yourself for me, who have no claim upon you, who can never repay you."

"It is not my way to work for payment. At least, it never has been, although soon now it may be. And as for ruin..." he broke off. "I've said all I have to say on that score. So, if you please, we'll close the argument."

But she did not please. Her grey eyes considered him steadily out of her white, determined face. "I do not choose to do you the injustice of believing you. And I never shall. I am not an ingrate. That is why I cannot suffer you to add to a debt which I can never pay. I will not continue a burden on you. I spoke like a foolish, stupid child when I said that I could not face the world alone. After all, I am a grown woman, and better women than I can hope to be have done so."

"If there were the need for that, I'd not deny you. But there is not. I, too, am for France. I have little choice. In Paris I may find friends, fellow-exiles at least, who may be able to help me to a living. Since, then, we both go the same way, what more natural than that we should go together?"

"I had not said that I would go to France." She was smiling at him across the table, but her lips were quivering, and her eyes were moist. "Do you think I am so easily deceived? Do you think I do not understand your subterfuge? No, no, my dear, generous Marquis, I

177

can accept no more. I should be ashamed. Sooner than let you do more, I will go back."

"Into hell?" he asked.

She made a little gesture of helpless assent.

Alverley rose. "So be it, since you are determined," he said in the quiet tone of acceptance, and then added: "You'll need an escort. I'll come with you."

"To Berlin?"

"If that's your destination. I brought you away. I'll take you back."

"Oh, you are quite mad," she cried. "What reason is there in that?"

"None; I have assumed that you prefer to dispense with reason. Therefore, whether it's Paris or Berlin, I shall go with you. So be good enough to make up your mind. I put my fate in your hands."

Her distress deepened. "This...this is to force me to continue in your care."

"Until you find a care in which you would prefer to be."

"But it's impossible. Impossible! Must I repeat that I will not continue a burden on you?"

"It's a burden I shoulder joyfully. So let us have done. Do you dream that I will allow you to return? Or that I will abandon you to take your chance of the world? I should be a poor friend, indeed. You insist that I've ruined myself for you. Perhaps I have. I have lied and cheated and deserted so that I might pluck you out of Prussian clutches. Why?" He rose as he asked the question, and stood as if waiting for her answer. She looked up in fresh surprise, to meet an odd intentness in his glance that brought her a vague disquiet. "I ask you why? Don't you know the answer, Dorothea? Don't you see that you matter to me more than anyone else in the world, more than all the rest of the world? Haven't you suspected that I love you?"

He had seen fear and perplexity alternating in those eyes of hers during these last three days of their intimate association – three days that seemed to hold a lifetime – but never such awe as he now beheld in them.

"Ah, don't!" she cried. "Don't! You are not to say this to me. You are not to..."

"Don't misunderstand me," he broke in. "I ask for nothing beyond the leave to serve you; nothing beyond the joy of giving, surely the sweetest of all joys to him who loves. Here is nothing to alarm you, my dear."

"And I?" she asked him. "I am to accept, to take? Is that to be my part?"

"Since thus you will give me happiness, will you deny me?"

She considered him still a moment before she shook her head. A smile of wistful understanding crept slowly across her face. "This," she said, "is just another generous subterfuge born of pity for my plight. Your chivalry will not suffer you to leave me to my fate. I understand, and I thank you. It is good. It is noble. But...it cannot be."

"What cannot be? The prospect of enduring my company?"

"Not that, indeed. Never that. You know that is not what I mean."

"What else, then?"

Again there was only distress in her countenance. "It is impossible that you...that you should have for me the feelings you..." She broke off, to begin again. "How could I be deceived? You... Monsieur le Marquis, you are a great gentleman, a great nobleman in your own country..."

He interrupted her. "I see. I see. I am a great gentleman. I am a great nobleman. I am good. I am chivalrous. I am noble. Therefore I cannot love you. I make you my compliments upon your logic. It is unanswerable. But it also happens to be true that I am a proscribed fugitive, an outcast from my own land, a penniless, fortune-hunting adventurer, at such shifts to make a living that I did not disdain the service of the King of Prussia even when I had discovered that it was not the service for a gentleman. In fact, Mademoiselle, my nobility is ignoble. I can understand that a woman who is pure and good and adorable should scorn to have such a fellow in attendance upon her."

"How perverse you are!" she reproached him.

"Come. That's better. You begin to discover my faults."

"Oh, no. For you make of perversity a virtue."

"How foolish is this wrangle, Dorothea. My only virtue is that I love you; my only merit that I appraise your worth."

Solemnly she gazed at his solemnity. Her bosom strove within its confining corsage. "I am to believe this, then?" There was in the question an almost piteous note, as if she implored him not to deceive her. "Can you be sure that it is not just pity for my helplessness? That…"

"This is to confuse cause and effect. Far from being born of pity, my love aroused the pity that sent me to rescue you. Had that not occurred to you? Faith, it leaps to the eye."

She gave it thought a moment. Then, timidly, with lowered eyes, "Since when…" she began, and there broke off as if afraid.

But he had understood. "What do I know since when? Perhaps since I played the father to you, and admonished you to beware of princes."

He came round the table as he spoke, and stood beside her. "Who knows if it was not jealousy that prompted me? It is very likely. We never quite know ourselves. But this I know, and this you may believe: that if I could offer you marriage and you would have me, I would end this argument by making you my wife." He took her hand, bowed over it, and bore it to his lips.

"My dear!" she whispered, and looked up at him through tears.

"Do not let me trouble you," he begged. "Just give me the happiness of serving you, and take what comfort you can find in the knowledge that I am beside you to that end. That is all I ask."

"And I, then…" she was beginning, when he checked her.

"Hush." His hand rested lightly on her shoulder, a caressing repression. "I require no answer. I'll order the horses."

Chapter 20

Cüstrin

At about the time that those fugitives from the ferocity of the King of Prussia, the Marquess of Alverley and Dorothea Ritter, were making their way to France in the pursuit of their platonic adventure, unconscious as yet of either its oddness or its perils, the fate of Prince Frederick was being balanced and decided. It is even possible that by their flight those two may have contributed to the tragic solution of the matter, although it was as well for his peace of mind that Alverley never suspected this, not even later, when he was actually reproached with it. Certain it is that Frederick William's rage was swollen by the thwarting of his infamously cruel intentions concerning Dorothea Ritter, and it may well be that the escape of one victim made him the more remorselessly tighten his grip upon those that remained.

So far as his son was concerned there are the best of grounds for supposing that Frederick William seriously considered putting him to death. For it is difficult to believe that if he did not entertain the notion he would have allowed the world to think so. That the world did think so, and was shocked and alarmed, we know from the representations that were made to his Majesty, enjoining him, for his own sake, to practise mercy. From the Low Countries, from Sweden, from England, from Russia came letters of intercession, and it was even rumoured that the Emperor was about to take action in the matter. If the anguish of the Queen and the prayers of the royal family weighed for nothing with the King, yet before that body of world opinion Frederick William shrank from placing his son in the class of the Infante Don Carlos, the Czarewitch Alexis, and other victims of a royal father's rage.

He resolved his ugly problem at last by the dreadful expedient of putting Fritz to death by proxy. Once upon a time, he may have reasoned, there were whipping-boys for princes, and his present notion was merely an extension of that aforetime practice. Under his hand and apt for the office, as Fritz's intimate friend and associate, was von Katte, who had presumed to criticize his Majesty's conduct towards the Prince.

So his command went forth to the Schulenberg court martial that sentence of death be passed upon Katte.

A shudder of horror ran through court and army at that barbarous order, to which an added barbarity was to be supplied in the very manner of Katte's death. Intercessions poured in upon Frederick William. Katte's father, the Lieutenant-General, appealed to the King in person, to no purpose. His grandfather, the Marshal of Wartensleben, begged his grandson's life as a return for the blood which he and his son had shed in the service of their country.

"Your Majesty will not wish," his supplication ended, in the well-worn terms from the Book of Genesis, "to bring down my grey hairs in such sorrow to the grave."

Majesty was merely irritated by these prayers. He answered that in sparing the man torture he had shown all the mercy that could be expected; that an example must be made; and, finally, that he forbade anyone to speak to him further of this matter. He proclaimed that to maintain himself he would at need cut off the heads of a thousand Kattes, and he seized the chance for yet another fling at the King of England, the Red Cabbage, in whose encouragement of the Prince's insubordination he persisted in believing. The English must learn that he would tolerate no interference in his realm.

So Katte's doom was settled. Word of it was conveyed to him in his prison by Major Schacht, in natural loathing of a task from which he had vainly sought to be excused. Staggered though he might be by the incredible intimation, yet Katte received it with an outward composure of utter dignity. He met with courtesy Schacht's expressions of sorrow and of detestation for the odious task imposed upon him.

"Your distress," he said, "is kind. If I am to die I have at least the consolation of knowing that by my death I give proof of my devotion to Prince Frederick."

But that his quick mind and his young body, so rich in the energy of life, were in anguished revolt at this monstrously unjust extinction we know from the passionate letter he wrote to his father, craving forgiveness for the sorrow that he brought upon him. We see in it how high had been his ambition and how bitter was this relinquishment of his hopes.

The King had decreed that he should suffer at Cüstrin, where the Prince was imprisoned, and characteristically he had prescribed down to the last detail the macabre pageant that was to strike terror into the Prince's soul. Accordingly to Cüstrin Katte was conveyed by Schacht.

There on a chilly morning of early November the Prince was aroused at five o'clock by an officer, Colonel Reichmann.

In the last few weeks there had been a relaxation of the rigour of his confinement. Not only was his table less esuriently served, but he had been allowed books, pens and paper, and he had discovered channels through which to correspond with the outside world and in particular with the Princess Wilhelmina, who still shared his disgrace. Also he found Grumbkow actively courting him, from which he inferred that his stock was rising and that the end of his chastisement was in sight. In such an atmosphere he was recovering his normal spirits. He read Racine, and plagiarized him in the course of some exercises in French prosody, composed a song or two, and began to be impudent again to all who came in contact with him. This note of impudence was present in his greeting of Reichmann that morning when he had been told the time.

He knuckled the sleep from his eyes, and yawned. "You've taken to early rising at Cüstrin. But why the devil disturb me?"

"A special occasion, Highness. There is to be an execution this morning, and his Majesty's orders are that you attend it."

"An execution?" His tongue clove to the roof of his mouth. The blood drained from his face. He fell to trembling. Had he been but a wretched mouse between the paws of that gross cat, his father, allowed to feel himself escaping merely so that the agony of recapture should be the sharper?

He glared at Reichmann. "An execution!" he stammered again, in fearful inquiry.

"Rittmeister von Katte's, Highness, for his share in your Highness' escapade."

If this relieved him of one terror, it supplied him with another.

"Katte! Katte!" The Prince flung himself out of bed. "No, no, no!" he screamed. "Lord Jesus! It must not be."

"Calm, Highness! Calm, I beseech you."

But no calm was possible. Conscience was astir for once in that arid, egotistical soul, stirred by shock into activity; and conscience denied him calm, scarcely permitted him relief in the discovery that it was not himself who was to die that morning. It was he, conscience pitilessly reminded him, who had brought Katte to this pass, betrayed him to it, indeed, in his endeavour to avert his father's wrath from his own head.

"It cannot be, Reichmann. It must not be," he raved. "Send word to the King. Tell him he may disinherit me, or kill me even if he wishes. But Katte must not die for me. He is my friend, my dearest, loved friend. Oh my God!" He beat his brow with his fists; he ran almost naked about the room. "Katte! My dear Katte!" he wailed. "This must not happen to you. I could never forgive myself. It must not happen. I shall die of remorse." Then, passionately, he fell again to imploring Reichmann to postpone the execution until his appeal could reach the King. He would willingly submit to anything the

King might choose to impose upon him if only this horror might be averted.

The distracted Reichmann brought him gradually to understand that it was beyond his authority to order a delay, that he dared do no other than carry out the positive orders of the King.

At last the Prince was persuaded to dress himself. But his despair was not to be soothed. He was still raving and sobbing, alternately cursing his father, reviling himself, and praying for help to a God in whom he ostentatiously published his disbelief. Thus until a few minutes before seven, when the drums began to roll outside.

Two officers entered the cell, and, using compulsion, conducted him between them to the window, Reichmann following close. Thence in the half-light of the November morning he beheld the ramparts above the Oder, and the scaffold dressed upon them, with its ominous butcher's block beside a heap of sand. About it were paraded a hundred and fifty men of the garrison, whilst issuing at that moment from the gateway of the citadel the Prince beheld a body of military police escorting Katte. The drums fell silent as the Rittmeister came into the Prince's view, walking sedately between two clergymen, his hat under his arm.

The Prince gasped and fought for breath, clawing the bars of his open window. "Katte!" he called. "Katte! Mon cher Katte! In the name of God, pardon me. Pardon me."

The doomed officer broke step to peer upwards through the dim light. It was a moment before his eyes discovered the Prince. Then he raised his hat aloft in salute. His voice rang steady. "Monseigneur, you have nothing to ask of me," he answered, and went on.

He stood composedly on the scaffold through the formality of the reading of the sentence of death. Then he took off his coat and his wig, delivering them together with his hat to an orderly. He put on a white cap, opened wide his shirt at the neck, refused to have his eyes bandaged, and knelt on the sand.

"Lord Jesus…" he began, and ended there.

The headsman's glittering sword made an arc of light in its sweep, and Katte's head rolled away.

The Prince, having beheld the death that might have been his own, that might yet be his own, swooned into the arms of the two attendant officers.

BOOK TWO

The King

Chapter 1

The Amorist

Frederick William, Elector of Brandenburg and King in Prussia, died in May of 1740, ten years after Alverley's flight from Brandenburg. He was not yet fifty, but so dropsical, as a result of excessive guzzling, that life had become a burden which he must have been glad to lay down.

Although in the last years relations between father and son had notably improved, yet Frederick bore this bereavement with exemplary resignation, which is to say that he shed no tears over the grave of a father of whom he was glad to see the last.

The late King's subjects were in much the same case. The rest of the world remained indifferent.

Not so, however, when in the following October the Emperor Charles VI suddenly departed this life, of a surfeit of mushrooms. Europe held its breath, waiting to see what changes might follow. France, in particular, was exercised; and this because divided into two camps. In one stood the party which, still clinging to Richelieu's policy towards Austria, accounted this an opportune moment to fall upon the hereditary foe; in the other stood old Cardinal Fleury, of clearer, saner vision, who realized that the Austrian menace to France had ceased with the Bourbon occupation of the throne of Spain. He perceived, further, that the honour of France demanded fidelity to the Pragmatic Sanction of which she was one of the signatories, guaranteeing the Habsburg dominions to Maria Theresa, the daughter of Charles VI. And he still further perceived that peace was of paramount importance to the prosperity of France, which he ruled for the youthful Louis XV.

There were rumours that the Elector of Bavaria, who for value received was also a signatory of the Pragmatic Sanction, and who was now aspiring to the Imperial Crown, was about to dishonour his signature by laying claim to some of Maria Theresa's inheritance. The disquiet which this caused Cardinal Fleury – threatening as it did the peace of Europe – was presently deepened by such vague news as he received of the conduct of the new King of Prussia, a conduct of such contradictions and mystery, that the old Cardinal, for all his shrewdness, found it difficult to fathom. Brooding upon this brought him to remember that in the Prison of the Châtelet lay one Charles Stuart-Dene, Marquess of Alverley, of whose antecedents his Eminence had lately had occasion minutely to inform himself.

This imprisonment of Alverley's supplied a climax to ten hard years of striving with poverty and misfortune. If he had not been made bitter by the fact that this poverty and misfortune had been shared by Dorothea Ritter, it was because of the bright courage with which she faced whatever tribulations fate brought into the joint existence which circumstances had thrust upon them. There were times when he reproached himself with having committed her to a life of such dismal uncertainty by his inadequacy to fulfil the duties he had assumed when presumptuously he had taken charge of her. She, however, was derisive of these moods. Upbraiding, she insisted, should be addressed to her and not to him, for she was a burden without which he might have walked lightly. From her, she would assure him, there could be only gratitude for a shielding affection which had never faltered and which she had proved able to do little to deserve. This in all those years was their only source of disagreement, and in all the disappointments and privations they endured they were sustained by a love that set a background of light to their darkest days.

You perceive that the events had not justified the optimism in which Alverley had entered France, nor had his light-hearted prophecies at Wittenberg been realized.

On their first coming to Paris he had sought acquaintance with other Jacobite exiles in refuge there, in the natural hope that the bond of common politics would deserve him their assistance in his need. Most of them he found to be in little better case than his own, whilst pride forbade him to take advantage of the only help offered to him by the few who at least were well supplied with funds and ready to place a purse at his disposal. The assistance that he sought was not financial. For it was not in his nature to accept loans which he perceived no prospect of repaying. He had looked for introductions at Court, through whose influence he might have entered French service. Some such introductions were actually supplied him. But political conditions, from which it resulted just then that England and France must always be found in opposite camps, made it inevitable that an Englishman, even if a Jacobite, should be viewed without kindness by the French Government.

Once this was realized, and once Alverley had conquered the dismay it caused him, he addressed himself to finding some other means of livelihood. By then the slender resources with which he and Dorothea had quitted Germany were running low. Alverley discarded a title which it seemed to him that penury made ridiculous, and in the comparative anonymity of Mr Charles Stuart-Dene accepted an appointment as tutor to the two sons of the Comte de St Maur, of which the good offices of Lord Henry Fitzjames had procured him the offer. Besides teaching the lads English and German and a smattering of the classics, he gave them instruction in horsemanship and fencing. It was not a lucrative appointment, but at least it enabled him to live in the modest lodging which he occupied with Dorothea, over a grocer's shop in the Rue de l'Arbre Sec, behind the Louvre. They were known to their grocer landlord and to the world in general as Mr and Mrs Stuart-Dene. For they had come to realize that the pretended relationship of brother and sister, however symbolical of the platonic intent in which they had first set out, was not one that could conveniently be maintained. Nor would Nature suffer that two young persons, confessedly lovers, in such constant and intimate association should – whatever the original resolve – indefinitely continue in that chaste relationship.

In the Rue de l'Arbre Sec, in '33, a daughter was born to them. It was no joyous event for Alverley, for whilst the child lived but some few days, a puerperal fever suspended the mother for some weeks between life and death. Dorothea's latent vigour and Alverley's unremitting care of her, given in anguished devotion, triumphed in the end.

Six months later Alverley's employment with the Comte de St Maur came to an end. The Count desired that further to form themselves, as the French express it, his sons should make a tour of Germany and Italy under Alverley's care. But since this would have entailed leaving Dorothea alone in Paris, he was constrained to decline the proposal, and another tutor was engaged in his place. Some months of penurious anxiety followed, during which the little that Dorothea's illness had left of their exiguous savings was absorbed. They were rescued at the eleventh hour by a recommendation from Monsieur de St Maur to the Duc de la Ferté, and Alverley entered the ducal household as tutor to his grace's only son.

With such fluctuations of fortune they lived through the ensuing years precariously, but in the main happily in the fond sustenance which each derived from the other.

In 1737, when Alverley's employment with the Duc de la Ferté came to a natural end, another ugly hiatus followed, resolved at last when the chair for English became vacant at the Lycée of Louis-le-Grand and was obtained for Mr Stuart-Dene by the powerful influence of the Duke. The pay was wretched, but Alverley was able to supplement it by taking a few private pupils, and meanwhile Dorothea was earning some odd louis as a painter of miniatures, an art which she had perfected under poor Katte's influence.

Of Katte's dreadful fate they had been informed soon after they reached Paris. Dorothea had written for news of her father to

Theresa, and it was from Theresa that they first heard of Katte's execution. Some months later, when Pastor Ritter was restored to liberty, but with health gravely impaired, they received from him a more detailed account of the event, confirming a horror which to Alverley had seemed incredible. His grief was profound; for he had come to love Katte as a brother; but deeper still was his anger against the abominable tyrant who had perpetrated that murder, and deepest against the craven prince who, in order to shelter himself, had treacherously delivered up Katte to his ineffable father's wrath.

It was because of this that when in 1740 the death of Frederick William opened for him once more the gates of Prussia, the very notion of returning to Berlin and renewing relations with Frederick, with all the advantages which this might offer, was so repugnant that rather he preferred to struggle on in the straitened Paris circumstances.

"I would willingly return to Berlin," he said, "if in doing so I could avenge poor Katte's murder. Since that is beyond my power, I'll not think of it."

To this repugnance Dorothea opposed no argument. It would have been different had her father still lived. But the old pastor had died in that same month of May that saw the end of Frederick William. To the end Dorothea had been in affectionate correspondence with him; for although she had frankly avowed her circumstances, refusing to find cause for shame in them, the old scholar had judged as a man rather than as a cleric, and if he deplored the situation, yet he recognized the circumstances that had created it and did not allow prejudice to condemn her.

His death disclosed that for all his unworldliness the pastor had been thrifty. Dorothea inherited not only the house in the Nikolaistrasse with all that it contained, but some further house property in Berlin acquired by her father's savings. An administrator was appointed through the intermediary of the faithful Theresa, and whilst for sentimental reasons the house in the Nikolaistrasse was to remain for the present untenanted, the rents from the other properties were remitted regularly to Dorothea. They amounted only to a modest sum, it is true, but it sufficed, at least, to mitigate the penury of their existence.

It was in that summer of 1740, when Alverley and Dorothea had determined to make the best of the little that was theirs rather than seek better fortune in Prussia that the Comte du Plessis de Mazan first became one of Mr Stuart-Dene's private pupils. A wealthy young nobleman in the middle twenties, Monsieur de Mazan was a nephew of the great Duc de Richelieu, in whose footsteps as an amorist he was bidding fair to follow closely. He entertained diplomatic ambitions which his powerful connections at court should make it easy to gratify, and because of this sought lessons in English at the hands of Mr Stuart-Dene on the recommendation of the Comte de St Maur.

These private lessons were given by Alverley in the Rue de l'Arbre Sec. He was no longer lodged in the garret, but occupied quarters on the floor immediately above the shop. If far from luxurious, they were yet pleasant enough, and there was even a clavichord in the little salon that served them as a living-room.

In the course of his twice-weekly attendance there, Monsieur de Mazan had repeatedly met Dorothea, whose womanhood, now that she was in her twenty-eighth year, more than fulfilled the lovely promise of her adolescence. Subconsciously schooled perhaps by years of association with Alverley, she had come to bear herself with the calm self-assurance of a woman of birth, and if normally she was of a gravity that commanded respect, yet she had not forgotten how to display an endearing gaiety.

Monsieur de Mazan permitted himself respectfully to admire her. A collector of bonnes fortunes, the respectful approach was a cardinal feature of his technique. When coming for his lessons he would bring, now a choice nosegay, now a bonbonnière, now some similar trifle, which he would entrust to Alverley: "For Madame, with my respectful homage."

Shown her miniatures, the Count expressed voluble wonder at so much talent, spoke, not very appositely be it confessed, of Watteau and Lancret, to their disparagement by contrast, and finally, one day, offered to commission a miniature of himself and to give her sittings for it.

She was amused, and frankly laughed. "But I am incapable of working from life. I've always protested that you exaggerate my ability. Now you enable me to prove it. I am no more than a copyist All my miniatures are copies of ordinary portraits."

"Is it possible?" He flattered by incredulity. "The work of such charm, such certainty of line, such delicacy of tint! Such dazzling art! Madame, I am persuaded that you mistrust your great talent. I will not believe that you could not as readily succeed if you worked from the original. If you will make trial upon me I will very gladly accept the risk."

She shook her head. "Bring me a portrait, and I shall be happy to reproduce it in miniature. More I cannot do, believe me."

"But it is not the same thing at all. Can you not persuade her, Monsieur Dene, at least to make the attempt?"

Alverley smiled upon this earnestness, so flattering to Dorothea. "None could persuade her to attempt what she believes beyond her powers, just as she needs no persuasion to do what is within them."

"You reduce me to despair." Monsieur de Mazan sighed. "Enfin! If I cannot have what I would, I must take what I can."

"The beginning of all philosophy," said Alverley.

On the following morning, a half-hour or so after Alverley had left home for the Lycée, and whilst Dorothea was still busy with her household tasks, there came a knock at the door. Supposing it some tradesman, she went to open, and to her surprise found Monsieur de Mazan upon the threshold. He was followed by a servant carrying a slim, flat parcel, some two feet square. There was no embarrassment in her surprise, for all that he found her in a plain linen sacque, her head tightly coiffed in a turban that completely enclosed her gold-bronze hair, her arms bare, and a feather duster in her hand.

"Monsieur le Comte!" Under her faintly raised eyebrows her clear grey eyes were steady.

He bowed from the waist, his tricorne over his heart, a gorgeousness of blue and gold. "Madame! I permit myself to bring you the portrait."

"Oh! The portrait! Let your servant place it in here."

Instead, however, he took the parcel into his own hands, and dismissed the lackey by a gesture.

"By your leave," he said, and advanced into the room.

She closed the door, and followed, coming to stand beside him whilst he set the picture upright upon the arms of a chair, and removed the wrappings. With her head slightly tilted she critically surveyed the portrait. "It is very beautiful work."

"It is by Lacour."

"So I perceive."

"And it will give you pleasure to copy it for me in miniature?" He seemed to plead.

"Great pleasure – for three louis," she laughed.

He laughed with her, as at an excellent jest. "You amuse yourself at my expense by pretending to give importance to such a detail."

"I do not give it importance, Monsieur le Comte. It possesses importance. We are poor people."

He faced her smiling, a darkly handsome man, perhaps a little heavy in the lips, and with the eyes of a faun. He was moderately tall, exquisite in his appointments and graceful in his movements. "That is not surprising since you are no better at a bargain. I am, I hope, too honest to take advantage of your innocence. We will say five louis."

"It is too generous."

"For such exquisite work? You do not know your worth, Madame."

"You shall have of my best," she promised him.

"It is much to deserve."

He smiled again, whilst her eyes, shifting from portrait to original, noted for her purpose that full redness of his lips, the brightness of his dark eyes. "It is very well," she said. "How soon do you require the miniature?"

"Oh, but at your leisure, Madame. Entirely at your leisure. It does not press. Art is not to be hurried."

"I shall not try your patience, Monsieur le Comte. It only remains to thank you for the commission."

This was clearly polite dismissal. But he made no shift to go. "It is for me to thank you for undertaking it." His dark eyes considered her with undisguised admiration. "Has none ever painted your portrait?" he asked.

"Why, no."

"When it happens, be painted as you are now, in some such turban. A ravishing effect. Whilst we lose the glory of your tresses, yet the very loss lends your countenance, in its noble pallor and chaste severity, an austere perfection, a nun-like glamour."

She laughed outright. "This is to make a sonnet of me."

"You inspire no less, Madame. And I do not jest. I am intensely in earnest when I beg you to be painted just so."

"And I am no less in earnest when I remind you again that we are poor folk. We do not have our portraits painted."

"That is what I find shameful."

"But why? If there were no poor, there would be no rich. It is by such contrasts that the world is made."

"Not always rightly made. For instance, it is not right that such as you, a woman of your beauty, your talent, your incomparable air, should hide in such mean surroundings the graces that would adorn a court." His sweeping gesture implied scorn of the humbly furnished, rather shabby apartment.

She overspread her resentment by a serene coolness that was unconsciously modelled upon Alverley's. "You want to flatter me. This, I assure you, is court enough for me."

"But it should not be. That is what I find intolerably wrong. A precious jewel set in brass."

"Ah!" She looked him challengingly between the eyes. "And the remedy?"

The poor gentleman, as ready as another to believe what he hoped, mistook the nature of the challenge. "Do you need that I point it out? Why should you waste yourself amid these poor tatters, in drudgeries that are almost sordid, when you may command life's best?"

"I am willing enough to command it. But will it obey?"

"Try it, Madame." A sudden eagerness robbed him of some breath. "Or let a friend assist you."

"A friend?" Her calm was unruffled. "I like to have things clear. You mean a protector perhaps?"

"You have said it, Madame. A protector."

"Yourself, for instance?"

"If you should find me worthy."

"How am I to judge?"

He drew nearer. "Ah, Madame. I could so easily convince you."

"I do not doubt your willingness. Just as I do not doubt that to be the real purpose of your visit. Confess, sir, that the miniature is no more than a pretext." Her voice remained pleasantly level. "But what need? It is too plain. You arrive at a moment when you know that my husband is absent, when you will be sure to find me alone."

If she thought to put him out of countenance, he disappointed her.

"Can you blame me, Madame, when I tell you that I am drawn by a power beyond my strength to resist?"

She laughed. "How practised you are! How practised in the arts that destroy a woman's balance."

He drew back. "I perceive that you mock me, Madame."

"It is the best that I can do. After all, you are a pupil of my husband's, and my husband depends upon his pupils for his livelihood. And I am to earn five louis to paint you a miniature. You will understand that I cannot afford the luxury of annoyance."

He became wistful. "It would be less offensive, Madame, than this derision. But I understand, I think. You regard me as a mere hunter of good fortunes, an opportunist in gallantry. You do me a great wrong. Let me confess all. It is not mere chance that has made me a pupil of Monsieur Dene. Nor is it so necessary for me to learn English as I have pretended. One Sunday, a month ago, riding on the

Cours la Reine with Monsieur de St Maur, I saw you walking with your husband. All that I know now of what happened to me in that moment is that the need to see you again was the most urgent that I have ever known. Monsieur de St Maur told me who you were. It was as if Destiny were at work, and I could scarcely credit the good fortune that made it so easy to gratify my wishes. What do I say – my wishes? My irresistible needs. For I loved you, Madame, from the moment of that passing glance."

"And you hoped that poverty in alliance with feminine frailty would render you irresistible in turn. Since it does not so fall out, shall we close this conversation? You see, it happens that I love my husband."

He was fiercely scornful, betrayed by irritation. "That poor pedant!"

"Poor, unfortunately. And a pedant, no doubt, since he teaches languages. But not on that account an object for any man's commiseration. It was commiseration, was it not, that you expressed? It was not, by any chance, contempt? However! It is no matter. We will forget all this if you please, Monsieur le Comte." She smiled sweetly. "I should be sorry to lose a client, and deprive my husband of a pupil. Sorrier still if he should be caused annoyance or anxiety. Therefore, oblivion will be best. I will work on the miniature without delay." And she moved to the door to open it for him.

He bowed low with every token of submission. "Madame, in all things and in all humility your servant; your very faithful servant."

He went off in some bewilderment. The experience was entirely novel and contained much to mystify him. The insistent thought that he had been mocked was countered by the gentleness of her dismissal. Was he to conclude that she was – as she seemed to represent herself – at once prudish and mercenary? That whilst rejecting his advances, she muffled the rejection, lest, as she had said, she should lose a client and her husband a pupil? Impossible that a genuine prude should be so calculating. Besides, prudery never failed of indignation when assailed. A genuine prude would angrily have shown him the door at the first hint of his purpose. So that either she mocked him – and he found it hard to believe that a prude could ever exercise the self-control to do so – or else she employed a wanton guile as a whetstone to his desires, leaving the door open to further advances by the pretence of mercenary considerations and the covert assurance that her husband must be left in ignorance of what had passed. Out of his wide experience Monsieur de Mazan came hopefully to the latter conclusion: a nice instance of ex hypothesi judgment.

Alverley, returning home in the course of the afternoon, found the Count's portrait displayed on the easel, and Dorothea at work upon the miniature copy. He stood considering the canvas.

"When did this arrive?"

"Monsieur de Mazan brought it, himself, this morning."

"Himself? What impatience that he could not wait until tomorrow when he comes for his lesson. It's a flattering eagerness."

"An eager gentleman, Monsieur le Comte," she laughed, and worked on.

"You do not like him?" said he, on an inference from her tone rather than her words.

She shrugged. "He is amusing with his fatuities."

"Fatuities? Yes. You judge shrewdly. A coxcomb." He studied the portrait. "It is all written there. The painter possesses vision. He has set the fellow's nature upon the canvas."

"I hope my copy will prove faithful," she jested. "Truth is not to be treated lightly. And I am to have five louis for it. Monsieur de Mazan insists."

"Ah! He is more generous than I should have judged him."

She worked so diligently that when on the following evening Monsieur de Mazan came for his lesson, the miniature was almost finished. He professed himself as delighted with her reproduction as amazed at the facility that enabled her to make such speed.

By the time his exercises in English grammar had come to an end she had put the finishing touches to her work. "It will be dry by tomorrow," she told him. "If you will send for it then, it will be ready."

Instead of sending, he came, himself, next day, again in Alverley's absence. This time he was greeted with a frown.

"I hoped, Monsieur, that I had persuaded you to be wise. I asked you to send."

"How quick to misjudge me," he complained. "What cruel anxiety to find fault. Though I may lack the power to command your love, yet I cannot think that I deserve your hate."

"This is foolish. I do not hate you, Monsieur."

"Come. That is already something."

"I only desire that we understand each other, once for all."

"The echo of my own desire," said he. "But – alas! – you do not permit me to understand. However, this is no deliberate violation of your wishes. I did not send because there is something further that I desire of you – of your art, Madame. May I not come in?"

She had kept him on the threshold, holding the door whilst she spoke to him. At his request she now stood aside and allowed him to enter.

He sauntered forward, leaning on his gold-headed cane, his three-cornered hat under his arm.

"You have wrapped up the portrait. That is premature. The exquisite miniature you have done is for myself. I now require another one, for my mother, if I can persuade you to undertake it."

"Of course." She agreed without warmth. She was a little taken aback. She could not dismiss the suspicion that this, again, was no better than a pretext. "But first be sure that you approve the one I have made." She proffered him a shallow little box of white pasteboard.

He opened it, and in a long silence he contemplated the little picture, done on ivory. "You but increase my wonder with every fresh revelation of your talent." He sighed, closed the box and put it in his pocket. He drew forth his purse, and laid ten louis on the table.

"What is this?" she asked.

"For the two miniatures."

She frowned at the gold pieces. Then she laughed. "You make me wealthy."

He was quick to take this for a cue. "That, did you permit it, would be my loftiest ambition. It should be yours to dispose of all my possessions. And how you would grace them!"

Quietly she answered him: "I thought, Monsieur le Comte, that we had exhausted that topic."

"Can I help forgetting it when I behold you? The other day I commended the turban. That lent your face a nun-like aspect. A blasphemy, as I perceive, when I see your loveliness enriched and crowned by the glory of your hair."

She lowered her eyes under his smouldering glance. "Let me thank you for this further commission," she said quietly, as if she had not heard the rest. "I shall lose no time in executing it. It will be ready when you come to my husband for your next lesson."

He continued intently to regard her. Then he sighed again and shook his head. "Is it possible that the good God who made you so beautiful should have given you a stone for heart?"

She laughed outright. "No, Monsieur. It is not possible. But whatever my heart may be made of is no affair of yours or of any man's, saving my husband."

"Oh, this insistence upon a husband!" he protested irritably.

"You make it necessary." Firmly she led the way to the door, so firmly that Monsieur de Mazan must perforce take his dismissal.

When Alverley came home that afternoon the ten louis still lay on the table where the Count had placed them. "What is this?" he cried, at the sight of so much gold, twice as much as he earned in a month at the Lycée. "Into what Pactolus have you been dipping your bucket?"

"They come from our good patron, Monsieur de Mazan. He has commanded a second miniature, this time for Madame his mother."

"My blessings on his filial piety. May he have a grandmother, an aunt or two, and perhaps some sisters whom he would wish to favour similarly."

"I hope not."

He looked at her sharply, his levity arrested by her tone.

"I am sick of his face," she explained. "To paint it twice is at least once too many."

He came close, and took her by the shoulders. Gravely his dark eyes searched her face. "He has not by chance given you any other reason?"

"What other reason could he give me?"

"It is what I am asking you. He prefers to come when he knows that I am absent. He pays extravagantly."

"If he chooses to be a fool need it trouble you, Charles?"

"That depends upon the nature of his folly. If he should have the presumption to trouble you…"

Her laughter interrupted him. "What am I that I should be troubled by him, or any man? You do not flatter me, my dear. Adventures are to the adventurous; gallantry for women who invite it."

"Not always. There are enterprising men who do not wait for invitations, and Monsieur de Mazan may well be of them. Those languorous eyes, those full lips, this prodigality of gold do not inspire confidence in me."

"Nor in me," she laughed. "Which forearms me against the need."

Reassured, he kissed her, and let the subject drop.

She went to work with such application that when Mazan came for his next lesson, two days later, the second miniature was thrust upon him together with the original painting, although he begged her to keep the latter yet awhile.

"It is possible that I may require yet another of your exquisite copies."

"In that case you can bring me the portrait again. But I hope you will not, for I weary of repeating the same work, and no longer do justice to the subject."

"Modesty, Madame, goes ever hand-in-hand with real talent." Under her husband's eyes it was the best that the poor man could do. When he left that evening she imagined that she had seen the last of his advances. This was to underrate both his judgment of her case and his pertinacity. To her amazed annoyance, one morning a week or so later, he presented himself again. She received him standing stiffly in the half-open doorway, one hand upon the door barring the entrance.

"Monsieur de Mazan!" Her tone was a rebuke, and in a breath she added: "You will excuse me, sir. I am busy and pressed for time. I can undertake no more miniatures at present."

He was solemn. "Alas, Madame! It is no matter of that. I would it were. I fear that I am the bearer of unhappy tidings. They concern Monsieur Dene. Suffer me to come in and explain."

If still mistrustful, at least she was startled into compliance. She not only admitted him, but offered him a chair, and seated herself to face him.

"I have thought it best, Madame, that you should hear this from a friend, and hear it with the assurance that all is not lost perhaps. You will be aware of the deep interest that my uncle, the Duc de Richelieu, takes in the affairs of the Lycée Louis-le-Grand. Because relations between France and England are unhappily not of the best, the governors of the Lycée, moved by stupid political spite, have taken it into their heads to abolish the chair of English."

This was grave news. The loss to Alverley of that regular employment would mean a return to the penury and hard shifts through which they had formerly struggled. She made no attempt to dissemble her dismay.

"I perceive your concern, Madame. It distresses me profoundly. But do not yet despair. It is because at the same time I can bring you a message of hope that I have preferred to give you this news rather than have it reach you from another who would have nothing to add to it."

"That is kind, Monsieur," she said, and waited.

He looked round the homely room, uncarpeted and sparsely furnished, yet not without a certain grace. The amenities might be few, but there was a gulf between them and the wretchedness that must attend their curtailment. Before the easel stood her work-table, bearing her palette and a cluster of brushes in a piece of blue faience pottery. These and the open clavichord, with a sheet of music on the stand, and a bowl bearing a cluster of autumn flowers, were evidences of the cultured tastes of the room's tenants. If the morning sunlight streaming through the open windows betrayed the worn and faded tapestry of the settle and chairs, yet it revealed how well polished was the woodwork, how well swept the floor.

"Happily there is a chance that this misfortune may be averted. After all, there are good arguments against the governors' narrow views. My uncle's influence with them is paramount, and my own influence with his grace sufficient, I think, to persuade him to bid them leave things as they are."

"That would be the action of a true friend."

"What other action could you expect from me? My dear, you know, I hope, that there is nothing I would not do for you. If my heart bleeds to behold you, so queenly, so peerless, in quarters so mean and unworthy as these, with what horror must I not think of you deprived of even these poor shards?" He rose, and ran on with a warming eloquence. "When will you consent to hear the voice of reason, Dorothea? To accept the gifts I should be proud to bestow on you?"

Her eyes grew sad as they considered him. "And thus you spoil all," she reproached him. "You besmear your good action."

The faint note of scorn stirred him to annoyance. "That good action is not yet performed. It is for you to say whether it shall be; whether your husband is to lose even this beggar's competence which he earns at Louis-le-Grand."

"So!" Her grey eyes looked up at him steadily, coldly. "It is a bargain that you offer. I should have known it. I am stupid sometimes, through faith in human nature. I should have seen, of course, that a true friend would already have done what you say it is in your power to do at so little cost."

"Can you really be angry with me that I snatch at every chance to win you? Why will you play with me, Dorothea? Do you think I am so easily deceived? Do you suppose I don't realize that if you had been serious in rejecting my love, you would at once have shown me the door? That you did not proves that your heart was not untouched, that it responded to the passion you had aroused in me."

"That is how you read me, is it? It proves your wits to be no better than your honour. I told you, sir, that I already have a lover. He happens to be my husband."

This time he was really dumbfounded. "It is incredible!" he cried at last "Are you really so infatuated that for the sake of this poor starveling pedant, this wretched gutterling without even the wit to value so priceless a treasure as yourself, one who is utterly unworthy…"

"Not another word, Monsieur!" She was on her feet, standing as tall as he and eye to eye with him, her face white, her glance hard with contempt. "Wait!"

Checked by this sudden cold fury and the consciousness that in his irritation he had blundered fatally, he stood silent whilst she swept to her work-table. From its drawer she took a purse, and from that purse under his wondering eyes she counted out four louis.

"For each of the miniatures I painted for you, my price was three louis. You chose to pay me five, which I was so foolish as to accept, not perceiving that what you added was a bribe, a payment on account of value to be received."

"Madame!" he cried out in repudiation.

"Pray take back these four louis, and go. Go, and do not presume to set foot here again. As I do not wish my husband to be distressed or annoyed, you will send him a line explaining as you please – lying should offer you no difficulty – that you are unable to continue your lessons. Here is your money."

She held it out. Livid with anger, he did not move. "You insult me, Madame."

Her lip twisted into a smile. "Is the prerogative of insult to be yours?" Then under stress of a sudden overmastering passion, the bonds of her restraint were burst. Her voice soared to stridency. "Must I be plainer still before you will understand? Must I tell you that you are vile? Take your money, I say. Take it and go! Canaille!" And she flung the coins in his face just as the door opened, and Alverley stood at gaze under the lintel.

Chapter 2

The Edict

Monsieur de Mazan recoiled, not so much before the golden missiles as before the opprobrious epithet unthinkably inapplicable to a man of his exalted birth. In the blindness of his fury he was conscious neither of the sound behind him, nor of the sudden change in her countenance, the fear that swept over it at sight of Alverley standing so attentively still.

"Madame, you shall be sorry for this. Remember it when your miserable husband is on the pavement, as he soon will be, I promise you."

"Monsieur le Comte," said a gentle, level voice behind him. "I think you are distressing Madame, and that is something that I cannot permit. I believe I heard her tell you to go. It is not for such a mirror of the courtesies as yourself to disregard a lady's dismissal."

Monsieur de Mazan swung round. The urbane tone of mockery was an excruciation to nerves already raw. "You listen at keyholes, do you?"

Alverley actually displayed amusement. "And if I did, have you a right to complain? It is my own keyhole, after all. And this is my house. You were forgetting it, I think. There is the door, Monsieur. It is all that I have to offer you. Unless you should prefer the window."

Monsieur de Mazan stood tense and menacing. "Insolent!" he cried, in the tone of the great gentleman speaking to a lackey. "Out of my way, rascal!" And he struck Alverley across the body with his cane, a wanton gesture of contempt and rage.

Alverley stiffened. He bowed slightly. "Bien!" he said, his voice crisp. "Since you insist, my friends shall wait upon you."

The Count had already reached the door. He checked, and turned. He could not believe his ears. "You said?" he asked.

"That my friends shall wait upon you."

"Your friends! Upon me?" Amazement overspread his face. Then he uttered an angry laugh. "Why, you presumptuous English oaf, do you imagine I would consent to meet your kind? For what do you take me?"

"I must hesitate to tell you in the presence of a lady. Certainly not for a man of honour. Nevertheless, I'll pocket my pride, and send my friends to you."

"Warn them that they shall have a whipping from my grooms when they arrive. That is all the satisfaction you shall have from me." He strode out, and slammed the door so that the air shook.

Alverley came to Dorothea, and put an arm about her quivering body. "My dear!" he soothed her. "Tell me what occurred."

She told him all, to be reproached at the end for not having told him sooner.

"I did not want just this to happen," she defended herself. "I thought I could handle him. And so I could have done if, like a fool, I had not lost my temper in the end." Then fervently she begged: "You will let this go no further."

"There is something," he answered quietly, "that I owe both to you and to myself."

"You do not owe it to me to put your life in danger. And what need? As a schoolmaster so much is not expected of you."

"You saw how he counted upon that."

"Let him. What does it matter? What would become of me if…if anything happened to you?"

"At the hands of that fribble? Have no uneasiness." He patted her shoulder and kissed her in token that the matter was dismissed. As he turned aside he caught a gleam from the gold scattered on the floor. "Your gallant has left his louis, after all."

"I do not want them."

"Use them to pay for Masses for his soul when I have done with him."

Some reassurance she could gather from his quiet confidence; for the rest, she was of too true a temper to seek to dissuade him from a course that he accounted dictated by his honour. But under the outward calm which she imposed upon herself, her mind was in anguish for two days.

It might have been longer but for the promptitude of Alverley's action. On the very day of the scene with Monsieur de Mazan he presented himself at the Prussian Embassy in the Rue St Honoré. It had come to his knowledge some time ago that his old friend and fellow-aide-de-camp, the Freiherr von Katzenstein, was now there as military attaché.

Amazement at sight of him was followed by uproarious joy in the Baron. "Charles! Is it, indeed, you?" He was enfolded in a wrestler's hug. "But where have you been these years? Whence do you spring? And how is it with you?"

Even as he questioned, his kindly light eyes were running over his visitor, and growing solemn as they remarked the plain and rusty suit of black.

"But it is a miracle! A resurrection! Stéphanie will swoon with excitement when she hears that you have been found. You remember my little Stéphanie? She is still waiting," he jested, "for you to come back and marry her. And she's grown very marriageable. As tall as my shoulder. But I chatter. It's news of yourself I want."

Alverley rendered a brief and limited account that left Katzenstein indignant. "A teacher of languages! You! Had you, then, no friends at court? And how long have you known that I am here, that you have not come to me before? A teacher of languages! God save us! But that's over now. I am leaving France next week. His Majesty wants me at Potsdam. And you'll come with me. That will make me doubly welcome to him. Fritz will be overjoyed to have you beside him again. He often spoke of you, and at one time even employed agents to discover you. Indeed, I wonder that you haven't, yourself, thought of seeking him since his accession."

"I have thought of Katte," said Alverley grimly.

"Ah!" Katzenstein's handsome, kindly countenance became overcast. "That was an ugly affair."

"A very ugly affair. A foul crime."

"Yes. It shocked the world. But things have changed in Prussia since those days, as you'll find. For, of course, you are coming back. You can count upon Fritz's affection for you."

"It is gratifying," said Alverley, politely evasive. "What presses at the moment, however, is my need of a friend who knows me for what I am. An impudent fellow, presuming upon his station, has thought it safe to lay his cane upon Mr Stuart-Dene, a humble schoolmaster, and refuses him satisfaction because of his lowly birth. Dare I ask you, my dear Katze, to carry a message to him from the Marquess of Alverley?"

At first the Baron was taken aback by the sinister request. When, however, he had recovered from the shock, and recalled the reputation as a swordsman which Alverley had enjoyed in Berlin, he ended by finding amusement in the situation. "Faith, it should be interesting. It has a dramatic flavour. It will be diverting to discover to this gentleman the wolf inside the sheepskin he rashly belaboured. Who is your victim?"

"The Comte de Mazan."

Katzenstein's brows went up. "Old Richelieu's nephew? Better and better. I know the dog. If you are really resolved I am at your service, of course."

Thus it fell out that late that evening Monsieur de Mazan was waited upon at his mansion in the Faubourg St Germain by the Freiherr von Katzenstein accompanied by Colonel von Holtzenfeldt.

In a salon of green and gold magnificence the Comte de Mazan hastened to give an effusive welcome to these distinguished foreign visitors.

"My dear Baron! My dear Colonel! To what do I owe the honour?"

The Prussians clicked their heels, and bowed with cool formality. Katzenstein replied for both.

"We permit ourselves this intrusion on behalf of our friend Milord the Marquis de Alverley."

"I do not think I have the honour of his acquaintance. I do not recall the name. But it suffices that he is your friend. In what can I serve him?"

"By indicating two friends of yours with whom we can make the necessary arrangements for a meeting which you have rendered inevitable."

"Messieurs!" Monsieur de Mazan's affability was completely effaced. "But what is this? I do not understand. I have said that I do not even know your Marquis de... What did you say was his name?"

"Alverley. You know him very well, Monsieur le Comte. But by his family name of Stuart-Dene."

"Stuart-Dene?" Slowly Monsieur de Mazan's face changed colour. "If this is a jest, sir, I must deplore its taste. Stuart-Dene is a poor pedant whom I have hired to give me lessons in English."

"Monsieur le Marquis de Alverley, like a good many other exiled Jacobites, is at odd shifts to make a livelihood. Whilst this endures he does not choose to be known by his title; a commendable reticence. I should not be acting for him if there were any doubt of his identity. It happens that he is an old friend of mine, and was at one time my fellow-aide-de-camp to his late Majesty King Frederick William of Prussia."

For a long silent moment de Mazan stared in stupefaction at the Prussians. "I see," he said, at last. "I see. But it goes without saying that I was not aware of this. If Milord Alverley chooses to travesty himself as a roturier, he has, it seems to me, little right to complain if he is treated as one."

"That, Monsieur le Comte, if you will permit me to say so, would be a novel argument to advance in a court of honour. Also, I am afraid, it would be inadmissible. A blow has been struck. That is very grave, as you will admit, and we have no choice but to press for satisfaction."

"The blow was struck upon Stuart-Dene, the schoolmaster; not upon Milord Alverley."

"Unfortunately it is impossible to separate one from the other."

"You will have to separate them. You are losing your time, gentlemen. The circumstances are too unusual, too contemptible. I must refuse to take them seriously."

"I permit myself to remind you again, Monsieur le Comte, that a blow has been struck. Milord Alverley cannot but take it seriously."

"But Stuart-Dene, the teacher, is under no such necessity."

Colonel von Holtzenfeldt put in a word, impatiently. "The argument pursues a circle."

"Precisely. Therefore, we can arrive nowhere. There is an edict against duelling, and I do not propose to expose myself to its consequences for the satisfaction of a person who veils his identity under an alias. That, sirs, is my last word."

Katzenstein and Holtzenfeldt looked at each other, and then the Colonel spoke again. "You allude to consequences, sir. Have you reflected what must be the consequences to yourself of this refusal? Have you considered that you leave Milord Alverley no alternative but to cane you in public?"

"Monsieur!" Mazan was outraged. "Do you dare?"

"It is not a question of what I dare, but of what my friend will certainly dare. As you will then no longer be in ignorance of his true identity, you will have to choose between meeting him and being excluded from the company of men of honour."

The Count flung about the room in a passion. "Dieu de Dieu! I am caught in a snare, then?"

"I am afraid you baited it yourself, Monsieur le Comte," said the Colonel. "But there it is. You now know exactly where you stand."

The bravest of the brave with women, with men Monsieur de Mazan was not brave at all. Hitherto he had conducted his life with circumspection, careful to give offence only to those whose inferior social station excluded active resentment. Here, in the case of this schoolmaster-marquis, he was hoist at last with his own petard, or would be unless he adopted what he believed to be the only remaining way out.

He strove to appear calm, and contrived to be pompous. "Messieurs," he delivered himself, "had I known with whom I dealt it is unthinkable that I should so have used a gentleman of Milord Alverley's quality. It naturally follows that, aware of it now, I should wish unhesitatingly to offer my apologies. That, messieurs, I am sure will satisfy the Marquis as an honourable issue to this unhappy incident."

Katzenstein smiled in undisguised amusement. "It sounds well as you state it, with your own particular eloquence. But translated into common terms how will it sound? Monsieur de Mazan struck a man whom he believed of too humble a station to claim honourable satisfaction. When, however, it unexpectedly transpired that the man was of a station at least equal to Monsieur de Mazan's own, rather than grant the satisfaction required, Monsieur de Mazan abased himself in an apology. How will the world judge that, monsieur? What term do you suppose it will apply to it?"

"Sir! Is it your aim to insult me?"

"Far from it. I actually warn you of the insults that will await you if you persist in your present attitude."

"Just as I, sir," added the Colonel, "have warned you of the public caning that is equally inevitable."

Thus at last – scrupulously following their instructions that no compromise was admissible – they broke down Mazan's resistance. It gave way suddenly in an explosion of passion. "Enough! Your masquerading friend shall have his way. It is an infamy. But I am weary of arguing. Since he prefers my point to my apology, my point he shall have. I shall give myself the pleasure of killing him."

When they met in the Bois on the following morning, Monsieur de Mazan failed to fulfil his threat, although the fury of his attack showed the earnestness of his intentions. The encounter was brief. When that fury had spent itself against an easy, practised guard, Alverley ran him neatly through the body, and left him in the care of his friends.

Katzenstein would have carried Alverley off at once to his house to celebrate the victory and renew acquaintance with the impatient Stéphanie. But Alverley, excusing himself, postponed that visit until the morrow. His immediate duty was to relieve Dorothea's anxieties, and he was naturally in haste to fulfil it.

This relief, however, was to prove short-lived; for that same evening Alverley was arrested by the police of the Lieutenant-General, and carried off to the Châtelet.

"Do not be alarmed," he told Dorothea at parting. "This is no more than a formality to satisfy the edict. When the facts are disclosed, it will be seen that the provocation was too grave to be disregarded by a man of honour. You may be confident that I shall return in a day or two."

Things, however, were not to run the course that he so confidently predicted. De Mazan came of too powerful a family, and the head of it, the old Duc de Richelieu, was demanding the application of the edict in all its rigour, whilst Alverley, not merely a foreigner but an exile, and therefore a foreigner without the protection of an embassy, could command no influence to oppose to that which was being exerted against him.

At his examination he was brought to perceive that his fate hung upon the life of Mazan. If the Count died, his own life would probably be forfeit. If the Count survived, imprisonment in the Bastille, perhaps for years, was the likely end of the matter.

He was plunged into despair, and this by no means on his own account. In his thirty-eight years he had quaffed so much of the bitter wine of life that he could almost welcome ending it. And to end it a victim, as he felt himself, of a vindictive injustice, seemed to him an apt conclusion, in harmony with the course of it. But there was Dorothea, utterly dependent upon him, to be left without provision or protection at the mercy of the Mazans of this world. Sensitively governed by his sense of duty to her, he raged now at his impotence. Often had he upbraided himself in the course of the last ten years for his presumption in taking charge of Dorothea's life, for the penury to which he had committed her, for his utter failure to discharge the responsibility assumed in a manner befitting his station, in the manner which he accounted it her right to expect. But never had his upbraidings been as fierce as now, when he beheld her in danger of finding herself cast destitute and defenceless upon the world. It was in Alverley's nature, as it is in all fine natures, to harbour a higher sense of his duty to others than of the duty of others to himself. Hence he must now bitterly reproach himself with having set considerations of honour above considerations of Dorothea. He should have foreseen every possible consequence of his action before plunging into the encounter with de Mazan. Under the anonymity of the schoolmaster he could have taken the blow, and let the matter drop, especially since by what had happened they were rid of the Count and his importunities. In this he did himself injustice; for it was not for the blow that he had set out to punish Mazan, but for the insult to Dorothea.

He had reached the very nadir of despair on that morning, two weeks after his arrest, when an officer, a lieutenant of the Maison du Roi, entered his cell to surprise him with a summons to the presence of Cardinal Fleury. Casting about him for a reason why the great minister who governed France for the young king should thus send for him, he bethought him of Katzenstein. He conceived that the Count, exerting ambassadorial influence, might have pleaded for him with the Cardinal and obtained him some measure of consideration. Hope revived. At least he was afforded an opportunity of stating his case to a man who, out of his renowned uprightness, might prove sympathetic.

Chapter 3

Cardinal Fleury

In a spacious, lofty, sumptuously furnished salon of the Palace of Versailles, whose windows, reaching from floor to ceiling, overlooked the terraces, the fountains that had delighted the Sun-King, and a long sweep of park, now vague in the mists of a November morning, the Cardinal came to the waiting Lord Alverley.

His Eminence was tall and spare, and in the scarlet silk that clothed him from head to foot, from skull-cap to slippers, would have been imposing but that his back was arched under the burden of his years. He counted more than eighty. His face, grey and bloodless, was finely featured and still handsome, shrewd yet kindly, and the eyes, although dulled by the arcus senilis, still preserved something of their earlier glow.

He advanced slowly, leaning upon a crutch-handled ebony cane.

"It is good of you, Monsieur le Marquis, to give yourself the trouble of waiting upon an old man." The words must have sounded ironical but for the gentle, even voice that uttered them.

Alverley bowed in silence, and waited.

His Eminence reached a table on which there were writing materials. The chamberlain who attended him advanced an armchair of gilded wood upholstered in blue satin, and placed on the table a little volume bound in white vellum.

The Cardinal lowered himself into the chair, and dismissed both the chamberlain and the officer who had escorted the prisoner, bidding them wait in the antechamber. Whilst they were withdrawing, the old eyes, deep in their sockets, made an intent study of the Englishman. He considered the tall, well-knit figure, so straight and soldierly in its well-worn suit of black; the rather narrow patrician face, appearing the narrower from the breadth of brow; the dark, kindly eyes, in contradiction to the bitterly humorous lines of the tight mouth.

As the door closed, his Eminence broke the silence in his quiet, gentle, infinitely courteous voice. "I am desolated, Monsieur le Marquis, that you should be in your present position, and I hope that it may not prove beyond my power to be of some service to you."

Brighter glowed the hope that had been lighted in Alverley's black despair. He bowed again, outwardly impassive. "Your Eminence is very gracious."

"I am sorry to gather that you have fared none too well at the hands of fortune. But at least you appear to have known how to retain the regard and affection of some persons of rank. Your friend, Monsieur le Baron de Katzenstein, who left Paris a week ago to return to Berlin, has paid me one or two visits on your behalf. He has told me a good deal about you, and I have been able to learn a good deal more from other sources. Unhappily I was not able to give the Baron the reassurances he sought before he left. I had to tell him frankly that the edict is very definite, and that Monsieur de Mazan's uncle, the Duc de Richelieu, is pressing for its enforcement. It is at least fortunate that since his departure Monsieur de Mazan's condition has sensibly improved, and this morning I was relieved to learn that he is considered out of danger. That, in itself, lessens the difficulties, since it lessens the penalties to which you are liable."

He paused there, as if to give Alverley an opportunity of speaking, and Alverley, with his new-born hope making rapid growth, took advantage of it.

"Your Eminence has perhaps not been informed that the provocation came from Monsieur de Mazan. He struck me with his cane. I sent my friends to him, confident that any court of honour must hold that I could do no less, and therefore acquit me of blame."

"You do not mention how you provoked the blow. For I take it that Monsieur de Mazan must in his turn have suffered some provocation."

"The provocation of being caught in a dishonourable situation."

"Ah!" The Cardinal produced from his scarlet robes a gold snuff-box, and quietly tapped it. "I understand from Monseigneur de Richelieu that the quarrel concerned a woman."

"A lady, Eminence," Alverley corrected. "Yes."

"In effect, your mistress."

Momentarily Alverley's lips tightened. "In effect," he admitted. "But I could hold her in no greater honour if she were my wife."

His Eminence held a pinch of snuff between thumb and forefinger.

"Unfortunately others may not do the like. If the lady had indeed been your wife, the case would be altered, and the courts might justify your action. As it is, I see little hope of that, especially as the prosecution will be pressed by Monseigneur de Richelieu. However…" He paused, applied the snuff to his nostrils, and closed and pocketed the box. "There is a possibility that I might find employment for you, should you be willing to undertake it. In that case, of course, the service of the State must override every other consideration.

"But I keep you standing, Monsieur le Marquis. Be seated, I beg."

He indicated a chair, beyond the table. Alverley took it, with a word of thanks, wondering why the Cardinal should be so long in coming to the point.

"From what Baron von Katzenstein told me, I understand that you were, during your sojourn in Berlin, intimate with King Frederick of Prussia when he was Crown Prince."

"I was closely associated with him, Eminence. Yes. I know him well."

The Cardinal leaned forward a little. "Excellent." The old eyes became of a searching keenness. "And with such exceptional opportunity for judgment what estimate, may I ask, did you form of his character?"

For a moment Alverley hesitated. "Your Eminence desires me to be quite frank, of course."

"As if I were your confessor, my son."

"I found him presumptuous, vain, affected and perfidious."

Audibly his Eminence drew in his breath. His white eyebrows went up. "You make it evident that you do not reciprocate the high regard in which Katzenstein tells me that you are held by Frederick of Prussia. And perfidious, eh? Perfidious. You will have good grounds for that?"

"The best. An instance should suffice. Once, when he planned to escape from the brutalities of his father, and, being caught, supposed himself in danger of his life, he cast the blame upon his best friend, Hans Hermann von Katte, and, taking shelter behind him, flung him to the headsman."

The Cardinal nodded thoughtfully. "I know, of course, of that barbarous murder; the civilized world was shocked by it. But I did not know that the unfortunate young man was betrayed by his friend the Crown Prince. You are quite sure of it?"

"I have it on the word of King Frederick William, himself. I was his aide-de-camp at the time."

"So Katzenstein told me. Yes, yes. And you had this fact from the King, himself?" The old man's eyes were veiled. He sat in thought for a moment. "Perfidious, eh? Perfidious," he muttered, as if to himself. "In describing him you have not mentioned ambition. Tell me now: did you find him ambitious?"

Alverley's lips were scornful. "Of an ambition rooted in vanity. Ambitious to be a poet, a man of letters, a philosopher, even a musician, with none of the equipment to be any of these things. His education had been neglected, misdirected. Yet a natural ability he certainly possesses, and he was avid of learning, but merely, I think, so that he might gratify those vanities."

"This is interesting. Very interesting. I am much obliged to you for your frankness, Monsieur le Marquis, although it merely serves to deepen a mystification I am anxious – most anxious – to dispel. From what I gather from other sources – particularly from Monsieur de Valori, his very Christian Majesty's ambassador to Prussia – it is possible that the King Frederick of today and the Crown Prince Frederick you knew ten years ago are very different persons. Of course a man may change a good deal in ten years, from adolescence to manhood, but not in essentials; not in fundamentals. At least, that is my experience in the course of a long life. It has been wisely said that the Ethiopian cannot change his skin nor the leopard his spots, which means that a nature never really alters; its seeming changes are merely the intensification of its inherent traits. And yet..." He sighed. "This man presents me with a baffling problem.

"I am being entirely frank and open with you, Monsieur le Marquis, as is necessary in view of what I have to propose."

Alverley inclined his head in silence, wondering.

From the table his Eminence took up the slender volume in vellum.

"You speak of him as a dilettante, an aspirant to literary fame; and in this, Monsieur de Voltaire, with good grounds for judgment, confirms you. I have here a treatise by King Frederick, published last Spring, entitled *The Anti-Macchiavel*. Its impeccable French and elegant turn of phrase are due, no doubt, to Monsieur de Voltaire, who revised and edited it. So far, then, as literary merit, your Prince is merely a crow in the plumage of a jay. But the actual sentiments must be his own, and no sentiments could be loftier. The work is a complete and righteously indignant refutation of Macchiavelli's cynical gospel of opportunism. He pillories Macchiavelli throughout as an infamous corrupter, a monster of crime, a charlatan of hell."

His Eminence had opened the book whilst speaking, and was turning the pages. "Listen to this," he said, and began to read: " '*The desire for aggrandizement with the spoils of another will not occur to the mind of an honest man or to him who desires the esteem of the world.*' And then there is this: '*I ask myself what can induce a man to raise his power upon the misery and destruction of other men, or how he can believe that he will make himself illustrious by creating miseries.'* Indeed, wherever you open the book, you come upon sentiments of the same noble character; so that the work constitutes no less than a very solemn contract in which this Prince has engaged himself with mankind."

He set the volume down, and looked at Alverley, who remained silently puzzled. "You offer no comment, Monsieur."

"What am I to say, Eminence? There is nothing here to surprise me. I perceive but the expressions of the presumption and vanity of which I spoke. Yielding to a cacoethes scribendi, and urged by conceit to appear arrestingly before the world, the poetaster has turned philosopher. He has found a facile subject for criticism in Macchiavelli, whom he can have read only in translation, and whom he has probably imperfectly understood; and with the assistance, as your Eminence says, of Monsieur de Voltaire, he has produced an essay of a pinchbeck glitter with which he hopes to dazzle mankind."

Meditatively the Cardinal stroked his chin with a hand that was the colour of old ivory. "That is very possibly true; probably even. You suppose, then, that this work is insincere; that it does not represent his true sentiment?"

"Oh, as to that, on the contrary, Eminence. They are just the sentiments I should expect in a prince who is absorbed in dilettantism, in phrase-making, flute-playing, the writing of bad verse and the composing of worse music, a prince utterly without military ambitions."

"Ah! Without military ambitions?" The Cardinal spoke sharply, raising his voice for the first time. "You speak very confidently, Monsieur le Marquis."

"With good reason, Eminence. He was a soldier only under compulsion from his father. He was filled with horror, an effeminate horror, of all things military. I have heard him speak of his uniform as his shroud."

The Cardinal pondered the words, then sighed again, and shook his head. "Yet, consider me this, I beg, and perhaps you will perceive

221

the contradiction, the enigma which I cannot read. He inherited from King Frederick William an army of between eighty and a hundred thousand men, recruited and impressed, per fas et nefas, by fair means and foul, throughout the Empire, an army exceptionally trained and superbly equipped, a preposterous army for a ramshackle State amounting to perhaps no more than say twice the marquisate of which you, yourself, have been dispossessed. Yet to this army, already so disproportionate, Monsieur de Valori informs me that your Prince, whom you describe as without military ambitions, has added in the last few months since his accession sixteen new infantry battalions, five squadrons of hussars and a squadron of heavy cavalry. In addition, military stores in great quantity are being assembled in Brandenburg and cannon is being cast. You perceive the riddle? Can you read it for me?"

"Indeed, I cannot. Your Eminence surprises me."

"Do you think you could read it if you went to Prussia?"

"If I went to Prussia? I do not understand."

"I will endeavour to make it clear. An ambassador sees only what he is permitted to see. Monsieur de Valori can inform me only of physical facts. But he is powerless to fathom intentions. That, sir, is where you could serve me. In urging grounds for your release Baron von Katzenstein assured me with great emphasis that I should earn by it the gratitude of the King of Prussia, who out of his old regard for you would rejoice in your return and be glad to give you employment in his service." He paused there before adding: "At the King's side, it should not be difficult for you to discover his true aims."

Alverley audibly caught his breath. "And betray them to your Eminence?" A sneer swept across his face. Abruptly he rose. "I fear, Monseigneur, that I am in no case to resent the insult."

"There is none intended." The Cardinal's voice was sharp. He waved an authoritative hand. "Sit down, sir, and hear me out."

"Is it possible that there can be more?"

"A great deal more." The old voice became very gentle again. "Do me the honour," he begged, and motioned him to sit. "I am an old man in urgent need. Not for myself, God knows. I am beyond the age of all that. But for France. Perhaps for the world. I think you misunderstood me."

"I understood your Eminence to ask me to become a spy."

"Why employ so ugly a word for an office which differs little from that discharged by every ambassador?"

"What an ambassador does he does openly. He does not sail under false colours. He does not go slyly or treacherously about obtaining information."

His Eminence smiled. "Do you know no more than that about ambassadors? I can assure you that they very often do. Unfortunately, because of their declared office, opportunity is commonly denied them. That is where you could not only serve me, but justify me in serving you. For if I should enrol you in the service of the State, I should then be able unanswerably to ordain that the edict shall not be invoked against you. Short of that there are no grounds upon which my intervention in your favour would be tolerated. But will you not sit? I think that I can conquer your scruples. If I fail, at least, I am sure, we shall part friends."

Alverley resumed at last his chair, his indignation soothed by the almost pleading note, the winning courtesy, and something else. It was in vain that he sought to ignore the reminder that a chance of escape was being offered him from the terrible situation in which he found himself. This chance might be an ignoble one, of which in the end he might consider it impossible to avail himself. But Cardinal Fleury spoke of conquering scruples, and the matter – being one of life and death – was not to be settled impetuously.

His Eminence resumed. "I have said, sir, that I am not asking you to serve me personally. My age should be evidence enough that I am no self-seeker, since I have no future for which to build. My chief concern, I repeat, is for France. Next to that, I am thinking of humanity. At this moment the peace of Europe is delicately poised. A spark struck in Prussia may start a conflagration in the Empire that will eventually set the whole of Europe in a blaze. War, that negation of law between men, is a horror conceived in hell, and never so vile as when made by Germans, as all history teaches down to the comparatively recent instance of the Thirty Years War. Holding this view, you will conceive with what ardour I desire to see peace preserved. Further, as minister of the King of France, I account it my duty to strive to maintain it because the prosperity of France demands it. Let this lend you patience with me, even if in the end you should find it impossible to serve me. Consider also that there is a certain nobility, if not in the actual service, at least in its object."

He paused there a moment as if collecting himself, fingering the gold cross that gleamed against his scarlet breast.

"Praemonitus, praemunitus," he murmured. "Forewarned of an evil, we often may avert it. What I need to know is whether the King of Prussia is arming for war, and, if so, against whom he intends it. It is inconceivable that it should be against Austria, for not only is Prussia one of the guarantors of the integrity of the dominions of the Queen of Hungary, not only were the Hohenzollerns raised to royal rank by the Habsburg Emperor, not only is Frederick heavily in debt to the Habsburgs for subsidies received from the late Emperor, but Monsieur de Valori assures me that King Frederick professes the warmest friendship for Maria Theresa, the firm resolve to adhere to the Pragmatic Sanction, and the intention to support her husband's claim to the Imperial Crown.

"Perfidious was one of the terms you applied to him. But perfidious in that quarter and to that extent is not humanly credible. The man would stand before the world as a monster of ingratitude and dishonesty, a scoundrel without honour – and that is not the role for a vain man.

"But if not against the Queen of Hungary, then, against whom does he arm? Or is this arming a mere continuation of the vain, parvenu ostentation which made his father squander his substance on a great army which he had no thought ever to employ? You will perhaps realize, Monsieur le Marquis, of what importance it is to me to know the answers to these questions, in order that I may take my measures."

He paused there before concluding. "I have completely opened my mind to you, and even something of my heart. I ask you again: Will you go to Prussia for me?"

It was a long moment before Alverley replied. His eyes, now wistful, frankly met the Cardinal's steady gaze. "Your Eminence knows that this is not a task for a gentleman."

The Cardinal slowly shook his head. "It is not so simple as that, my friend. If I did not account you a gentleman I should not be paying you in advance with your forfeited liberty, if not, indeed, your forfeited life. Nor should I have been at such pains to show you the merit, the nobility even, of the cause you will be serving. Is this to weigh for nothing?" And as Alverley, in the grip of his scruples, perceiving merely sophistry in the Cardinal's arguments, made no immediate answer, his Eminence added: "Agree, and you walk out of this room a free man in the service of the King of France."

Alverley smiled awry. "Whilst if I refuse I go back to the Châtelet to await trial and sentence. That, Eminence, is the coercion, is it not?"

The Cardinal made a little gesture of repudiation. He raised his shoulders and spread his hands. "Against the law, relentlessly pressed by Monseigneur de Richelieu, I can do nothing unless I can show that what I do is to the advantage of the State."

Alverley stared straight before him, whilst temptation continued to wrestle with his preconceptions, with the instincts of his class; but even as he struggled and debated within himself, he knew that honour fought a losing battle, that temptation would overthrow it in the end. Temptation's arguments were too strong. They offered surcease of that black despair into which he had been plunged by the thought of Dorothea's plight if he were taken. They urged that duty to Dorothea demanded that he should purchase life at any price. Having made this breach in his defences, temptation went swiftly about enlarging it. Did honour really demand sacrifices from him where Frederick of Prussia was concerned? What did the man know of honour who had treacherously sent the trusting Katte to his death? The old, vindictive rage in which he had heard of Katte's end surged up in sudden strength. Did not Katte's soul cry out for vengeance upon his murderers? And should Alverley, then, deaf to that cry, immolate his liberty, perhaps his very life, for a scruple concerned with the perfidious popinjay who had immolated Katte? Had he not once said, himself, that he would willingly return to Berlin if it were in his power to avenge Katte's murder? And was not this the chance to do so?

Thus he questioned himself, until it seemed to him that honour, itself, whilst barring his way on the one hand, was urging him forward on the other. And forward he must go, both as the avenger of Katte and the protector of Dorothea. The love which he had borne Katte and the love which he bore Dorothea were not to be denied. Thus, he found himself at last almost wondering that he should have hesitated.

He sighed, and again a wry smile twisted his lips. "I am at your orders, Monseigneur."

His Eminence sighed in his turn, but with manifest relief. "I am glad for your sake as well as for ours." He sat up, and passed briskly to instructions.

In Berlin Alverley would place himself in contact with the French ambassador, Monsieur de Valori, for whom his Eminence would give him a letter. To Monsieur de Valori he would deliver such reports as he might have for the Cardinal, in order that the ambassador might forward them by his own channels. Then came the matter of supplies, over which the minister displayed a noble liberality, and, finally, the provision of a laissez-passer, duly signed and sealed, which ensured the bearer complete freedom of movement. In this the Cardinal enlisted the assistance of a secretary summoned from the ante-room.

At last all was done and Alverley, once more alone with the Cardinal, stood to take his leave.

"You will remember," said his Eminence, "that in going free you are paid in advance, and that the only bond upon you is that which your own honour imposes." Sharply he added: "Why do you smile, Monsieur?"

"Not from mirth. Is it possible, Monseigneur, that the irony escapes you?"

The Cardinal tinkled his little bell to summon the chamberlain, and slowly rose. "It is not good, my son, to possess too keen a sense of irony. Anxiety to scoff does not make for the perception of truth." His ivory-tinted right hand was raised in a vague Sign of the Cross, in benison. "The Lord be with you."

Nevertheless, Alverley's sense of irony was not checked, for as he said long afterwards, "And so, with the blessing of the Church and pledged in honour, I went forth to tread dishonour's path."

Through the murk of that November day a chaise conveyed him back to Paris, to the Rue de l'Arbre Sec, alone and free.

He took the staircase in leaps, and came breathless to his own door. It opened to his knock, and against the familiar background of their room Dorothea confronted him, a pallid, woebegone Dorothea, with dark shadows under her grey eyes. For an instant those eyes, which looked preternaturally large, seemed to grow still larger. Then, with an inarticulate cry, she sank against him, almost swooning.

With cherishing, supporting arms about her, he drew her in, and closed the door.

"Charles! My dear! My very dear! Is it you? Is it really you? Free!"

"Free, child. Free," he assured her.

"Oh, my dear, my dear! I have prayed. Dear God, how I have prayed!"

"As I have. And we are answered."

They came to the settle, and sat down together, his arm still girdling her. There was no fire in the little stove, and the room, in a disorder normally foreign to it, was cold. But they did not heed it.

She stroked his face, as if to assure herself by touch that it was really he. Tears were running down her cheeks, and through them she was laughing foolishly.

"I can't believe it. I can't believe it."

"Assure yourself," he bade her, and displayed a paper bearing the seal of France. On it she read:

"Be it known by these present that the bearer, Charles Stuart-Dene, Marquis de Alverley, is travelling in the service of the State. Wherefore let every assistance be rendered him, and let none hinder him at his peril."

To this was appended the date and Cardinal Fleury's signature.

"Are you convinced?" he asked.

"But how does it happen, this miracle?"

For the first time in the ten years of their association he told her less than the truth, yet all the truth that he could bring himself to utter. "Katzenstein has proved a true friend. He pleaded for me with Cardinal Fleury. Pleaded in the name of King Frederick of Prussia. Told his Eminence that I am required by his Majesty. And...and political considerations induced the Cardinal to listen. That is all, save that we go back to Berlin. Does that content you, child?"

"So that we are together, my Charles, Paris or Berlin, it is all one."

He drew a sigh. "Life will be easier now, I hope. Katzenstein was convinced that Fritz will give me employment."

"I am glad for you. But I have never found life hard; not until this last dreadful fortnight. I must have died, I think, had you not come back," she said, which left him reflecting that but for her it was not likely that he would have done so.

Chapter 4

The Return

Berlin lay under a shroud of snow when they reached it in the first days of December, Alverley still describing himself as Mr Stuart-Dene and Dorothea as his wife. They put up at the Brandenburger Hof, in the Zeughaus Platz of wistful memory, holding as it did the house that once had been Katte's.

Of wistful memory, too, particularly for Dorothea, was the Nikolaistrasse, with the house in which her happy youth had been spent. They went, as on a devout pilgrimage, to view its exterior. More was denied her for the moment; for although the house stood untenanted and was now her own, she possessed no key.

As from across the street they paused to look at the white-fronted, narrow dwelling, her eyes filled with tears.

"No doubt," said Alverley, "it would be a proud day for you when the Crown Prince of Prussia first crossed that threshold. But how you must have barred the door against him could you have guessed what he brought you."

"He brought me you, Charles," she reminded him.

"One of the lesser evils in which he dealt. What have I brought you?"

"The dearest gifts for which a woman may hope. If, tomorrow, Charles, you went from me, forsaking me, I should still have only gratitude for the happiness of these ten years."

"Dear heart, you are easily made happy."

"Not easily. No. But I am of those who prize what they possess instead of bewailing what they lack. Only those are happy; and you, too, I think, are of those."

"Not quite. For I bewail at least what you lack."

"And thereby enrich me at your own cost, which is not right."

"Nothing could be more right, my dear. Courage, selfless devotion and loyalty such as yours deserve the best a man can give."

"And have you not given it?"

"It has been my endeavour. But, God knows, I have never had much besides. Let us hope that it will be different now; that Fritz will make my fortune."

But as if a reluctance weighed upon him, he seemed in no haste to put the matter to the test, and it was some days before he went to Potsdam to wait upon his Majesty.

Meanwhile there were other visits to be made. On the morrow of their arrival in Berlin they hired a sleigh, and drove through the frosty air to the village of Koepenick, where Theresa dwelt with a sister who was married to a horse-leech.

In a little white house, set back from the road in a diminutive garden that lay now under drifts of snow, they found a Theresa grown stouter and greyer with the years, but as youthful and warm of heart as when she had kept house for Pastor Ritter in the Nikolaistrasse. She almost swooned from joy to behold these visitors. Her eyes streamed with tears as her great arms enfolded and crushed Dorothea against her opulent bosom.

"Schatzli! Schatzli!" she sobbed in ecstasy, and held her off, the better to contemplate her. "How lovely you have grown. Dear God! That your poor father might have lived to see this day!" Then her eyes went beyond, to the tall figure standing behind Dorothea. "And my lord, the margrave, still at your side, as on the day ten years ago when he took you away."

"You know the fate that joined us," Dorothea reminded her.

"Do I not?" sobbed Theresa. "How could it have fallen out otherwise?"

"Or better?"

"That may be, too. When I look at you both, after all these years, I must believe it."

Over the wine and cakes that Theresa's sister brought them they sat and talked in the homely room, made stuffily cosy on that winter's day by the great porcelain stove and the smell of burning peat suffused from it. Their words evoked the past. Theresa told of the pastor's last days, of his peaceful end, and of the modest inheritance left for Dorothea in the hope of her ultimate return.

Before they parted it was arranged to the happiness of all that on the morrow Theresa should come to Berlin, to reopen the house in the Nikolaistrasse and to resume her old functions there with her young mistress. By this arrangement Alverley was made free to pursue the business that brought him, and in pursuit of it, three days later, by when Dorothea was safely installed again in her old home, he went to wait upon the Freiherr von Katzenstein in his fine mansion on the Spree.

Into a lofty salon of splendours, of rococo panels lined in damask, great crystal lustres, many mirrors and much gilding, a liveried servant conducted Lord Alverley, sombrely elegant in a suit that was new, though still of the black expedient to a gentleman of limited wardrobe. Into that room to greet him swept a young woman who radiated an exuberant vitality. She stood tall, on long, vigorous limbs, in a riding-habit of green velvet, ample of looped skirt, but tightly laced over a generous breast. On her golden head she wore a black tricorne, white-plumed and edged with gold lace. Under this her healthy, fresh-complexioned face, with bold, dark eyes and full, sensuous, well-cut lips was of an arresting beauty. She was all laughter as she confronted his wondering solemnity. She hailed him in a voice that was richly musical.

"Quixote! But have you quite forgotten me?"

He knew her then, and was the more amazed. "Time has dealt so nobly by you that I may be forgiven. Out of my little Dulcinea has been wrought a Juno."

With a laugh she held out both hands to him. He took them, and was bearing her right hand to his lips, when she withdrew it and proffered him her cheek. "I am not yet so old that you must prefer my hand. Let that wait until I have a husband."

"Faith, they are laggards in Brandenburg that you are still a maid, my lady Dulcinea."

"I have been waiting for you, Quixote. Is that not Dulcinea's part? And did I not swear I would?"

"In order that you may mock me. Well, well. I take my revenge," he said, and kissed the proffered cheek.

"Revenge is sweet, they say. Do you find it so?"

Her father laughed behind her. "Lord, Charles! Does the rogue practise upon you?"

"Practise," she cried. "I? It was Monsieur Charles who practised. Did you not see I was the victim?"

"A willing, self-immolating victim if I know you, baggage."

"Amusing herself at an old man's expense," said Alverley.

"Old!" she cried in horror.

"I must be, since you already found me so ten years ago."

"But now I find you ten years younger at the least, save that you are just as solemn."

"He's old enough, anyway," said her father, "to mistrust your guile. A wretch, Charles, that grows more shameless with increase of inches." But the arm he set about her held her close, and the eyes he bent upon her glowed.

Alverley stayed to dine with them, and they were merry with reminiscences until the talk turned upon his Paris imprisonment and his deliverance by Cardinal Fleury.

"I wonder what softened the old man in the end," said Katzenstein. "He was so very uncompromising with me when I pleaded for you."

"Nevertheless," Alverley answered, truthfully enough, "you appear to have left a seed in his mind that ended by germinating in my favour."

Then Stéphanie must press to know why he had fought the duel that had resulted in his arrest. "Was it for a lady that you fought, Quixote? For another Dulcinea? If so, don't tell me, for it would break my heart."

Alverley evaded. He could not bring Dorothea into discussion even though she remained unnamed. "It was a very simple affair," he said. "I was in poor circumstances, living under a plain name, and supporting myself by tutoring. A bumptious gentleman, presuming upon his birth, was unmannerly to the poor roturier he supposed me. It became necessary to put aside my humble mask. That is all."

"And you killed him?" Her dark eyes flashed.

"No. He is recovering. But he has enough. As for me, I had broken a law, which his powerful family was urgent to invoke against me. But for your father, it is likely I should have ended my days in the Bastille, or worse."

"It makes me very happy to know that we could serve you," she told him warmly. It was her way, encouraged by the doting Katzenstein, to account her relationship with her father so close a partnership that what either did was to be regarded as done by common consent, as the joint act of both. "We are proud to have done so. Are we not, papa?"

"To be sure we are. And it ends better than I hoped from Cardinal Fleury's attitude. Anyway, it was high time that you came back to your friends here, as Fritz's welcome will show you. Not in years have I seen him so concerned as when I told him how I had left you. He even went so far as to send for the French ambassador, with whom he was urgent on your behalf. However, here you are, and you arrive at the right moment. We are on the eve of great events. Fritz is not like his father. He does not maintain a mighty army merely for parade purposes. He is athirst for glory."

"He is greatly changed, then."

"More than changed. It's a metamorphosis, as you'll see."

He was to see it on the following morning, when, at last, he went with Katzenstein to Charlottenburg, where, at the moment, the King was residing.

Alverley had observed for himself the complete absence of troops from Berlin, which in the old days had swarmed with them, and he had learnt – for it was common knowledge – that they had recently been removed and sent to Crossen, on the Silesian border, where, it was reported, an army of some twenty thousand men was now assembled. Was, then, the quest of glory of which Katzenstein spoke to entail an irruption into the territories of Maria Theresa, after all? This seemed unthinkable, as Fleury had argued, considering the obligations under which the Hohenzollerns lay to the House of Habsburg, and the fact that Prussia was in honour bound by the Pragmatic Sanction as well as for value received to maintain the Queen of Hungary in her possessions. Frederick, as Fleury had correctly reported him to Alverley, was loudly professing fidelity to this, an unswerving friendship for her Majesty, and the determination to secure the Imperial Crown to her husband, Francis of Lorraine. Perfidious though Alverley had pronounced Frederick, yet not even Alverley could believe that he, or any man who desired to stand well in the eyes of the world, would carry perfidy to such lengths as the rejection of all those obligations and professions.

And yet, what could an army at Crossen portend but a menace to Silesia? Alverley must reserve judgment until he could discover more. So it was with a mind that he strove to keep open that he climbed into Katzenstein's sleigh, to be driven to Charlottenburg.

The parting that morning from Dorothea had been fraught with a certain sadness. They had stood together in the old familiar room that was haunted by the ghosts of Katte, of Ingersleben, of Spaen, and even of that mincing, effeminate Crown Prince for whom all those had suffered. The place looked just as it had looked in those departed days. On the green-panelled wall hung the smiling portrait of Dorothea that Katte had painted, and about it some of Dorothea's early miniatures, whilst from the overmantel Dorothea's rather sombre picture of her father frowned down upon them out of its oval frame. As of old a piece of blue Delft stood on a console, to hold flowers in season; the needlework tapestry of the chairs was still the same, if a little more rubbed and faded. It was hard to conceive that ten years were sped, impossible to exclude those insistent ghosts.

"I shall miss you, Charles," she told him wistfully. "I do not say it to trouble you, but as an expression of what you are to me. In all these ten years since I left Berlin with you, and saving that dreadful time of your imprisonment, we have never been parted for more than a few hours."

"That is all that will part us now."

"For today, yes. But if you succeed, if the King gives you employment, you will be in his following; you will take up residence with him. That is the separation in my mind."

"I would avoid if it I could."

"You could if you would," she ventured timidly.

"But we must live, my dear, and for that I must earn."

"You could do as you did in Paris. You could teach. Meanwhile we have a home here, far better than we knew in those happy days; and I am not without a little money to make us safe until your pupils come. Then, too, I can still paint." She took his face between her hands, she spoke softly. "Would not this content you?"

There was a tightening at his heart; for he had learnt to deny her nothing. Yet this he must deny her, since he was in honour bound to the mission, the quite dishonourable mission, upon which he had returned. It was the price he must pay for life and liberty, and there was the gold that had been advanced him for the purpose. But of this, prudence and even some shame kept his lips sealed.

"It would content me if I could do no better," he answered her. "Better for us both."

She pressed him no further. Although the parting now foreshadowed tormented her, yet in the selflessness of her devotion she would not urge it. She sighed and smiled. "I understand. That is your world, though you almost taught me to forget it. Go then, my dear. But come to me when you can."

"I do not need the injunction." He kissed her tenderly, and went.

Chapter 5

Charlottenburg

In the spacious, lofty library that was full of light from the tall windows and made luminous by the many mirrors in silver frames set between the bookcases with which the walls were lined, the young King received his visitors.

In a vast fireplace of green marble framed in copper, a great fire of logs was blazing. Above it a portrait of King Frederick's grandmother, who had given her name to this great domed palace built for her, smiled demurely down. The picture was framed in silver, like the mirrors, and like another portrait, by Rosalba, of a girl with black eyes and a wide, laughing mouth. It was an odd accident that this work-room of a man whose attitude towards women was fundamentally contemptuous, should be graced by no portraits but those two.

Frederick sprang up from his work-table when the kammer-hussar announced the Freiherr von Katzenstein. He put his head on one side, and peered with his big, short-sighted eyes at Katzenstein's companion. He was in the uniform of his guards, blue with red facings, and the star of the Black Eagle over his heart. Alverley observed this not only in wonder, remembering the Prince's antipathies, but also that the coat was well worn and rubbed, and that the riding-boots, innocent of spurs, had also seen hard wear and were rusty from lack of blacking,

The King's face was leaner, sallower, harder and more weasel-like than of old. It was framed in a tight military wig with a little stiff pigtail, instead of the blond curls that had so enraged his sire. Strange, reflected Alverley, that he should dress like this now that there was no one to cane him for dressing otherwise.

"C'est toi, Katze!" He smiled a welcome, and came forward, holding out his hand. Despite his militarization, he still minced in his step and leaned forward as he walked, and that the fop survived under the workmanlike exterior was perceived in the rings that loaded his fingers and in the heavy perfume he exuded.

"I bring you an old friend, sire."

"An old friend? You could bring me nothing I like better. Friendship supplies the first essential of a man's happiness."

He was, you will remember, qualifying to be accounted the philosopher-king of Monsieur de Voltaire's anointing. It behoved him, therefore, he conceived, to be uttering these didacticisms at every opportunity. Having spoken he gave attention to Katzenstein's tall companion in black. His blue eyes became alight with glad surprise.

"Morbleu, Marquis!" He flung out both hands. "So you've come, after all, and in spite of Katze's lack of hope of your deliverances. I have been expecting you these six months, ever since my accession; and I am not pleased with you that you did not come until Katze urged it." His hand tightened upon Alverley's with a warmth exceptional in one to whom physical contacts were repugnant.

"Your Majesty is very gracious. Katzenstein will tell you that I required little urging. Had I thought that I could serve you, sire, I should have arrived sooner." The words were civil enough, but the tone was oddly cold and formal.

"Service? Who talks of service? Is service the only purpose on which a king is to be approached. We have memories to link us, you and I."

"Your Majesty's recollection honours me."

"Did you expect less? Ah, yes, I know. The reputed short memory of princes. But I hope I am not of those. You belong to the unhappy days of my youth; to that little band of good fellows who mitigated the wretchedness of those times, and so kept me from suicide. You are one of those who suffered for me. Could I forget that?"

"My sufferings, sire, amounted to little compared with those of my poor cousin Katte."

The King's lips twitched. His glance faltered. "Ah! Katte!" he murmured.

Then Katzenstein was saying the things that Alverley should have said. "If all princes had memories as faithful as your Majesty's, then every man would have his due."

"Ah, Katze, but then I pride myself upon being something besides a prince." With a sweeping gesture he indicated the bookcases. "This is my real kingdom. Or, rather, the kingdom in which I aspire to reign. You will remember, Alverley, the library my poor Duhan was at such pains to assemble for me, so cruelly dispersed by my father. I have done my best to replace it, as you see."

Taking this for an invitation, Alverley looked about him, whilst Frederick launched into pedestrian talk upon the joys of intellectual pursuits, and the only true power, to be acquired by enrichment of the mind.

"Your Majesty is, indeed, to be felicitated." Alverley commended the collection, whilst continuing to inspect it. "You have assembled here the best that the centuries have produced."

"So I have supposed, and I rejoice that you confirm me. I regard you as something of a judge, Marquis."

"Your Majesty flatters me." He was giving a glance at some volumes on Frederick's writing-table, and more particularly at an enormous map spread upon a supplementary table beside it.

"But come," said the King, with that winning charm he could exert when so disposed. "Let us sit by the fire, and talk like old friends."

To an officer who had risen from a writing-table set near one of the windows he waved a hand in dismissal towards an inner door. "I shall not need you for a while, Feuerwach."

The officer, a tall, handsome young man, with a high-bridged nose and dark, liquid eyes, bowed in acknowledgment of the order, then paused to bow again, smiling, to Katzenstein, who, with a lift of the hand, gave him greeting. "Ah, Gottfried! Good day to you." To the King, when he was sitting down after Feuerwach's departure, "He gives satisfaction, I hope," he said.

His Majesty shrugged. "He does his best, which could not be much worse. He has no Latin, knows no English, and his French spelling is atrocious. Also he's religious and fond of women. In fact, he's a fool. Still, he cuts a good figure in uniform, and since he's your protégé, Katze, I suppose I must suffer him. His shortcomings will matter less once I've replaced Mannteufel. That was an able fellow." He sighed. "Why are clever men so commonly dishonest?"

"Did your Majesty prove Mannteufel's dishonesty, then?"

"Prove it? No." The thin mouth tightened, drooping at the corners. "He wouldn't be at large now if I had proved it. But he was too friendly with the Austrian ambassador, and I suspect that he was selling me. That was enough, Katze. I don't take risks. So I sent him back to his regiment. But to the devil with Mannteufel. I want to hear of you, my dear Alverley. Katze has told me how you got yourself into a French prison; and, faith, he left me little hope that you would get out of it. That old shaveling Fleury was not to be moved by him. Yet moved he seems to have been in the end. How did you work the miracle?"

"Cardinal Fleury must have been more impressed than he avowed by Katzenstein's solicitations; and then the fact that Richelieu's nephew recovered made it possible for his Eminence to practise the clemency Katzenstein had urged."

"Let us give thanks. But apart from the little that Katze tells me, I know nothing of you in all these years."

"There is not much to know," Alverley answered, by way of introduction to the brief and sketchy account he supplied of those ten years in France.

The King was thoughtful when the tale was told. He sat up in his armchair by the fire. "It seems to me that I have more to answer for

than I knew. Well, well, we must see what amends we can make."
Then through his graciousness came a gleam of malicious humour.
"The story ran, Alverley, that you abducted Pastor Ritter's pretty
daughter."

"'Abducted' is not quite the word, sire. My departure was
concerned with rescuing her. Your Majesty must know the horrible
fate with which she was threatened."

But the King still mocked. "Sheer knight-errantry, eh? I trust that
you were suitably rewarded."

Alverley preserved his sobriety of countenance. "Nor is 'knight-
errantry' the word, sire. 'Duty' would describe it better. The duty of
a friend. The duty to a lady in dire straits, and in some sense a duty
to your Majesty."

"To me!" The King was taken aback. He laughed. "Voyons donc!"

Alverley explained, in his cold, formal voice. "I acted as I
imagined your Majesty would have me act, and in order to spare you
the pain that must have been yours if this lady, innocently
compromised by you, had suffered the dreadful consequences
intended."

The King was sobered. He abandoned mockery. "Ma foi, it was
well done, an action that every chivalrous heart must applaud. Poor
Dorothea! What has become of her? Do you know?"

"Your Majesty will not think so meanly of me as to suppose that I
forsook her. You will be glad to learn that she is once more in Berlin,
in her own house."

The King's eyes narrowed momentarily. The shadow of a cynical
smile flitted across his lips, instantly effaced by Alverley's gravity. The
question that stirred the royal humour was spoken, nevertheless.

"She has come back with you?"

Alverley inclined his head. "The logical sequel, sire."

"Ah, yes. I suppose it would be." Frederick shifted once more in
his chair, and again his manner changed. It became effusive. "I must
pay her a visit one of these days when I have leisure. It will be
pleasant to revive happy memories in that music-room of hers."

"Where first your Majesty made the acquaintance of Katte," said Alverley quietly.

The King sighed. "Do I not remember it?" He fell pensive, staring at the fire. Then he roused himself to a sudden briskness. "But we have to think of you, Alverley. This good Katze has told you, I know, that you could count upon employment here. He knows me, you see, as well as I know myself. My difficulty is to discover the right employment for you. If you had seen service in these years it would be easy, and you'd arrive most opportunely. Soldiers are my present need."

Katzenstein interposed a reminder. "Are you not perhaps forgetting, sire, that your most urgent need is to replace Mannteufel? Whom could you find better suited than Alverley? He certainly possesses those qualifications which you say that Feuerwach lacks."

"Morbleu!" The lean face was alert. His Majesty took a moment for thought. "I wonder, indeed, that I hadn't thought of it. It's to be considered if it would suit you, Alverley."

"The question is, rather, whether I should suit your Majesty."

"Ye–es." The King spoke meditatively, his eyes keenly on the Englishman as if measuring him. "You are certainly as qualified as was Mannteufel, and in addition you are fluent in English, which he was not. That may be useful." Brutally he added: "And you would not be likely to sell me, since you could hardly have an interest in doing so."

"Also," put in Katzenstein, with the freedom he alone had licence to use, "Alverley is a man of honour."

"So was Mannteufel. So are you all. Until you find honour unprofitable. I prefer to put my faith in a man's interest. That is the only thing to which he is never false." He looked at Alverley, who inscrutably returned the stare. "You say nothing."

Alverley smiled. "I am not used to protesting my honesty," he drawled. "I leave it to be assumed."

Frederick smiled in his turn, ingratiatingly, as if to make amends. "And I assume it. Readily. I'll think of this. But the emoluments are lean. Of course you would live with me, at my charges, and you would have the pay of your rank: a captaincy, let us say. It is not Peru, of course…"

"It will serve, sire."

"Then let me sleep on it. Wait on me here again tomorrow at the same hour."

He rose with sudden briskness, to signify that the audience was at an end, and they rose with him. He held them a moment with amiabilities, expressing again his delight in Alverley's return, and so dismissed them.

In the sleigh, on the way back to Berlin, Katzenstein was congratulatory. "Am I a false prophet, then? Did I not foretell a warm welcome for you and sure employment?"

"I am not yet employed."

"Are you not? Postponement of decision until tomorrow is only Fritz's way of dissembling his satisfaction at having secured a man so admirably suited to his needs. Fritz does not give readily, though he can be generous when he must. In your place, Charles, I'd demand a colonelcy."

"I am content," said Alverley.

He was little concerned just then with dreams of ambition. As the sleigh glided swiftly, to the muffled thud of hoofs and the jingle of the horses' bells, he sat considering in silent gloom how of all the offices he might have sought none could have supplied him such opportunities as that which he was offered for the task on which he came. It was as if Fate were determined to leave him no escape.

That night, in the quiet of his room in Dorothea's house, he drew up his first report for Cardinal Fleury. So as to provide against accidents he cut a broad point to his quill, and wrote in heavy, vertical characters not to be identified with his normal writing, and left the letter unsigned. By way of a clue, however, he employed the opening sentence: "As your Eminence said, the Ethiopian cannot change his skin." After this he proceeded to report that the King of today differed from the Prince of yesterday only in that his vanity and presumption had been directed into fresh channels, oddly enough, those very channels which in youth he had found distasteful. That he was educating himself as a soldier and preparing for war there could be no doubt. And since his troops in the last few days had been massing at Crossen, the only possible inference was that despite all his protestations of friendship for Maria Theresa, despite all barriers raised by honour against the enterprise, this war was to be made upon the Queen of Hungary.

Alverley added details in support of both his contentions. His inspection of the library at Charlottenburg during the little time he had been able to devote to it had by no means been as perfunctory as it appeared. That considerable collection of books was entirely French, not only in original works, such as those of Voltaire and Montesquieu, but in translations from the ancient classics, Caesar, Livy, Thucydides, Suetonius, Plutarch, and so forth, from more modern authors, such as Ariosto and Tasso, and even from those of recent German philosophers, like Leibnitz and Wolff. Besides, there were a great number of works on the military art: on his Majesty's table – whence it was to be assumed that they were subjects of present study – lay a volume of Turenne's campèigns, together with a theoretical work on strategy by Folard and another by Fouquieres. More significant than any book, however, as an indication of military aims, was a large-scale map of Silesia spread out for study, bearing notations in red which Alverley had lacked leisure to examine closely, but the implications of which, he urged, were clear.

With this report under sealed cover he took his way early on the following morning to the house of the Marquis de Valori, beyond the Schloss. Promptly admitted to the ambassador's presence, he found himself keenly and coldly examined by a short, slight, frigidly elegant gentleman of consequential manner.

"I have been expecting you, Monsieur le Marquis. His Eminence Cardinal Fleury has informed me that you would seek me. But I do not apprehend in what capacity you are here."

"I come, Excellency, as an observer."

"An observer?"

"Of the policy of the King of Prussia."

Monsieur de Valori's frown implied mystification. "I do not think I understand. That is more or less my own function. What can you observe that is hidden from me?"

"His Eminence assumes that I may command opportunities denied the ordinary ambassador."

"Opportunities? I still do not understand. Is there any reason why you should not be frank?"

"Only that my instructions from his Eminence limit me to handing your Excellency my reports, in order that you may forward them by your own couriers. I have the honour to bring you the first of them."

Still puzzled, the ambassador took the sealed package, and thoughtfully turned it over in his hands. "You do not choose to tell me more? Such as how you come by the matter contained in this?"

"That is not important. But I can tell you the substance of the report. It is to the effect that the King of Prussia is about to make war upon the Queen of Hungary."

Monsieur de Valori's lip assumed a more definite curl. "You will forgive me if I describe that as rashly preposterous. I am able to tell you, sir, that his Majesty is the Queen of Hungary's staunchest supporter, as he has everywhere repeatedly announced." The ambassador went on to add those various additional heavy reasons why no prince with the faintest spark of honour could harbour the intentions Alverley supposed.

"I am entirely of that opinion," said Alverley. "But I am also aware that Prussian troops are massing at Crossen."

"Can you imagine that Maria Theresa is not informed of it? Further, she perceives what you appear to have overlooked: that King Frederick has inherited his father's taste for playing the drill-sergeant. Those troops, as I have sure information, are being assembled for manoeuvres. A man of the levity of the King of Prussia is not a man to make war. His soldiering is mere play-acting, a pretence, like his study and patronage of the philosophers." With a superior smile Monsieur de Valori added: "It is evident, sir, that you do not know King Frederick." He paused there, before asking

244

contemptuously: "Do you still wish me to forward this report of yours?"

"If your Excellency pleases."

The Frenchman was annoyed. "I warn you that it will make you ridiculous."

"I have never been afraid of that," said Alverley, and took his leave of the omniscient ambassador.

A couple of hours later he was at Charlottenburg, being very cordially received by the King. As Katzenstein had predicted, his appointment was definitely confirmed, and he found himself at once being instructed in detail in the duties of his office. Of so confidential a nature were these that it was manifest that very soon the royal mind must lie entirely open to him.

Indeed, so little secrecy did Frederick practise with him that whilst the Englishman shared with Captain Feuerwach a work-room adjacent to the royal library, the King required his almost constant personal attendance in preference to that of his fellow-secretary. This was no more than natural since he regarded Alverley as the more competent, which undoubtedly he was, and the more discreet, which undoubtedly he would have been but for Cardinal Fleury.

In these circumstances it is not surprising that Alverley did not deserve the affection of Captain Feuerwach.

Chapter 6

Statecraft

That shrewd psychologist, the Marquis de Valori, who saw with such penetration into the character of the King of Prussia that he could be contemptuous of other men's judgments upon it, conceived nevertheless, after his interview with the mysterious Lord Alverley, certain misgivings as to his own reading of the signs.

To allay these he sought audience of the King some few days later, and upon being received by his Majesty was dumbfounded to behold at his elbow the English nobleman, glittering in the red-faced blue and silver of the Guards. He betrayed, however, no recognition of this officer and begged for the honour of a private audience.

The King, seated at his writing-table, waved the ambassador to a chair. "We are private, Monsieur le Marquis. This is my military secretary, Milord Alverley."

That supplied a further shock to the sensibilities of Monsieur de Valori. Nevertheless, the ambassador of his very Christian Majesty bowed formally to the Englishman, who as formally returned the bow, accepted the chair indicated by King Frederick, and loosed his silver-braided sable pelisse, set his sable muff on the floor beside him, and plunged straight into business. He announced that he did himself the honour of coming, in order that he might be in a position to inform his government upon his Majesty's views on the Pragmatic Sanction.

The lean, foxy face of the young King became expressionless.

"They are, I hope, identical with those of the government of his very Christian Majesty: that those sanctions are binding only in so far as the integrity of the dominions of the Queen of Hungary is concerned."

Monsieur de Valori pursed his lips. "But not the Imperial Crown?" he asked.

"That is certainly not included. Therefore we are not in conflict, even if, as is freely rumoured, France intends to support the claim of the Elector of Bavaria."

"Pardon, sire," ventured the Frenchman, with obvious diffidence, "but our information – indeed, it is common knowledge – is that your Majesty's declared intention is to support the claim of the Queen of Hungary's husband."

"That does not bring us into conflict on the question of the Pragmatic Sanction, which is, I understand, the subject of your inquiry. As I have said, the Imperial Crown is not, nor could be, included in it."

Monsieur de Valori, however, was too shrewd not to perceive that his real question remained unanswered. Therefore, he was driven to bluntness. "I am to take it, then, that your Majesty will uphold the Pragmatic Sanction?"

Frederick sat back, and his big, myopic eyes stared coldly. "What else could I do in honour?"

"Nothing else, sire, I agree."

"Then the question should not have been asked."

"I agree again, sire. I can only hope that your Majesty will forgive it on the score of anxieties aroused by current rumour."

"What have I to do with that thousand-tongued beast?"

Valori's eyes strayed to the soldierly figure standing behind the King, and Alverley guessed the scornfully triumphant thought in the ambassador's mind. Actually, his own settled convictions were shaken. But when the Frenchman had departed, a royal chuckle reassured him.

"What impatience to read the future! Valori is reputed shrewd. Yet he can allow himself to imagine that I should declare myself before the proper time."

Monsieur de Valori was not the only one to imagine it. A couple of days later came Captain Guy Dickens, the representative of King George II, seeking audience on the same subject, and standing upon less ceremony than his French confrère. The plump little Englishman revealed himself as hard as he appeared benign. He began by courtesies, in which Alverley, again present, was included. The King raised his brows at this, looking from one to the other.

"You are already acquainted?" he asked sharply.

"I have that honour," said Captain Dickens.

Alverley amplified. "An old acquaintance, sire. It goes back to the days when Captain Dickens was the intermediary between the Crown Prince of Prussia and King George." Superfluously, yet with peculiar stress, he added: "Back to the days of Katte."

The King's face was darkened by recollection. "Ah, true!" he said. "For the moment I had forgotten. You have been in Berlin a long time, Captain Dickens." He sat silent for some moments, his head on his hand. Then, sharply, with an invitation to briskness, "However," he said. "You will have messages for me."

"On the contrary, sire. I come to ask what messages your Majesty may have for King George."

"But I have none."

"Is it possible? A month ago your Majesty did me the honour of indicating your intention to stand with England and Holland in support of Queen Maria Theresa, and so we reported to Vienna. I confess, sire, that I now find it difficult to reconcile your declarations to Vienna, London, and the Hague with the present troop movements on the borders of Silesia. Nevertheless, in reporting these to the government of his Britannic Majesty, I trust to be able to add assurances that the indivisibility of the Austrian succession will be respected."

The King flared in annoyance. "What the devil do you mean by that?"

"The Pragmatic Sanction."

"Does England intend to support it? I hope not; for that is certainly not my intention."

Captain Dickens did not trouble to conceal his surprise, less perhaps at the fact than at this frank admission of it, which to Alverley was even more startling. But he answered quietly: "England is bound in honour by her engagement to support it. As, indeed, is your Majesty."

This bluntness brought Frederick to his feet in anger, real or assumed. "My engagements? What are you saying? I have entered into no such engagements."

"The late King, your Majesty's father..."

"My father? What have I to do with engagements into which my father may have entered? Let me tell you, sir, that I am bound by none that I have not myself contracted or ratified. Please understand that."

Captain Dickens became prim. "I permit myself again respectfully to remind your Majesty of your letter of the tenth November last, in which you expressed yourself as acting in concert with England and Holland, and I beg you to inform me in exactly what terms I am to write now about these matters."

The King's lean, pallid face turned red under the envoy's steady regard. "You go beyond the bounds of your office, sir," he exclaimed. "I cannot believe that you are instructed to ask me any such question. A presumption!" he growled, and turned away from the table, to stalk to the window. He stood there, drumming on a pane with his fingers, and staring out at the snow that was beginning to fall, veiling the park from his view. He turned again, and stood stiff and straight, his hands behind him, the flush still on his cheekbones, lending a glitter to his eyes.

"Whether you are acting upon instructions or upon your own presumptuous responsibility, my answer is the same. You have no more right to inquire into my designs than I have to ask you about England's armaments at sea. And let me add this: I have nothing in view but the general good. Austria as a power is needed for fighting

the Turks. But she must not be of such might in Germany that three
electorates cannot control her. You English are like the French. You
seek to keep all the princes under your thumb. But I am not to be
driven by either of you. As for you English, again you are like the
Athenians, who wasted their time making speeches whilst Philip of
Macedon prepared to attack them." The scornful curl of his lip
became a malicious sneer. "In conclusion, pray inform my uncle
George that I wish him that he may not be beaten by the Spaniards.
That is all I have to say to you, Captain Dickens."

Alverley's surprise, as he listened impassively, was less at the
matter of the King's speech than at the effrontery with which he
unmasked, and revealed himself for a prevaricator. We know, from
the terms in which Captain Dickens informed his government of the
interview, that the ambassador's emotions were identical.

Frederick, however, provided for this by a communication of his
own.

"I can guess what that jack-pudding will report," he told Alverley,
when the British ambassador had departed. "We must anticipate it."
He grinned in enjoyment of his own cunning. "Draft me a letter to
King George, telling him bluntly that I am going to Silesia in
consequence of certain information that has reached me that Austria,
in conjunction with France, is preparing to invade Germany, and
must be anticipated. Explain that the expedition is necessary, in fact
a duty, as the only means of saving Germany from the rapacious
intentions of the Court of Vienna."

"Will King George believe it?" Alverley permitted himself to
wonder.

"So long as he believes that I believe it, that will suffice."

Alverley addressed himself to his task in the persuasion that King
Frederick was of those who would rather lie than not. This
persuasion was to be confirmed on the very next day at an audience
even more surprising than the two that had gone before.

The Court of Vienna had been completely reassured by
Frederick's repeated and explicit protestations of friendship and
fidelity to his obligations. Nevertheless, reports of the movement of

troops, the purchase of horses, and the accumulation of stores on the Silesian border appeared to Maria Theresa to be matters for investigation. Accordingly she dispatched to Berlin as her envoy the Marchese Botta d'Adorno with the object of obtaining clear enlightenment.

He was received by Frederick with all the effusive charm with which the young King flattered those whose services he needed or whom it was his purpose to hoodwink. On this occasion not only was Alverley in attendance, but also Frederick's minister Otho von Podewils. A short, stocky man with a big head and strong features, he was son-in-law to Grumbkow, now dead, and, unlike Grumbkow, quite incorruptible. He enjoyed Frederick's fullest confidence.

The Marchese Botta was no easy victim of Frederick's wiles. In the course of his journey he had seen with his own eyes the military preparations that were being made, and finding them to exceed all that had been reported at Versailles, he could be in no doubt of their purpose.

Amiably the King hoped that the envoy's journey had been pleasant. The lean, astute Italian took advantage of the opening to utter a sly warning. "Far from it, sire. The roads in Silesia are in a terrible condition. Broken by flood, they render movement laborious and difficult."

The keenness of his dark eyes went unrewarded. The King merely smiled, and his tone was casual. "A pity. But the worst that can happen to those who use the roads will be to arrive a little muddy." From that, abruptly, he passed to solicitous inquiries touching the health of the Queen of Hungary, who was known to be pregnant.

Botta assured him that her Majesty had never been in more vigorous health or better spirits, and, compliments thus set aside, came to his purpose. "I permit myself to be entirely frank with your Majesty."

"I esteem nothing so much as frankness."

"You may be aware, sire, that the Grand Duke Francis holds and has expressed the view that there is no prince in the world who prides himself more upon his honour than your Majesty."

RAFAEL SABATINI

Frederick inclined his head in acknowledgment. "I am proud to deserve the Grand Duke's good opinion."

"Therefore, despite all rumours, the Court of Vienna neither can nor will believe that the assembly of troops on the Silesian border, which I have seen for myself, can portend any evil intentions towards her Majesty."

"I rejoice to hear it."

"It remains, then, for our complete reassurance to learn the purpose of these military measures, information which I do not imagine that your Majesty can have any reason to withhold."

Thus, as Alverley conceived, the envoy placed his Majesty with his back to the wall, compelling him to declare himself where refusal to do so could be only tantamount to admitting the intended treachery.

The King, however, betrayed no distress. His smile was as easy as it was friendly. "Of course I have no reason to withhold it. As will now be manifest to you, I am, indeed, going to Silesia. But I am going there as the Queen of Hungary's good friend, to defend her hereditary rights against her enemies, and especially against Saxony and Bavaria, who are ready to attack her."

It was a moment before Botta recovered from the shock of this impudence. When he did, he was entirely formal. "I respectfully beg your Majesty to remark that neither Saxony nor Bavaria displays any sign of attacking us."

Slowly Frederick shook his head. His great eyes were wistful.

"Your information cannot be as precise as mine. Or else you do not read the signs aright. It is impossible that you are not aware that the Elector of Bavaria is laying claim to certain parts of Queen Maria Theresa's heritage."

"Against that, should the Elector attempt it, I can assure your Majesty that my sovereign will know how to protect herself. All that she asks of your friendship, sire, is that you be content to look on."

"It is evident, then, that she does not realize the peril. Bavaria will have the full support of France. Can you doubt it? France's aims are to place the Imperial Crown on the Elector's head in order thus to

252

create a puppet emperor who will dance to her piping. That does not suit my views. Since this must be plain to you, let it serve, if nothing else will, as a guarantee of my good faith and of my firm intention to procure the Imperial Crown for the Grand Duke. Believe me, my friend, Austria is in great danger, and stands in need of allies. Let me beg you to convey that to your sovereign, with the assurances of my unswerving good will."

Thus dismissed, Botta, for all his shrewdness, departed without knowing what to believe.

The door had scarcely closed upon him when Podewils broke the silence in which he had witnessed the interview, and by what he said revealed to Alverley how fully he was in the King's knavish confidence. "I cannot think, sire, that Botta is deceived."

"That no longer matters," snapped Frederick. "The time for action has arrived. The troops are ready. If I don't take advantage of this, then I am in possession of something that I don't know how to use. If I do, my ability will be applauded. Why do you frown, Baron?"

"Because, sire, to me it does not appear so simple. There remains the question of right. However well-founded might be your Majesty's claims to the Silesian duchies, there exist solemn treaties, which Austria will produce, under which the House of Brandenburg has allowed itself to be induced to renounce those claims."

"Renounced for a mess of pottage," snarled Frederick, working himself into an artificial heat. "A fraud was practised upon us. It is for you to establish that, and at the same time to establish this question of right."

"It will not be easy, sire."

"That is your affair. I leave you to work at it. As for the question of actuality, you may leave that to me."

That evening Alverley wrote his second letter to Cardinal Fleury on the subject of statecraft as practised by Frederick of Prussia. It informed his Eminence that the extent and variety of King Frederick's falsehoods defied the belief of any who had not, like Alverley himself, been a witness of them. He dealt briefly with the three widely divergent stories told by Frederick: to the French that he was bound by the Pragmatic Sanction to uphold the integrity of Maria Theresa's dominions; to the English that he must anticipate the attack upon Germany dictated by the rapacity of Maria Theresa, acting in conjunction with France; and to Austria that he was going to Silesia in order to protect Maria Theresa from the rapacity of Saxony and Bavaria. All this in order to lull suspicion and mask his intentions until he should be ready to strike and take his victim unawares. For that time, when it came, he had prepared the further lie that the treaty under which for value received Prussia had forgone all claim upon the Silesian duchies had been fraudulently obtained. Finally, Alverley was in a position positively to inform his Eminence that Frederick was on the eve of invading Silesia for purposes of conquest.

On the morrow, in Berlin, he found occasion to wait upon the French ambassador with this dispatch.

Monsieur de Valori's manner was of a studied offensiveness. "I owe you an apology, milord, for the doubts I last expressed to you. I had not realized how exceptional were your opportunities for…observation. That was your word, I think."

Alverley kept his countenance. "Your Excellency perceives the rashness of judgments upon insufficient evidence."

"True." Coldly the ambassador surveyed the Englishman. "There are occasions when even evidence strains belief."

Alverley perfectly understood the sarcasm. "That is perhaps because evidence is not always what it appears to be."

"I am thinking of those occasions when the evidence is unmistakable."

"I fear we shall not understand each other, Monsieur le Marquis. Evidence, after all, is only that which we see, and human vision is limited to surfaces." To put an end to this civil exchange of incivilities, he added: "My dispatch is urgent. I beg that it may be forwarded without delay. I take my leave." He bowed. "Monsieur!"

He went off outwardly calm, but inwardly enraged by Monsieur de Valori's contempt, the contempt with which he must be regarded by all men of honour who knew the facts, the contempt with which at times he could not avoid regarding himself. His temper was not improved by the fact that almost on the doorstep of the Embassy he ran into Captain Feuerwach. The officer paused, civilly to pass the time of day with him, yet Alverley thought that he raised his brows as he glanced up at the lily-escutcheon over the ambassador's door. It served to suggest to Alverley that he be less open in any future visit he might pay Monsieur de Valori.

He sought Dorothea, to tell her in confidence of his impending departure for Silesia with the King.

"And so this separation widens," she reflected sadly. "It is what I foresaw from the moment that you decided to seek service with his Majesty."

"It is only for a little while," he answered her. And then, still smarting from Valori's sarcasms, he added the reassuring admission of a new-born resolve. "I promise you that I shall not long continue in this service, and then we shall be free to do as we choose."

This was to bring her surprise, even dismay. "Do you mean that you will quit it because of me? I should not want you to do that."

"I shall quit it for both your sake and my own. It is a service in which there is no honour. So be patient for a little while, my dear."

"I don't understand."

"Just believe, and be patient as you have always been."

Chapter 7

The Masked Ball

On the following night, which was that of 14th December, a masked ball was given by Frederick's young queen. This in her own Palace of Schönhausen where she dwelt apart, for, on the death of his father, Frederick had flung her out of his life, refusing further to cohabit with her.

Thwarted by Frederick William in his desire – for which his mother had so assiduously intrigued – to marry an English princess, Frederick had, with contemptuous indifference, accepted the wife chosen for him, Elizabeth of Brunswick-Bevern, a gentle, comely, happy-natured little lady who deserved a better fate, and who nowise resembled the malicious portrait left us of her by the Margravine of Bayreuth.

After an initial period of indifference, in which he found pretexts to avoid her, Frederick had permitted her for four years to share his residence at Rheinsberg, during his father's lifetime. Then, on Frederick William's death, he had definitely put her from him, and given her a separate establishment. She had accepted this with characteristic docility, and we do not gather that her natural gaiety was diminished by the separation. In spite of it and of his general indifference to women, Frederick insisted that officially all honour should be paid to his queen – which in a sense he regarded as honour paid to himself – and in order to set the example, he chose, at the very moment of departure for Silesia, to attend this ball accompanied by his staff. Under their dominoes they were all in uniform, for word had gone forth that they were to march that very night.

In the great gallery, ablaze with the candlelight from the ponderous crystal chandeliers, reflected from mirrors, flashing from gildings, a glittering company ebbed and flowed about the space left clear for the dancers and so maintained by the heavy red ropes held by lackeys, made to serve as human posts. Ante-rooms and alcoves opening from this gallery served for the overflow, offered rest from the exertions of the dance, or refreshment for those who sought it, whilst in a blue and gold salon into which Alverley wandered he found Marshal von Schwerin holding a well-patronized bank at faro.

Masked, and cloaked in a domino of purple silk, Alverley mingled with the onlookers about the green table, to watch the fall of the cards. The luck was running strongly in the bank's favour, and gold was piling high in front of the burly, jovial Schwerin, the greatest gambler, just as he was the most experienced soldier, in Prussia; indeed, he was already a soldier of European reputation.

Two or three officers were amongst the punters. One of these was Alverley's fellow-secretary, the Junker von Feuerwach. He had unmasked as had most of the players, and his handsome dark face was pale; a gleam of moisture showed below the line of his wig. He staked heavily as Alverley looked on, turned his card, and breathed a curse. Schwerin chuckled hoarsely as he raked in the gold.

"Too lucky with the women, Feuerwach, to be lucky with the cards. No man can have it all ways. You know the proverb."

There was some laughter; but the Junker answered only by a twitch of the lips meant for a smile, and the production of another rouleau. And then Alverley's attention was claimed by a high-pitched, dissembled voice at his elbow.

"You do not play, Monsieur le Marquis. Perhaps you, too, know the proverb."

He turned to meet the gleam of a pair of eyes from a black satin mask. Above it there was a tight, powdered wig from which sprouted

an osprey tipped with diamonds, like sparkling drops of water;
below it a fair white bosom generously displayed, and below that a
shimmer of green flounces that Watteau might have designed.

Alverley laughed. "If you drew a bow at a venture, Madame, I
betrayed myself by turning. What forfeit do I pay?"

"Your hand for the next quadrille," the voice squeaked. "Unless
you can name me in your turn."

"Should I attempt it when by succeeding I must be the loser?"

"What do you know of that since you do not know me," she
squeaked again.

"There is the siren melody of your voice to assure me that under
your mask is a loveliness to intoxicate a poor man."

Light laughter answered him. "You arm yourself in sarcasm. That
argues fear of this intoxication, as you fear the cards. Therefore you
look on."

"Nay. It also happens, Madame, that I am poor."

"The more reason to be venturesome. Poverty will limit your
losses, whilst Fortune, if you trust her, may flood you with her
wealth."

"Ah, but then I never had cause to trust her; that is, not until you
came."

"And now?" the dissembled voice challenged him.

"Now?" he echoed. "The quadrille is about to start. Come."

"You do not answer me," she complained, but went with him, her
hand upon his arm.

In the doorway they were confronted by Katzenstein in a colonel's
uniform and unmasked.

"Behold me, Count, your daughter's captive," said Alverley.

Stéphanie snatched her hand from his arm. "Monster!" she cried.
"You were mocking me. You dared to dupe me."

"The duper duped," laughed Katzenstein. "Most salutary."

"Oh, and instructive for me," said Alverley. "I've heard some
opinions of myself."

"They were masked, sir, like my face."

"It follows, then, that they were merciful. I think I'll resign you to your father, Mademoiselle."

"Nay, I want none of the baggage," her father protested. "I've a louis or two to stake. Does Schwerin hold the bank?"

"Unless he's finished flaying Feuerwach."

"Is that the victim? Then he's more in need of rescue than you are."

"That's fatherly," said Stéphanie. But Katzenstein was already elbowing his way towards the faro table.

Returning later in quest of him, when the quadrille was done, they were met by Feuerwach. He was pale and seemed in some disorder. But he bent his stately height before the lady. His voice was muted.

"I claim the honour of the dance you promised me."

She hung closely upon Alverley's arm, the rise and fall of her breast announcing her recent exertions. She chose to answer him in the dissembled falsetto. "I wonder for whom you are mistaking me."

"No mask could baffle my eyes when they seek you, Mademoiselle Stéphanie."

He was mocked by her ripple of laughter. "Your eyes possess more faith than vision, sir. Seek your Stéphanie behind some other visor."

She attempted to draw Alverley on. But Feuerwach, frowning, put himself resolutely in her way. "I have found her behind yours," he insisted. "I should never forgive myself if I had not."

"You have been answered, sir," she squeaked back at him. "You become importunate."

"This is to test me. But it does not succeed. You dare not use your own voice. It would belie your words."

She looked up at her escort. "Pray desire this gentleman to let us pass."

"In effect, sir, you cannot have remarked that you are in the way," said Alverley pleasantly, and by that simple speech turned resentful dislike into implacable hostility.

Of course there was in the Junker a strong predisposition to it. The half-playful attempt to thwart him was merely a spark to highly inflammable material. Resentment of this foreigner's favour with the King, of the fact that he was admitted to royal confidences from which the Junker was excluded, had been growing daily since Alverley's coming to Charlottenburg. Feuerwach's nerves moreover were raw at the moment from losses to Schwerin of far more than he could afford, for he was by no means wealthy. Of late his hopes of fortune had been based upon alliance with Katzenstein's richly endowed daughter. Seeing her so possessively intimate with this Englishman, whose cool deportment was in itself an irritation, Feuerwach recalled that it was Katzenstein who had brought Alverley to Charlottenburg. He asked himself what was the link that bound the Count and the Englishman, and he was taken with a furious fear lest this newcomer should supplant him in his suit of Stéphanie just as he conceived that he was supplanting him in the favour of the King.

He drew himself up, and looked down his handsome nose at Alverley.

"I do not care to be taught manners, sir."

Alverley felt the little hand quiver and tighten on his arm, as if to enjoin restraint. He laughed. "I should not presume to teach. I merely remind you of them."

"It is all one. I resent it."

Stéphanie spoke suddenly in her natural voice. "Then you should not make it necessary, sir. And we are blocking the doorway. Please allow us to pass."

Other dancers pressed behind them. Without making a scene it was impossible for the Junker to continue to offer hindrance. Moreover, Stéphanie's resumption of her own voice. Abandoning pretence, robbed him of all pretext, and so, at last, defeated, he stood aside.

"We are obliged," said Alverley. "Come, Dulcinea."

If he had intended further to embitter Feuerwach's defeat he could not better have achieved it than by the employment of that name, of which the Junker did not know the origin. What he perceived in it was evidence of an intimacy already far closer, and therefore far more dangerous to his hopes than he had suspected. His jealous rage welled up as the pair swept past him. His furious glance pursued them as they went to mingle with the crowd about the faro table, where Katzenstein had now taken the bank from Schwerin. He was actually moving to follow when suddenly the King, in pink and silver, stood beside him, and baffled his intentions by a sharp command that sent him off in the opposite direction.

It was striking midnight.

His Majesty went on into the room, the company opening out to give him passage. He came to Alverley's elbow, and Stéphanie heard him say: "It's time to pull on our boots and tighten our girths. Pass the word. We march in an hour."

He moved on, to tap Katzenstein's shoulder where he sat, whilst Alverley took a hurried leave of the lady, and departed on his errand.

It was carried out swiftly, and so quietly that the company remained without suspicion of what was afoot. Whilst the dance continued uninterrupted the members of Frederick's staff and some score of officers besides slipped away for reassembly in an hour's time at Charlottenburg.

As Alverley, his task accomplished, was leaving in his turn, he came upon a group at the head of the great staircase, in which the tall figure of Katzenstein was conspicuous. From this group Stéphanie, now unmasked, detached herself and crossed to intercept him.

He paused, smiling. "I am happy in this chance to kiss your hand, Dulcinea."

But her full lips did not reflect his smile; her fine eyes were solemn. "My father will not admit it, but it is war, is it not?"

"More or less, I believe."

"And you are going?"

"My place is with the King."

She held out her hand. Her lip was tremulous. "Bonne chance, Quixote. Come back safely and soon."

"I am by nature obedient," he answered lightly, and bent to bear her fingers to his lips.

Out of the corner of his eye as he straightened himself he beheld the Junker von Feuerwach marching upon them, with a brow of thunder. But before he reached them Katzenstein had come to set an affectionate hand on Alverley's shoulder and move with him to the stairs.

"Au revoir, Charles. I do not come with you on this quest of glory. My duties are assigned me here, worse luck. Take good care of the King." He gave the shoulder a final pat. "God keep you."

He turned and stepped back to his daughter's side, and from the expression of Feuerwach's face as he stood before Stéphanie, Alverley accounted it as well that she should have parental protection.

Chapter 8

Pandora's Box

"The desire for aggrandizement with the spoils of another will not present itself to an honest man or to one who desires the esteem of the world."

Thus the Philosopher-King in one of the passages from his Anti-Macchiavel, which Fleury had read to Alverley.

In spite of this and many other expressed sentiments of a similar sublimity, the Philosopher-King rode away on that winter's night to his troops at Crossen for the purpose of doing precisely what he says that no honest man could do But, then, he does not appear to pride himself upon honesty, for somewhere in his memoirs – that monumental misrepresentation of facts, which this Prince of Liars entitles *Histoire de Mon Temps* – he explains that whilst willing enough to behave honestly, only a fool would do so in a world of rogues.

Elsewhere in that illuminating work he writes: *"It is an established principle in a policy of invasion that the first step in the conquest of a country is to obtain a position there, and that is what is most difficult."*

He overcame the difficulty in the case of the invasion of Silesia, by the novel expedient of making war without troubling first to declare it. And lest this should not be sufficient for the overwhelming of an unprepared and unsuspecting victim, he was further at pains, as we have seen, to lull and disarm that victim by professions of friendship and suggestions of alliance. And when eventually he had occupied the victim's territory, obtained and made good his position there as the first step towards its conquest, he must still be impudently protesting that he came, not as a conqueror, but as a friend and protector.

It is a technique which has found favour and imitation with subsequent admiring students of his career, who have described as political genius a similar course of brazen, shameless falsehood. The credit of its invention, however, must remain Frederick's own.

This rape of Silesia may be dismissed in a few words. After all, it is an oft-told tale. Utterly undefended and in the main ungarrisoned, Silesia was an easy prey, and within some four weeks the whole of it was occupied by Frederick's troops, with the exception only of the strongholds of Glogau, Brieg and Neisse. By false pretences and the assistance of traitors within, he contrived even to enter the independent City-State of Breslau, and ordered the Protestant ministers there to preach to the text: "We have neither taken other men's land nor holden that which appertaineth to others, but the inheritance of our fathers, which our enemies had wrongfully in possession a certain time."

Meanwhile, at the very moment of crossing the frontier – "crossing the Rubicon", he called it, already conceiving himself another Caesar – he dispatched his Grand Marshal, Count von Gotter, to Vienna to proffer an olive-branch on the point of a sword. Despite all his "thirst for glory" – as he described his emotions in a letter to Voltaire – he preferred to avoid the hazards of battle if he supposed that chicanery would serve his turn.

Gotter was a man of handsome, virile presence, resonant voice and authoritative manner, and in choosing him for his ambassador Frederick was probably guided by his contempt for women and the belief that it should not be difficult for a man of such commanding male endowments to obtain persuasive empire over a young queen. This showed a poor conception of the spirit of Maria Theresa; and, anyway, the Grand Marshal never reached her presence. Both her pride and her advanced state of pregnancy supplied obstacles. Gotter was received instead by her husband, the Grand Duke Francis, and to the Grand Duke he delivered the King of Prussia's impudent, crafty message.

"I come to Austria bearing in one hand a guarantee, in the other the Imperial Crown for your Royal Highness. The troops and the resources of my master are at the disposal of the Queen of Hungary, an offer which she cannot fail to accept at a time when she stands so much in need of the support of a prince as powerful as the King of Prussia together with his allies, Russia and the maritime powers.

"Since, in view of the situation of his states, the King my master would be exposed to great dangers, he hopes that the Queen of Hungary will offer him nothing less than the Duchy of Silesia as the price of his alliance. I should warn your Royal Highness that no one could be more firmly resolved than the King of Prussia. It is for his Majesty a necessity to occupy Silesia, and if he is not assured of the immediate cession of this province, his troops and his resources will be placed instead at the disposal of the Elector of Bavaria and the King of Saxony."

This brutal language, offered on behalf of a poet, flute-player and peace-loving philosopher, smote the Austrian Court like the explosion of a bombshell.

"Have Prussian troops already entered Silesia?" the Grand Marshal was asked, and when he had admitted it he was dismissed by the Grand Duke with Maria Theresa's answer: "Go back to your master, and tell him that so long as a single Prussian soldier stands on Silesian soil we will die rather than enter into discussions with him."

And to this the Grand Duke added: "Your master's father accounted himself honoured when permitted to hold the basin and napkin to the father of the Queen of Hungary. The son would do well not to forget it."

It was not an answer that pleased Frederick. He did not care to be reminded of the parvenu character of his paltry kingship. Besides, the display of firmness was embarrassing. If it persisted he might have to fight, after all. So back again to Vienna went Gotter with a more modest demand, this time for Lower Silesia only, backed by the offer of a loan of a million thalers.

By the time the Grand Marshal returned, with a second refusal, as haughty as the first, Frederick was already back in Berlin. He had come home in triumph, leaving Schwerin in occupation of Silesia, and he had published to the Courts of Europe an apologia for his action, in which the advancement of claims was mingled with hypocritical protestations of his regard for the interests of Maria Theresa and his determination firmly to support the House of Habsburg in any circumstances that might arise.

It is to be presumed that these circumstances did not include the second refusal with which he was now confronted. It disconcerted him, and it disconcerted his minister Podewils even more.

Frederick's assertion through Gotter that he was in alliance with Russia and the maritime powers, England and Holland, was just another impudent falsehood. He had no such allies. Himself, he may have accounted it a mere anticipation, for he was certainly depending upon the rivalry between England and France to bring one or the other into alliance with him.

England, however, faithful to her pledge to uphold the Pragmatic Sanction, looked with stern disapproval upon Frederick's violation of the same pledge. In France Cardinal Fleury still contrived to restrain the party, headed by Belle Isle, that was clamouring for war. His hands may well have been strengthened by Alverley's reports which made clear the dishonesty and untrustworthiness of the King of Prussia.

Despite the misgivings of the prudent Podewils, who protested – and with greater truth than he could possibly have foreseen – that Pandora's box had been opened and all the evils were escaping from it, Frederick did not see how he could now do other than persist in the course to which he was committed: strengthen his hold upon Silesia and stand on the defensive, defying Austria to turn him out. To this end he increased the troops there to thirty-five thousand, entrusting to old Prince Leopold of Anhalt the raising of yet another two thousand in the Mark.

These and other matters, such as the collecting of siege materials and instructions for their conveyance by the waters of the Oder, kept Alverley busy during the bare three weeks the King spent in Berlin. Yet he found time to visit Dorothea almost daily, and to assure himself that all was well with her.

He had occasion also to visit Monsieur de Valori, for the purpose of handing him for transmission to the Cardinal a secret report of the latest Prussian transactions. A few days later he called upon the French ambassador again, this time on the King's instructions, in order to sound him on the subject of his government's attitude towards a possible alliance. If only the traditional anti-Austrian feeling of France could be rendered active, Frederick's last doubt on the issue of the campaign ahead would be dispelled.

Monsieur de Valori was as chilly as usual with him. "Really, sir, I find it difficult to know how to treat with you. At one moment you come to me as the agent of Cardinal Fleury, at another as the accredited representative of your sovereign."

Alverley was taunted into an answer that affords a glimpse of his mental attitude. "Your excellency is profoundly in error. I am no man's agent but my own. That is something which you will not understand and which I am not disposed to explain. Therefore if you will confine yourself to forwarding my dispatches without troubling about their nature it will be pleasanter for both of us. For the rest, you need know me only as his Majesty's military secretary, in which capacity you now behold me." And he passed on to the business with which the King had charged him.

Coming on the following morning into the royal library he found Feuerwach with his Majesty.

Frederick hailed him with a queer smile. "Ah, Alverley. This good Feuerwach tells me you have been visiting the French embassy."

Alverley understood the malicious humour of the King, just as Feuerwach, taken aback and flushing indignantly, misunderstood Alverley's silent stare.

"No use to deny it," cried the Junker. "You were seen."

Frederick chuckled. "You were seen, Alverley. Observe how faithfully I am served."

It was only now that Feuerwach understood that he was mocked.

"So have a care what you do," laughed the King in cruel enjoyment of Feuerwach's confusion. Still laughing, he dismissed him. "You may go."

He waited until the door had closed upon the Junker, who departed in seething resentment. "Oh, he takes an interest in you, Alverley. He also reports to me that you frequently visit a house in the Nikolaistrasse, where dwells a certain Fräulein Ritter. Evidently he intends that my military secretaries shall be not only faithful, but – unlike himself – of puritan morals. Or has he some other purpose?"

"It is what I shall take the liberty of asking him."

"Oh, no, no." Frederick held up his hand. He was suddenly very much the master. "This matter is not to be pursued. I forbid it. You understand?"

"At your Majesty's orders."

"Good. And now, what of de Valori?"

"He is to take the feeling of his government; but there is no indication from him that the proposals will be welcomed."

"Then it remains for me to contrive that they shall be. Boldness is necessary. When it is seen that I have broken the eggs, I shall be surprised if the war party in France will not wish to share the omelette, whatever the old Cardinal may do. Decidedly boldness is necessary."

"Audaces fortuna juvat," murmured Alverley.

"What is that?"

"Fortune favours the bold. A maxim poor Katte was fond of repeating," Alverley sighed. "Yet it did not avail him."

The King's eyes were veiled at this mention of his dead friend. He was silent a moment, and when next he spoke it was as if he had not heard. "Yes, boldness," he said again, "is required. The French will come to heel when they've been given proof of my quality."

In order to give them proof of this quality Frederick was off again to Silesia in mid-February, and three weeks later the weakly defended city of Glogau surrendered to his troops. By that time, however, Austrian mobilization was complete, and an army under the elderly but indifferently experienced Neipperg was advancing through the mountains of Moravia to the relief of Neisse.

Frederick made his dispositions, giving prominence amongst them to instructions for the event of his own death in battle. His body was to be burnt, Roman fashion, and the ashes taken to Rheinsberg in an urn, whilst a monument was to be erected to his memory akin to that of Horace at Tusculum. To his intimates he proclaimed that he would not survive defeat. If the glory which he sought should elude him there were opium pills in a box which he wore next to his skin. This talk of suicide as an alternative made little impression upon Alverley. It merely served to remind him of how Frederick had constantly harped upon that same theme in the old days, when he was Crown Prince.

Chapter 9

Mollwitz

The King's baptism of fire and first taste of glory – tempered by some ignominy – came at Mollwitz in the early days of April.

For a week there had been marching and counter-marching and manoeuvres for position, in the course of which Neipperg had contrived to neglect most of the measures he should have taken. Through the snow and mud of that laggard spring the two armies moved northwards along parallel lines on either side of the River Oder, until at last, finding his supplies diminishing and Neipperg lying across his lines of communication, Frederick was obliged to fight.

The necessity brought him into that state of premature despair, to use Voltaire's phrase, which, like the threat of suicide in the event of disaster, was to be chronic with him in the campaigning years ahead. He spent, on the eve of battle, a sleepless night, much of which was consumed in the writing of a couple of letters in the manner of a man taking leave of the world.

The cold of the following morning, which was the 10th April, did not help his courage. But at least it served to supply an explanation of his shivers as, wrapped in his pelisse, he took final counsel with Marshal von Schwerin.

The snow, which had been coming down heavily in the last two days and lay thick upon the ground, had now ceased to fall. But overhead the sky continued ashen, and it was in a wintry morning light that the King viewed from his encampment the flat and dreary landscape, flanked on the right by the black mass of the forest of Hernsdorf, and extending mistily ahead to the distant village of Mollwitz, about which the Austrian host was marshalled.

In contrast with the gloom of the King, Schwerin was in excellent spirits, cheerfully confident of the issue, as well he might be, considering the vast preponderance of Prussian strength. His knowledge of this was based on the reports of some Austrian deserters. From these he had learnt that Neipperg brought no more than nineteen thousand men, with only nineteen guns, to oppose to the twenty-two thousand Prussians with fifty-three light and heavy guns.

The odds, when disclosed to him, put heart into the King, and at ten o'clock the word was given to move forward in the orthodox two lines, each with the infantry in the centre and the cavalry on the flanks, the heavy guns ahead. The advance was on a front of two miles, which was to prove too wide for the space between the wood of Hernsdorf and the marshy brook of Neudorf, on the left. Hence a hasty constriction attended by some disorder, which was not rectified until a little after midday. Then, at last, the Prussian guns opened up on a body of white-coated cavalry that was covering the Austrian deployment. Galled by this fire, Römer, a soldier of dash and ability who commanded the Austrian horse, took matters into his own hands, ignored Neipperg's instructions, and ordered his buglers to sound a charge.

The Prussian preponderance lay in its infantry, which was twice as numerous as the Austrian. In cavalry, on the other hand, the Austrians were half as strong again as the Prussians, and, moreover, were accounted the finest in Europe. They were to give proof of it now.

On a slight eminence to the rear of the right wing, which had been thrust forward, the King had taken his stand with a group of attendant officers which included Alverley and Feuerwach as well as Katzenstein, who this time had accompanied the army. Thence they watched the white Austrian phalanx as it came thundering down upon them at the gallop. The shock when it occurred proved irresistible. Under the impact the foremost ranks of the Prussian horse gave way, recovered momentarily, to be broken again by the Austrians, who were amongst them, riding them down, sabreing and scattering them.

Frederick, white-faced, stood in his stirrups, cursing.

"Stand, you dogs! In God's name, stand!" he was yelling, as if he could be heard at that distance and above the roar of battle.

Schulenberg – that same Schulenberg who had presided over the court martial that sentenced Katte – was in command of the Prussian horse. In an attempt to retrieve the disaster, he brought a squadron in good order from the extreme right, and flung it on the Austrian flank, hoping by this diversion to disorder it. But Römer wheeled his dragoons, to meet the charge, and it broke and scattered upon them like water upon a rock. Thereupon the Austrians drew off, re-formed, and charged once again. Down they came upon the sorely shaken and half-disordered Prussian squadrons, and through them Römer's dragoons tore and ploughed, overwhelming them in helpless rout.

Almost before the battle reached the rearmost ranks, immediately ahead of the King, these were giving way in panic, turning aside and fleeing across the front of the first line, heedless even of their own infantry fire of which they thus ran the gauntlet. In the tail of this panic-stricken mob came the King, himself, who must have been swept away had he remained at his observation post. He galloped on, his attendants following, until he reached the extreme left of the line. Here, whilst the main mass of fugitives ahead of him went plunging through the Neudorf brook, still in headlong flight, he thrust his way through the infantry ranks of the left wing, and came to shelter behind it. Thence, gibbering and grimacing, he watched the Austrians, a mile away to the right, making an end of what Prussian squadrons Schulenberg's desperate efforts had rallied.

After that, from the open space by the brook, alongside of a row of gaunt poplars, where the King had drawn rein, he beheld the cavalry of the Austrian right similarly overwhelming the Prussian left, whilst in the background the Austrian infantry was now advancing to the attack.

This was more than Majesty could bear. He groaned and cursed in a breath, and upon Schwerin who came up to him at the gallop he turned a scared, distorted face.

"Hell and the devil!" he greeted the Marshal, quavering. "This is ruin! Ruin! Those cowardly hinds won't stand. Damn them! Do they want to live for ever?"

Schwerin, splashed with mud from head to foot, his face bathed in sweat, sought to steady him. "Courage, sire," he implored. "All is not yet lost. Our infantry will prove more than a match for theirs. We should yet avert defeat."

"Avert it? Look yonder!"

The Prussian cavalry of the left, utterly demoralized now by the Austrian charge, was streaming away in full flight for the shelter of Neudorf, with the white-coats furiously upon their heels.

"What remains, my God? Neipperg's whole line is advancing."

Schwerin dashed the sweat from his brow with his gauntlet. He was livid. Yet he sought to reassure the King. "The infantry will not break as easily," he asserted. "But I confess that in the pass to which things have come, your Majesty were better off the field. Your life is too precious to the State to be endangered."

"My life?" cried the King, in a voice of despair. "What does my life matter now?"

"It is your Majesty's duty to your people to preserve it. I implore you, sire, to go." And as if giving the King a direction for his flight, he added: "We shall fall back upon Oppeln."

A moment the King stared at him out of an ashen, distorted face; then suddenly he wheeled his horse, and was off, riding hard in the direction of the Oder.

Of those who had been in immediate attendance upon him, Alverley, Feuerwach, and Katzenstein set out to follow. With them went Fredensdorff, the King's valet.

It was now three o'clock in the afternoon, just an hour and a half after the Prussian guns had first opened fire.

Alverley's last view of the battlefield was of some squadrons of Austrian horse which, having cloven right through the Prussian wing, had left the fight to go and pillage among the Prussian baggage carts in the rear.

Another baggage train was drawn up across the path of the royal fugitive, on the banks of the little river Neisse in the shelter of a coppice. Through this the King and his four followers squelched their headlong way, startling the carters and camp-followers and spattering them with snow and mud.

"Save yourselves!" Frederick yelled to them. "Be off, on your lives! All is lost!"

Thus he communicated his panic to them, and they began to scatter on the instant. Of some hussars who were with them, four, for lack of direction, fell in behind the royal party.

The warning was no more than in time, for round the coppice at that moment, also intent on plunder, swept a troop of Austrian dragoons to pounce upon the baggage carts. They sighted the fugitives, and it is probable that some camp-follower betrayed the presence of the King amongst them, for a moment later, with a view-hallo, a half-score of these dragoons gave chase.

The King was superbly mounted, on a powerful grey; but not all his father's objurgations had succeeded in improving his horsemanship, and he rode out of rhythm, with humped back and dangling legs. Naturally his party must let him set the pace, and it was not fast enough to outdistance the dragoons. For a couple of miles or more the chase endured with a steadily lessening gap between pursuers and pursued. The King, looking ever and anon over his shoulder, swore at last that the Austrians were gaining on them.

"Burn their souls! They'll have me yet, those sons of dogs!"

Alverley was already aware of it. If they continued thus they must end by being overtaken and charged from behind. At some point, unless they were content to be butchered like sheep, they must turn and stand. Therefore, in his view, they had best turn at once. He took command.

"Katze, ride on with the King. And you, Fredensdorff. Feuerwach and I and these hussars will try to hold them."

"That's it!" gasped the King, still galloping. "That's it. Hold them! Hold them at all costs."

Katzenstein demurred at being sent off. He would stand with them.

"And leave me to ride alone?" cried Frederick in a frenzy. "By God, Katze, you'll keep with me, if you please."

Already Alverley was slackening rein, and falling behind. Feuerwach, nowise relishing the Englishman's assumption of command, perforce must do the same. "We are to see fine things now," he sneered.

"If you doubt it you may ride on with his Majesty." Alverley wheeled his horse, and brought it to a standstill, waiting for the four hussars to come up with him. "Halt, my lads!" he commanded. "We must stand to meet them if we value our lives. It's our only chance."

Because they perceived it, they obeyed. In flight there was no hope of escape from the better-mounted Austrians. Moreover, after the fashion of Prussian horsemen, they were armed with carbines. In battle this was a source of inferiority, since it converted them into a sort of mounted infantry; but in a rough-and-tumble such as they now faced it gave them a definite advantage. It was not, however, more than they needed with the heavy odds against them.

They ranged themselves in line across the road, with the two officers on the extreme right; they drew their carbines and held them at the ready.

"Hold your fire yet," Alverley ordered. But already he was too late; an instant ahead of him a corporal who was of the party had given the word, and even as he spoke they let fly their volley at the white-coats, who were charging in a mass, without any sort of order.

Had the Prussians held their fire they might have done a little better. As it was, one Austrian rolled out of his saddle, and the horse of another went down, shot under its rider. Yet a third, unable to

pull up in time, hurtled into the fallen horse, and came down on top
of it, flinging its rider headlong. There were yells and curses, and a
moment's confusion among the pursuers.

"Courage!" Alverley steadied his men, who now drew their sabres.
He stood up in his stirrups, and waved his sword. "Charge!" he
commanded.

Quick to perceive the advantage that lay in this, they spurred
forward to meet the foremost three who rode abreast a little ahead of
the remainder. They were received with an irregular fire of pistols
hastily plucked from the holsters. The corporal went down with a
bullet in his head, whilst Feuerwach's horse sank screaming under
him. But Alverley and the three remaining hussars charged on.

Alverley rode to take the outside horseman on the left in flank,
and so crashed into him that horse and rider rolled over in the snow.
In the next moment he was, himself, beset, and being sabred. He was
armed with no more than a gentleman's sword, but it was of the type
known as a coliche-marde, very heavy in the forte of the blade. On
this he took the thrashing Austrian sabre and deflected it, yet not so
completely as to avoid a grazing cut on his brow. As it fell away he
dropped his point and ran the dragoon through the body.

The three Prussian hussars were already ahead, at cut-and-thrust
with four of the dragoons. Alverley looked behind him, to see how it
fared with Feuerwach. The Junker, unhorsed, but on his feet, was
desperately defending himself from the onslaught of the fifth
Austrian, leaping aside as the mounted man sought to ride him
down. It could have been only a matter of moments before the
Junker would have been destroyed but for Alverley's prompt action
in drawing a pistol and firing at the horseman. Having seen him
topple out of the saddle, Alverley turned again, and rode on into the
mêlée ahead, drawing his second pistol as he went. Already a man on
each side was down, and a second Austrian was being carried off the
field by a frenzied horse that had been cut across the muzzle. Only
two of the dragoons remained, and Alverley's approach was about to
reverse the odds when a pistol-bullet struck him in the left shoulder,
almost knocked him off his horse, and caused him to drop his sword,

which together with the reins he was holding in his left hand. His knees tightened convulsively on the flanks of his mount, and he recovered his balance and retained his seat.

He levelled his pistol, but his aim was unsteady, and the shot went wide. Then the dragoon who had shot him charged, and Alverley, defenceless, could do no more than wrench his horse aside. A pistol cracked behind him, and the Austrian horse, shot in the breast reared wildly and crashed over backwards.

That was the end of the battle, in which Alverley himself had accounted for three of their ten opponents. The only mounted Austrian left was not disposed to stand before four Prussians even if one of them was unhorsed and another so wounded as to be useless. He backed away, wheeled round, and was off as fast as his horse could carry him.

There was no thought of pursuit. The victors, breathing hard, were glad to sit idle for a spell and watch him go.

Then to Alverley, who sat his horse half-blinded by blood from the sabre cut on his brow, came the voice of Feuerwach at his side.

"We are quits, I think. I could not have borne to have been left in your debt."

Alverley groped for his holster with the empty pistol, and thrust it in. Then he dashed the blood from his eyes, and looked down. The Junker's unreasoning hostility annoyed him. "There was no debt," he answered curtly. "We were in action, and that, you should know, imposes definite duties."

"So! So much the better, then."

"I am not in very good case, sir. I have a ball in my shoulder, besides this cut. If you'll take command, we'll get on."

Of the Austrians, three were dead, three were wounded, and of the remaining three, two were too bruised and shaken by the falls they had sustained to offer any resistance. In addition two of their horses were down and lying useless in the snow, which had been churned into blood-stained mud. On the Prussian side, the corporal lay with a bullet in his brain and one of the troopers with a cloven skull; a third was wounded in the thigh, but only lightly, and when his fellow had patched him up he was able to mount again.

Feuerwach possessed himself of the best of the now ownerless horses, and leaving the Austrians to fend for themselves, he led the way briskly from that shambles, the two surviving hussars electing to continue with them.

As they rode south they could still hear in the distance, some three miles away, the intermittent roar of cannon, which told them that the battle still raged before Mollwitz.

With two wounded men in that party of four, progress was perforce slow. Out of Alverley's handkerchief and another supplied by Feuerwach, the unwounded hussar had contrived a bandage for Alverley's brow, which at least had the effect of staunching a cut that was only superficial. The wound in his shoulder, however, was causing him such loss of blood that in the end, with swimming senses, he could ride at no more than a walking pace. By then they had come nearly a dozen miles, and dusk was falling. They had only the vaguest notion of where they were, and but for the faint gleam of the river they were following they must have accounted themselves lost.

Feuerwach riding ahead cursed the slowness of the pace, yet dared not push on and leave his companions. Wherever they might be, he knew that it must still be many a mile from Oppeln, and he was beginning to wonder if they would ever reach it when his eyes met the yellow gleam of a lighted window a little ahead and to the left, almost, as it seemed, at the very edge of the water. He swung aside, to head for it, leaving the road and striking across a piece of open ground, ploughing through a snowdrift that reached nearly to his girths.

As he advanced he was caught in a broader beam of light from a door that was suddenly opened, and a harsh voice challenged him.

"Who goes there? Answer, or I fire."

"Count von Katzenstein!" cried the Junker, who had recognized the voice. "I am Feuerwach." He slid from his horse, and found Katzenstein beside him.

"How is it with you? Is Alverley safe? Ah! Come in, then; come in. His Majesty is here."

In the fewest words Katzenstein explained that they had reached Oppeln only to be denied admission and to be fired on. The Austrians were in the town. So the King and his companions had turned back, hoping to reach Breslau. But they had got no farther than this mill-house on the outskirts of Löwen.

Without thought for Alverley, whom one of the hussars was assisting to dismount, Feuerwach strode ahead into the stone-flagged kitchen, stamping the snow from his boots until he stood arrested at sight of the King.

Frederick was standing in the middle of the mean room, watching him with febrile, blood-injected eyes. He had cast off sword-belt and sword, his coat was unbuttoned, his neck-cloth loose and soiled, his wig wet and bedraggled, with patches of powder caked upon it, and he was splashed with mud from head to foot. For a moment he stood silently glowering at the newcomer. Then, without greeting or sign of recognition, he turned on his heel and paced away towards the fireplace. There Fredensdorff, the valet, was busy with a metal pot, whilst the miller on his knees was coaxing the wood into a blaze with a pair of bellows. A fragrant smell of coffee pervaded that cavern of a chamber.

Katzenstein came in, supporting the staggering Alverley. The two hussars, hearing that the King was in the mill, did not dare to intrude. They had gone off with the horses, and were seeking the straw of an outhouse, where the wounded one could be tended by his fellow with the assistance of the miller's wife.

"Here is Alverley, sire," Katzenstein announced. "He is wounded."

Dully Frederick looked round at the Englishman, who stood there faint, his countenance leaden-hued below the blood-stained cloth that bound his brow and increased the ghastliness of his appearance. His Majesty advanced a pace or two and stopped. "Alverley? Faith, I never expected to see you again." It was the most casual of comments, without trace of feeling. Not so casual, however, was what followed, on an obviously sudden fear. "What the devil do you mean by coming here? Are you followed?"

Alverley contrived a ghastly smile. "Be easy, sire."

Feuerwach asserted himself. "We should never have intruded here, sire, if we had been followed. I should never have permitted it."

"I hope not," was Frederick's surly answer, on which he turned aside again, to resume his restless pacing.

Katzenstein, summoning the miller to assist him, gave his attention to Alverley, who was clearly in urgent need of it. His upper garments, now full of blood, were removed, and the ugly wound in his shoulder laid bare. The miller fetched water and linen for bandages, and the wound was washed and dressed. The extraction of the bullet must wait. They dealt similarly with the cut in his brow, which was only slight. They patched him up at least effectively enough to prevent further loss of blood. The miller found him a fresh shirt, of coarse linen, fetched him a draught of Schnapps, and, wrapping him in a blanket, set his coat and waistcoat to dry.

Whilst this was doing, Feuerwach, having asked the King's permission, had gone to seat himself weary and morose by the fire.

Across the hearth Frederick stood, gloomily receiving the coffee Fredensdorff had brewed for him. He drank it off, scalding-hot as it was, without wincing. When he signified that he would have no more, the valet poured cups for Katzenstein and Feuerwach, to which some spoonfuls of brandy were added.

Slowly the King paced towards Alverley, who was leaning back in his chair, seeking ease for a shoulder that was now growing stiff and painful. His Majesty came with dragging feet, his hands clasped behind him, his shoulders bowed. He halted before the wounded man, and stared at him. When presently he spoke, his voice was acid and mocking.

"It was your idea to hold off those Austrian dogs, and I suppose that I owe you my life this day. But don't expect me to thank you for it. It was no kindness to preserve me, now that I face the ruin of all my hopes." Overcome by the contemplation of his misfortunes, he turned abruptly away in tears. "Oh, my God! My God! It is too much! Too much! Oh, my God! Do not punish me so heavily!"

Alverley did not answer as he might that Frederick in his weariness of life should have stood with them against the Austrian pursuers; nor did he remind his Majesty of the opium pills with which he had provided himself for just such an emergency as this, but which lay now, forgotten, in their box. In silence, with a faint, pitilessly scornful smile on his pale lips, he watched the King as he paced the stone floor of that mean chamber, sighing and groaning and calling upon the God in whom he had widely published his disbelief. Alverley hoped that the spirit of poor, murdered Katte might be looking down now upon this torment of self-pity of the false friend who had betrayed him to his death. He was certainly far from sharing the awe in which the others, equally silent, looked upon that agony of a king.

Time passed, and Alverley, exhausted, fell into a doze where he sat. He was roused by a sudden stir in the room. Over by the fireplace, Feuerwach and Fredensdorff were afoot and alert. The miller had vanished. The King stood in mid-apartment, grey-faced, wide-eyed, listening. Outside there was a stamping of hoofs, and in the doorway stood Katzenstein, as before, musket in hand, calling a challenge into the night.

"Wer da?"

A voice answered him in an excited shout. Quick steps and the rattle of a sabre followed, and an officer in the green of the Prussian hussars, his dolman hanging torn from his shoulders, appeared in the doorway. Katzenstein was announcing him.

"A messenger from Marshal von Schwerin, sire."

"Schwerin? To the devil with Schwerin!" The King scowled at the officer. "What then?"

The hussar removed his calpack, and stood to attention. "May it please your Majesty, I was on my way to Oppeln, to announce a great victory to your Majesty."

"A great... Are you drunk, sir?"

"Your Majesty's infantry redeemed the day and broke the Austrian utterly. Neipperg, driven from the field in defeat, is falling back on Neisse. Marshal von Schwerin awaits your Majesty's orders."

His Majesty's mouth had fallen open, his glazed eyes stared without intelligence. Then when at last his mind had mastered this incredible message, his only emotions were dismay and rage at the part he had played, and horror of the ridicule of which he already saw himself the butt.

"Hell and damnation!" he roared to the uncomprehending amazement of his witnesses. He reeled aside, sank to a stool, and took his head in his hands. But in the next moment he had rallied. He was on his feet again, wild-eyed, his mouth dilated in a grin that was not mirthful.

"Neipperg driven from the field in defeat! And I... I... Death of my life! Here's a lesson against hasty judgments, against premature conclusions." He stood up again, suddenly. "Where is von Schwerin?" he cried in his shrill voice.

"He is being taken to Ohlau, sire. He is wounded. But the army remains encamped at Mollwitz, awaiting your Majesty's orders."

"My orders? You hear, Katze! The horses. Have them fetched. We ride at once."

It was in his mind, as a last hope, to reach the camp before daybreak and to create perhaps the illusion amongst all but those who had actually witnessed his flight, that he had never left it. Reflection, however, showed him that this was too much for which to expect belief. And so, in the end, he adopted a less incredible alternative. Having succeeded in reaching Mollwitz before daylight he boldly gave it out that when the battle was in doubt he had ridden off to fetch, as reinforcements, the six thousand men who were known to be with the Duke of Holstein at Frankenstein, in order that with these he might fall upon the Austrian rear. It was a fantastic explanation, to which the most casual study of a map must give the lie. But it sufficed, at least with the ignorant rank and file, to stifle an account that must utterly have ruined his reputation. We also know that it stifled Alverley's hopes of seeing this accomplished.

That victory of Mollwitz, when all is said, was by no means overwhelming. Actually the Prussian losses, of close upon five thousand men, were heavier than the Austrian; but their great preponderance in numbers could better support it. The issue was mainly due to the great steadiness of the Prussian foot, and partly to the disorderly conduct of the Austrian cavalry after the rout of the Prussian horse. From the terrible discipline by which Frederick's infantry was controlled, the extraordinary precision of movement into which it had been drilled, and the iron ramrods with which old Dessauer had equipped it, enabling it to load and fire three times as fast as the Austrians with their ramrods of wood, it proved itself at Mollwitz an engine of warfare more formidable than any that had yet appeared on a field of battle.

Marshal von Schwerin, disabled by his wounds, had counselled a pursuit of Neipperg, in the hope of utterly destroying the Austrian army whilst it still staggered under the shock of defeat. Frederick's return, however, frustrated this. His spirit had been so sorely shaken that he was content to accept in thankfulness what had been achieved, and fearful of any course that might yet jeopardize the laurels won for him.

Chapter 10

Klein-Schellendorf

Those nations which, like Prussia and mainly for value received, had guaranteed the integrity of Maria Theresa's heritage, had viewed Frederick's invasion of Silesia with disgust and horror, deepened by the treachery in which he had masked his designs and the impudent falsehoods with which he had afterwards justified them. It was supposed that he went deservedly to his ruin in measuring himself against the might of Austria, sadly though this might had been diminished by the Turkish war and the need to keep garrisons in Italy. When, however, the battle of Mollwitz had betrayed the Austrian weakness, those nations which had condemned Frederick's brigandage were inspired to reconsider the situation and calculate the extent to which they, too, might plunder a queen who seemed unable to defend her property.

In addition to Bavaria, whose Elector aspired to the Imperial Crown, Spain, Sardinia, and Saxony disclosed themselves for predatory enemies, and their ranks were joined almost at once by France, despite all that Cardinal Fleury could do to exclude her. Mollwitz had so immeasurably strengthened against him the hand of Belle Isle and the war party that he was compelled to bow to their wishes, and this actually to the extent of concluding an alliance with the King of Prussia, whom Alverley's reports and the fulfilment of his predictions had taught the Cardinal utterly to mistrust. Nor did it lessen this mistrust to see his Prussian Majesty, for thieving purposes of his own, recklessly ready to promote the invasion of Germany by her hereditary foe, and let loose in Europe a war that must drench her soil in blood before all was done. For the promise of Breslau and Lower Silesia as his share of the plunder, Frederick undertook to give his support to France and his vote in the imperial election to the Elector of Bavaria.

As a result, in the late summer, Belle Isle crossed the Rhine at Strassburg with forty-two thousand men for the support of Bavaria, whilst a second French army of about the same strength pushed into Westphalia for the purpose of containing any movement from Hanover by King George II. For England, at least, had remained faithful to her undertakings under the Pragmatic Sanction. Hostile to the ignoble scramble to rob the Queen of Hungary, the country was clamorous for intervention on her behalf.

No sooner were the French armies over the Rhine than Frederick was resuming activities. Schwerin was sent to take possession of Breslau, in flagrant breach of a guarantee which Frederick had given that free city that its independence should be preserved. The occupation was effected by treachery, in true Frederickian manner. On a pretence that Breslau was about to be assailed by the Austrians, Schwerin obtained permission to pass a regiment through in order to defend its approaches. In the wake of this regiment, however, came bread-wagons, which were left to block the gates whilst other troops poured in and overwhelmed the unsuspecting city before resistance could be organized. It was a trick that delighted Frederick, as his memoirs show.

Despite her high courage, Maria Theresa, seeing herself beset on every side, listened to the advice of England, which urged her to negotiate a peace. She addressed herself for the purpose to her two most formidable foes, France and Prussia. She offered Luxembourg to France; to Prussia she offered the coveted lands of Lower Silesia in return for an alliance under which Frederick should assist her with ten thousand men and give his vote for the Imperial Crown to her husband, Francis of Lorraine.

The Cardinal courteously, and Frederick brutally, rejected the proposals, each informing the other, as in honour bound by their alliance, of the offer and its rejection.

The Prussian army was encamped before Neisse at the time, and Frederick, himself, had taken up his residence in the dilapidated Castle of Klein-Schellendorf. Thither to wait upon him with the Cardinal's messages came the Marquis de Valori.

He was cordially received, and bidden to dine without formalities with the King. Frederick, practising none of his father's parsimony in such matters, spread his table with a prodigality to rejoice both gourmet and gourmand, and he paid the Frenchman the compliment of giving him to drink some of the best wine that ever came out of Burgundy. Schwerin dined with them, the joviality of his broad countenance marred by the livid scar of the sabre-cut he had taken at Mollwitz. Alverley, his wounds now healed, was of the party, as were also Feuerwach, Katzenstein, and Podewils.

The King was in excellent spirits, lively in his talk, which was entirely francophile, concerned with French literature and French philosophy, and peppered with witticisms borrowed from Racine, Corneille, La Rochefoucauld and some others. Warmed by the generous wine, he pledged the King of France in terms of warmest affection, protesting the satisfaction he took in the present alliance.

"To me," he declared, "this is far more intimate even than a brotherhood in arms, proud though I am to find myself in such an association with the King your master. It is an alliance of the spirit. I can assure you, my dear Marquis, that no Frenchman is more French than I am."

"That leaps to the eye, sire," agreed the insincere Valori, who beheld in Frederick merely a German pretending to be French.

"You perceive it," said the King, well pleased. "Then you will understand how chimerical it is for the Queen of Hungary to send me her proposals. My engagements with France are so solemn, so indissoluble, so inviolable, that it is blindest folly to imagine that I could be induced to treat with a court which can never be anything but irreconcilable towards me."

Monsieur de Valori smiled as he answered: "The very Christian King will be gratified and flattered by these noble sentiments of a loyalty which I can assure your Majesty that he entirely reciprocates."

"Assure him, sir, that I am too much of an honest man to violate my engagements." Frederick laughed scornfully as he added: "What fools they are who imagine that I should commit the treason of turning my arms in their favour against my friends, however gross the bait they offer me."

That evening, when Valori was departing, Alverley sauntered casually forth to take the air, on a pretext of dissipating the fumes of Frederick's too generous wine. He crossed the courtyard with the ambassador, as if escorting him to his quarters.

"It is stimulating," said Valori, "to hear his Majesty's enthusiasm." His tone made it clear that for once he condescended to seek the opinion of his companion.

"For those who are easily stimulated," said Alverley.

"Ah? Is that an implication that he may not be sincere?"

To this direct question Alverley returned no direct reply. "You know, of course," he said, "that the Austrian proposal reached his Majesty through the British ambassador to Prussia. It is quite true, not only that it was formally rejected, but that Lord Hyndford was informed that loyalty to his allies made it impossible for the King of Prussia to consider any proposals whatsoever."

"But then..." Monsieur de Valori was beginning eagerly.

"I haven't finished, Excellency. It is also true, and you may inform his Eminence of it, that a second letter has since gone to Lord Hyndford, informing him that he would confer a special pleasure on his Majesty by visiting him here at once."

Monsieur de Valori pulled his lip, thoughtfully. "That is certainly odd. You...you are sure of it?"

"I, myself, wrote both the letters."

"Ah!" The Frenchman considered again. "Odd, certainly. Yet why conclude that the King's object is to make terms?"

"I do not conclude it."

"What then?"

"I conclude nothing. I merely state what has occurred."

"I see. That is to say, I don't see at all, especially after the enthusiasm for France which we have just witnessed. What you tell me is unthinkable. Or, at least, what is to be inferred from it. If King Frederick intends to be false to his engagements, why should he have written the first letter, rejecting all Austrian proposals?"

"As to that I can only guess. In order that he might send a copy of his letter not only to Cardinal Fleury, but also to the Elector of Bavaria."

Valori was impatient. "But in God's name, sir, to what purpose if he means to play us false? It does not make sense."

Alverley shrugged. "It is his way to work underground. A human mole, our Fritz. Sometimes I suspect that he loves intrigue for intrigue's sake. His mother did; so it may be in his blood. It flatters his monstrous vanity to make dupes."

The cold contempt of his tone brought Valori to a standstill. They had reached the entrance to the wing in which the Frenchman was lodged. In the half-light he peered at his companion.

"You puzzle me, Milord," he said. "The only thing I understand about you is that you do not love the King of Prussia."

"It does not happen that I have any cause to love him."

"Tiens! Yet it is common knowledge that at Mollwitz you saved his life, and almost lost your own in doing so."

Alverley did not choose to explain himself. "It is human, I suppose, to be inconsistent." Briskly he went on: "If your Excellency will meanwhile inform Cardinal Fleury that Lord Hyndford is expected here, his Eminence shall have word from me after the visit has taken place. Good night, Monsieur le Marquis."

Frostily the Frenchman returned the salutation, and on that they parted. Sauntering back across the vast quadrangle, Alverley overtook a tall man in whom he had no difficulty in recognizing Feuerwach. It did not occur to him that the Junker's perambulations might be concerned with himself. Yet he might have imagined that Feuerwach's discomfiture when last he had reported Alverley's movements to the King would have the effect of rendering the Junker doubly vigilant in the hope of yet justifying himself and so triumphing not only over this defeated Englishman, but also over the King who had mocked him.

Alverley was to realize this on the following morning when the King casually asked him: "What had Monsieur do Valori to say to you last night?"

"To me? Little beyond expressing his stimulation at your Majesty's enthusiasm for France."

"Aha!" There was malice in Frederick's laughter. "That should buttress their confidence in my intentions. Do you know, Alverley, that actually I don't trust Fleury. I don't trust any priest. A false, slippery tribe. I'd as soon trust a woman. It is in my mind that this Cardinal is plotting treachery against me."

"Could there be evidence of that?" wondered Alverley, in his cold, aloof manner.

"Evidence? There are signs. These fools can't hoodwink me."

To Alverley two things were clear. One was that Feuerwach continued to spy upon him under the spur of his hostility; the other, that Frederick's talk of French treachery was just a cunning scoundrel's common method of justifying treachery contemplated by himself.

How well he judged the King was shown when at the end of that month of September, Lord Hyndford, who had replaced Captain Dickens as British ambassador to Prussia, arrived at Klein-Schellendorf in response to his Majesty's invitation.

The King of Prussia was in considerable strength, actually twice as strong as Neipperg, whom he was facing at Niesse. But he was still haunted by the memory of Mollwitz, with its near escape of disaster, and of the despair into which he had been plunged that night at Löwen. He had been made to realize that the path of glory is fraught with perils, and that if he could obtain by trickery what he sought, he would be a fool to fight for it. It is possible that he had read Sully, and had taken to heart the great Frenchman's assertion that "The conquests achieved by the fear that arms inspire are often more extensive than those resulting from their actual employment."

Hence the invitation to Lord Hyndford, and hence, when Lord Hyndford presented himself at Klein-Schellendorf, the protocol that was drawn up.

Frederick came to that meeting fresh from renewed assurances to Valori of his unswerving fidelity to the alliance with the King of France, and from writing in the same strain to the Elector of Bavaria. As a piece of pure supererogation in treachery, Alverley was instructed by Frederick to compose a letter to Belle Isle protesting his Majesty's enthusiasm for the great part played by the very Christian King in supporting the Elector and confounding the evil designs of the King of England, and asserting that no Austrian intrigues would ever succeed in detaching Prussia from the alliance.

Yet on 9th October, with the ink scarcely dry on that letter, Frederick, accompanied by Alverley and Major Goltz, was sitting down in a chamber almost as bare and cheerless as a guardroom in his quarters at Klein-Schellendorf, to discuss with Hyndford, with Marshal Neipperg, and yet another Austrian representative the terms of the proposed agreement with Maria Theresa.

Under this agreement the Queen ceded to Prussia all Lower Silesia including the city of Neisse, and the King of Prussia engaged himself never to demand from her any further territorial cessions. Inviolable secrecy was to be observed on the subject of this pact until the general peace, and for this Hyndford and the Austrians pledged their honour, as set forth in the protocol. It was further agreed that until the following April a part of the Prussian army should go into winter quarters in Upper Silesia; and in order to dissemble the design the siege of Neisse should continue for fifteen days, at the end of which it should surrender with the honours of war. Neipperg should then be free to take his army wheresoever he listed, whilst the King of Prussia should refrain from any offensive movement against the Queen of Hungary or her allies.

Thus, having by his alliances intimidated Maria Theresa, Frederick had obtained by chicanery and without striking a blow all that he immediately coveted; and he had so disposed that by further treacheries he might presently extend his acquisition to those territories upon which he had now engaged himself to make no further claim.

Chapter 11

The Cardinal's Message

Before the middle of November, his work accomplished, and whilst the farce of the siege of Neisse was being played out, his Majesty was back in Berlin, savouring the applause of subjects who rejoiced in the cheaply achieved aggrandizement of Prussia and in the prospect of a general peace, which they deluded themselves was now in sight. They lacked von Podewils' perception that Pandora's box had been opened.

A couple of days after the return to Charlottenburg, Alverley was at work with Feuerwach in their own cabinet, when an usher brought him word that Monsieur de Valori requested the honour of a word with him.

"With me?" Alverley was taken aback at what he accounted a gross imprudence. But Feuerwach's watchful expression made him defiant. "Admit him."

Feuerwach rose. "You'll desire to be private, no doubt." His tone was sly.

"I can't conceive it," was Alverley's cold answer.

Valori came in, his fur pelisse hanging loose on his slender figure, his muff dangling at the end of his left arm. He checked when he saw that Alverley was not alone, and then bowed with Gallic grace to each of the officers.

"Could we be private?" he asked Alverley. "I have a personal communication for you."

"I was supposing it," said Feuerwach promptly. "Give me leave."

Valori's eyes followed him as he went out. "Do I gather that the gentleman permitted himself to sneer?"

"It is possible. It is his one accomplishment. But this visit, Monsieur le Marquis?" He lowered his voice to a murmur, his eyes stern. "Is it prudent?"

"I hope so. I have a message for you from his Eminence."

"Just so," said Alverley, with a glance at the door by which the Junker had departed.

"Ah, but wait. It is to inform you that the British Embassy in Paris is seeking to discover your whereabouts."

Alverley put up his brows in fresh astonishment. "But why in Paris?"

"You should better be able to answer that question than I. It must have come to the knowledge of the British Government that you resided there at one time."

"But I was known then only as Mr Stuart-Dene."

"Exactly. That is the name under which you are being sought."

"I cannot conceive to what purpose."

Valori shrugged. "That is not a matter for us. All that I am instructed to do is to inform you of the fact at once, so that you may take your measures. Oh, and I am to add that no information has been supplied to the inquirers."

"I cannot imagine the object," Alverley repeated, "or what measures I should take. However, pray convey my thanks to his Eminence for the message."

He paid the ambassador the compliment of escorting him across the antechamber. The room was empty save for the usher on duty. At the door, in the act of leave-taking, Alverley spoke in a quick murmur. "I am preparing a report of the first importance for his Eminence on certain events at Klein-Schellendorf. I shall have the honour to wait upon you with it tomorrow morning."

The ambassador bowed formally. "I shall expect you."

Within the hour, Feuerwach, being summoned to the King's library at a moment of Alverley's absence, was informing his Majesty of that visit, his tone portentous.

"Your Majesty will probably laugh at me again. But I consider it my duty to inform you that a while ago Monsieur de Valori was here to see Milord Alverley on a personal matter."

The King, at his writing-table, looked up from the document he was studying. "Tiens!" There was faint amusement in his big eyes, a faint curve to his thin lips. "And what am I to make of the knowledge, if you please?"

"The matter was so private, sire, that I was bluntly asked to leave them alone together."

"You expect me, of course, to be surprised. But I don't think I can gratify you."

"Your Majesty sees no…inconvenience in this…intimacy of your confidential secretary with the French ambassador, in these repeated visits passing between them?"

"What inconvenience do you wish me to see?"

It began to be clear to the Junker that, as he had predicted, he was again being derided. He drew himself up and swelled with dignity. "It is not for me to suggest that to your Majesty."

"Then what the devil is it you are suggesting? Do you expect me to share your emotions concerning Stéphanie von Katzenstein?"

The dark, handsome face turned crimson with indignation, to Frederick's secret delight. There was no sport he loved better than to prod a sensitive nerve and watch the victim writhe. With more manifest mockery he added: "Why, in God's name, don't you marry the wench, and so acquire peace of mind? That is if such a state is possible to a man of your temperament when married to a handsome woman."

"Your Majesty is pleased to mock me."

"What else? Shall I take you seriously when you forget that I am King of Prussia, and conceive me a puppet to dance according to the strings you pull?"

"I protest, sire, that I have no object but your service."

"You are forgetting the hope that it may jump with your own, and so ease your love-pangs." Abruptly he changed the subject. "Here, take this document. You'll find my instructions on the margin. Deal with it accordingly."

Feuerwach withdrew in dudgeon, yet glad to escape the stings of a caustic tongue against which there was no defence in kind. The very limitations of his intelligence rendered him more prone than the average man to believe what he hoped. The royal mockery had the effect of making him stubborn, turning suspicion into conviction that Alverley was engaged in treachery. To establish this was, indeed, now the incentive of a furious desire to avenge himself upon the royal mocker by proving his mockery misplaced. He proceeded to consider measures.

He would have been less aggrieved could he have suspected that, for all the derision to which he had been subjected, some of the poison he had distilled was at last taking effect upon the King. Having had his malicious amusement with the Junker, his Majesty sat thoughtful for a little while, and when presently Alverley came to take up his duties, he was greeted in terms that once again informed him of Feuerwach's hostile vigilance.

"Ah, Alverley. I hear you had a visitor this morning."

Alverley's imperturbability remained untroubled under the intentness of the royal gaze. "Monsieur de Valori," he quietly answered. "He brought me a message from Cardinal Fleury." And coldly he added the import of the message.

A suspicion once formed will seldom need to seek for nourishment. What, wondered Frederick, and quite reasonably, could be Cardinal Fleury's interest in Lord Alverley that he should trouble himself with his lordship's affairs? He confined himself, however, to a display of mild interest. "What should that portend, do you suppose? – Nothing evil, I trust."

"I can think of nothing good, sire. But conjecture is idle." Alverley spoke with that chill aloofness he now habitually used, and which no warmth of Frederick's could succeed in thawing. For the first time Frederick gave heed to it, and wondered.

"I did not know…" he was beginning, and there broke off. He had been about to voice his surprise at Fleury's concern. "No matter. I have a letter here from Monsieur de Belle Isle. The Marshal is indignant, I think." He resumed his confidential manner. "He informs me that Neisse has surrendered to my troops after a siege that offers, he says, some curious features." His Majesty chuckled. "He is aggrieved that Schwerin should have made no attempt to pursue Neipperg. He complains that this is something he cannot understand, and he permits himself the impertinence of pointing out to me that this leaves in being an Austrian army which a little timely energy might easily have destroyed. He gives himself unnecessary trouble to show me that even a Marshal of France may have his glimpses of the obvious." He sighed with mock chagrin. "I am afraid that Monsieur de Belle Isle is bitter. Compose me a soothing letter for him in your best manner, Alverley."

"But on what lines, sire?"

"Need you ask? Say that Marshal von Schwerin's action is as incomprehensible to me as it is to Monsieur de Belle Isle, and that it must be explained by circumstances not at present apparent to either of us. Protest that whilst I am beyond measure vexed at the turn of events, I must withhold judgment until I possess more information than is contained in Schwerin's present report." He looked up, grinning. "It is hateful to have recourse to such deception, but in a world of scoundrels it is impossible for a king to be honest."

"And not only for kings, sire."

"Ah! You have discovered that, have you? Well, well! We did not make the world." He held out Belle Isle's letter, and waved Alverley to his writing-table. "A propos, my dear Alverley: I hope that Dorothea is in good health."

"In excellent health, I thank you, sire."

"And happy, too, I trust."

"I do my best, sire." Alverley spoke without embarrassment.

"I am sure you do. You have been a good friend to her." After a pause he added thoughtfully: "And to me, too, in that matter. For I must have had her on my conscience if you had not rescued her from the danger to which I unintentionally exposed her." He sighed, and then his malicious grin made its appearance. "But, no doubt, there were compensations, oh?"

It required all Alverley's self-command to conceal the loathing Frederick inspired in him. "If it had been in my power, Dorothea Ritter would long since have been Marchioness of Alverley."

"You may be more fortunate than you suppose, then, in that it did not lie in your power. I say this although I have the deepest regard for Dorothea and many happy memories connected with her."

"I think," said Alverley, his eyes steadily meeting the King's, "that she deserved and commanded the regard of all who knew her in those old days. Katte, I remember, was devoted to her."

The King's glance faltered and slid away from Alverley's. "Katte!" he echoed. "Ah! How that name is ever on your lips! How his memory haunts you!"

"Does it not haunt you, sire?"

"Me? Morbleu!" He fell into thought, and Alverley, watching him, wondered were the eyes of his mind looking again from the window of his Cüstrin prison at the butcher's block by the heap of sand and the headless body under a cloak. His Majesty's next words hardly suggested it.

"For old times' sake I think I shall pay Dorothea a visit. She has come back to dwell, I understand, in the old house in the Nikolaistrasse. It would revive old memories to see her again in that setting: the green-panelled room, the polished clavichord and the rest, and the gaunt old pastor, who never really liked me, who conceived his daughter's virtue imperilled by my visits."

"An idle fear, sire," was Alverley's dry comment.

The King stared. "Peste! I don't think that is a compliment. But I quite understand that it should be your thought."

"My conviction, sire."

"Ha!" Frederick recovered his grin. "Such faith belongs to the age of chivalry. It does more credit to your heart than to your head; like your notion of marrying her if you were free to marry. Marriage is seldom a successful association; never between parties from different social classes. In Dorothea you have found yourself a charming mistress; and you have me to thank for it. Never commit the folly of repining that you cannot make her more."

"I should never account it a folly, sire. For I never met a woman who would make a nobler wife."

"Not even Katzenstein's daughter?" And now his Majesty was sly.

Alverley, however, refused to yield sport. "Not even Mademoiselle von Katzenstein."

Frederick burst into laughter. "Well, well! Persuade Feuerwach of that and perhaps he'll hate you less cordially. He has hopes in that quarter, and I think he imagines that you are thwarting them." Then, abruptly, as was his way, he put an end to frivolities. "But we neglect our work."

The wish he had expressed to revive old memories his Majesty gratified upon the very next day. But not for their own sake. They supplied the pretext, not the reason, for his visit to the Nikolaistrasse. The impulse came from that poison of suspicion that Feuerwach had succeeded in instilling into the royal mind. The dose was very slight. But suspicion is essentially an emotion of the mean, and there can have been few meaner souls than that of Frederick hereafter to be called the Great.

True, what Feuerwach had told him had not in itself sufficed to arouse misgivings. There was, after all, no reason to suspect Alverley merely because he was on friendly terms with the French ambassador. What had really set Frederick brooding was Alverley's own admission that Valori had brought him a message from Cardinal Fleury. It had instantly occurred to the King as odd that the great minister should be on such terms with a man who had been so very negligible whilst in France. And the more he considered it, the more odd did it seem. His Majesty recalled how Katzenstein had lamented that all his appeals to Cardinal Fleury on Alverley's behalf had been coldly rejected on the ground that his Eminence could not intervene to suspend processes of law considering the powerful court influences that insisted upon their fulfilment. Yet in the end suspended them he had, and in so doing, as it now appeared, had conceived such an interest in Alverley that he went to the trouble of sending him through Valori the message which Alverley described.

Of course, his Majesty recognized, some simple and innocent explanation might dispel the oddness which his brooding brought him to perceive. But that explanation it was certainly desirable to possess considering the confidential position which Alverley occupied. Too cunning to seek it from Alverley, himself, by questions that must put him on his guard if he had anything to conceal, Frederick conceived the idea of seeing what he might extract from Dorothea.

Chapter 12

Soundings

Count Otto Podewils was giving a banquet to be followed by a ball which his Majesty had promised to honour by his presence. Since his military secretaries were among the guests, and Alverley would, therefore, be safely bestowed, the occasion served excellently for that interview with Dorothea.

His Majesty drove into Berlin early in the day, and in a second coach Alverley and Feuerwach followed him to the Schloss, materially altered since his father's day, and rendered more suitable for a royal residence. Some of the court officials, however, still had their quarters on the ground floor, and with these his Majesty had an accumulation of business to transact, reports to receive and orders to issue. With such matters of home affairs neither Alverley nor Feuerwach was concerned, and they were relieved from duty until the morrow.

For Alverley this was the opportunity to place his dispatch in the hands of Monsieur de Valori. On reaching Berlin, his first visit was to Dorothea. After that, from the Nikolaistrasse, he set out on foot for the embassy, hard by in the Nikolaiplatz. Fully aware at last of how relentlessly he was being spied upon by Feuerwach he deemed it well to take precautions. At Dorothea's he had exchanged his cockaded military tricorne for a plain round hat that overshadowed his face, and he had covered his uniform by an ample plain black cloak, justified by the chill November weather.

Instinctively, from an unquiet conscience, he looked sharply about him as he left the house. There were few wayfarers, and these went briskly and unconcerned. The only loiterer was a drunken trooper across the way, who leaned momentarily against a doorpost, singing softly in maudlin tonelessness. As Alverley walked briskly down the street he was vaguely conscious that that droning voice kept pace with him, as the drunkard lurched along, going in the same direction.

In the slush of melting snow, by the fountain in the middle of the square, a little knot of townsfolk had gathered about a bear-leader and his dancing bear. To the sound of pipe and drum the great shaggy beast, erect on his hind legs, shambled, grunting, within the length of his chain. As Alverley entered the embassy, the trooper, reeling fantastically, joined the laughing group of spectators.

Although when Alverley came forth again the bear and his leader and the spectators had departed, the trooper still lingered by the fountain with two or three disreputable idlers. He was, however, no subject for my lord's attention, and Alverley paid no heed to him. He went back to the Nikolaistrasse, there to exchange boots for silk stockings and buckled shoes, and otherwise to set such order in his apparel as the occasion demanded. Thence in a sedan chair that he had ordered he had himself conveyed as dusk was closing down to the palace of Count von Podewils.

Within a very little while of his departure, another chair was borne down the Nikolaistrasse to Dorothea's door. Out of it stepped the King, wrapped to his nose in a fur-lined cloak, ostensibly against the cold, actually against the chance of recognition.

His coming might have startled Dorothea had she not been prepared for it by a word of Alverley's on his Majesty's intention. As it was she momentarily almost shared the panic in which Theresa brought her word that his Majesty was in the music-room.

She kept him waiting whilst to do him honour she arrayed herself in her best, indeed her only gown of ceremony. It was of black

301

velvet, and from the fullness of the hooped petticoat the waist arose slender and supple to the swell of her breast which the low-cut bodice revealed by contrast of an almost startling whiteness. She wore no jewel, and no ornament beyond the little ruff of lilac muslin about her neck, and her glossy chestnut hair, with its occasional golden gleams, was innocent of powder. But she required no adornments to stress the nobility with which nature had invested her, and which time had matured, and this Frederick acknowledged to himself when she sank before him in a curtsy that might have resulted from long practice at Versailles.

To raise her he put forth his hand, excessively jewelled as usual, and as usual not excessively clean. It was an unusual condescension, for latterly he had been developing an increasing repugnance to physical contacts.

"Madame, I vow to God you've ripened in queenly fashion. Almost I look in vain for my little friend, the pastor's daughter."

"Not in vain, sire. She stands before you. Older in years, no doubt, but unchanged in heart."

"You reassure me, parbleu." He looked about him and became sentimental. "The dear, familiar room! What memories haunt it for me. What happy hours we spent here. What peace I found in the refuge it offered me in those bad old days. Do you remember, Dorothea?"

"So much that I could still play you one of the airs your Majesty composed."

"That is sweet flattery. From all the cares that burden me I still find solace in music, relief for a surcharged heart in the songs I write. Alverley once quoted to me a wise Scot who said that if a man were permitted to make the ballads of a nation, he need not care who should make the laws. How well that Scotsman knew his world! Alas, my dear! It is my tragedy that Destiny has put upon me the burden of making laws when all my nature craves to be making songs."

"You are the master of both, sire."

"Master? I am master of nothing. A king, child, is a servant, the servant of the State. Were it otherwise I should have found time before now to pay you this visit, and to seek here to recapture be it no more than a lingering fragrance of the past."

"The poet still lives in you, sire. You make it plain."

"You discern it?" he cried, having intended that she should. "You were always acute and sensitive, Dorothea. But I keep you standing. Let us sit." He disposed himself upon the settle, whose striped brocade was of a faded blue. But when Dorothea would have taken a chair opposite to him, he stayed her. "Nay, nay. To the clavichord, I beg. Make good your boast that you still remember a melody of mine."

His big eyes glowed with admiration as they followed her movement across the room. The rise and fall of her hoop lent her such an air of lightness that she seemed almost to float. Then whilst she played an air that he had forgotten, he listened in a sort of ecstasy.

"Did I truly compose that?" he asked as the last chord faded. "It is not too bad. It should have sounded well on the flute. But I must do better when leisure serves."

He rambled on, pouring forth a stream of sentimentality with occasional mock-heroics, and so this master of obliquity came artfully to his real purpose.

"I am much to blame for the trials you have suffered. It is something, my dear, for which I shall never quite forgive myself; for which there are amends to be made. It was," he added with a lapse into levity, "a bitter irony to me at the time to think that they punished you for a sin which I never had the happiness of committing."

"Nor the occasion, sire," she reminded him, her voice chilly.

"As you say," he agreed submissively. "Ah, well! I hope that life was not too hard for you in France."

At once she recovered her momentarily obscured brightness. "I did not find it hard at all, sire. Indeed, it was a happy time for me. That is," she added more thoughtfully, "until the end came. That was horrible; the worst horror I have had to face; worse even than that from which Charles rescued me here."

"Poor child!" He was the incarnation of tender sympathy. "Poor child! I am thankful to think that, at least, Alverley enjoyed the powerful protection of Cardinal Fleury."

"Ah, but that did not come until all hope was lost."

"Still, it came. Let us be thankful. Blood counts, my dear. It was impossible that the Cardinal should permit a man of Alverley's birth and rank to go to the scaffold."

"Yet there was a moment when I believed he would."

"What do you tell me? But then, they have queer minds, these priests. I have no faith in them. Their sense of right is oddly warped, oddly influenced at times. I have often wondered what influence worked upon the Cardinal."

"Who shall say? But at least he proved a good friend at the last."

"He might have proved so earlier, and thus saved you those days and nights of anguish."

"That is true. Still, I must be thankful."

"To fate, perhaps. But certainly not to Cardinal Fleury. What, after all, did he do? What, when all is said, is an order of release? It would cost him nothing."

"Ah, but he did a little more. A good deal more, sire." She was warm in defence of the Cardinal to whom Alverley owed his life, and generously anxious to publish his goodness. "We had no savings, and Charles' imprisonment and loss of occupation had left us almost without means. If his Eminence had not opened his purse to Charles the order of release might have availed us little. We might have had to remain in France at least for a time, exposed to the vengeance of the Richelieu family."

"What?" crowed Majesty. "The old skinflint opened his purse, did he?"

"Liberally, sire."

"Faith, almost you make me respect the shaveling. Of course money would help. But even so, I still marvel that you succeeded in leaving France; I mean, that Monseigneur de Richelieu and his friends offered no obstacle."

"It would not have mattered if they had. Charles was furnished with a safe-conduct from his Eminence."

"A safe-conduct? What is that, after all? Vindictive men pay little regard to safe-conducts; that is, unless they are of a very special kind."

"Perhaps that explains it, sire. Charles' announced him as an agent of the State, travelling on the King's business. It secured us protection everywhere, and prompt relays. Judge, sire, if I have cause to remember his Eminence in my prayers. He made our journey out of France very different from our journey into it."

"I see. Yes, child, you are right. You have reason to be grateful to him. Yet you must have been reluctant to leave. You have become so very French. Not only your air and deportment, but your very speech has all the grace, the very intonation of the beau monde. How right is Alverley to say that he never saw a woman who would make him a nobler wife."

For the first time in that interview colour flooded her face and neck. Her eyes increased in brightness. "Does he say that?" And then, as suddenly, the brightness faded and her glance grew wistful. "It is Charles who is noble."

He stayed yet awhile, and their talk was again of music and of poetry. But it was now all make-believe on his part. His object was accomplished. He had taken his soundings. He had extracted from her all that she knew of Alverley's relations with Fleury. It did not amount to very much, and that to which it amounted might mean nothing. Yet two facts he had gleaned which were, at least, worthy of attention: the Cardinal had supplied and liberally supplied funds for the journey to Prussia of a man who was a stranger in the grip of a law against which he had offended, and this at the risk of incurring the hostility of the powerful Richelieu family; he had supplied this same unimportant man with a safe-conduct which described him as an agent of the State; and he had done all this suddenly, within a week or so of protesting that he dared not interfere, unmoved by the powerful intercessions of Katzenstein, with all the weight of the Prussian Embassy behind him. What had induced the sudden change?

Frederick knew his world well enough to realize that when motives for an action are not manifest on the surface it is prudent to seek them beneath it. Remembering that Alverley belonged to a caste that prided itself upon its honour, and considering the esteem and admiration which the man had always inspired in him, he found it repugnant to his instincts to believe that this English nobleman could indeed have become a spy in the pay of France. Yet life is sweet, and the urge to preserve it has corrupted many an honourable man. What if the Cardinal had taken advantage of this? Frederick deemed it well that whilst still reserving judgment he should practise vigilance.

It might have led him nowhere had not Feuerwach also, and more effectively, been practising it. Indeed, the Junker, desperately spurred by events at Count von Podewils' ball that evening, went to such dangerous lengths as recklessly to gamble his career upon the issue.

More than ever that night did Alverley seem an obstacle to the realization of Feuerwach's ambitions and desires. Stéphanie von Katzenstein, in a dazzling brilliance of gold brocade, white throat, sparkling gems, and still more brightly sparkling eyes, was in possessive charge of her Quixote. Over the inlaid polished floor, in which as in water were reflected the thousand candles in the prismatic lustres overhead, they moved together in the minuet. Together, when the dance was done, they sought the monstrous buffet in one of the tapestried antechambers, where iced wines of the Moselle and Champagne were served from huge golden beakers by lackeys in the lilac and silver liveries of Podewils. There, amid the throng of heated dancers, they pledged each other, and laughed together.

About them surged the chattering courtly throng: powdered and brocaded gallants, officers in tight uniforms and white-stockinged silken legs, women whose waists seemed slender even when they were not, by contrast with the flounced ballooning skirts from which they sprang, their white breasts, dazzlingly displayed, adorned with gems to draw the eye, their faces crudely raddled as the mode dictated.

At a little distance, standing tall in the crowd, they beheld the handsome, dark face of Feuerwach, wearing a more than usual darkness. His liquid eyes were upon them. Having met their glance, Stéphanie turned her back upon him.

"Dear God!" she cried. "I believe that tiresome Junker is struggling towards us." She tugged at Alverley's sleeve. "Come this way."

Glass in hand he went with her, moving inside the barrier of the crowd. It was an uneasy progress, of much jostling and constant apologies. But it brought them at last to the end of the long buffet, and down two steps into a semi-circular alcove that made a vast niche for a marble Antinous.

"Here we should be out of his sight and safe. It's a persistent, persecuting gentleman whom there's no evading. Compassionate me, Quixote."

"Is so much needed?"

"That and more. Hasn't my father told you that he hopes that I will marry the man? And so does the man himself."

"Him I can forgive; but not your father."

"I can forgive neither. I would rather die a maid."

"That is the last danger that will ever threaten you."

"Do not be too sure. My pretensions are high."

"They could be no higher than your deserts."

"I thank you. Yet the fault is yours." She laughed. "I told you ten years ago that when I grew up I would marry you. Yet now that I am grown up, you do not gratify me."

"Alas! I could not if I would."

"It were more gallant to say that you would if you could."

"Mere gallantry will not help me."

"Nor me. I am seeking someone who resembles you, and Gottfried von Feuerwach does not resemble you at all. Be thankful."

He raised his glass. "I drink to the success of your quest," he laughed. "It is all that I can do."

And then Feuerwach arrived to interrupt their laughter. He spoke with attempted lightness. "You are merry."

"Don't be misled," Stéphanie answered. "We laugh so that we may keep from weeping. We mask a cankering sorrow in a grin."

"Or," said Alverley, "to quote a young English poet, 'laughing wild amidst severest woe.'"

"You are mysterious. What is your woe?"

"Nay," she denied him. "We guard it jealously. We share it with none."

"Nor should you inquire," said Alverley. "For, to quote the same English wit, 'where ignorance is bliss 'twere folly to be wise.'"

It was more amusing to Stéphanie than to Feuerwach. He looked down his nose at Alverley. "Mon Dieu!" said he. "Is it possible that there are wits in England?"

"Do you ask so as to seek instruction, or merely to be uncivil?"

"Oh, but to seek instruction," Stéphanie answered for him. "The young gentleman knows his needs."

"And now you also practise wit, Mademoiselle," said Feuerwach. "It's plain the English humour is infectious."

"Oh, not to all. I suspect that you would be proof against it, Monsieur."

"That is, indeed, my hope. But I'll remove myself, to avoid the risk."

As, uncivilly, he turned away, her question followed him: "I wonder why you came."

Lacking a fulminating answer, he chose not to hear. And he was assisted by the fact that his attention, with that of all the company, was claimed elsewhere. His Majesty, in white silk stockings and gold-laced coat of cinnamon velvet, was entering the ballroom, looking more like the prince of ten years ago, modelled on a French fashion-plate, than the severely military figure that had since emerged from the foppish chrysalis.

He was in a smiling mood, displaying all that graciousness of which he was master at need, using an engaging camaraderie with the men, which came naturally, and a gallantry with the women which was more strained.

He had Podewils by the arm, and moved down the polished floor with him, pausing here and there for a greeting or a quip. Thus he came in time to Alverley and Stéphanie.

"Why, Stéphanie! You grow less human every day."

She looked up from her curtsy, frowning. "Less human, sire?"

"More angelic, his Majesty means," Alverley explained.

Majesty laughed. "Oh, no. I mean at once more and less than that. I mean divine. And female divinities are not angelic."

"I am content, sire," said Stéphanie.

"You are always modest. And you take contentment more readily than you give it. Your future husband, for instance, has just departed as if the furies were driving him."

"I do not know the gentleman. But again I am content, sire."

He wagged his head. "Too much contentment, my dear. Too much contentment. Beware of it." He was passing on, but paused to look back at her companion. "I have been to pay my homage to your Mademoiselle Dorothea. The years have been gracious to her. I felicitate you, Alverley."

Stéphanie held her peace until his Majesty was out of earshot. Then, "Now we are both warned," she laughed. "You, that a husband has been chosen for me; I, that your affections are pledged elsewhere."

"His Majesty delights in subtlety."

"Your Mademoiselle Dorothea will be Dorothea Ritter, I suppose." She looked at him frankly, as a sister might have looked. "You are deeply attached to her, Quixote?"

"With a devotion that destiny has imposed upon me."

"Was it destiny or knight-errantry? You see, I know the story: how to rescue her from an infamy you broke your career and ruined yourself with the late King."

"No man who counted himself her friend would have done less."

"Or yet could have done more. Your Dorothea is to be envied."

"I, should be happier if I could believe it. Our paradise is not without its ugly snake."

"Is any paradise? In mine there is the Junker von Feuerwach. But I am not for his coils. Not even if royal authority comes to support my father's."

"Poor Feuerwach!"

"Do you commiserate him? He is no friend of yours."

"The poor man conceives it right to be my enemy. Insensate jealousy has falsified his views. He accounts me in his way. I understand his resentment."

"And understanding, you forgive it," she commended him. "To understand all is to forgive all. The difficulty lies in understanding."

"You read Montaigne. A noble grammar of life, and that is its noblest precept. But you do not, yourself, practise it where Feuerwach is concerned."

"Because it does not suit me. I am a woman, after all."

"For which every man gives thanks, my dear."

"Saving my father, who comes to remove me from temptation."

The tall figure of Katzenstein bore purposefully down upon them.

"A word with you, Charles. Lord Hyndford was at Charlottenburg, seeking you, on a matter, so he said, of extremest urgency. We did not know where to look for you. But I undertook that you should wait upon him at the embassy, at noon tomorrow. I trust that will suit your convenience."

"What business can the British ambassador possibly have with me?" wondered Alverley, taken by surprise.

"I gathered that it is concerned with inquiries from England. Perhaps the same as those you heard were being pursued in Paris."

"Perhaps. But what those were is equally mysterious. However, no use to waste thought in conjecture when I am invited to ascertain."

"That means that it will suit your convenience to wait upon Lord Hyndford at noon tomorrow."

"The immediate question is will it suit the King's convenience to give me leave?"

"Little doubt. But here comes his Majesty."

The King, sauntering back at that moment, heard the request with raised brows.

"You become persona gratissima with the diplomatic body, my dear Alverley. First you are sought by the French, and now by the British."

"I suspect that the reason may be the same, sire."

"No need to explain. It is a praiseworthy quality in a military secretary." The sub-acid tone of the commendatory words was attributed by Alverley to Frederick's natural habit. "By all means make your time your own tomorrow. It is not likely to be an eventful day."

Chapter 13

The Eventful Day

The morrow was to prove his Majesty a false prophet in declaring that it would be uneventful. Indeed, in its earliest hour, a little after midnight, on his return to Charlottenburg from Count von Podewils' ball, he found news awaiting him that was to banish sleep for that night.

Prague had fallen. It had succumbed to the combined assault of French, Bavarian and Saxon troops. Frederick perceived at once – nor was great perspicacity required – what must follow out of this Austrian discomfiture. The hesitating powers, Spain and Savoy, would hesitate no longer. By that victory the imperial crown was now assured to Charles Albert of Bavaria. The entire situation was completely changed, and it was for the King of Prussia to review his own position and assure himself of where his profit lay.

He reviewed it, and his vision, obscured by no considerations of honour, was clear and swift, worthy of one whose nature was to be summed up by Maria Theresa in the simple, deadly phrase "ein böser mann" – a wicked man.

The Klein-Schellendorf agreement had fulfilled its purpose. It had given him possession of Lower Silesia without a fight, and he took the view that he should be failing in his duty to himself and to Prussia if now that Maria Theresa was more sorely beset than ever on every side, he permitted himself to be bound by his declaration that he had no further territorial claims on Austria. By dishonouring the Klein-Schellendorf treaty, by a prompt and timely return to the alliance which he had secretly betrayed, the rich lands of Upper Silesia should now be his for the taking. After all, he had had the prescience to sign nothing. The protocol of Klein-Schellendorf bore no signature beyond that of Lord Hyndford, the intermediary acting for both parties. And when all was said, it was not in itself a treaty of alliance, or even of peace. Here again the author of the *Anti-Macchiavel* had been more knavishly careful than Macchiavelli, himself, would have condoned. It was merely an agreement to enter into such a treaty by December, and this subject to the condition with which Frederick had saddled it, that the secret of it must be inviolably preserved. He had warned Austria that any leakage of information would compromise him with France and Bavaria and make it impossible for him to fulfil his part.

It was quite clear to his Majesty what course he must now pursue. What was not so clear was how to pursue it plausibly, how to mask dishonesty, how to avoid unnecessary proclamation of his knavery. But he did not doubt that study would discover the way.

He sat alone in his library, preoccupied with this question, on the following morning when Feuerwach presented himself, pale with excitement, his eyes febrile from lack of sleep. Informed by his spy – the drunken trooper who had followed Alverley – that the Englishman, half disguised, had paid that secret visit to the French embassy, Feuerwach, urged by his jealousy, determined upon a desperate gamble. This had proved fruitful beyond all his hopes.

On the previous night the horse ridden by Monsieur de Valori's courier had stumbled and fallen heavily on the road between Berlin and Potsdam. The courier had pitched forward on to his head, and lay stunned by the fall. When he recovered consciousness he found himself at the side of the road. His horse was gone, and so was the heavy wallet that had been attached to him by a chain about his waist. Whether his fall had been the result of accident or design, it was certain that he had been robbed, and nothing remained but to

313

trudge, bruised and shaken, back to Berlin and report the matter to Monsieur de Valori.

Meanwhile the embassy wallet had reached the hands of the Junker von Feuerwach, and was taken by him to Charlottenburg in the very early hours of that morning. Too deeply committed to stop at half-measures he had snapped the lock. But when it came to the seals of the two packages within, one bulky and the other slim, he hesitated. It might not be wise, he argued, to burn all his boats. Nor was it necessary. Among the King's secretaries there was one Stultz, who was very skilful in the matter of seals. Feuerwach, too, impatient to wait until daylight, had not hesitated to drag the fellow from his bed at three o'clock in the morning, and set him to work.

Stultz drew a thin, flat, heated blade under each seal, so carefully and skilfully that he raised it undamaged, giving access to the contents of the packages. It was with these that the Junker sought the King.

Frederick, engrossed in his problem, was irritated by the interruption.

"Not now, Feuerwach. Not now. Come to me later. In a couple of hours. I have nothing for you at present."

"But I have something for your Majesty," was the bold retort. "Something very grave, which you should know at once." He displayed the wallet.

"What the devil's that?"

Feuerwach told him. A frown gathered and deepened on the royal brow. There was even some consternation in the royal glance. "God in heaven! Are you out of your senses? To interfere with an ambassador's dispatch-rider!"

"If your Majesty will glance at this, I think you will justify me. You will see how right I was to mistrust that Englishman's traffic with Monsieur de Valori."

"Eh?" Frederick was suddenly reminded of his own vaguely nascent suspicions of Alverley, strengthened by what yesterday he had drawn from Dorothea, but momentarily eclipsed this morning by the news of the fall of Prague.

Without another word, he took up the sheet that Feuerwach had set before him. He studied the seal. "I do not know the arms."

"A makeshift, sire."

Frederick contemplated the heavy vertical writing. "This is not Alverley's hand."

"A counterfeit, sire." Feuerwach trembled in his excitement. "The matter will leave your Majesty in no doubt. For if the statement is true, and unless it is Count von Podewils who is selling you, only the Englishman could be in possession of the facts."

But the King was already reading, and his eyes goggled as he read:

"Your Eminence's judgment that the Ethiopian cannot change his skin, or the leopard its spots, is more justified than ever before."

From that beginning the letter went on to give in detail the story of the secret agreement of Klein-Schellendorf negotiated by Lord Hyndford.

When he had read to the end, the King sat white and still for some moments, tight-mouthed, absorbed in thought. When at last he stirred it was to ask: "Is there anything else?"

"Isn't that enough, sire?"

"I asked you if there is anything else."

"Nothing else, sire. Monsieur de Valori's package contains documents of various kinds. All quite normal. There is a dispatch partly in cipher, and..."

"No matter." Frederick was brusque. "Make me a copy of this letter. At once. Bring it to me as soon as it is done."

"Your Majesty sees now what grounds I had for..."

"Yes, yes." The King was curt and sneering. "You are shrewdness incarnate, Feuerwach. Copy me that letter. And not a word to a soul about this. Not a word, you understand."

When Feuerwach came back with the copy, he found the King pacing the library, his hands behind him, his eyes on the ground.

315

"Very good. Set it on my table. Those seals, Feuerwach, can they be replaced so as not to show that they have been tampered with?"

"Easily, sire."

"Have it done at once. Restore the packages to the wallet, and have the wallet taken immediately to Monsieur de Valori. Send a note with it to explain that it was found in the possession of a highway robber arrested this morning. Say that he had broken the lock evidently expecting to find money. Express the hope that nothing is missing, and my profound regrets that such an outrage should have been committed in my realm."

Feuerwach was aghast. "Your Majesty will allow Alverley's letter to go?"

The King's stare was like a blow. "Have you the impertinence to question me? Do as I tell you. At once."

Feuerwach went out sulkily, realizing that there is no gratitude in princes.

Frederick moved across to his table, sat down, and chuckled maliciously. He had solved his problem.

Chapter 14

The Messenger

Punctually as noon was striking from the Cathedral Lord Alverley ascended the marble staircase of the British embassy to his appointment.

In a room of some richness, softly carpeted and hung with precious tapestries, a portrait of his Britannic Majesty King George II presiding from the elaborate rococo overmantel, Lord Hyndford awaited him.

There were two persons with his lordship: a tall, fair stripling, of some seventeen or eighteen years, elegantly dressed in mourning, and a paunchy little man of middle age, also in black, whose bands and small, tight wig announced the churchman. A moist skin gave his round-featured, rubicund face the appearance of being varnished; benign little eyes twinkled perpetually through black-rimmed spectacles.

Alverley, however, hardly observed him. His attention entirely for the youth. There was something arrestingly familiar about his looks and air. He was very pale, as if from emotion, and his clear blue eyes returned his lordship's gaze with strained intentness.

The ambassador stepped forward with a word of gracious welcome for his guest. "We sought your lordship yesterday, unfortunately without success. However, that is mended now. I have

317

a presentation to make of a gentleman who has been anxiously seeking you up and down Europe for the last three months." His gesture designated the stripling, who, as if it beckoned him, advanced an eager pace or two. "My Lord Alverley, this is the Earl of Revelstone."

"Revelstone?" For an instant Alverley was bewildered, as well he might be, for Revelstone was one of his own titles. Then understanding broke upon him like a flood and swept away utterly his mantle of imperturbability, leaving his emotions naked. The blood drained from his lean face; his voice came in a choking cry: "My God! You are Jack. My Jack."

It made an end of the lad's hesitating anxiety. He sprang forward, and seized Alverley's hand. He was bending to kiss it, when abruptly he found himself enfolded in his father's arms.

"Jack!" Alverley was murmuring, and again, "Jack!"

"Father!"

Hyndford looked on and smiled; the little parson in the background turned aside and blew his nose.

Alverley had taken his son by the shoulders, and was holding him at arms' length, to scrutinize him. "God's my life! Jack! Why didn't I know you at once? It's because you favour me, I think, more than your mother. That is why. Besides, how was I to expect you?" He loosed his hold, and let his arms fall to his sides. "But I don't understand. This is so utterly incredible. I had scarcely hoped ever to see you again."

The youth's eyes were moist. His voice was unsteady. "I thank God you don't say that you had hoped never to see me again."

"How could I have said that? How could you think it? Why?"

The lad's glance avoided his father's. He displayed embarrassment. "You have been used very ill, and I... After all, I remained with my mother. She and I might well have seemed as one in your eyes, and...and... Oh, I can't quite explain myself. But I feared..."

"You explain yourself perfectly. But what a groundless fear! And yet... I am glad you harboured it. It tells me much. It explains that you should seek me."

"Not entirely. There is a more definite reason. I bring you news."

Lord Hyndford interposed. "Give me leave. You will have much to say to each other; and my task is done – a novel one, of presenting a son to his father."

The clerical gentleman begged leave to efface himself also. He was presented to Alverley as the Reverend Nathaniel Culver, tutor to my Lord Revelstone. He professed himself honoured, and at the same time happy that their search for Lord Alverley should at last have succeeded. Then, in the charge of Lord Hyndford, he went out on tiptoe, as if leaving a sick-room.

Alverley drew his son to a settle, and sat down with him. He had already guessed what must be the news the lad announced; the mourning in which he was clad supplied the clue. Nevertheless he asked: "And now, Jack, what have you to tell me?"

"First, sir, my mother... She died four months ago."

Alverley lowered his glance. "It is what I was supposing." He was thoughtfully silent for a long moment. Then he spoke on a sigh. "Poor Marion! So charged with life. It stays in my memory that I loved her very dearly once, whilst all that followed to sunder us has almost faded from it."

"You are generous, sir."

"I would not have you think so. It is not a question of generosity. Perhaps the knowledge that she is dead shapes my thoughts of her. God give her peace."

"She sought it in the steps she took to make amends to you. She realized at the end how much she had wronged you, and her last endeavours were to have the ban lifted from you. She charged me to find you and to bring you word that she had succeeded, and that his Majesty has been graciously pleased to accord you full reinstatement."

Alverley threw up his head, his eyes suddenly alight. "Reinstatement! I may return home? I may go back to England?"

"To all that was yours. You may return when you please. There is only one condition."

"Ah?"

319

"That you take the oath of allegiance."

The momentary apprehension was banished. Alverley laughed outright, "If Paris was well worth a Mass, Dene is certainly worth an oath."

"That means that you will be coming home with me." The lad was eager, his hand tightening on his father's arm.

"As soon as ever I can order matters. There is a good deal to arrange, but nothing that will take long."

He was thinking of several things at once, and of Dorothea most of all. His debt to Fleury he could account discharged. Indeed, his commitment might be said to have ended when France entered into alliance with Prussia. What he had done since, and especially the report of the Klein-Schellendorf treachery, had been rather in discharge of his debt to the King of Prussia. And this he must now leave, content in the persuasion that once the secret understanding with Austria was made known, Frederick would stand branded for all time as a liar and a cheat.

There was the matter of resigning his commission and his secretaryship. But in this he could conceive of no delay being imposed upon him. There was no lack of officers in the Prussian service qualified and eager to take his place. And, anyway, if Frederick did not choose to give him leave, he would go without it.

With Dorothea his course was clear. As a commencement he would tell his son of her existence and of the place she filled in his life.

"It is opportune," he said, "that you travel with a parson. I shall have need of his services. There's a chapter of my biography with which I should acquaint you at once, Jack. You sought me lately in Paris, I believe."

"First in Rome, at the Court of the Pretender. It was there we had word of you as last heard of in Paris, and so…"

"But you never heard why or how I went there. That is what I am now to tell you."

The boy listened soberly, almost sadly, and said nothing until Alverley brought the story of Dorothea to a close on the words: "This lady goes home to England with us as Lady Alverley." There was something of challenge in his tone, as if he were uttering an ultimatum that admitted of no discussion.

His son, however, was far from displaying any hostility. If the news troubled him he dissembled it. Very soberly he answered: "I can only rejoice, sir, that you should have found this solace in your long and bitter exile."

Alverley patted his shoulder. "God bless you for that," was all he said. "And now let us find Lord Hyndford and your Mr Culver."

He did not, however, linger when they had been found. On a promise to return to dine at the embassy, where Revelstone was meanwhile lodged, he went off on foot, with buoyant step, to the Nikolaistrasse.

Dorothea came swiftly and gaily into the music-room, where he awaited her; and then at sight of his transfigured countenance she checked. "What has happened to you, Charles?"

He laughed as he took her in his arms. "My looks do not belie me, then. What has happened, do you ask? Of all things the most unexpected. I bring you great tidings. We are going home to England."

"To England?" She was suddenly breathless. "How is that possible?"

"The ban has been lifted from me by King George. I am reinstated."

Slowly the colour faded from her face. "Reinstated..." she echoed. "What does that mean?"

He took not more than a score of words in which to tell her, and at the end he asked: "You will be happy in England, Dorothea?"

"You...you wish me to go with you?"

"Did you suppose I was thinking of leaving you behind? You will go as Madame la Marquise, as my lady Margravine."

Her eyes were scared. Her lip began to tremble. "Is that what you wish, Charles? What you really wish?"

"Have I ever given you cause to doubt that I should wish it once it were possible?"

"You...you know...you owe me no such duty."

"Did I mention duty? My dear, I owe you... What do I not owe you? My greatest thankfulness in this hour is that at last – at long last – I can discharge the debt." And then he added: "This son of mine has thoughtfully brought a parson with him. We'll be married tomorrow, my dear, at the British embassy."

A moment still, with quivering lip, she stared up into his smiling eyes. Then she buried her face against his breast, and fell to weeping.

Chapter 15

Calamity

Alverley reached Charlottenburg in the dusk of that last day of November. It was beginning to snow again as he rode out of Berlin, and the wind was keen and piercing. But he carried within him a glow to deride the weather's inclemency.

At the palace he went at once to report himself, as his duty was, to the King. He found his Majesty in his library, at his work-table, in a blaze of candlelight, studying a map and making notes upon it – a map, Alverley observed, of Silesia, Upper and Lower. There was a cup of steaming broth at his elbow. A great fire blazed on the hearth. The place had a cosy, intimate air.

His Majesty looked up. "Ah, Alverley!" The lean, weasel face was pallid, and the eyes that searched the Englishman's face were cold and unfriendly. His thin lips assumed a quizzical curl. "Prague has fallen," he announced, and added in the same breath: "That will make an end of the Klein-Schellendorf agreement. You perceive that, don't you?"

"Hardly, sire."

"You are dull, then. But no matter. Whether you perceive it or not, so it is. I do not think that I have anything for you tonight."

"By your leave, sire, there is a personal matter with which I have to trouble your Majesty."

"Continue."

"Circumstances have arisen which make it necessary for me to resign the commission I have the honour to hold in your Majesty's service."

Coming when it did, Frederick found this resignation suggestive. His eyes narrowed. "Circumstances?" he queried, drily. "Do you choose to tell me what they are? Or do you prefer that I guess them?"

"I think they would defy your guessing, sire." And briefly Alverley told him what had occurred.

It was so far removed from all that Frederick had been suspecting that blank astonishment overspread his face. But the balefulness of his glance was not diminished. "I am to felicitate you, I suppose. You will eagerly be looking forward to going home."

"Naturally, sire."

"Ah, well. We must take order about it." Alverley became aware of an oddness in the King's manner, and was puzzled. His Majesty turned to his cup of broth. From a basin beside it he added a teaspoonful of ginger, stirred it in, and drank the scalding fluid at a draught. He set down the empty cup, flung himself back in his chair, and fetched from his pocket an agate snuffbox that was studded with diamonds. He tapped it as he spoke. "The moment is not of the most convenient. I have reason to be reluctant to part with you. Abundant reason. You are so deeply in my confidence. I don't think I shall ever again trust anyone so implicitly."

"Your Majesty is very kind," said Alverley without warmth.

"Kind, am I?" He sniffed. "I wonder." He raised the lid of his snuffbox, and helped himself, neglecting to offer a pinch as was his habit with his intimates. "This affair of Prague will give me a lot of work, which I was not expecting quite so soon. The Austrians have displayed a singular incompetence in the matter. But, what would you? It is their normal manner." His glance became fixed. "The Ethiopian cannot change his skin, or the leopard his spots."

From Alverley, standing erect before the writing-table, with the sense of calamity suddenly upon him, there was not so much as the flicker of an eyelid.

"You recognize the quotation?" said Frederick pleasantly, after a moment's pause.

"It is from the Book of Jeremiah."

"So! From the Book of Jeremiah." His Majesty sat forward suddenly, and laughed. "You are, yourself, an exemplar of its truth. Do you know, Alverley, that much though I have found to admire in you, I have admired nothing more than your imperturbability. An enviable quality. It attracted me to you in the early days of our acquaintance. It is quite Oriental in its perfection; the very culmination of bon ton."

"Your Majesty is pleased to flatter me," said Alverley, ever in that cold, formal tone of his, well knowing that he was being mocked, but still betraying nothing of his apprehensions.

"I study to give every man his deserts," was the sly answer. Then the King's manner became brisk. "However. You interrupt me, and I have much to do. You may go now; but come and see me early in the morning. There are one or two matters on which I shall require your help, and we'll settle then the question of your departure. Good night, Alverley."

Alverley brought his heels together. "Sire!" he bowed, and withdrew.

From under drooping eyelids the King's eyes watched his departure. When the door had closed he flung himself back in his chair and breathed an oath. He was still perplexed. Everything pointed to Alverley's guilt. Yet, was it possible, he asked himself; for a guilty man to bear himself with such unruffled calm under the hints which his Majesty had calculatedly let fall. Only to an innocent man could those hints fail to be clear.

Their purpose, however, was to apply a test. If Alverley were, indeed, as everything seemed to indicate, a spy in the pay of France he would know now what to expect, and he would not wait for it.

Irritably Frederick tinkled a little hand-bell, and to Feuerwach, who came swiftly in answer to the summons, he issued his orders sharply.

"Alverley has gone to his quarters. Follow him, and keep watch. Should he attempt to leave the palace tonight, you will at once arrest him. You will enjoy the task, I know." It was not in his nature to miss the opportunity of that sneer. "You will confine him to his quarters under guard. But – understand me – only if he attempts to leave. Otherwise, you will not interfere with him. Is that clear?"

"Perfectly, sire. Your Majesty still entertains a doubt of his guilt?"

"A faint hope of his innocence," Frederick growled in correction. "But that is no affair of yours. Carry out my orders. March!"

Feuerwach, sharing neither his Majesty's doubts nor his hopes, went off with alacrity, convinced that at last he had got this damned Englishman where he wanted him. He had not a doubt of the doom awaiting him. Neither had Alverley. Impossible to misunderstand those mocking, baleful allusions of Frederick's. The King played cat-and-mouse with him. If the claws within the velvet pads had not at once struck him down, it was, he supposed, because of the sport he was likely to afford the sly, feral nature of the King. He conceived how Frederick would exult in the game, how his vanity would flatter itself by a sense of his clever cunning in tormenting a victim with doubts before finally destroying him.

There was, he realized, no time to lose. The night, at least, was his. Of this he was assured by Frederick's order to be in attendance early tomorrow. It remained, then, only to seize the advantage afforded him by Frederick's sinisterly playful humour. Let him at once rejoin Dorothea and his son, and let them put as many leagues as possible between themselves and Berlin before morning. After all, it was a matter of only fifty miles to the frontier of Saxony, and by hard riding they should cover the distance before daybreak.

Back in his quarters, he dispatched his kammer-hussar to order his horse and to bring it at once to await him in the forecourt. Then, hurriedly, he assembled those of his belongings that were of consequence, and made of them a little bundle in a cloak. With this he set out.

As he came down the wide main staircase he saw Feuerwach lounging in the hall below. By the light of the courtyard lanterns the

Junker had already seen Alverley's orderly waiting with the horse, and he had casually informed himself of the purpose of this. A couple of guardsmen were on duty in the hall, besides the liveried porter, who solemnly paced the marble pavement.

In excellent humour Feuerwach now put himself in Alverley's way, and addressed him with a smile.

"You are thinking of leaving us, Marquis?"

"I have to ride into Berlin."

Feuerwach shook his head, still smiling. "Not tonight, sir."

"How? What do you mean, not tonight?"

"I have orders – the King's orders – to arrest you. I must ask you for your sword". Over his shoulder he called sharply: "Guard!"

Then Alverley understood that he had walked into a trap, and perceived precisely how it had been baited. The attempt to escape after his interview with the King was to supply the final, culminating proof of guilt.

He laughed as he unbuckled his sword, and to Feuerwach his words were an odd echo of the contempt in which the King had spoken to him. "I am glad, at last, to be the means of affording you some enjoyment, Feuerwach."

But if the Junker must swallow contempt when poured for him by Majesty, here he could throw it back with interest. "That's to follow when I see you hanged, as hanged you will be, you foul spy."

This was to bring Alverley up with a round turn. It was to plunge his soul into sudden shame, to suffuse his mind with agony. That crude, unanswerable insult brought him to realise exactly where he stood, and how the shame to which he was doomed must touch others as well as himself. What but an ignominy must his memory now be to his new-found son, the boy in whose eyes he had seen the glow of pride and affection only some few hours ago, on that day of days? As agonizing was the thought of Dorothea, whose steadfast loyalty through every trial was to be cheated at the last, who would never now be Marchioness of Alverley, as that day he had so proudly promised her. And there were others whose esteem he had won,

Katzenstein and Stéphanie and some lesser ones, whose high regard for him would now be changed to scorn.

Crushed under the burden of his punishment he sat in his quarters, behind a locked door, with a guard on his threshold and another under his window. Could a more bitter irony, he asked himself, be measured out to him? It was a refinement of fate's cruelty that discovery should wait to strike him down in the very hour that had brought him triumph and exultation. He had been lifted so high that very day only to be cast down with a violence that broke his brains and shattered his very soul. Despair almost drove him mad.

There was little, a very little, that he could do to mitigate the blow that must fall upon those two who loved him. Of that little he bethought him at some time after midnight. He took pen and paper, and sat down to the bitter task of writing his apologia to his son and to Dorothea. The task, the orderly marshalling of his thoughts to its accomplishment, brought him a meagre measure of peace, enabled him at least to repair his shattered self-control. He was aware that before being delivered – if they ever were delivered – these letters would be scanned by his judges, and would afford support to his indictment. This, however, did not weigh with him, persuaded as he now was that evidence against him was already complete, since manifestly his letter to Fleury was in the King's possession. That quotation from it could leave no doubt of this. It would suffice for the hanging which the exulting Feuerwach had said awaited him. The utmost for which he could now hope was that these passionate letters he had written, by allowing a glimpse of his motives, might serve even with his judges to remove a little of the stain that must smirch his memory.

Chapter 16

The Last Audience

Coffee was served to Alverley by his gaolers in the morning.

They found him carefully shaven, his hair dressed and powdered, and his blue-and-silver uniform scrupulously worn. Thus the ravages of a sleepless night were the less manifest.

Soon an officer – a lieutenant whom he did not know – brought him word that the King commanded his attendance. After a moment's surprise he thought that he understood. Frederick's natural humour would be to bait a man in his situation.

The snow had ceased to fall in the night, and the morning was clear and bright. Pale sunlight flooded the library, setting a golden sheen upon the grey panelling and the array of books.

The King, always a bloodless creature who felt the cold intensely, stood roasting himself, with his back to the blazing fire, when Alverley was brought in. With a wave of the hand he dismissed the escorting officer, and when alone with the prisoner, half the length of the room between them, his cold, hostile eyes looked him over from head to foot, his face forbiddingly set. In silence he crossed to his writing-table, took thence a document, and proffered it.

"Cast your eyes on this. You will recognize it."

Alverley took the sheet. It was the copy of his letter to Fleury. Outwardly calm, disdainful even, he glanced at it whilst the King malevolently watched him. Then he returned it.

"I let you see it," said the King, "in order to save time and argument. It will serve to show you how fully we are informed. You perceive that it supplies the culminating link in the chain of evidence that will hang you." He dropped the sheet on to his table, and stalked back to the fire, to resume his position there.

"That you will be hanged you must realize. It is necessary, pour décourager les autres. And this although I really should reward you; because nothing at present could profit me more than this treachery of yours. I want you to savour the irony of this." A sinister flippancy had crept into his manner. "That letter of yours to Cardinal Fleury is most opportune. It goes forward to its destination, with seals apparently intact. Perhaps I surprise you. Let me explain."

He addressed himself to this, urged by that monstrous vanity which must ever make him parade the low cunning which he accounted cleverness, or perhaps just by schadenfreude, that enjoyment of another's pain.

"I told you last night that the fall of Prague makes it necessary to tear up the treaty of Klein-Schellendorf. That offered me a problem. Your letter to his Eminence resolves it.

"You'll recall that it was a condition of the treaty that the secrecy of it should be sacredly kept by Austria until after the ratification next month. Your letter does what is necessary. For when France thunders indignation at my breach of my alliance with her, I, knowing nothing of your letter, must assume that it is Austria that has betrayed me. That frees my hands; it relieves me of the obligation of being content with Lower Silesia, and it justifies me in going forward to fresh conquests at the side of my old allies."

Alverley perfectly understood, and whilst he did not trouble to efface the contempt from his steady eyes, the King smiled in complacent mockery. He moved aside, and dropped into a chair by the hearth.

"You see?"

"I see," was the cold answer. "But not why your Majesty should tell me all this."

"Is it not clear? In order that you may savour the irony of your treachery's frustration to my advantage."

"Is that really the case? I wonder. By this fresh campaign of brigandage you will have added to the impetus you have given to a war that may yet involve all Europe and drag on through years of bloodshed and desolation. When as a result you will have made your name accursed in the end, you may come to a different view."

Frederick quivered as if he had been struck. "You are, indeed," he sneered, "a student of the prophet Jeremiah, as you had already proved." With a snarl he added: "A pity you will not live to see what you foretell."

"At least I shall die content in the certainty that it will follow."

With curling lip and baleful eyes the King silently considered him. At last – "You are bitter, Alverley," he scoffed. "Almost you depart from the phlegm I have so admired in you. Perhaps it is natural. Here are you, after years of penurious exile, suddenly reinstated in your possessions; you tell me that you have just held in your arms a well-grown son whom you had little hope of ever seeing again, and you find yourself free to reward by a foolish marriage the fond constancy of a woman you love. How enviable yesterday was your lot. But, my friend, you were drinking your wine before it is out of the press. You may well resent the hangman's little knot that is to frustrate all this happiness."

Alverley's answer came laden with contemptuous wonder. "And God willed that you should be born a prince!"

"In His omniscience," Frederick laughed.

Alverley shrugged impatiently. "May we not make an end? Has your Majesty not mocked me enough, Commodus-like?"

"Commodus-like?" Frederick raised his brows. "What is that?"

The question handed Alverley a whip wherewith to lash his Majesty where he was most tender; and Alverley did not hesitate. His scornful gesture swept the bookcases. "In these translations of the classic authors, which your Majesty lacks the learning to study in the original, you may read of the Emperor Commodus, and how it was his vainglorious practice to go down into the arena armed with a sword, to measure himself against a gladiator whose only weapon was a blade of lead. Having slain the helpless victim, the Emperor struck a medal in honour of the glorious deed."

The King sat very still, looking at him, his face the colour of clay. The malevolence of his glance must have terrified any but a man who, accounting himself already on the threshold of eternity, had nothing more to fear in life. In the ears of this prince who claimed in his pretentiousness to be recognized for a philosopher, a poet, a scholar, a man who walked as an equal among the learned and the wits, echoed and re-echoed the disdainful words: "These translations of the classic authors which you lack the learning to read in the original." The rest was nothing to him. The comparison with Commodus he could bear. But the taunt that all his scholarliness was spurious, his learning superficial, was like a mortal blow to his soul.

Yet in a moment he had mastered himself. He must not allow his wound to be perceived. He chose to dissemble his pain in a crackle of laughter, and showed himself able to meet classical allusion with classical allusion.

"You remind me of Petronius Arbiter doling insolence to Nero when ordered to open his veins. But you remind me of him in no other way. For Petronius was, after all, a gentleman, whilst you... Pah! You are so base a creature, so false to your birth, that you can fill the office of a spy. But perhaps your conduct is not so viewed by the English code of honour."

Alverley gave him back sarcasm for sarcasm. "Your Majesty should remember that in the matter of honour I have for some time been to school in Prussia."

"So! You cannot rise above pert insolence. Give thanks that you have not my father to deal with. For the half of that speech he would have had you torn asunder on the rack before hanging you. As for me, your poor taunt does not touch me." Again he must be justifying himself. "You lack even the wit to perceive that what I do as Frederick von Hohenzollern is one thing; what I do as King of Prussia, in the service of the State, quite another. In a world of knaves, duty to my realm demands that I meet knavery with knavery. But I explain myself, I think."

"Unnecessarily, sire."

Frederick glared at him, but still did not dismiss him. Nor was it only so as to protract the torment that Frederick detained him. He had become aware of a force of hate in Alverley that was hardly to be explained by the situation. He was reminded by it of the cold, aloof manner, only half-noticed at the time, in which Alverley had almost repelled the favour he was conscious of having shown him. It was to probe it that he now protracted the audience. "So do not you," he snapped. "And there is need for it. After all, Milord Alverley, whatever you may have become, at least you were born a gentleman. In Paris, I know, you were in sore straits for money. That old shaveling, Fleury, must have paid you handsomely to become his spy."

This, at least, Alverley could deny. "No money would have bought me," he said with a sudden vehemence.

"Then, in God's name, what did? What was the inducement?" Frederick's tone abruptly changed. It became one of injured reproach. "You baffle me. I have actually been your friend. I have shown you every favour and consideration. You, yourself, were so conscious of it, that you counted upon this friendship to enable you to crawl into a position of confidence from which you could the better betray me. Could conduct be more vile? What have I ever done to you, Alverley, that you should requite me in this fashion?"

And then, at last, very quietly, Alverley gave him the explanation that he sought. "You murdered Katte."

"What?"

The King slewed round in his chair, directly to face him, his countenance blank, his voice suddenly hoarse. "What? I did what?"

Alverley repeated the charge with elaboration. "Meanly, cravenly, treacherously you murdered Katte, my cousin, whom I loved as a brother; you murdered him in order to mitigate the rigours you dreaded as a punishment for your play-acting levity."

Frederick bounded out of his chair. "God of God!" He shook a clenched fist in Alverley's face. His voice was now a scream. "A lie! A foul, damnable lie! You dare to face me and utter it? You dare to make that infamous invention a pretext for your own vileness? God's death! Play-acting, you say. Who is the play-actor here? You, yourself, who hope to prevail by this imposture, well knowing how poor Katte died."

"Oh, yes. I know. I know that he was beheaded at Cüstrin, flung to the headsman by your treachery. A scapegoat for your offences."

Frederick's face was convulsed. "Dare you persist in that lie? My God! My God! That I should listen to it! I, who loved Katte; loved him better than any man I have ever known." The words came in panting sobs. There was froth on the King's lips. "You cruel, infamous dog! I shall rejoice to see you hang. By that horrible lie you have killed what pity there was in me."

Outwardly Alverley was still unmoved. "If it is a lie, then your father was the liar. I have it from him, every detail of that betrayal, as he had it from the pastor who attended you at Cüstrin, I even remember his name. It was Burmeister. You imagined that he was sent to prepare you for death. In your cowardly panic you made Katte your scapegoat. You pleaded that Katte had persuaded you, seduced you – that was your word to the commissioners who examined you – seduced you into your intended flight, when the truth was that only out of his great affection for you had that staunch soul consented against his better judgment, against the advice I gave him, to lend you his assistance."

"It is all false. False as hell!"

Quietly the accusing voice asked: "If it is false, sire, how came Katte implicated at all? Who else possessed the knowledge necessary to betray him?"

This was a thrust in Frederick's very vitals. His mouth fell open under the shock of it. He stared at the questioner out of a livid face from which all intelligence had been effaced. Then he rallied. "There was Keith," he cried. "Keith knew. It was Keith who betrayed me, and so he may have betrayed Katte."

"Keith? Keith had fled. And how many weeks lay between Keith's flight and Katte's arrest?" A bitter smile flickered across Alverley's lips, and then the narrow, high-bred face became set and stern. "The price that Cardinal Fleury offered me to come and spy upon you was my life, which Count Katzenstein will have told you was forfeit. What loyalty did I owe you that I should boggle at the proposal? None. What I did owe you was something on Katte's behalf, and Fleury's offer supplied me with an opportunity to pay off at least a part of that heavy score. And let me add, without vainglory or to seek excuse, that I was concerned to save my life for the sake of another victim of Hohenzollern ruthlessness and your own levity, one whom my death would have left shipwrecked on the world. I speak of that tender child whom your father had condemned to be stripped and flogged in public and then imprisoned for life in a fortress dungeon."

"God of Heaven! Will you make me answerable for that, too?" Frederick exclaimed, so reduced and overwhelmed by the sternness of Alverley's denunciation that, by a crowning irony, the accuser was now become the accused. In his own defence he quavered on: "As for the rest, if you are not lying about this Pastor Burmeister, then it was he who lied; lied to save me; bore that false tale of a confession to my father. It may be that Katte's name escaped me. It may be. How should I remember? I was too distracted at the time to know what I said. And the chaplain may have taken advantage of that. But that I accused Katte... As God hears me, nothing could be more false. I swear it. I would have died for Katte." Mastered by emotion, his voice faltered, his eyes filled with tears. "I... I implored them to let me die in his stead."

He turned away, and went to the window, dragging his feet. There he remained, with his back to the room, and Alverley observed that his shoulders were heaving. Presently, still without turning, he was speaking again, in bitter plaintiveness.

"I have endured much in my life, but nothing that brought me greater pain than Katte's death. I all but died of it, myself; as they could tell you who were at Cüstrin with me; and I shall never know a crueller, more wicked accusation than that I was a party to his death.

"You have used in other ways a brutal frankness amounting to lèse-majesté making your hatred clear, and…"

He checked there, and abruptly swung round, urged by a sudden fierce suspicion that Alverley was playing a part, that he had been inspired to use the Katte affair as a pretext, a defence, a justification of his own infamy: to mantle his role of a spy in that of an avenger. Fiercely he disclosed the reasoning upon which that suspicion was based.

"Yet, with this pretended hatred in your soul, at Mollwitz you saved my life at the risk of your own, and nearly bled to death in doing so. Is it likely that you would have done that if what you now say is true? Is it? Answer me."

Alverley did not hesitate. "At Mollwitz I shared your belief that you were defeated and ruined. I was content that you should live on, despised for your treachery and presumption; that is, if you lacked the courage to swallow your opium pills and die by your own hand as you had threatened."

It was an answer that instantly destroyed the King's suspicion, and in destroying it aroused an anger that restored him much of his malignancy.

"So!" he said. "So! Yet now, with a noose about your neck, you might make capital of it. You might claim your life in payment of that debt. Why don't you? Is it because you prefer even in your extremity to be venting your malevolence?"

"It is because I would not have your Majesty conceive yourself under an obligation to me." And he added, not too happily perhaps, "Prevarication is not among my faults."

"Ha! To be sure you are a grand seigneur, a gentleman, a man of honour. I was forgetting. I was considering you merely as a spy."

"Must you still be mocking me? Even now, when you know the motive from which I acted? Let it satisfy you that I am content to go the way of Katte."

The King's eyes fell away from Alverley's steady glance. His face darkened again. "Katte!" he echoed. "Katte! That name was always on your lips, and I never suspected that you were using it to stab me. But then neither did I suspect that you believed that I... Oh, God!" He turned his back upon Alverley, as before, to face the window. He remained so, in silence, whilst Alverley stood, impatiently awaiting his dismissal, never suspecting the dark conflict in the King's mind.

An old wound had been reopened in his soul, the wound dealt him by conscience when he had seen Katte's head fall under the sweep of the headsman's sword. It was not only Alverley whom he had sought to deceive by his bluster, his outcries, his fierce protests that the denunciation was a lie. He had sought, and primarily, to deceive himself, to salve that old wound, as he had ever salved it, with the sophistry that he could not be held responsible for that horror at Cüstrin because none could have foreseen so dreadful a consequence to his avowal to the chaplain. Yet the sense of fearful guilt had always been there, hidden away in the secret recesses of his soul. It was now as if Alverley had torn it thence to cast it in his face, to compel his recognition of it.

At long last he mastered himself and moved from the window. He had taken the resolve that conscience had imposed upon him, perhaps because in this matter of Katte conscience could bear no more, perhaps because of a hope that thus he might cease to be haunted by the ghost of Katte which Alverley had raised in such dread vigour.

He paced slowly back to the hearth, his head bowed. He had a part to play, and he must play it, he told himself, in kingly fashion. He set his shoulders to the green marble overmantel, straightened himself, and looked bleakly at his prisoner. He spoke slowly, as if weighing each word.

"Your vindictiveness I can understand, since you believed what you did. Understanding it, I can even condone it. But not the method you chose to gratify it. That must always deserve my scorn, and the scorn of every man of honour, even your own scorn if you have a spark of honour left.

"Perhaps if I had suffered by your actions this audience would have a different ending. But as it happens, and as I have shown you, your treachery has served me well. In fact, it leaves me in your debt. And I am in your debt for my life, which you saved at Mollwitz. Whatever the motives out of which you acted, the profit in each case is mine. It is almost amusing, is it not? Anyway, it happens that I care no more to remain in your debt than you have said that you care to be in mine.

"In payment, then, and also as a sacrifice to the shade of my poor, dear Katte, out of love for whom you profess to have acted, I bid you take your wretched life, and go."

It was a moment before Alverley understood. Then the shock of that understanding almost shattered his self-control. Having stood firm and arrogant in the face of doom, he fell to trembling upon being suddenly confronted again with life and all that life now implied to him. Out of the dark he came suddenly into the blaze of high noon, and he was dazzled. He threw up his head, as if to speak. But the King raised a forbidding hand.

"I do not desire you to thank me. This is no gift. It is a quittance I give you with your life, and in the same disdainful spirit as that in which you tell me that you preserved mine at Mollwitz." With increasing harshness he added: "It is possible that I may regret this weakness. So see to it that you are beyond the frontiers of Prussia within forty-eight hours, and never venture within my reach again." He flung out an arm, histrionically, to point to the door. "Go!"

Alverley recovered his momentarily shaken self-mastery. He brought his heels together, bowed stiffly, then turned and walked firmly out.

Thus they parted in mutual contempt.

Rafael Sabatini

Captain Blood

Captain Blood is the much-loved story of a physician and gentleman turned pirate.

Peter Blood, wrongfully accused and sentenced to death, narrowly escapes his fate and finds himself in the company of buccaneers. Embarking on his new life with remarkable skill and bravery, Blood becomes the 'Robin Hood' of the Spanish seas. This is swashbuckling adventure at its best.

The Gates of Doom

'Depend above all on Pauncefort,' announced King James, 'his loyalty is dependable as steel. He is with us body and soul and to the last penny of his fortune.' So when Pauncefort does indeed face bankruptcy after the collapse of the South Sea Company, the king's supreme confidence now seems rather foolish. And as Pauncefort's thoughts turn to gambling, moneylenders and even marriage to recover his debts, will he be able to remain true to the end? And what part will his friend and confidante, Captain Gaynor, play in his destiny?

'A clever story, well and amusingly told' – *The Times*

Rafael Sabatini

The Lost King

The Lost King tells the story of Louis XVII – the French royal who officially died at the age of ten but, as legend has it, escaped to foreign lands where he lived to an old age. Sabatini breathes life into these age-old myths, creating a story of passion, revenge and betrayal. He tells of how the young child escaped to Switzerland from where he plotted his triumphant return to claim the throne of France.

'…the hypnotic spell of a novel which for sheer suspense, deserves to be ranked with Sabatini's best' – *New York Times*

Scaramouche

When a young cleric is wrongfully killed, his friend, André-Louis, vows to avenge his death. Louis' mission takes him to the very heart of the French Revolution where he finds the only way to survive is to assume a new identity. And so is born Scaramouche – a brave and remarkable hero of the finest order and a classic and much-loved tale of the greatest swashbuckling tradition.

'Mr Sabatini's novel of the French Revolution has all the colour and lively incident which we expect in his work' – *Observer*

Rafael Sabatini

The Sea Hawk

Sir Oliver, a typical English gentleman, is accused of murder, kidnapped off the Cornish coast, and dragged into life as a Barbary corsair. However Sir Oliver rises to the challenge and proves a worthy hero for this much-admired novel. Religious conflict, melodrama, romance and intrigue combine to create a masterly and highly successful story, perhaps best known for its many film adaptations.

The Shame of Motley

The Court of Pesaro has a certain fool – one Lazzaro Biancomonte of Biancomonte. *The Shame of Motley* is Lazzaro's story, presented with all the vivid colour and dramatic characterisation that has become Sabatini's hallmark.

'Mr Sabatini could not be conventional or commonplace if he tried'
– *Standard*

TITLES BY RAFAEL SABATINI AVAILABLE DIRECT
FROM HOUSE OF STRATUS

Quantity	£	$(US)	$(CAN)	€
FICTION				
ANTHONY WILDING	6.99	12.95	19.95	13.50
THE BANNER OF THE BULL	6.99	12.95	19.95	13.50
BARDELYS THE MAGNIFICENT	6.99	12.95	19.95	13.50
BELLARION	6.99	12.95	19.95	13.50
THE BLACK SWAN	6.99	12.95	19.95	13.50
CAPTAIN BLOOD	6.99	12.95	19.95	13.50
THE CAROLINIAN	6.99	12.95	19.95	13.50
CHIVALRY	6.99	12.95	19.95	13.50
THE CHRONICLES OF CAPTAIN BLOOD	6.99	12.95	19.95	13.50
COLUMBUS	6.99	12.95	19.95	13.50
FORTUNE'S FOOL	6.99	12.95	19.95	13.50
THE FORTUNES OF CAPTAIN BLOOD	6.99	12.95	19.95	13.50
THE GAMESTER	6.99	12.95	19.95	13.50
THE GATES OF DOOM	6.99	12.95	19.95	13.50
THE HOUNDS OF GOD	6.99	12.95	19.95	13.50
THE JUSTICE OF THE DUKE	6.99	12.95	19.95	13.50
THE LION'S SKIN	6.99	12.95	19.95	13.50
THE LOST KING	6.99	12.95	19.95	13.50
LOVE-AT-ARMS	6.99	12.95	19.95	13.50
THE MARQUIS OF CARABAS	6.99	12.95	19.95	13.50
THE MINION	6.99	12.95	19.95	13.50

ALL HOUSE OF STRATUS BOOKS ARE AVAILABLE FROM GOOD BOOKSHOPS OR
DIRECT FROM THE PUBLISHER:

Internet: www.houseofstratus.com including author interviews, reviews, features.

Email: sales@houseofstratus.com please quote author, title and credit card details.

TITLES BY RAFAEL SABATINI AVAILABLE DIRECT
FROM HOUSE OF STRATUS

Quantity	£	$(US)	$(CAN)	€
FICTION				
THE NUPTIALS OF CORBAL	6.99	12.95	19.95	13.50
THE ROMANTIC PRINCE	6.99	12.95	19.95	13.50
SCARAMOUCHE	6.99	12.95	19.95	13.50
SCARAMOUCHE THE KING-MAKER	6.99	12.95	19.95	13.50
THE SEA HAWK	6.99	12.95	19.95	13.50
THE SHAME OF MOTLEY	6.99	12.95	19.95	13.50
THE SNARE	6.99	12.95	19.95	13.50
ST MARTIN'S SUMMER	6.99	12.95	19.95	13.50
THE STALKING-HORSE	6.99	12.95	19.95	13.50
THE STROLLING SAINT	6.99	12.95	19.95	13.50
THE SWORD OF ISLAM	6.99	12.95	19.95	13.50
THE TAVERN KNIGHT	6.99	12.95	19.95	13.50
THE TRAMPLING OF THE LILIES	6.99	12.95	19.95	13.50
TURBULENT TALES	6.99	12.95	19.95	13.50
VENETIAN MASQUE	6.99	12.95	19.95	13.50
NON-FICTION				
HEROIC LIVES	8.99	14.99	22.50	15.00
THE HISTORICAL NIGHTS' ENTERTAINMENT	8.99	14.99	22.50	15.00
THE LIFE OF CESARE BORGIA	8.99	14.99	22.50	15.00
TORQUEMADA AND THE SPANISH INQUISITION	8.99	14.99	22.50	15.00

ALL HOUSE OF STRATUS BOOKS ARE AVAILABLE FROM GOOD BOOKSHOPS OR
DIRECT FROM THE PUBLISHER:

Order Line: UK: 0800 169 1780,
USA: 1 800 509 9942
INTERNATIONAL: +44 (0) 20 7494 6400 (UK)
    or +01 212 218 7649
(please quote author, title, and credit card details.)

Send to: House of Stratus Sales Department House of Stratus Inc.
24c Old Burlington Street Suite 210
London 1270 Avenue of the Americas
W1X 1RL New York • NY 10020
UK USA

PAYMENT

Please tick currency you wish to use:

☐ £ (Sterling)   ☐ $ (US)   ☐ $ (CAN)   ☐ € (Euros)

Allow for shipping costs charged per order plus an amount per book as set out in the tables below:

CURRENCY/DESTINATION

	£(Sterling)	$(US)	$(CAN)	€(Euros)
Cost per order				
UK	1.50	2.25	3.50	2.50
Europe	3.00	4.50	6.75	5.00
North America	3.00	3.50	5.25	5.00
Rest of World	3.00	4.50	6.75	5.00
Additional cost per book				
UK	0.50	0.75	1.15	0.85
Europe	1.00	1.50	2.25	1.70
North America	1.00	1.00	1.50	1.70
Rest of World	1.50	2.25	3.50	3.00

PLEASE SEND CHEQUE OR INTERNATIONAL MONEY ORDER.
payable to: STRATUS HOLDINGS plc or HOUSE OF STRATUS INC. or card payment as indicated

STERLING EXAMPLE

Cost of book(s):..................... Example: 3 x books at £6.99 each: £20.97
Cost of order: .... Example: £1.50 (Delivery to UK address)
Additional cost per book:.............. Example: 3 x £0.50: £1.50
Order total including shipping:.......... Example: £23.97

VISA, MASTERCARD, SWITCH, AMEX:

☐ ☐ ☐ ☐ ☐ ☐ ☐ ☐ ☐ ☐ ☐ ☐ ☐ ☐ ☐ ☐ ☐ ☐ ☐

Issue number (Switch only):

☐☐☐

Start Date: **Expiry Date:**

☐☐/☐☐   ☐☐/☐☐

Signature: _____

NAME: _____

ADDRESS: _____

COUNTRY: _____

ZIP/POSTCODE: _____

Please allow 28 days for delivery. Despatch normally within 48 hours.

Prices subject to change without notice.
Please tick box if you do not wish to receive any additional information. ☐

House of Stratus publishes many other titles in this genre; please check our website (**www.houseofstratus.com**) for more details.